MW00574831

BLOOD
TO
DUST

L. J. SHEN

Copyright © 2016 by L.J. Shen
All rights reserved.

No part of this book may be reproduced or transmitted in any way,
including electronic, mechanical, photocopying, recording or any other
means without the explicit written permission of the author, except for
brief quotations of the book when writing a review.

This is a work of fiction. Names, characters, brands, places, incidents and
even facts are the product of the author's imagination. Come to think of it,
especially facts. Any resemblance to actual people – alive, dead, or
somewhere in-between, is completely coincidental and is just in your head.

All song titles and lyrics in this book are the property of the sole copyright
owners.

Cover Designer:
Letitia Hasser at R.B.A. Designs

Interior Designer:
Jovana Shirley at Unforeseen Editing,
www.unforeseenediting.com

Editor:
Vanessa L. Bridges at PREMA Editing

For coffee, thanks for seeing me through this journey.
For the Beat Generation authors, without whom I would've never become one.
Last but not least, for my readers. You awesome motherfuckers.

*"She's mad, but she is magic.
There's no lie in her fire."*

—Charles Bukowski

Once upon a time, there was a boy.

The boy was sad and lost and violent, but inside him, lay peace.

He is sitting on the porch in his ivy-laced, putrid front yard,
fisting his hair, his eyes blank and clean. He is beautiful, the boy.
The lord gave him a bad life and good looks, even though the boy
would have preferred it the other way around.

A woman standing behind him is screaming and bawling
and pounding her bloody fists against his back.

That woman is his mother.

Under his feet lies a man with a fractured skull, the contents of his head
spilling on the yellowed grass. Broken pieces of a vase adorn his head like
Jesus' crown of thorns and a sharp shard is stuck to his temple.

That man is his father.

Up above, heaven frowns at what the 22 year-old boy has
just done, and down below, hell shakes its rusty gates open.

In the distance, sirens are wailing their arrival. Closer. Nearer. Louder.

Once upon a time, there was a girl.

The 20-year-old girl was sheltered, privileged and of pedigree,
but inside her, laid a storm.

She dangles a shiny pair of new keys in her small palm,
an unusual smile playing on her face. These keys will soon
unlock a glitzy apartment she has rented all by herself. Her parents
are thought to be rich, but every dime paid on this condo belongs to her.
The money is bloody and tainted... *but it's hers.*

In this same exact moment, the boy is being plucked by two
burly officers from his porch as they read him his rights.

His run-down house in Stockton is only an
hour away from her swanky apartment.

She is smiling.
He is not.

This is the story of a boy and a girl fighting storms and
trying to find peace in the most unexpected place.

They try and find it in each other.

PRESCOTT

Time.

A wise, vile man once told me that it moves differently according to circumstances. Sometimes it's slow. But sometimes. . .it slips so fast between your fingers, your life is over before you had time to reflect on it.

See, life is like an hourglass. Sometimes you're up, and sometimes. . .well, you're *down*.

And right now I'm down, baby. So. Flipping. Down.

"My idea of fun is killing everyone. . ."

I hear him before I see him, his voice sing-songs in a whisper. He loves whispering. A whisper is much more powerful than a scream.

"My idea of fun, is killing everyone. . ."

I gasp. *No*. Shit. God, no.

"My idea of fun, is kill...Oh. Prescott, darling, fancy bumping into you this late at night." His posh English accent cuts through my ears. Seb's hands find the back of my neck and he thrusts me face-first into the nearest graffitied wall with a thump. I drop the stress ball I was squeezing a second ago, knowing that now I need it more than ever.

Warm blood snakes from my forehead into my mouth and I lick it wordlessly, careful not to show any sign of distress. He twists my arms behind my back in one hand and shoves my head into the wall with the other.

Bang.

"Here, Love, you look thirsty. Might want to get another taste of your own blood. After all, that's the only thing you'll be feasting on for the next few days, I suppose."

My head is smashed against the concrete before swinging back from the impact. Seb spins me around so I face him. A polite smile tugs at his lips. He grabs my pink duffel bag—a girly Nike—and tucks it under his arm. The sleepy Oakland pavement seems absurdly narrow and suffocating now that he is here next to me.

SEB

Pointy nose, non-existent lips, delicate frame and pasty skin, wired with blue and purple veins. He sways his hips when he walks, his fingers long and thin like a ballerina's. *Likes*: flamboyant suits, Gucci loafers, screwing young boys, preferably between the ages of thirteen to nineteen. *Dislikes*: the law, sloppy attire. *And me.*

"Let me guess—blow? Meth?" He tilts his head down, his grin spreading like a contagious disease. "*Crack-cocaine?*"

"If I tell you, I'd have to kill you." I head-butt him on a whim and feel his skull crashing against mine, ignoring the sharp, white pain that's dotting my vision. "And that's just too tempting."

Fisting my hair with a snarl, Seb jerks me toward a white van with tinted windows that's blocking my way out of the street. I guess our small talk is over. "Still got a sense of humor, I see. Lovely. You'll need it where you'll be."

I spit blood on his suede shoes. My head feels like it's split in two, but I'd never let him see how much it hurts. Seb rolls open the sliding door of the van and shoves me in. I roll across the dusty floor, my back hitting the opposite door.

He towers over me, leaning his narrow waist against the van.

"I see Blackhawk's aristocratic life is still not enough for little Prescott. Oakland? Really?" He shakes his head with a laugh and slams the door. The vehicle rattles. So does my heart.

Time is definitely not on my side right now.

We ride for about an hour before the van comes to a full stop. I spend the journey trying to crack the doors and windows open, bang the divider between the back and front seats and knock on the walls until my hands are swollen and purple.

Hysteria burns my throat, sending flames of panic through the rest of my body. I know exactly who he is taking me to.

Godfrey.

The door to the backseat swipes open and Seb stands in front of me again, equipped with two of his muscle men, one on each side. Godfrey's bulldogs, no doubt. I draw a breath and sit at the corner of the van, making a show of examining my nails.

These very men taught me how to look darkness in the eye and defy it, even when I stand no chance. If I show weakness, they win.

I will die a graphic, painful death wordlessly just to spite them.

"Get up."

"Make me."

"Happily." He shrugs, snapping his fingers once and nodding toward me. The two gorillas climb into the van and pull me out, each of them clasping an arm. I'm not dumb enough to try and break free; they can tear me limb from limb and make potpourri out of my skin, so I just watch the floor as they carry me—my toes floating above the sidewalk—into a warehouse I don't recognize in an area I'm not familiar with.

Once inside, the florescent lights hit me hard.

Then Seb hits me harder. Elbow shot straight to my cheek.

I collapse to my knees, blood trickling from my split lip and my chin, and it's when I'm on all fours that I catch the footfalls of Godfrey's orthopedic shoes. Rumor on the street is those are the only ones he wears nowadays—his legs will never be the same after what I did to him the night of the barn—and they're squeaking against the tiles like chirpy mice.

Screech.

Screech.

Screech.

Stop.

"Prescott. So nice of you to drop by." He rolls the word *drop* on his tongue, not allowing the pun to escape me. I may be down on the floor, but my chin is still high and defiant. "Funny, I don't remember you paying me any visits when I was in state prison."

I raise my head proudly, my eyes adjusting to the bright light, and toss a bloody, scarlet smile, compliments of his right-hand man.

"Don't be sad. I promise to visit your grave regularly."

He flashes his teeth, even though he is anything but amused, and jerks his index finger sideways. "Sit her arse down, tie her up to this chair." He cocks his chin in the same direction. I let the muscle guys do as he said, watching him through hooded eyes as I calculate my next move. Godfrey looks delicate, brittle. San Dimas prison did the job I couldn't finish, and weakened him even more. His limp got worse and his cheeks hollower. But I know better than to think it'd work in my favor.

It's when the king is about to be dethroned that he is the wickedest.

GODFREY

Sixty-something, English, head overflowing with cotton-white hair and a matching moustache, hobbles toward me, each leg creating a semi-circle as he puts it forward. *Likes:* Money, watching others writhe in pain and his son, Camden. *Dislikes:* when people cross him…*and me.*

Godfrey has a quad cane with tennis balls shoved onto each end. He clutches it in his hand to the point of pale knuckles. White stretch walker shoes, Bermuda shorts and Hawaiian button-up shirts are his uniform. He always looks like a retired tourist.

The police are less likely to pick on a tourist.

"What's in the bag, darling girl?"

"I busted your knees, your hands are fine. You can unzip it and see for yourself," I chirp, and am immediately rewarded with another smack from Seb. My body crashes against the dirty floor, a coat of dust sticks to my tongue.

"Camden misses you." Godfrey's voice floats above my head. Calm. Collected. *Crazy.* "He's coming stateside next month. Eager to see you."

Eager to kill me, more like. I shudder into my Prada dress.

"I'm guessing that's why my heart is still beating in my chest?" Said organ pounds so fast it almost burns a hole through my skin, spattering on the floor.

"Yes." Godfrey bends down to my eye level and taps my nose, feigning endearment. "And no. I'm going to let my son do as he pleases with you after you stew in misery. Beat you, shag you, gang-rape you. He'd be more than happy to tick all three boxes. But after he's done with you, you'll be delivered back to my loving arms. And trust me, Prescott, there's no fun in a bullet to the head. I have quite the plan for your death. You'll be made an example, a lesson for all to see." He trails his long, delicate finger on my neck, stubbing my chin to tilt my head upwards.

Our eyes click, the air between us super charged—light a match and the whole place would explode. A wide smirk spreads across his wrinkly face.

"It'll be a beautiful death. Gaudy, dazzling and inventive. A bit like you, come to think of it."

I gulp, chancing a glare at Seb and the muscle men. They stand behind Godfrey cross-armed, their masochistic glee barely contained by their tough charade.

"But first things first—accommodation." His tone turns cheery and he straightens his stance, clapping his hands together. "Prescott Burlington-Smyth had me locked up in prison for a few good years. . .and now she's going to have a taste of her own bitter medicine. She's about to learn a lesson about *time*. How awfully slow it moves inside four, thick walls of nothing. Bring me Beat and Ink. Now."

Two men charge into the warehouse in perfect timing. Godfrey always was one for punctuality. One is a chubby, short man in a ski mask and blue coveralls. The other is a tall, built guy. He's wearing black, ripped skinny jeans like a second skin, with a book rolled into his back pocket, military boots—unlaced—and a matching black hoodie. His straight dark hair is modernly slicked back, a Guy Fawkes mask covering his face. You can see from his form, posture, and the lazy way he carries his muscled body, that behind the mask is a man who sees more pussy than a pack of Tampax.

Godfrey saunters behind an office desk and falls onto a chair, resting his cane behind the table. Seb hands him my Nike bag as the masked men slouch on two plastic stools in front of their king, ignoring me completely. The chubby one in the ski mask straddles the back of his chair. Years of living in the back alley of life made me fluent in body language, and what his body says is perfectly clear—he's scared. Black hoodie guy, on the other hand, stretches his legs forward, the ridges of his bunching biceps and triceps visible even through the thick fabric of his clothes as he hooks his arms behind the back of his chair. Relaxed. Comfortable. *Peaceful.*

Well, he *is* the size of a tank. I need to be careful with this one. One punch from him and I'd be liquefied.

"See Little Miss Goldilocks over there? She's my job for you." Godfrey cocks his head my way as he unzips the bag. He takes out the drugs I was about to sell. The Glock, Taser, pepper-spray, fake passport and one hundred dollar bills wrapped together and stuffed into a sock. He also takes out the plane ticket to Des Moines dated for a month from now, placing everything on the desk like incriminating evidence. Lifting his crusty old eyes back to me, he pulls his lips downwards, faking a devastated frown.

"Shame, really. So close to escaping your fate. . .yet oh-so far."

If Godfrey thinks I am going anywhere without his blood all over my hands first, he is suffering from Alzheimer's on top of his new physical disabilities.

No. I wanted to stick around until the very end, kill him, Sebastian and Camden, generate some money and find my brother.

Preston.

Where the hell are you, Preston? It's not like you to disappear without a word.

Beat and Ink turn to look at me for the first time. Their masks mean I can't read what they're feeling, but I sure know what they're seeing.

And they're not seeing a typical drug dealer who spent the last five years selling coke and crack in the bowels of Stockton.

My long, honey-blonde waves, perfectly trimmed and impeccably shiny, are now matted to my bloody forehead and neck, big hazel eyes running in their sockets as they inspect them back. I'm wearing a designer, gray mini-wool dress that compliments my curvy body. Soft wide thighs and narrow waist. I look like the perfect victim. Scared. Beautiful. Innocent. . .

Though, I'm anything but the latter.

Ink goes back to staring at the drug lord. But Guy Fawkes—or Beat, as Godfrey refers to him—throws another glance my way before folding his log-wide arms over his pecs.

"The fuck, God?" he snarls.

They nicknamed him God? Is he leaving me with brain-damaged people?

"The fuck is you not asking any questions, Beat my lad. I expect you to keep her in the basement until Camden arrives next month," Godfrey orders dryly. "And if you want your balls left intact, she better not run away."

Beat shakes his head, chuckling on the brink of laughter. At least someone finds humor in my dire situation.

"I'm not down with this shit." His leg bounces under the table. It's so long and muscular, it sends the table shaking every time it hits it. "Thought you needed help with blow and weed, *not* kidnapping and trafficking."

Ink coughs, shifting unnervingly in his seat. "Yo, man," he says, leaning into Beat's shoulder with a whisper. "It's *Godfrey.*"

There's a moment when their eyes meet behind the masks, locked in a silent battle. It's a moment too long, and it will cost them a lot—because I realize that these two are far from friends. Works in my advantage.

"Trafficking?" Godfrey looks both startled and offended, playing with the zipper of my bag. "The only traffic she'll see is a few passing cars on her way to your house. This girl is not crossing borders. She's crossing forms, from living to dead. Just keep her in one piece and underground until my son's arrival. Doesn't take much more than a few brain cells and working limbs to do that."

Beat tips his head back, slipping his massive tan palms under his mask and rubs his face in frustration. He glances my way again, and I ball into myself, trying to look like a lost lamb. Ink nods vehemently to Godfrey's every word like he is reading from the Bible. He'll do whatever the hell Godfrey tells him to, like the majority of the human population. But the mammoth Beat guy. . .he's got some backbone.

"No." Beat stabs a finger on the desk, dragging it from end to end. "This is where I draw the fucking line. I'll pack a bag and pay you three months upfront for the rent. Count me out. This doesn't sit right with me."

Beat stands up to his full height, which is approximately the stature of an average-sized building.

"Oh, don't play the bloody saint now, Beat." Godfrey shoots up, hammering him back to his chair, spitting a yell. "You've killed before. You can babysit a little blonde girl for a few weeks. No one's asking you to slit her throat. That's for us to do."

Lookie here. One of my mysterious captors is also a *killer*. Fun times. I'm *so* happy I met Camden. *So* happy our fathers were in business, and we ended up hooking up. *So* happy I'm now tied to a chair in a warehouse, about to be thrown into some psycho killer's basement. Fun, fun, fun.

"I'm not doing it." The dark, tall guy states with conviction, his tone eerily peaceful. "Find another sorry ass to drag into your shit-show. I ain't hurting the girl."

"We're doing it," Ink snaps, nodding to Godfrey and resting a hand on Beat's shoulder. He is staring at the big guy, but talking to his boss. "We don't want any trouble, God."

Beat has none of it. When he stands up again, his chair flies to the floor with a bang that makes the whole room gasp. He storms toward the door before Godfrey's voice makes him halt mid-step.

"The Aryan brothers are close." The old man leans forward on his desk, his arms straining to hold him upright without the walking stick. "They're still on the lookout for you, and all it takes is one"—Godfrey grabs my Glock and points it at Beat, squeezing one eye shut—"little. . ."

He releases the safety with a soft, deadly click, his finger applying pressure on the trigger. "Push."

His hand moves up and he fires a bullet a few inches shy of Beat's head. Nausea slams into me and the room spins as I drift in and out of consciousness. I can still hear Godfrey's voice hovering like dark clouds over restless skies.

Beat hasn't moved an inch.

"Pshh. Little Prescott meant business when she got armed. Loaded, are we?" He blows air into the barrel mockingly and continues. "Trust me, son, you don't want to cross your loyal, truest friend. I might decide to lead them straight to your door if you do."

Color me intrigued *and* on death row. This Beat guy is full of surprises. I'm going to be a hot target next to this guy. God, I have to find a way to ditch these two clowns. I'll figure it out when they take me.

"It's not up to us." Ink shoots up from his seat, clasping Beat's arm. "It's your goddamn life, man. She's just a nameless chick."

Just a nameless chick. He has no idea how close he hit home. I used to be a sister, a daughter, a girlfriend and a friend. A poet, a dreamer and an honor student. But now. . .now I'm alone, left to fend for myself, with no one to look out for me. Some would say I'm taking my situation too lightly. I'm not. I'm looking at it from the outside, providing sarcastic commentary. Why? Because looking at my situation through a stranger's eyes is all I can do to survive. After what I've been through, allowing myself to become intimate with this thing called a soul is practically a death wish. No. I'm stuffing reality, jamming it under mundane thoughts, and looking at the whole thing like it's a terrible B-movie.

"Just follow the orders, pawn," Godfrey instructs, his eyes returning to mine. He is stroking my gun, looking like he is using every ounce of self-control in his frail body not to shoot a hole in my forehead. "Camden arrives in California in thirty days. He has a wedding to attend in London first. We cannot miss it. After all, it's *his*."

My throat bobs involuntarily, my nose nipping like someone's punched me square in the face. Camden's getting married? It's been a long time since I've last seen him. Up until now, I stupidly believed that I still knew him. But the guy I left behind wouldn't marry anyone who wasn't me. By the time we parted ways, we were much the same. Our guards were up so high, we couldn't even see beyond the walls we'd built.

I was his sun and his stars, his water and air. And in my eyes, he was beauty and art, witty and smart.

Now I want to kill him, and he. . .he wants to cage me.

Godfrey snaps me out of my reverie.

"Now take the girl away before I cut her open and sell her inner organs to the highest bidder. A few things before you go—one: Do. Not. Fuck her. She belongs to Camden, and if he wants her as a belated wedding gift as a sex slave until she's dead, it's for him to decide. Two—don't buy into her prissy charade. The girl might be of pedigree, but she is the epitome of ruthless, and she *will* try to run away. I'd expect nothing less from the daughter of a dirty politician. Three—" He takes a deep breath, rubbing his thin eyelids. "Do. Not. Fuck her. I said it before, but I'll say it again. My son is quite smitten with this one. I want her untouched and, as much as I hate to say it, unviolated. Don't hit her too hard and don't rape her. She's Camden's."

This could have been touching if Godfrey wasn't a kingpin with enough blood on his hands to fill a river, and Camden wasn't a tailored, spoiled brat who lived off his father's fortune and name. I hope my ex doesn't plan on reproducing. The world needs more Archers like daytime TV needs more *Friends* reruns.

"No one's gonna touch anyone," Ink reassures, placing his gloved palm on his heart. He is standing close, too close. I hate it when men get too close.

The pulse in my neck is so strong, I'm worried my veins will burst. Sebastian walks behind me, untying the rope that chains me to the chair.

"Oh, and a word of advice," Seb states casually with a deliberate tug that wounds my wrists, yanking me up to my feet. "Keep your masks on or blindfold her at all times. If she does get away, she will hunt you down and make fashionable jackets out of your skin. Make sure there aren't any sharp objects anywhere near her—for the exact same reason. She can fuck you over so hard you won't be able to walk straight for years." He rubs the small of his back, probably reminiscing about the last time I saw him.

Seb circles to my front and throws an uppercut straight to my nose one more time before I leave. My head swings backward and my skull finds the wall. I'm shaking, squeezing my eyes shut so I don't cry.

Happy thoughts.

Iowa fields.

White summer dress, cold against my warm skin.

Chocolate covered cherries.

Don't cry. Don't cry. Don't. Cry.

"Farewell, little rascal. Next time I see you, I'll tuck you in goodnight before your eternal slumber." Seb kisses my bleeding forehead gently, licking his lips—and my blood—with a smirk.

Ink's mouth drops into a stunned *O* through his ski mask.

Beat's smiling mask is trained on Seb. *They* don't know that last time I met him, I pushed Seb from the rooftop of a barn.

He was lucky he fell straight into the arms of his boss, otherwise, he'd be as broken as Godfrey.

Beat slingshots Seb against the wall, twisting the collar of his crisp shirt into a heap of wrinkles. "Hitting girls now, Sebastian?" he hisses, grasping Seb's jaw and squeezing so hard, the impending sound of a bone breaking fills the air. "And here I thought you couldn't get any worse than you were in San Dimas."

Seb laughs and pushes the big guy away.

"A girl? She's the fucking devil. Her ex-boyfriend calls her *Diabla*. That's Diablo with a cunt. All yours now. Have fun, mate."

The ricochet of Godfrey and Seb's laugher dances against the naked walls of the warehouse as Ink leads me to the door by the arm. Beat is hot on our heels, and panic takes over my feet, making me stumble like a drunk.

I don't want to leave.

I don't want to stay.

Not that it matters. I'm screwed either way.

"We need to search her for potential weapons." Ink tugs at the fabric of my dress. Beat grunts from behind us. We pour into the thinning summer night, the stars above me dimmed by pollution and the coat of tears I resist shedding.

My stress ball. I need it. *Now.*

"I volunteer," Ink snorts, his palm stroking the curve of my ass hesitantly. *Scared.*

My brain kicks into action and I realize what's about to happen.

"I'd like Beat to search me."

We stop in front of a rusty Toyota Tacoma—I think it was red at some point—and Ink fumbles for the keys in his coveralls.

I don't want to fuck my way out of a bad situation. It's always been a hard limit for me. But this time, I just might make an exception in order to save my life. Godfrey wants me untouched. The minute one of them sleeps with me, I have leverage over him. The master plan would be to run away, but considering their physical advantage, it's wise to have a plan B.

Now, I'm not sure which one of these idiots is more likely to hand me the *Out-of-Jail* card. Ink seems affected by my looks, but too mortified by Godfrey and his crew. Beat, on the other hand, isn't intimidated by the English gangster, but doesn't look like a guy who is struggling for pussy. Offering him sex would be like selling STDs to a street hooker.

"You don't get a say in this shit," Ink announces with borrowed authority. I can hear the uncertainty leaking from him. He's what I call an *easy job*. If it were just him watching over me, I would have been dancing in Iowan cornfields far away from here by now, Sebastian and Godfrey's heads tucked in that Nike bag.

"You make me uncomfortable." I yank my arm away.

"What, and the other guy makes you warm and fuzzy?" He sounds genuinely offended.

Beat inches closer behind me, and I feel the heat of his body drifting into mine. He's close. Hot-jock-leaning-against-your-locker close. It's going to be hard to bypass someone his size.

"You think I'm nice?" His breath moves through the plastic of his mask, tickling my ear. I shudder down to my toes. His mouth smells like peach. How bad can a guy who smells like a peach be?

"Nice-r." I clear my throat, my eyes still trained on Ink in front of me. Ink shakes his head, indicating that I'm dead wrong. The air becomes chilly. Why hadn't I noticed it's so chilly?

Because it's not. It's August in California, and I'm cold because I'm frightened.

"Let's test your theory. I'm going to touch you now. Move without permission, and I'm breaking your arm."

My busted lower lip splits open again as I scowl. He definitely looks like a guy who makes good on his threats.

"Okay." I lick my bloody lip, my voice tender.

Beat kicks my legs open and brings my arms up, patting me down dryly, like airport security. His rough fingers stroke the curves of my shoulders as he moves down from my skull to my outer breasts, circling them lazily. Down to my stomach, lower to my tensed inner thighs, then he pushes the fabric of my mini dress away to make room for his warm paws.

Every muscle in my body is ready to plow forward, to run away, to try and hurt him; the memory of every experience I've had that started this way demands for me to take action. But this. . .it doesn't feel like a violation. The sour taste of bile has yet to explode in my mouth.

His hands move down my legs, stroking my ankles. . .then he stops.

"Got something inside?" He squats down, hooking one of his thumbs into my ankle boot. His masked face is eye level with my pelvis, and warmth spreads along my bones like hot wax.

"No," I lie. There's still a slight chance he won't check.

But he checks.

Beat jerks my boot off and a Swiss army knife falls with a *clank* on the concrete pavement. I let out a sigh and drop my head. Shit.

Happy thoughts.

Frozen yogurt with Preston down at the local mall.

Curling up on the egg-swing with a Mia Sheridan book.

Water lilies blooming over the artificial pond in the Burlington-Smyth's garden.

A genuine smile from a stranger.

Beat stands up slowly, his gleeful mask zeroing in on my face. It all looks like a scene from a horror movie.

And I'm the victim.

"You know I can hurt you without leaving physical marks." His thumb brushes my lower lip, like he's about to kiss me, and chills run marathons up and down my arms. "Don't test me, Boots. I can make sure you suffer in more than one way your country club ass isn't used to."

Maybe it's because his finger is on my bleeding lip, and maybe it's because his tone is the most peaceful I've ever heard, but the threat runs deep.

"I'm so s–sorry." I stutter my way into heated cheeks. He doesn't answer, just shoves me lightly in Ink's direction, announcing in a flat tone, "Let's blindfold her. No way in hell I'm driving with this shit on my face. Wait here."

He strolls to the other end of the deserted parking lot, giving us his back, while Ink digs his fingers into my arm like a nervous child. Ink is twitchy, fidgety and judging from the wet pools under his armpits—scared shitless. I watch as Beat pulls off his black hoodie in the darkened corner of the lot. His back is defined with arches and muscles. Tan, and not only from the sun.

Manual worker, probably not Caucasian, I make a mental note in case I'll need to identify him in a police station someday. Still optimistic, as you can see.

Half of Beat's back is tattooed to its last inch, and the other half is completely ink-free. The tats end along his spine, making him look like half a man, half a machine. I watch his hard body flexing as he produces my Swiss knife, flips it open and uses it to rip his black shirt into long pieces.

He works the knife skillfully. Every movement is methodical, deliberate, almost like he is piecing it together into something magnificent, not tearing it apart to become a weapon against me.

Maybe he's a butcher. Everything about him sounds dangerous.

Killed before.

Just got out of San Dimas Prison.

Got beef with the Aryan Brotherhood.

Just imagining Godfrey's neck, instead of Beat's shirt, being ripped into shreds makes my thighs quiver.

"You did this to him?" I point my chin to Beat's half-tattooed back. Ink snorts smugly.

"Damn right I did."

Ink is a tattooist. And a stupid one at that, because milking intel from him was as easy as getting a cab driver to tell you their life story.

Beat strides back bare-chested, his hoodie swung over his tattooed shoulder, with strips of black cloth clutched in his palm.

"Hands," he orders sharply. I raise my hands forward, wrists glued together. He takes one piece of black cloth and binds my hands to one another. It doesn't hurt, but I won't be able to break free.

And Mr. Tied-Me-Up-and-Not-to-a-Bed took my Swiss knife.

"Turn around."

I spin on my heel and he wraps a second black cloth over my eyes. Utterly blind and completely helpless, the realization that I'm in trouble runs deeper. Beat and Ink might not be as dangerous as Godfrey and Seb, but they're still capable of doing very bad things to me.

"Hop in," Ink rasps behind me. The truck door swings open by the sound of it, but I stay rooted to the ground.

"I have no idea where I'm going," I seethe. Beat grunts again. I feel him pick me up—the bulge of his biceps hard and round—and rest my frame on the beer-scented seat. My dress rides up, and I know they can probably see my panties. I try to wiggle it downwards.

"Can you pull my dress down?" I only manage to swallow some of my humiliation, my voice soaked with raw shame. A moment of silence ticks by before I feel the tips of his fingers pulling the hem of my dress toward my knees. A shiver breaks up my spine, crawling its way to my skull. Probably just fear, I tell myself.

"Thank you."

He shoves me by the shoulder so that I'm lying in the cab and slams the door behind me.

"Don't lift your head unless you want me to shoot a hole straight into it." Ink barks, and someone slams the passenger door shut. "Enjoy the ride."

"I fully intend to," I bite, my eyes staring at the pitch black cloth with a woodsy, masculine smell. They underestimate me. That's exactly how I like my rivals.

They think of me as a rich bitch, a frail little toy.

Little do they know that I'm not a toy, I'm a storm.
And I'm going to rip their lives apart.

Beat and Ink spend the ride talking about Godfrey and Seb. I figured they all met in a magical kingdom not too far away called San Dimas State Prison. But I couldn't care less if they've all met through a knitting club. I put the pieces of Godfrey's operation together as I try to make sense of it all.

After I arranged for Godfrey and Sebastian to get thrown into prison, I became a small-time drug dealer, nibbling into a negligible piece of the NorCal drug cartel cake. I had three streets I worked in Oakland, Richmond and Stockton. Crack heads knew better than to mess with me especially after, early into my gig, I broke someone's jaw with my Glock when he tried to fondle me. There's a lot I can tolerate, but sexual harassment is a hard limit.

Cocaine. Weed. Crack. Even super-glue. If you can get high on it—I had it in my pink duffel bag. The suppliers I worked with gave me a fifty percent discount for tipping them off about the whereabouts of all the drugs Godfrey and Seb smuggled past the border before they got caught.

Yup, that's me.

Small. Blonde. Tailored. *Fearless.*

Godfrey Archer and Sebastian Goddard knew I was biting at their business on the outside, and I'm not going to lie—part of me sold drugs because I needed the money, but a bigger part did it to taunt them.

I heard that they were already targeting the inmates who were about to get parole, collecting soldiers to help them reclaim their empire. Recently, I changed streets. Dropped most of my clients and always met my regulars on different pavements so I wouldn't get caught.

Apparently, the client I was supposed to be meeting today, Joe, tipped off Godfrey and sold me out. *Asshole.* But that's how Godfrey works—buying friends and collecting debts.

I'm sure Beat and Ink owe him a favor. A big one, too. A favor that he cashed in tonight, in the form of me.

The men flip radio channels. My lack of sight sharpens my other senses. I detect Beat's husky, monotone voice. Growls are his favorite method of communication, and peace is the ambiance that pours from this huge man. He doesn't speak much, never raises his voice and is unimpressed with his companion. Ink's voice matches his body language: high, pitchy and articulate as an artichoke. He talks a lot, but says very little. A definite sign of stupidity.

"Can you believe this shit?" Ink spits. "Ain't nobody got time to babysit this rich kid. She's bangin', though."

Beat grunts in response. Maybe he doesn't share the sentiment.

"We can't tap that, but maybe we can get away with a BJ. Whaddaya' think?"

"If I find out you as much as grazed one of her fingernails, I'm handing you to Godfrey by the balls." Beat sounds so serene, you'd think he just offered Ink a pampering vacation in Bora Bora.

"Whoa, what do you care about this sorry ass chick?"

"I don't." He's detached, composed, unreadable. . .and scary as hell. "But that doesn't give us the green light to act like bitches."

Is it a good time to tell him Prince William won't be calling for etiquette tips anytime soon?

"Whatever." Ink disregards Prince Asshole of the East Bay. "I just hope she ain't gonna cry all day. The walls are thin, and you know how I need my morning naps."

"Don't worry," I shoot from the backseat. "My emotions are rare and treasured. I won't waste them on the likes of you."

Beat grunts. "Where's that quote from?"

"A little dark and twisted place called my head," I rub my tied hands against my face. The cloth is itchy, and it smells like Beat. It's not a bad smell. Spicy and fresh, with just a twinge of sex thrown in. Something male. Something dangerous. *Something musky.*

"Bangin', we've got ourselves a smartass." Ink snorts. I hear a smack Beat must've awarded him with.

"Your dark, twisted place might be worth visiting, kid." The compliment is aimed at me.

"Thanks. That means a lot coming from the guy who just kidnapped me," I deadpan.

"Shorty's got a mouth on her," Ink complains.

"Yeah, well, shorty's in luck. Our walls don't answer back," Beat says, slamming a lid on the conversation.

They pull up to the curb and drag me into what I presume is their house. I resist, digging my heels into the ground. Kicking, screaming, making a scene. Praying that someone will hear. My body twists from side to side as they usher me in. Someone tries to clap a hand over my mouth when they realize my yells can draw attention, and I bite it hard until my teeth meet. A slap to my cheek whips my face, my head crushing against a stone-hard shoulder.

16

Even before I feel the small, damp palm, I know that it's Ink and not Beat. I stop shouting because: 1. It stings like a thousand needles pricking my cheek, especially since Seb has already banged my head against every surface we came across earlier this evening. 2. The door behind my back shuts with an earsplitting bang, and hushed rage electrifies the air.

"What did I say about touching the girl?" Beat's large body pins Ink to the nearest wall by the sound of bones hitting concrete. "I'm letting you off with a warning." I hear something snapping. Not a bone, maybe a ligament. Ink cries in pain, howling like a dog who'd lost a fight. "Next time, your glowing career at flipping burgers is going to end on the grounds of two broken arms. No warning. No second chances. Understood?"

Ink is trying to swallow a scream, and I hear a slap that did not land on my face. I jump back anyway. Beat receives his answer in the form of a hard gulp I can actually hear.

"Words, idiot. Under-fucking-stood?"

"Yes." Ink's voice tells me he, too, is terrified of Beat's commanding presence. The power in the room is distributed haphazardly: I have none, Ink has very little, and Beat. . .he rules this place.

"Don't fucking touch her," he warns. "Ever. Again."

My burning cheek and I are relieved when I feel Beat's calloused hand pushing me through what I believe is their hallway.

"Come on, Country Club. I'll see you to your room."

Just when I think I have a real shot at forming some sort of a dialogue with this bizarre man, he throws me in his basement—laced with a dingy scent and moldy temperature. The deadbolt snaps from the outside.

"No." A small voice escapes my paper-dry throat. "No, no, no!" I'm throwing my bound fists against the door, begging.

Tied, blindfolded and in desperate need to pee, I start pacing in a pattern, trying to figure out how big the room is and what's inside. I'm hungry and dirty from my own blood and having been touched by Sebastian and Godfrey. And it kills me, knowing that it should have been the other way around. *I* was supposed to target them, not them me. If things had gone according to my plan, I would have killed Godfrey and Sebastian by the end of August. By September, I would have been on a plane to Iowa, sipping overpriced Coke and munching on peanuts on my way to a new, better life. A life where it wouldn't matter that my parents disowned me, that my lover ruined me, that my brother is still missing and that I became a savage who uses bold tricks to see the next day.

You just couldn't let it slide. Yet again, you had to let your ego override your welfare.

But even as guilt brews within me, I know that I stayed here all this time not only because I wanted to slaughter Godfrey, Camden and Sebastian like wild beasts. I stayed in NorCal hoping I'd find my brother, Preston. MIA for the past four years, since right before my father's political empire collapsed. I was twenty-one at the time, and he was only eighteen. I wanted to stick around, let him know there was still a place he could call home in case he came back.

That place was me.

Mom. . .she paid infrequent visits in our lives, rolling in and out with her Louis Vuitton suitcase. He and Dad never got along. My father was too proud and too stupid to accept his gay spawn. Preston was deemed unworthy as a human being and unwanted as a son. I guess he decided to take off and leave the place where he wasn't welcome.

But Preston hasn't shown up tonight. Beat and Ink did.

Knowing I'll be stuck in this place for at least a few days, I need to keep tabs on the time and date. Camden arrives in a month, and no matter what—he won't get to me alive, well and willing.

I bite the tip of my index finger. The skin cracks and when I feel the thick, warm blood dripping down, I smear a long streak on the nearest wall.

The countdown begins.

PRESCOTT

Some hours later, the door whines and my head flies up. I'm sitting in the corner of the room, my knees drawn and my chin resting upon them. My fingernails are bent and broken, a bitter reminder of my futile attempt to break free. Shrinking into myself, breathing as quietly as possible, I wait.

I think I hear Beat's footsteps. They're slower in pace, wider in stride. He's very tall. Very calm, too. *Peaceful.* My lungs wheeze and I loll my head back. It'd take me weeks to get all the dried blood cleaned up.

"Food." He kicks the sole of my boot. So it is him. Somehow, it makes me feel a little less scared. He didn't want me here, and didn't slap me across the face. Unfortunately, in my world, this qualifies him as some sort of a black knight.

I hear the clank of a plastic plate being thrown in my direction on the floor, but don't make a move for it.

"You deaf?" he asks.

"You stupid?" I smart off. "I'm blindfolded and tied. How the hell am I supposed to get to this food? The power of telepathy?"

He offers me another grunt, and I immediately regret snapping at him. I feel his fingers working the black cloth that's tying my hands together, that peachy breath on my face again.

Once I'm free, he bends down, his warmth engulfing me, and places the plate in my hands.

"What's for dinner?" I lick my injured lips.

"Whiskey-glazed steak with a side of wine-tossed asparagus." He lets out a sniffle before adding flatly, "Wait, my bad. It's just a peanut butter sandwich."

"That's better. I'm vegetarian."

"I'll let our chef know." He offers me his own brand of sarcasm, his voice already descending. I realize that he's about to climb back up. I can't let that happen. Who knows when he'll check on me again? The prospect of holding my pee a minute longer is nothing short of tormenting.

"Wait!" I launch forward, crawling on the floor toward his voice. I don't hear anything, so I continue.

"I really need to take a shower, wash off all this blood. And I really, really need to pee." I shuffle my way back to the corner, taking a small bite off my sandwich, my teeth brushing against my fingers. "Please?"

I feel his palm pressing flat against the wall I'm leaning on. I swear it moves a little from the impact.

"Finish your sandwich. Make it quick."

I wolf down my dinner before he grabs my hand and leads me up the stairs. He stalks closely behind, and even though it's taking me forever to climb up the narrow staircase, he keeps his grunt-count to a respectable minimum.

Leading me to the bathroom by the arm, he throws the door open and we both walk into the tiny room. Still blindfolded, I feel the cold sink stabbing at my lower back, but the warmth of his proximity keeps me from shivering.

"I need my privacy." I lick my lips, feeling him everywhere. Not only is Beat physically big, he is also somewhat of a human furnace. I swear he radiates enough heat to photosynthesize a whole forest. I guess it's good, because I always know when he's around. But also bad, because why would it matter? It's not like I can fight him in any way.

"Dream on, Country Club." Another grunt.

"Please." My voice breaks. Usually, I'm counting on my caramel blonde hair and big Disney-animal eyes—which he unfortunately can't see right now—to get me out of trouble. I have a feeling this guy is harder to crack. "Just lock me in and stand guard outside. What can I do? Arm myself with a bar of soap? Try and break free through the sink's hole?"

Is he going to buy it?

Is he sensitive?

Is he hard-nosed?

Maybe he's both. He's got some serious codes going on—no beating women, no manhandling your victim—yet he essentially agreed to lock me in here. Then there's his tone and body language. *Peaceful.* Like he hasn't got a care in the world, which couldn't be further the truth. I've known him for a few short hours and I'm already privy to the fact that he was an inmate in San Dimas, has killed, owes Godfrey a favor and has the Aryan Brotherhood on his tail.

"Be warned,"—his peachy breath tickles my nose—"when people are bad to me, I'm worse. Don't tempt my demons."

Beat takes off my blindfold, but he's not thoughtless enough to show me his face. His black tee is pulled over his head, revealing a tattooed six-pack. Even his fingertips are full of blues and blacks. Yet, one side of his body is completely ink-free. Massive, menacing. . .and as much as I hate to admit it, *attractive.*

Sweet Statute of Liberty, if I need to screw one of them in the name of freedom, please let it be him and not the chunky tattooist.

Beat can still see me through the fabric of his shirt, but before I get the chance to make out his face, he dashes out of the bathroom and locks the door from the outside with a key.

"You've got fifteen minutes to do everything. Pee, shit, shower, get dressed. Starting now."

I don't argue or waste a second. I jump into the shower and pee as the stream of gurgling water splashes over my body. My bladder is burning with release, and so are the blistering fresh wounds Seb decorated me with. Slowly, I'm starting to feel a little better, think a little clearer.

The water is hot and violent against my strained muscles. There's only one bar of soap—I'm pretty sure Beat and Ink are sharing it (I'm guessing they're roomies by the two worn-out towels on the rack). Not very sanitary, but hygiene is a luxury I cannot afford right now.

I scrub my body and keep the water running as I try to pry open the overhead rust-stained window next to the showerhead. I stand on my toes, peeking outside, blinking away disbelief as the sight in front of me registers. A teenager with a beanie zig-zags his way on a bike in the middle of the road, the electric wires above his head tangled with shoelaces and sneakers. Beyond the sight of shotgun houses, wilting porches and the echoes of desperate, barking dogs is a Taco Bell.

Taco Bell!

I recognize the branch. I'm in Stockton. Whose streets I know, whose crack heads I studied, whose language of hardship and adversity I speak fluently.

I study my surroundings. The house I'm trapped in is a simple one-story, and the house right in front of it is probably an identical bungalow. It looks deserted, so yelling will get me nowhere other than on Beat and Ink's shit list.

But I'm guessing by the sound of traffic and the location of the fast food restaurant that we're close to El Dorado, one of Stockton's main streets.

Knowing where I am will work in my favor when I run away.

And I *will* run away. One way or the other. With or without Beat's help.

I always land on my feet.

I broke free from Camden, Godfrey and Sebastian. Getting rid of these two should be a walk in the park.

Beat's fist slams against the door three times, then he unlocks the door from the outside.

"Yo, Silver Spoon. Your time's up."

"Just one second," I call, turning off the faucet and stepping outside. I reach for one of the manly dark towels and cover myself up as I squat down to pick up my gray dress.

Hold on a minute.

Manly. . .Dark. . .Towels.

They might have a shaving razor. Holy hell, they might have a weapon in here.

I start flinging drawers open, still wrapped in a towel, desperately trying to find something to injure Beat with. I don't even care if he hears. Give me a razor and I will dice this 6'5 Goliath to pieces the size of Barbacoa. Talent can be outworked and rage can outweigh size. That's the motto I live by.

Beat bangs on the door again, and it wails on its hinges.

"Hey. . .you," he grunts. *He doesn't even know my name.* "If you make me open this door myself, you'll be fucking sorry."

I ignore him. He can't rape or harm me. Godfrey made that clear. Honestly? I'm not even that scared of him. He's been nothing but compassionate to me so far, in his own, angry, Stockton way. Damn it, though. They have absolutely nothing in these drawers. Empty, empty, empty. What's wrong with these men? Do they not live here, or did they think about this scenario beforehand? Probably the latter. I'm just about to turn around and pick up my dress when the door swings open and Guy Fawkes's face greets me again, bat-shit crazy galore. The drawers are all open. I threw most of their contents on the floor in my desperate search for a weapon.

This is not looking good for me.

I stumble back, but he shoots his arm out, yanking me by the towel flush against his body. I bump into his hard abs, my eyes zeroing in on the curves of his pecs.

Okay, I take it back. A little scared now.

"You wanna play like that?" he grits out, his voice hoarse. I gulp as I scan his eyes for the very first time. Honey brown, almost greenish. . .and *full.* So full. Full of things I shouldn't see. Of soul. Of pain. Of a story behind a man I mustn't personify.

Breaking eye contact, I pick up my dress from the floor. So what? Hot killer guy has a soul. Big fucking deal.

BEAT

Big. Broken. Maybe even a little good, underneath all those calloused layers life wrapped him in. Indebted to Godfrey, and is filed under Must-Recruit-To-My-Side. *Likes*: Reading (he had a book in his back pocket), the color black and sarcasm. *Dislikes*: Ink, Godfrey, Seb. . .*not me*.

To him, I'm still a clean slate. Although that's starting to change.

I'm waiting for a slap or a punch to arrive, every muscle in my body tensing, but he just stares at me through his mask with those eyes.

"What's your name?" he growls, not unlike a beast.

"Prescott."

"Stupid name."

"Allow me not to take offense, considering the fact that you call yourself Beat."

I'm sure he smiles behind this mask, though there's no way I could tell. His body relaxes, which prompts me to breathe normally again.

"You need some ground rules, Country Club, so let me lay them out for you, before you do anything stupid that'd land your ass in trouble. One—if I find you looking for a weapon again, you lose all privileges. No showers. No peeing. No getting out of the basement. For all I care, you will sit in your own shit and piss until the Archers come and pick you up. Two—you disobey, you'll be punished. Food will be scarce and in-between. Three—" his eyes close, and when they open again, there's a flicker of something devious in them, "I'm not like them. I have no interest in making this unnecessarily painful for you. But don't try anything that'd make me turn on you. I easily flip, and once I do. . ."

My nipples brush against the rough towel at his threat.

"I need shampoo, soap and tampons." I try my luck. "And a stress ball. If you're going to keep me here. . ." I trail off, thinking about the outside world I just caught a glimpse of. Squinting my eyes, shaking my head, letting the soft, wet strands of gold frame my face. "Just. . .please. It's worse than prison."

"I'll see what I can do," he surprises me by saying. I nod curtly. The shampoo and tampons are luxuries I can live without. The stress ball, though. . .I've never gone out of the house without one. Not since a shrink I went to after the baby ordeal told me I should try and use one to release some of my anger. That's what keeps me relatively sane. It's what also keeps me a drug dealer, as opposed to a drug user.

"Thank you."

He leads me back to my cellar, where he blindfolds me again. My hands are back to being tied. They want to keep me disorientated, and for a good

23

reason. Godfrey told them I'm not who I appear to be. But whoever I am, I don't want to be left with myself right now. With my thoughts, with my mind working overtime, trying to second-guess Camden and Godfrey's next move.

"Please don't leave." I draw a sharp breath. As much as I hate to admit it, the anxiety in my tone is not only due to my plan to have him warm up to me in order to gain his trust, but also because I genuinely hate the idea of spending the next few hours alone.

He doesn't respond, and I hear the door shutting and locking behind him.

I bang my head against the wall, letting the tears that've been threatening to escape loose. I've already been through so much, but I just have to pull through one more thing. I can take these guys down.

It's only Stockton. I'm already so close to home.

Home.

I don't have one, but I do have a place I can call my own. It's called revenge, and I will seek it, find it and soak in it.

NATE

"Oopsie. Someone forgot to wipe down the windows."

I'm on my knees, mopping pristine hardwood tiles. Looking up to the woman who had spoken to me, I throw the wet cloth I'm holding near an exotic plant she once told me was imported from Singapore and push to my feet.

"Yes, ma'am." My acceptance holds more authority than her command. She knows it. What's more—she fucking loves it.

"Or. . ." Mrs. Hathaway presses her elbows on the grand piano in her living room, its keys still virginal, having never been touched. She angles forward, offering me a perfect view of her plastic tits as she lifts one foot in the air and twists from side-to-side in her white mini-dress.

All I can think about is that she's leaving marks I'll have to clean afterwards. "You can come upstairs and help me pack for Tahoe."

Ignoring her suggestion, I brush past her heading toward the shed outside where she keeps my cleaning tools, the squeegee included. I can still see her face in my periphery. It's painted with pricey makeup and displeasure—both unappealing to my taste—and by the time I get back to the foyer, Mrs. Hathaway's already deep into her plan B. She's sitting on her upholstered gray leather sofa in nothing but a tiny black bikini.

"Should I take this or the leopard one?" She waves the printed bikini that's clutched between her pink fingernails.

"Ma'am, I'd make the worst fucking stylist. I still wear the same pair of Dickies from when I was sixteen." Fisting the squeegee, I walk straight to her floor-to-ceiling windows, dangling the wire of the bucket I'm holding. I've worked here since I was released from San Dimas, housekeeping and doing some light landscaping when Mrs. H's gardener Eddie is out of town. Godfrey hooked me up with this minimum wage job. And even though it's in Blackhawk—a good hour or so from Stockton—I can't afford to pass on this opportunity. A felon with manslaughter on his record? I'm shit-lucky to have any kind of job, especially with a parole officer watching my every move.

And I need the money.

Bad.

I've never been bothered by my poverty. Haven't known anything else. Where I come from, you inherit poverty the way you do your eye color or height. You can't escape it, but you sure can ignore it.

No money, no pride, no problem.

Materialistic things do nothing for me. I'm a fugitive who escapes reality with a good book. This is the first time in my life I really need money, and I need it to survive.

It's time to turn my back and leave Stockton as well as Godfrey's watchful eye. Saving up is crucial so I can disappear.

For now, I have a place. I share it with a guy called Irvin and pay Godfrey pennies for the rent. But that's the problem—relying on Godfrey Archer's goodwill? Better to slit my own throat right fucking here.

Mrs. H is still eyeing my ass, eyes so heavy with desire she can barely keep them open. I feel the ache between her legs for her. Rich girls love bad boys. The tattoos, the attitude, the danger.

The hopelessness.

They want to fuck something dark and damaged, but always with a condom, God forbid our bleak reality would rub off on them.

Mrs. Hathaway built a fantasy in her head and cast me in the leading role. In that fantasy, I'm a beast, taking her from behind, going in dry, fisting her hair, spanking her until she purples, claiming her like a savage and leaving marks that'd confirm her grave assessments about my nature. I know that, because she's not the only rich girl who's tried to get some since I was released.

I may be a felon, but she's a sexual harasser of the highest level.

When I'm done wiping her windows, I change from the swim trunks she makes me wear on my shifts to my usual attire. I stand in her drawing room (the fuck is a drawing room? I've no idea, but she keeps calling it that so I humor her) and she slaps cash into my palm.

That's just the extra she pays me for working in nothing but my trunks. She also gives me a payslip every two weeks.

"Have fun in Tahoe," I grunt, praying it won't lead to more boring-ass small talk. Rich people just love small talk. For them, time's not a luxury.

"Thanks," she says, stretching her long limbs. She's got the legs of an eighteen-year-old sorority girl attached to a body of a forty-six-year-old housewife who fights nature with plastic surgery and bullshit green shakes.

"Ever been to Tahoe, Nate? It's quite spectacular. A lot to see and experience."

Here comes brainless blather. I crack my neck and squint, not sure why she's asking a question with such an obvious answer. Where does a Tahoe vacation fit into my reality? Next she'll ask me if I have a place in Aspen.

"We can go together sometime if you'd like. Stan will be spending the summer in New York. His company is opening an East Coast branch."

I raise my brow in amusement, leaving no room for negotiation.

"See you next week, Mrs. H. Again, enjoy Tahoe."

I stop at a drive thru before I go back home. It's a ritual I keep religiously, the only part of my day I don't hate completely.

Stella, my beat-down Toyota Tacoma (it's okay to give it a name when it's your only reliable companion in this world) is red and blends, but I still pull my hoodie over my face just in case I'm being watched. The Aryan Brotherhood is breathing down my neck, always. Seeking retaliation for a crime I didn't do, forever.

Two weeks after I got out, they almost managed to off me, blocking my way out from a side street armed with baseball bats. I beat them up and ran away.

Four months forward, and the car I'd bought when I left prison with the little money my mother left for me was set on fire in downtown Stockton. It wasn't just a financial disaster, an inconvenience and a fucking warning—it also made the authorities and my parole officer suspicious of my doings.

The day after my car exploded, I stood in front of a freshly released Godfrey. I told him I was willing to work for him in exchange for his protection. God has been dealing with the AB since his Californian drug cartel expanded before he got thrown in the can. They respected him inside and out. We struck a deal.

Now, eight months later, I still feel like the bull's eye.

Godfrey claims he's got them by the balls, but I don't trust anything the man says.

I order two double cheeseburgers, and it's only when the cashier hands me the food, that I remember that God's girl is with us.

And that she's vegetarian. *Fan-fucking-tastic.*

I smack my steering wheel and swallow a curse. Another mouth to feed, and an irritating one too.

"Get me something for a vegetarian too. A salad or some crap," I grumble to the teenager who serves me. She ain't happy about me placing an additional order when I'm already at the window, but she complies.

God's girl.

More accurately—Camden's girl.

How stupid can you be to get your ass tangled with the Archer men by choice? I know that she's some rich kid from the Bay Area, and as I said before, I have my theory regarding rich girls and bad boys, but this one didn't just jump into bed with a baddie. She didn't just fuck a baddie without a condom. She practically made babies with him, in the form of poisonous maggots that are now eating her life away.

At least she can take a fucking punch.

Seb's a jackass for hitting a woman. But the mouth that's attached to this woman. . .uncontainable. Uncontrollable. Of course he would fucking hit her. She's so much stronger than he'll ever be. Baby dick syndrome sufferers won't tolerate women like Country Club. Probably why she's neck deep in shit.

I climb down to the basement, two stairs at a time, and find her exactly as I'd left her—tied, blindfolded and sitting in the corner. She drags a bloody finger on the wall, right next to another line of blood.

She's counting the days until Camden's arrival.

Her head snaps up the minute the door locks behind me and her posture straightens. She scrambles to her feet, her chin lifting in defiance.

"Who is it?" she demands, her voice sharp and entitled like Mrs. Hathaway's. Unlike Mrs. H, though, God's girl doesn't sound desperate. If nothing else, it makes her slightly less annoying.

"Dinner," I grunt, throwing the plastic container to her feet. The basement is mostly empty. Irv and I have nothing to our names and when we rented this shithole, it barely offered the basics of two beds and an old, saggy couch.

But there's a rotting wooden table in the corner that's been here since before I moved in and a few carton boxes where we store our useless shit. Nothing that could serve as a weapon. Clothes, books, some old family albums Irvin keeps of himself and his crew. That kind of stuff.

This means Silver Spoon sits on the floor, sleeps on the floor, and considering the long hours I'm out of the house, she'll probably pee on the floor soon. She only gets one bathroom break, and after Irv slapped her when she first arrived, I gave him the *Don't-Come-Near-Her* talk. Just to make sure he took the warning seriously, I stomped on his foot. He's been limping ever since.

"I'm thirsty," Country Club announces through blistered lips.

I go upstairs and fill her a bottle of tap water. When I hand it to her after untying her wrists, she drinks the whole thing in one gulp and wipes her mouth with a satisfied cluck of her tongue.

"Shower," she demands next, then adds a little question mark at the end of the sentence.

I already figured out that she wants me to think she's some kind of damsel in distress. But her mask is as unbelievable as my Guy Fawkes one. It's full of cracks.

She's not weak, she's strong. Even worse, her strength shines through, blinding every fucking person in her vicinity. There's nothing submissive about a girl with fire in her eyes who seeks revenge. Thin-skinned people don't go around laughing in the faces of people who hit them. This chick is a holy fucking terror. She acted like the warehouse scene was some kind of big, fat joke.

What have you done to deserve this, Blondie?

"Eat first," I order, turning to climb back upstairs.

"Then sit with me. I really need to hear something other than silence."

Having been in segregation, I know exactly what she means. When the silence is so loud, you want to tear the place down until the pain of bleeding fingers shout your screams for you. But the truth is I don't owe her shit.

And I definitely shouldn't play into her game.

"Got plans."

"Please." Her tone is anything but begging. "You have the outside world all day. All I have is you. Ten minutes is all I ask. We'll eat and then you'll go."

Ten minutes won't kill me, I guess. And whatever shit I'm dealing with right now, her problems are a hundred times bigger. I sit at the far corner of the room, opposite from her, and rip my brown paper bag open.

"Thank you," she mouths. We eat. God's girl's pretty disorientated. Trying to eat a salad while being blindfolded is a bitch. She stabs her plastic fork—I make a mental note to take it away when she's done—in the air, around her thighs, anywhere other than the plastic bowl before giving up altogether. Then she starts eating with her hands.

"Tell me about yourself," she says, munching on lettuce.

"This is not a blind date," I growl.

"Technically, it is." She grins at the pile of leaves sitting on her lap, her eyes still wrapped in the black cloth of what used to be my shirt. I don't humor her.

"You know, I majored in English Literature at UCLA." She pops a cherry tomato between her lips. They're the best kind of lips. Her upper lip is thicker than the lower one, creating a natural pout.

"Good for fucking you."

"The best life to live is the one people will judge you for." She brushes her upper lip with the tip of her tongue. "Dance with your demons, love carelessly. Selflessly. And most importantly, love yourself, even at your worst."

Wow. She's so fucked up. And nuts. I kinda' dig it.

"Did Ink hook you up with some dope? Are you fucking high?"

"It's a part of a poem I wrote in lit school. It was published in the campus newspaper." She pats the inside of her bowl.

I wanna get up and tell her to forget about the whole thing, but my ass is still rooted to the floor, because I shouldn't be intimidated by some rich kid.

"Let me guess," she rasps, "You graduated from the School of Hard Knocks?"

"Nope. Dropped out of that one, too. I'm a failure through and through. There's not even one competent bone in this body." I bang my fists on my chest like a gorilla.

She's laughing at my lame joke—it sounds genuine—and I notice her hands caressing the walls of the black bowl again. She's finished her salad but is still hungry. Of course she is. She hadn't eaten all day. Reluctantly, I scoot to her side and place my fries in her hand. I can raid the kitchen later. A small beam tugs at her lips. "Thanks. So why Guy Fawkes?"

"Easiest mask to get on the market."

"And why Beat?"

This, I don't answer.

"Let's see. . ." She nibbles on a fry, bobbing her head backward and contemplating. Her neck is thin. Pale. Fine. *I'd love to choke it.* "Ink is called Ink because he's a tattooist—wasn't difficult to milk that one out."

"Fuck-tard." I inhale, rubbing my face. That's another reason why I keep him away from her. Is it any wonder he ended up in San Dimas? The guy's so stupid it's borderline illegal. I've lost count of the times he's gotten us into trouble with his stupid mouth. Be it at a bar or just picking up fights with the teenagers on bikes across the road. This week he tells her what he does for a living (it's not even true. He hasn't worked in a parlor since he was released), next week he'll be sharing tips on how to sneak out of here.

"You probably thought of names together, so that means your name has a meaning, too. Beat, huh? Music? But you're too silent to be the partying type. Maybe you like to beat people up. . .but then you wouldn't be so shocked about Seb smacking me for fun. And maybe. . ." She leans closer. "Maybe I fell captive in the arms of an avid reader. Wouldn't that be something?" Her shoulder brushes mine. Something weird stirs inside me, signaling that my body's awakening from its normal dormant state.

"*Beat generation* fan. But who's your favorite? Fante? Bukowski? Burroughs?" She leans closer. My mouth twitches. *What. The. Fuck?* "Which one of these authors plays the strings to your lonely heart, Beat?"

"You done psychoanalyzing?" I stand up, taking her hand and jerking her up. "You've got fifteen minutes of peeing, shitting and showering. Hurry your ass up, Sigmund Freud."

She follows me up, and this time doesn't stumble on the stairs on her way to the bathroom. Quick learner.

"I need a few extra minutes to wash my dress. And maybe I could borrow a clean shirt from you while it dries?"

I don't want to pamper her, but these are the kinds of things you are granted in prison, no questions asked. "I'll wash it. I'm keeping an eye on you after your little stunt yesterday."

"What if I need to use the toilet?" her tone turns panicky.

"Then you should be happy to know I shared a cell with a guy who took shits less than a foot away from me while I was eating fucking dinner. In other words—I couldn't give a damn."

When we get to the shower, she peels off her dress. Her cream lace panties are thrown to the floor. Silently. Confidently. Assertively.

Her nipples, pink like cotton candy, spring free from her lace bra, and my eyes drop to the blindfolded girl's pussy. Completely shaved—or maybe waxed—her pussy is like a delicate flower. A sudden urge to rub my nose against it hits me hard. She reeks of privilege; her sleek body screams it. She walks like a rich person, talks like one, and her body is milky-white and scar-free.

Though by her odd behavior and deadly enemies, I have a feeling that despite her exterior, her interior is virtually disfigured.

Being a twenty-seven-year-old man who hasn't tasted pussy in five years sucks ass. My balls immediately tighten to the sight of her body, and I let out a surprised growl. I feel my cock twitching, and almost stumble back in awe.

What. In. The. Actual. Fuck?

After I got out of prison, I tried everything to get my mojo back. One night stands. Strip clubs. Hookers. I got a lot of offers from women, thanks to a face that can only be described as so pretty, I had to cover myself up with bad ink just to keep my ass from being torn by San Dimas's Gay for The Stay crowd.

Women courted me.

Old, young, beautiful and ugly. The model type, the curvy type, the everyone's-type type. But ultimately, none of them made me hard. You know, *really* hard. Hard and wanting and seeing everything through the fog of red, agonizing desire.

Don't get me wrong—I do get hard. All the time.

I get hard when I think about slitting the throats of Godfrey and Sebastian. I get so fucking horny when a vision of me, blithe and free, driving in a convertible sports car without worrying that the Aryan Brotherhood will spot me pops into my head. I jerk off to the beat of independence, freedom and peace of mind.

But never to a woman.

To put it nicely—the vehicle drives just fine, but the GPS is out of service. No compass, no guidance, no turn-ons.

I tried porn. Straight porn. Gay porn. I even watched porn involving a cow and a sheep I wish I could erase from my memory. Nothing turns me on.

And now there's a hot, blonde girl in my bathroom—naked and blindfolded, her nipples as erect as my dick is—and it terrifies me that I've finally found someone I'd like to dirty up, rub some of my filth on. Because she's pretty much the *only* person in the world who's completely off limits. Hell, I'd have fewer issues if I screwed the living, fully-grown cow I watched the other day.

But my balls. . .they demand to be emptied inside Country Club.

"Get in." I shove her into the shower angrily, and turn on the showerhead. This time she'll have to do it blindfolded. I pick up her filthy dress from the floor and twist the knob, rinsing it in the sink. She hums something I don't recognize underneath the stream of water and rubs her arms and legs behind the shabby plastic curtain, occasionally patting the tiles to try and find the soap. I bend toward her, flapping the curtain away and reach for the soap so I can give it to her, my hand brushing her bare stomach.

We both flinch at the contact, and for very different reasons.

"Beat!" Her voice pitches high. I growl.

"Relax, I saw you were looking for the soap. Here." I stick it in her palm, but use the opportunity to glare at her nipples again. They're like sweet fucking coins I'd like to toss between my thumb and finger. Her mouth pulls from displeased back to content as she continues humming, shutting the drape so I can't see her. "You said you'd buy me what I need for my shower."

"I never said it'd be today. I ain't Amazon Prime." I sniff, getting back to washing her dress. I've no idea why I said that. Actually I do. She was really fucking sad and really fucking vulnerable. "No fancy shit, God's girl. You'll only get the basics."

"My name is Prescott." She draws the curtain back sharply and pokes me in the shoulder.

"Shitty name," I drawl again. I hate it when rich people give their kids pompous names. Prescott's a last name. Not a first.

"Stop being mean just because you can't stand the fact that you like me," she says breezily.

I kind of like that she's still keeping things light despite her situation. It's badass. I watch the dirt and blood seep out of the fabric of her dress with fascination, swirling in circles of a black and red whirlpool down the sink. It's better than watching her body, knowing I can't destroy it.

"Pea." Her voice carries from behind the curtain. "Call me Pea. It sounds like a nickname I can get behind. Country Club and Silver Spoon are plain annoying. And don't 'God's girl' me, either. I'm no more his girl than you are his soldier."

She turns off the faucet and draws the curtain open. I pull my towel from the rack and hand it to her, looking the other way and hoping *my* soldier ain't saluting in her direction.

Luckily she can't see shit.

"Dry up. I'll hang your dress in the backyard. Fair warning: If you try and pull any more stupid shit, you will not be fed for three days."

I throw her dress over the clothesline and walk to my small bedroom— it's half a room, actually, Irv took the master bedroom before I moved in— and readjust myself in my jeans.

Yeah, sergeant Vela definitely saluted to our new tenant.

I sift through my stuff. I don't have many shirts and most of them are in poor condition. I pull out the newest one that I bought for my job interview with Mrs. H and walk back to the bathroom. Prescott awaits, silent, naked but dry. Her back is arched seductively, her ass round and her tits just the perfect size for my palm.

The minute I walk in, she parts those full lips into a shy smile. Every single move is deliberate. The little bitch is trying to seduce me, and it's working. I really do want to strangle her.

"Hi," she says softly.

"Bye." I throw the shirt into her hands and turn my back to her.

I catch her pulling my shirt over her head. It's so big on her small, curvy body, she could probably use it as a fucking blanket. I take her hand and guide her out of the bathroom. I'm eager to throw her in the basement so I can go back up and see if the smell of her spicy, sweet pussy stuck to my towel. Yeah, grinding my cock against a towel is just another low I might stoop to today.

"Beat, let's do dinner tomorrow."

"Pea, let's not," I snap.

"Please? Solitude is the kiss of death to the spirit." She wiggles her words at me like they're her curvy ass, and my cock jumps to attention again. Where's *that* quote from?

"No."

"We can exchange notes on Godfrey. I'm sure he screwed you over, too. That's his trade, and that's why you're holding me against my will. . .and against yours."

I don't answer her, but I pull my shirt up to cover my face and take off the bandage covering her eyes. Tonight, her hands won't be tied, either.

"Wait, Beat!"

"Bye, Felicia." I kick her little ass into the basement and slam the door behind her.

Good fucking riddance.

PRESCOTT

I see everything.

The basement must've leaked for years. Mold blooms on every corner of the ceiling, smeared on the walls like a horrific scream. The air is wet and smells of despair. Everything is bare. Gray bricks dotted with black filth. No amount of scraping and washing will bring this floor back to good condition.

Other than a small wooden table and some saggy carton boxes, there's no furniture.

No electricity.

Not even a dangling bulb hanging by exposed wire for comfort.

No. Light.

A part of me is woeful that he didn't leave the blindfold on. Then, at least, I could have convinced myself that this place was livable.

I see everything.

There's a row of windows high up on the walls, boarded from the inside by rotting wood. I will try and peel it off the minute I get my hands on something sharp.

Shaking violently, I rub my arms and light jog in a patterned circle to raise my body temperature. The mold makes everything cold. I circle the room, wishing I had a stress ball, before I hear it.

Boom.

I strain my ears, somehow knowing that another one will follow.

Boom. Boom. Boom.

It's steady, angry. I press one ear against the wall, squinting and pressing my lips together.

Boom. Boom. Boom. Boom. Boom. Boom.

Whoever it is upstairs that's doing it, is tearing the place down. Ripping it apart. Furniture crashing, walls banging, wallpapers stripped raw. Whoever it is is angry as hell.

Beat.

I see everything, and I hear everything.

He's frustrated. Mad. Pissed.

Just like me.

He's handicapped by Godfrey just as much as I am. We shouldn't be enemies, we should be allies. A coalition of revenge against these men.

The need to pull him to my side is so overwhelming, I even tried to seduce him in the bathroom. I don't know what came over me. I usually avoid sex. I usually avoid *men*.

I scrape the wall with my fingernail as I think about how I got here in the first place.

Camden.

Beat needs to know. He *has* to know that we're on the same team. He can't let them kill me.

"I met him at a charity event seven years ago. I was eighteen and he was thirty, and I basked in this powerful man's attention, like a lazy cat under the sun. Posh English accent, sharp suit—he wore Dior—and manners to die for. I'd never met a man like him before."

Beat's furniture-crashing stops, and I continue into the dusk, my voice hoarse but bold.

"I remember eyeing Camden behind my dad's shoulder. Howard Burlington-Smyth was talking to Godfrey Archer, and this was a big deal. Archer had a shady reputation, and my dad was the mayor of Manor Hill, a small, affluent town near Blackhawk. He had aspirations of becoming governor, and he needed money to kick-start his campaign."

Money Godfrey Archer had in spades.

Money Camden Archer wiped his ass with every morning.

"Officially, they were businessmen with properties all over northern California. Officially, this was all legit."

Swallowing painfully, I look up. I know why the commotion above me has stopped. *He can hear me.* Thin walls, thin floors. This paper house will crumble under the weight of my truth.

I'm going to rewrite my destiny by luring Beat to my side.

"That night, Camden took my hand in his and we sat underneath the stars, talking. Laughing. Falling. I was studying in Los Angeles and he was going back to England the next day. His dad let him run some of his London-based businesses. You know, keep the kid busy.

"Camden was an average looking guy. Plain, bland even. Ink blue eyes, thin lips and a bony nose. He had a lanky long frame with a hint of a beer belly poking out.

"I was young and impressionable and thought frat boys and college brats were beneath me. I wanted something different. *Something dangerous.*"

"The day after the charity event, I flew back to Los Angeles, disappointed with the loss of Camden. I thought our encounter would be forever shelved under 'What If?'

"What if he lived in California?

"What if I'd been bold enough to ask for his number?

"What if he was the love of my life and I let him slip between my fingers?"

Sighing at the young, juvenile Prescott, I squeeze my eyes shut and continue.

"But I soon learned that the Archers don't live well with 'if's'. They are more of 'when' kind of people. A first-class plane ticket to London waited at my dorm, along with a warm designer coat for the valley girl who has never had to brave English storms.

"I should've seen the red flags back then. They were flipping in the wind of an impending storm, but I was too young to understand what I was doing.

"I'd never been to London, but always wanted to visit. I thought I was falling for a bad boy, when in fact, I got caught in the web of an evil man. The thing about cold-hearted monsters is that in the dark, Beat, their touch is just as warm as any other person's.

"This was the beginning of my fall."

NATE

I bang my head against the wall behind my bed in a systematic tempo.

Boom. Boom. Boom. Boom.

I took it hard when she *made* me hard. I took it hard and I took it out on my walls and bed and stereo and laptop. It was unfair, yet made uncannily perfect sense that I'd want to fuck the only person who I shouldn't.

Finally, I was physically attracted to someone. But having her meant getting killed, and with all due respect to my cock and Silver Spoon, I'm sure she's a good lay, but not worthy of my head.

Then she started talking and my lame reason to keep her captive became even lamer.

She's hurt and broken in her own, fancy-ass country club way.

And I'm hurt and broken in my own, broke-ass ghetto way.

I know what she's feeling, but I shouldn't.

"Shut the fuck up, or I'm sending Ink to shut you up for me," I grunt when I hear her shuffling downstairs, muttering something about the moment she got on the plane to London to meet Godfrey's son. Irv's not even here. He works night shifts at a local fast food joint, but she doesn't need to know that.

Prescott zips it.

I sigh in relief, raking my bloody palms through my face and hair, leaving red stripes like war paint. God's girl. Country Club. Silver Spoon. All these nicknames won't do justice to the dancing flame that's trying to blaze her way out of my basement.

Pea.

PRESCOTT

Another day of nothingness eats at my soul.

Another day of trying to figure out how to break away or how to break Beat. Both will grant me my wish—freedom.

Like everything else, this is a numbers game. What are the odds of me running away without his help? Right now, with no weapon, slim. And what are the odds of him cracking for me? Perhaps they will get better tonight, with a little push from Mother Nature.

Time moves too slow and too fast, as it does in desperate situations. Sometimes, when I fall asleep on the cold floor, I wake up with a sharp inhale. My hair is slick with sweat and my throat burns after his hourglasses haunt me in my dreams. *Hourglasses.* I can't bear them anymore. I once slammed my fist into the new TV in my living room because I saw the opening to *Days of Our Lives*. Spent the night in the ER.

Time.

I'm running out of it.

Today I've decided that since I'm not blindfolded and tied anymore, I should go treasure hunting in the carton boxes under the table. There are some old clothes and family albums from one of the guys, but I don't know which, and they're so dated, the people in the photos are either too old or too young to be recognized.

Shoving my hand again into the damp box, I retrieve a simple-looking red book. When I open it, warmth flutters in my chest, taking over, making my heart beat faster.

THIS DIARY BELONGS TO

NATE THOMAS VELA

INMATE #21593

SAN DIMAS STATE PRISON, CALIFORNIA

No. Way.

There's no question it belongs to Beat and not to Ink. I'll bet anything I have that Ink barely knows how to spell his own name. Beat, on the other hand. . .the first time I saw him, he had a paperback rolled into his back pocket.

His nickname is homage to the literature movement.

I flip a page and read the first entry, my back pressed to the boarded windows, slivers of light licking at the yellow, crusty paper.

OCTOBER 23RD, 2010

IF YOU'RE GOING THROUGH HELL – KEEP GOING (WINSTON CHURCHILL)

Cafeteria. Red-rimmed eyes. Prepackaged meal. Still untouched.

"Took your time, but you've made it, boy." A squeeze on my shoulder throws me back to reality and I snap out of zombie-mode. Twisting my head in surprise, I see my old neighbor, Frank. As a kid, I spent a lot of time in his backyard helping him build shit from all the damaged stuff he had collected from street corners. Broken bikes and TVs were his favorites. I loved his willingness to fix broken things. I also loved his black eye patch. Thought he was a pirate. Or maybe a brave soldier who got injured in Vietnam.

He was neither.

Someone took his eye out with a swizzle stick in a bar fight.

I knew he was serving time here for drug trafficking because moments after the police dragged his ass out of his house five years ago kicking and swearing, his meth lab exploded and formed an atomic bomb-like mushroom cloud above our neighborhood. Took two weeks to get rid of that black shit.

I hunch the shoulder he's clutching in a shrug.

"Not much to do outside, huh?" He slides next to me with his tray and rips into his four bangers like it's Burger King. "Here, at least you don't have to pay rent."

I avert my gaze from him back to the cafeteria crowd, my eyes landing on the sea of bald, tattooed heads in front of me, lined up in layered, horizontal rows.

"Whaddidya' do, Nathaniel?"

"I killed him." I roll my tongue over my teeth.

He nods. "Finally."

Yeah. My dad left impressions everywhere. He was special like that.

"Plea deal?" He stabs something that vaguely resembles beef and smells like mothballs with his fork.

"Fifteen for manslaughter, parole in four." The judge said no man should so effortlessly and brutally kill someone else. If it was purely self-defense, Judge Chester argued—then why did I smirk as the cops read me my rights?

"How old will you be when you get out?"

"Twenty-six."

This awards me with a satisfied nod. Ha. My neighbor thinks I'm redeemable.

Think again, old man.

I came here with plenty of holes in my shoes and plenty of nothing in my belly. Life felt like I was sipping it through a narrow straw. I always gasped for more.

I have the whole sob story written in its predictability all over my resume. Bad school, bad neighborhood, bad family.

My only moment of deep breath was when I smashed a vase into Nathaniel Vela Senior's head. Between working as a janitor at the local mall and trying to stop my father from beating the shit out of my mother, there wasn't much room for chasing opportunities or grabbing life by the throat.

San Dimas was an upgrade, as far as I could see.

But I'm not like them, the young inmates.

Hungry and angry and boiling with barely restrained ire. I'm at peace with where I am. Hell, it's probably exactly where I should be.

"Plenty of jobs for you when you get out."

I throw him a condescending smirk and wipe my utensils with the sleeve of my orange uniform.

But Frank is not the type to be deterred by silence. He nudges me and laughs, spitting crumbs of minced meat on the table. His good eye is dry and rarely blinks. Probably for a good reason, 'round here.

"You still writing poetry, Nathaniel?" He hoots, choking on his food. I used to write under his oak tree as a kid. His place was quiet, mine—chaotic.

I don't indulge him.

"Might wanna keep your little hobby for yourself here. You're too pretty to walk those halls without guard escort as it is."

Taking a slow sip of my water, I stare ahead.

"Don't worry, boy. I got your back."

I'm not worried. Because in order to be worried, you need to care.

And I don't.

Peaceful, yet completely apathetic.

That was my state of mind before I got here.

And that's how I will most likely leave.

I'm running my bloody finger over the wall—for the third time since I got here—when he arrives with his Guy Fawkes mask and a brown paper bag. I sit straight and watch him intently. *Nate*. It's difficult to admit that he's my sunray in the rain, but that's exactly what he is. Weird, freaky, elusive. . .and comforting all the same.

"Soap, shampoo, Tampax, couple of clean shirts. . ."—he starts listing what he brought for me as he takes the items out of the bag, placing them in a neat row on the small wooden table, not even sparing me a glance—". . .two bottles of water, three bags of chips, chalk so you'll stop smearing blood all over the walls, I'd like my deposit back, believe it or not, a stress ball, a book. . ."

"What book?" I cut into his words, lolling my bloody finger inside my mouth, sucking it clean. His head twists. He wasn't ready for my question.

"Something I had upstairs."

I jump on my feet and pace toward him. The eyes behind the mask remain blank. He doesn't scan my body. He doesn't find me attractive, or if he does, he's extremely good at hiding it. My heart dives down with disappointment. It's going to be difficult to seduce him into making an epic mistake that'd grant me my freedom. Taking the stress ball from his hand and squeezing it fast and hard makes me feel instantly better, like I'm pumping some of the storm out of my body. It's been overflowing for days.

"*Dreams from Bunker Hill?*" I pick up the coffee-stained paperback with my free hand, brushing his tattooed knuckles, and not by accident. Each finger is inked with a cartoonish doodle. Ink was either drunk or is extremely untalented to have given him these horrible tats. My shoulder purposely bumps into his chest. He takes a step back, staring at me like I grew a pair of wings and a third green eye.

"I read it when I was fifteen." My tone is lenient. Nostalgic.

"Sucks for you. I'm not a library."

"You know what this is?" I brush the wrinkled spine of the book, still warm from its owner's touch. He folds his arms over his massive chest, staring at me through the mask. "This is you telling me that's why you called yourself Beat. Admit it. You want to talk to me, you want me to *listen*." I lick my lips, clutching onto the novel like I can squeeze Beat's heart's desires and secrets with it.

"You seem to know a lot about a nameless man in a mask you hang out with a few minutes a day," he grunts.

"Have dinner with me here."

"No," he says. "Your fifteen minutes of shitting, showering and washing your clothes have officially started. Move it."

Reluctantly, I drag my feet upstairs with my new toiletries in tow and watch as he pads into the bathroom, locking the door behind us.

"How come Ink is never around?" I take off my clothes.

"He works nightshifts."

That explains why we spoke freely last night.

"He's here tonight, though," Nate adds.

"So how come he hasn't checked on me even once?"

I swear he blushes under that mask.

I don't want him to think that I have a problem with the current arrangement, so I reassure him, by adding, "I'm not complaining. I like you better, for the record."

"Duly noted, now get your ass in the shower." He gives me a light nudge. I turn my back to him—showing him that I trust him and start humming under the stream of hot water, swaying my hips to a bad pop song. I love pop songs, because the Archers hate them.

Nate washes my dress again, even though there's no need. Maybe it soothes him to do something while he's here.

"Why were you upset last night?" I throw my head back and let the water wash out the shampoo he bought for me. It's hard to believe that only a few nights ago, I was still living in Danville, with a walk-in shower and four showerheads in my own giant bathroom. My usual shampoo is made of organic coconut and my body lotion probably costs more than his shoes.

"Finish up. I'm gonna hang this in the meantime." He ignores me and walks away, locking the door behind him. I quickly get out of the shower and resume my search for sharp objects.

Remember, Prescott, it's a numbers game. Nate's crack-up percentage is at about 15%, if not less. Camden will be here in twenty-seven days. . .

Time.

Godfrey was right. It slips between your fingers until you're dead. I need to find a way out of this place, fast. I can't rely on Nate's good heart if I have a slight chance to make it on my own.

I place one foot against the wall, grab the towel rack and pull it out with force. I use it to pop the lock on the bathroom door with a loud bang. There's no way either of them didn't hear the lock breaking in two.

Time.

I know my countdown starts now.

Ten.

I storm out with nothing but a towel. Once in the narrow, dim corridor, I run straight to the small living room and launch for the main door.

Nine.

It's locked. I swivel back and look around, eyes frantic, urgently searching for the keys.

Eight.

They should be here somewhere. Beat and Ink can't lock themselves in from the outside.

Seven.

I hear his heavy footfalls. The hallway is short, too short.

Six.

I spot the keys resting inside a fruit bowl, hidden between a few black bananas. I scoop them and jam the key into the lock with shaky hands. I can't do it. Dammit, I keep missing the hole!

Five.

Trying once.

Four.

Trying twice.

Three.

Come on. Come on. Come on.

Two.

Taking a deep breath, I jam the key again, twisting it left and right.

Click.

I swing the door open and trip through it, at first heavily, like I'm moving through sticky dough. I still can't believe my good luck. My pace breaks into a full-on sprint when I get used to the sudden fresh air. I'm out. My bare feet are hitting the dewed grass.

I'm out. I'm out!

I'm running into the pitch-black night, toward the lights, toward Taco Bell, toward freedom. Once I get there, I'll fall to my knees and beg the cashiers for help. They'll call 911. I'll be safe.

All I need is to get to the corner of this sleepy, wide-road boulevard. It merges with El Dorado, one of Stockton's main streets.

Liberty is at my fingertips, and I can almost brush it. Hell, I can already *smell* it. Nighttime breeze hits my lungs, the bloom of summer violent with its hopefulness. I gulp it in pleasure, gasping for more.

Stumbling upon shattered beer bottles, I race forward, wincing in pain but never stopping, my muscles straining under the rush of adrenaline.

I'm just about to round the corner into plain sight when a huge body football-tackles me into the grass of a front lawn.

My airway is cut by the attacker, who is pressing against my torso. Intentional? At this point, completely irrelevant, as I'm thrown back to square one. Muscular legs are straddling my body and he's using one hand to pin my arms above my head, the other to cover my mouth.

Nate.

I'm yelling, biting into his palm with everything I have, knowing that he is too good to hit me, too good to inflict pain upon me—though not too good to let me run away from the hands of those who would destroy me—but all I get is his low voice growling brokenly, "Sorry."

I pop one eye open, shocked. *He's sorry?*

"You're trying to save your life, I get it. But I'm trying to save mine, all right? We can do this cat and mouse thing, where you're trying to break free and I impose shitty rules to keep you from escaping. Or you can just accept that this is not going to happen. Next time, you'll be out of this house, Godfrey and Camden will escort you out."

I feel my chest trembling with tears. Hatred and terror block my throat, making it impossible to swallow. The possibility of not running away from here crashes into me for the very first time. And to think that I was so close. That I'm *still* close. Outside in the open, straddled by a huge masked man.

But this is a quiet side street in Stockton. On the corner of the street, three homeless people with loaded supermarket carts are yelling and throwing junk at each other.

A bum sleeps under a small shed he created for himself down the road, unmoved by our commotion.

There's a junkie sitting on the steps of a church not too far away, talking animatedly to her fingers.

Beat and I are nothing special here. Even if we were, no one is going to pick a fight with a guy so big and muscular. Not for me, anyway.

No one is coming to get me.

I open my mouth, intending to protest, maybe even beg—I'm not above begging at this point—when I feel him subtly grinding against me. At first, I think it might be by accident. But no. He's circling his hips against mine. I lift my ass on an instinct, wanting him to go crazy for me.

I'm going to smash your balls, Mr. Vela.

His cold zipper hits my bare lower stomach—just where the towel slits open. He's hard. Very hard. And I may be mistaken, but he's also as thick as Godfrey's cockney accent.

Beat moves lower, his swollen cock pressed against my sensitive flesh.

The hand that's clasping my mouth shut is now moving downward, the back of it brushing my erected nipple, going south, grabbing my ass roughly with a squeeze. I sigh, rolling my head against the concrete, wanting to submit to him but knowing I'm about to knee his balls and try to run again. . .

Then his head drops, his forehead meeting mine. I can smell the cheap plastic of his mask and the sweet scent of his masculine sweat. And that peachy mouth, the one I haven't even seen yet. He lets out a frustrated grunt.

"Let's go, Pea."

Nate scoops me up and helps me to my feet before I manage to damage his boys. We walk back to his house—I have no other option I'm completely imprisoned, clasped by this real-life gladiator. But when we walk in, something dawns on me.

He *is* attracted to me.

He is fighting this for Godfrey. For his life. But if I convince him that I can offer him a way out. . .game on.

There's a flicker of passion in him. . .and I'm about to set it to flames. Flames that'd burn every single plan Godfrey has for me.

Nate shoves me into the basement and locks me in.

"Last warning. If you don't want to end up blindfolded and tied again, you'll behave."

I sit on a blanket he brought down for me and wait until I hear his body sinking against his mattress, the cheap springs wincing under his weight. Taking out his diary from where I'd hidden it, I read another entry.

NOVEMBER 12TH, 2010

"GOING TO PRISON IS LIKE DYING WITH YOUR EYES OPEN" (BERNARD KERIK)

Losing yourself in repetition is easy, and that's what prison life gives you.

A structure so neat and linear, days mesh into weeks, then into months—and before you know it—even into years.

I miss Chow Time at 6:00 a.m. every day because I'd rather chew on my cellmate's leg than eat the breakfast they serve. And Pedro? His leg has seen some pretty rough shit, along with the rest of his crack-addicted body.

I'm a welder at the prison's general maintenance shop. At 32 cents an hour, I won't get rich, but at least I'll be able to afford some Ramen noodles from the canteen.

I work alongside an old English wiseguy named Godfrey. They nicknamed him God in here for a reason. With a distinctive limp that promises a good story behind it, he spends most of his time listening to classical music or hanging out with Seb— another British inmate who I think's gay by the way he looks at me. Ninety percent of the people here want to fuck me, but Seb? He looks like he wants to take my butthole on a dinner date and buy it flowers. Maybe even a piece of nice jewelry.

Frank told me that I shouldn't mess with Godfrey.

Beware of God, for he is very powerful and can seal your faith.

I fly low and work out. Read even more. Four or five hours of reading, every day. Skip the college classes and other bullshit programs they offer, as if you'll walk outta here into the open arms of society. If life gave you the San Dimas card, a full house is not in your future. Hell, you'd be lucky to have a roof over your head when it's all over.

But I go to the self-help class because they make you sign up for this crap, and because what else is there to do in this shithole? My options are limited, my time— boundless.

At dinner, I hang out with Frank and his Stockton crew.

San Dimas is known for county gangs. Forget about the blacks, the Latinos, the whites. Sure, there are jump offs between races every now and again. Mostly, though, we keep things civilized.

Other than the Aryan Brotherhood. They're a pain in everyone's ass.

Literally.

I walk into my cell today to see a guy I don't recognize. He's big, fat, with a homemade swastika tattoo adorning his meaty neck and the face of every illiterate hillbilly from the flicks. Bald, of course. Prison sucks the youth outta you.

"Can I help you?" I grunt.

"Na. But I can help you. Seen you around." *He leans his shoulder on the wall, one hand tucked in his pants. His eyes zero in on my crotch.* "You need protection."

Ignoring him, I reach under my thin mattress, tugging out a paperback. He clasps my arm, his hand greasy. "I said," *he grits,* "you're a pretty boy. Bend. Over."

I wait for him to throw the first punch, but he just jerks me closer. He's fatter, bigger. I'm lean but strong enough to take him. Then again I don't have the AB behind me in case shit goes south.

And it will absolutely go south, judging by the hungry look on his face.

But not the kind of south he'd like to stick his dick into.

"Look, man," *I say calmly.* "I've nothing to lose. Don't make me kill you. My ass ain't worth it."

He thrusts me into the wall with a thump, his nose brushing mine as he gets in my face.

"Eyes like whiskey, hair so soft, lips full like a girl's. You think people haven't noticed? Let's take a trip to the shower, pretty boy."

I'm about to do something that'd haul me into ad-seg for a long-ass time, when I notice a shard of glass making its way to my skin. The sharp edge travels along my neck before it passes my cheekbone, poking into the Aryan asshole's chin. Frank's crumpled-paper face follows the blade as his lips find the tattooed man's ear.

"Back off, Hefner. Can't you see he's just a kid?"

The Aryan guy's eyes never break contact with mine. I'm still sandwiched between him and the cracked wall when he lets a rotting sneer loose.

"Careful, old man. You're no shot-caller in here. We are."

Frank snorts. "Hefner," *he says, digging the shard into the man's skin.* "There's only one shot-caller, and that's God." *He refers to Godfrey Archer, not the almighty.* "Now, this one's not for taking. Get out."

Hefner's few working brain cells command him to fuck off out of my forty-eight-square-foot cell, and after an impotent stare down, he dissolves back into the murky hallway of our floor.

"I could've handled him myself." I tug my hair up. "But thanks."

Frank doesn't acknowledge my appreciation. Just shoves the shard into my hand, curling my fingers around it.

"Keep it safe. Goddamn, Nathaniel. You are too fucking pretty for San Dimas. You better toughen up or your asshole will be wide enough to push a watermelon through by the time you leave."

With that, my old neighbor turned rape-preventer walks away, leaving me and what's left of my pride feeling even smaller and less significant than my tiny room.

It's difficult to hate him when he's becoming more human with every page.

In fact, I want to show him how human I am, too.

He shut me up yesterday because he was bending, and I want him to break. Back to the master plan. Back to doing what I can to recruit him to my team.

It's my turn to show him that I'm real.

"The following weekend, I used that first-class ticket to London and paid Camden a visit."

Nate grunts quietly upstairs and wish I was there with him on a bed I've never seen, in a room I've never been in. A room that is undoubtedly not much bigger than his San Dimas cell.

"Camden lived in a Victorian building in Marble Arch, right in front of the big Primark, smack in the middle of London." I smile to myself, hugging my knees. I may hate Camden, but I've always loved his apartment.

"I didn't know what to expect. We didn't even kiss the first, and last, time we'd met. . .but he wooed me. Big time. That weekend, we went to amazing restaurants and enjoyed the best seats in the West End. And it took him exactly sixteen hours, from the moment I landed in London, to the moment I landed on his bed, where he drilled into me like there was oil at the end of my pussy."

My lips curve into a smirk. Nate is probably not so hot on hearing about another guy screwing me senseless. But I understand his silence as a green light to continue, so I do.

"By the time she left London, eighteen-year-old Prescott thought she was madly in love with Camden Archer, the flashy, English hot-shot with charming manners and a fine taste in music and films."

I hear his tender chuckle. "But let me tell you, Beat, it all went downhill from there."

"Whatever," he murmurs. The first time he's acknowledged my story directly.

"Let's do dinner tomorrow."

"No."

"I'll be good to you. Maybe even bad, if it's your type of thing," my raspy voice suggests through a smirk. "We'll both pretend that we have someone who cares. Everyone needs a friend."

I roll my stress ball in my hands, squeezing it until my fingers hurt.

I need.

I need my family back, and hugs, and to count my happy places every now and again. I need to be acknowledged and, as much as I hate to admit it, *I need him.*

NATE

My traitorous cock has betrayed me again.

I'm starting to think Godfrey deliberately put this girl under my supervision because he wants me to go fucking nuts. Never, in my entire life have I lusted after a woman. Women were low-hanging fruit for me to pick, sink my teeth into and toss after one bite. Prescott is no different. She's offering herself to me on a silver platter, with a side of grapes. But with her, I want it.

Why do I want it? Because she's broken like me.

Why do I need someone broken? Because she understands, never judges, and doesn't back down.

Broken people do things better; we learned how to make it in life without the missing parts other people have. Because when you're in the dark, you appreciate everything that shines.

She's not the most beautiful woman I've ever seen. She ain't the cutest or funniest. But she's shrewd and cunning. A chameleon changing her colors to adjust to the situation she's been thrown into. I know she's trying to manipulate me, and to some extent, she's succeeding.

It's fun watching her sweat for me, especially because in the outside world, I'd be her slave, polishing her expensive tiles in swim trunks and listening to her ramblings about Tahoe vacations.

Flashbacks of grinding against her like a fucking pervert have me walking around with a crimson red face all day. I'll never live this shit down.

I go about my usual routine, showing up at work. Thank fuck Mrs. Hathaway's still in Tahoe, because this dancing monkey is not in the mood to walk around half-naked just for her amusement. My body is humming with quiet rage, and I know exactly what will set it free, but I can't have it.

Godfrey would kill me if I touch her.

Throwing the Smiths vinyl record onto the gramophone—if there's one thing I love about this job, it's Stan Hathaway's record collection—I start working. Scrubbing, washing, vacuuming and dusting to the sound of Morrissey wording my misery ever so sweetly. My sorry ass would lick every inch of these Italian granite floors if I had to, just to save some money to run out of Cali-fucking-fornia.

I pick up my dirty backpack when I'm done and check my phone out of habit. I have four missed calls. Weird. No one ever calls me, other than the occasional fraud. I frown at my phone and redial the number on the screen, my pulse kicking up. The area code reads San Rafael.

I'm not ready for this phone call, and as the other line clicks alive, I know that my favorite person in the world is now dead.

Fuck, fuck, fuck.

I jump into Stella and call Irvin, telling him he needs to feed Pea and give her her fifteen minutes of bathroom time. I don't call her Pea, sticking instead with "God's girl."

I don't trust the bastard with her, but I need to drive to San Rafael to identify the body of Frank Donald Dixon. Dead, after four years in a coma.

Because of me.

Because of Hefner.

Because of God.

Because of the Aryan Brotherhood.

They're still after me.

I show up at the forensic laboratory and a grief counselor immediately greets me. A woman in her mid-thirties, thin with perfectly applied makeup and a haircut from the magazines. She shakes my hand, the grin that graces her face confirms blue blood runs in her veins. She explains that I'll need to identify him by a photograph. I was his only contact person. Me. How sad is that?

The last time I saw him was the day shit went down, and I dread the idea of seeing how he spent the last few years while I was eating four bangers and trying (yet failing) to stay out of trouble.

She sits me down and shows me a picture, and I nod, my face blank. It's him, all right. The last person who resembled family in my life is dead. No mom. No dad. No neighbor who showed me the ropes in prison. No one.

If I die on my way back to Stockton, no one will give a rat's ass. Just like no one gave a rat's ass about Frank. The grief counselor breaks the self-pity party I'm throwing by rubbing her palm against the back of my hand.

"Hey. I don't usually do this, but I'm almost done here. Give me ten minutes, and we can grab a drink?"

Everyone wants to fuck Nate Vela, but no one offers a shoulder to cry on.

I stand up, and she scans me up and down, her throat bobbing with a swallow. "Sorry," I say and pick up my keys and wallet. "Gotta go."

I spend the ride back home trying to come up with legitimate reasons to wake up tomorrow morning. So that. . .what? I could work a shitty job I hate under the supervision of a woman who pinches my ass and giggles, make minimum wage to try and escape a life I don't even have so the Aryan Brotherhood wouldn't kill me? So I could continue on existing, for no reason other than my basic, human instinct to survive?

I'm not even sure why I'm preventing Pea's escape. She probably has more of a life to live, and she certainly tries harder than I do. I'm just being a greedy bastard, saving my life instead of sparing hers.

Making a booze stop at a bar on the outskirts of Stockton, I come back to the house sauced as fuck. It's three a.m. Too late to check on her. Even if she's not asleep, we're not friends. I can't cry on her shoulder. Can't crawl into her lap. Even though she'd want that. Welcome me with open arms.

But she'd do it to save herself, not me.

I stomp my way to my room, kicking my boots against the wall and shouldering past a sleepy Irv, who wobbles his way back from another night shift.

It doesn't take a genius to see that I'm upset, but he doesn't care. We're practically strangers. Two people who share a roof because we can't afford not to.

Once I fall onto the mattress, I scrub my eyes, fighting the sting.

I wait for her to talk, because she always does whenever she hears me getting into bed. I can feel that she's awake. She waits for those fifteen minutes with me, longs for them as much as I do.

Oh, fuck. What the hell am I saying? I shouldn't want shit from her.

But right now, I'm too down to care. Don't care that I'm breaking for her, playing into her dangerous game, and that Irv is likely to hear us.

"Talk," I order, staring at my mold-stained popcorn ceiling, wishing it was the wood of a coffin. I need comfort, a distraction, and she's it. I'm Mrs. Hathaway's dancing monkey, and Pea? She's fucking mine. Pea doesn't answer.

"Goddammit, Prescott. My day was fucking brutal," I grunt. "Talk."

Nothing.

"Fucking talk!" I shout, rolling my body to the edge of the bed and slamming my fist to the floor. Irv raps the wall of his room three times. "Shut the fuck up, man. What're you doing drinking on weekdays?"

"Talk," I whisper one last time, ignoring Irv, knowing she can hear me. But she doesn't utter a word. This girl who seemed hell-bent on blabbing when I left her last night is now mute. What's changed? Has Irv done something to her? No. He knows I'd kill him.

Maybe she's given up on life too. Great fucking timing, Pea.

Bitch.

PRESCOTT

I hope I'm betting the right horse.

Nate just begged me to talk to him, and I threw the opportunity out the window, even though the original plan was to butter him up and win his heart, or at the very least, his dick.

Nate.

Ink gave me his name tonight. The idiot.

The mastermind showed up in the basement earlier than Nate usually does, probably before his night shift. I know that because Nate arrives when the owls start singing me my lullabies for the night. I was just marking Day Four with my new chalk on the wall when he came down, bringing canned food, his ski mask reeking of weed. I'm not used to five-star hotel service, but at least Nate—or Beat—brings edible food and snacks to see me through the next day.

"God's girl, you've got fifteen minutes, yeah? Let's go. I got a shift in half an hour."

I hated that he came for me. Then again, Nate is airtight and doesn't let me budge. Maybe Ink would give me more space, and I could run away.

"Okay." Excitement pushed me up to my feet, and I strode over to him.

"Keep your distance." He manhandled me, poking me up the stairs from behind. "Beat said you're a biter. Don't make me crush your teeth."

Huh.

Nate was trying to keep Ink away from me. I had a giddy feeling that I knew exactly why.

When Ink strode into the bathroom with me, I raised one palm up.

"Beat said I'm allowed my privacy in these fifteen minutes," I lied.

"Beat is not the fucking boss of me," he retorted chirpily, bulldozing his way in. The way his gaze licked my body confirmed that just like his roommate, Ink was ready for some action. But in his case, I moved uncomfortably, my eyes searching the room.

An hourglass moment pinched at my gut, telling me that Ink is just like them. *A taker.* But not again. Never again.

It was the first time I was grateful for Godfrey and his threat not to touch me. Ink was the kind of guy who'd let Godfrey cut his dick off with a butter knife—slowly and painfully—before disobeying orders.

"I need to. . .poop." I cleared my throat. He winced, I noticed it even through his ski mask. This was not a part of the peep show he had in mind. His round belly wobbled as he chortled. "Clean up after yourself." With that, he stepped out of the bathroom and locked the door from the outside. My stare lingered on the lock. Beat replaced it with a new one after I broke it the night before, and probably didn't tell Ink, seeing as he hasn't mentioned it.

I got down to business, weirdly happy with the fact that Beat wasn't here to witness me doing a number two, and even happier that he kept my attempt to run away to himself. I had a quick shower, after which I left the water running while I searched for a potential weapon. *Again.* But Nate wasn't stupid. After my attempt to break free yesterday, he removed the towel rack.

The towels were thrown on the floor.

Groaning, I yanked out the little metal wire that held the toilet paper and tucked it under my dress. It wasn't sharp enough to cause serious harm, but walking out of there empty-handed was admitting defeat. I knocked on the door from inside.

"I'm ready."

INK

Jittery, uncertain and conceited. Wants to be a tattooist but is too untalented to land a real job, so he is flipping burgers. *Likes:* belittling women, playing the tough guy and, well, ink. *Dislikes:* being talked back to, independent women and his life.

He opened the door, his eyes moving up and down my legs. "You scrub up good, bitch."

Eat shit.

"Thanks. You still look like rotten balls, even with a ski mask on," I told him with a straight face, and he almost slapped me, but this time withdrew his hand inches from my cheek.

Ink shook me by the elbow, pouring us into the hallway, and poked my back, more aggressively than necessary, on our way to the basement. That was Ink. He wasn't layered the way Nate was: sorrow, remorse, ruthlessness, heart, street-brain and compassion tossed into a personality of intriguing chaos.

"Who's coming for me tomorrow?" I enquired before he swung the door shut.

"Nate—er, Beat."

Nate.

While I don't want him to know that I'm reading his diary, the day I tell him his roommate ratted out his name is closing in After all, there's no guarantee I won't run away from Godfrey, and if I do, his life will be over.

Ink swung the door open and rushed in, pinning me against the wall. He dug his fingers into my throat, his ski mask sending hot air from his mouth. The rotten scent of bacteria and plaque assaulted my nostrils.

"Listen up, bitch. That was a mistake. Tell Beat I said his name, and you're dead. Get it?"

I nodded. He wouldn't kill me. He was far too scared of Godfrey. And Beat. And everything else. A prime example of a beta-male. While Nate is everywhere, oozing quiet power, Ink can stand inches from me and I wouldn't even notice. "Of course."

From the moment he left the basement, until the moment I heard Nate sinking into his bed, all I did was try to rip open the boarded windows with that small wire I stole from the bathroom. It got me nowhere other than bloody fingers and a cut wrist after my hand slipped against one of the rusty nails.

I need to change tactics. I need to lure Nate faster.

Considering the fact that talking my way out of this situation hasn't helped me so far, I've decided to try the opposite approach—silence.

NOVEMBER 18TH, 2010

"DEPRESSION IS THE INABILITY TO CONSTRUCT A FUTURE." (ROLLO MAY)

I get sick for the first time in my life.

The Vela men don't usually do weakness, unless it's booze.

I stay in my cell, nursing a fever and a bad case of the shits. Pedro and his pleas for methadone are pissing me off. The world is pissing me off. I'm not even twenty-two and my life is already over. The realization's a hard pill to swallow.

To make matters worse, Pedro's constantly eyeing the toilet bowl, trying to fish my shit out, because he wants to throw it at the corrections officers to make a scene. A scene will land him in the hole. But he'll get something to calm his raging withdrawal symptoms first.

That's what Pedro's counting on. He'd kill us both to get that shot in the butt. Beth, a corrections officer who I befriended, allows Frank to drop by with canned soup.

"Punk-ass kid." He spits his words, as he does when he forgets to put in his artificial teeth. I grunt into the lukewarm liquid, taking slow sips.

"You were less of a weirdo as a teenager, y'know?" He grabs on to my arm, yanking me upright. "That poetry messed with your head, Nathaniel."

"Name's Nate," I correct him. We've been hanging out every day since I arrived, but I never bothered to say something. Because I never bothered to talk. But today I'm angry at everything, Frank included.

"Whatever," he says, standing up and slapping the back of my neck. "What-fucking-ever."

DECEMBER 24TH, 2010

"THE FEAR OF DEATH FOLLOWS THE FEAR OF LIFE. A MAN WHO LIVES FULLY IS PREPARED TO DIE AT ANY TIME" (MARK TWAIN)

Christmas Eve I get word that Mamá's dead. One of the counselors calls me into his office and sits me down. He delivers the news in a hurry, eager to go home to his own functioning family, but uses the furrowed forehead expression, the one that's supposed to show compassion.

Is he sad for me? I don't know.

Who the fuck cares?

I'm twenty-two and completely orphaned.

I killed my dad and now my Mamá's gone, too. Hit by a plowed bus on her way back from sending me stamps. Lotta' rain. Lotta' fog. Bus driver was working overtime to make sure his kids would have presents under their Christmas tree. Got tired. Lost control.

Anyway, you know the rest.

The counselor asks me if I'd like to see a priest. Cry a little. Pray a lot. Pray. Hah! Pray to who? No one ever listens to me upstairs. My prayers fall on deaf ears no matter where they land. Heaven, hell, or the very earth I live upon.

Fisting my hair from its base, I answer with a headshake.

I spend the night in my bed, staring at the ceiling.

Unblinking.

Uncrying.

Unable to join everyone downstairs for the Christmas Eve charade.

And I'm all alone.

NATE

I drag my shades down and roll my lower lip between my fingers as I stare through the rear window.

Yeah, it's definitely them.

Stella merges into the highway as I try to lose the 1970 Ford Econoline van. White, rusty and fitting for these assholes. I spot it a couple of cars behind me. The faces staring back at me through my rear mirror are unfamiliar, but recognizable all the same.

I can spot an Aryan Brother from miles away, having been in prison for so long. Two big pink men. Fat, tatted and simple looking.

I can't lead them to my house. Gotta' get rid of them somewhere along the way.

Fuck, I thought Godfrey said he was on top of this shit.

Speeding onto the I-5, I duck my head low so that the back of my skull is covered by the cushioned seat. Cursing under my breath, I'm throwing glances to assess how many other cars I can bypass without raising suspicion. My pulse is wild, hammering against my ears, making my blood roar in my veins. Shaky, damp fingers choke my steering wheel. I push the gas pedal until my foot hits the floor. The van's following close behind. Now it's only one car away. It's ten p.m., too late for traffic, and the highway is deserted, other than a few random cars crawling along their journey to their point of destination.

Shit.

My eyes dart from the road back to the van, and a big guy with a tattoo on his cheek pulls his torso out of the passenger seat's window. Then I see it. A rifle. A fucking rifle.

Double shit.

He levels the rifle with me, one eye squeezed shut, the other focused on my head. I gulp hard and take a sharp turn to the right, switching lanes. If I don't take the next right exit, I'm dead.

Godfrey, you lying scumbag. Did you let them loose, or did you never have any power over them in the first place?

That's a question I'll have to deal with if I get out of this alive.

I veer onto an exit ramp and speed with everything I've got. Stella starts shaking to the point where everything clatters. Reluctantly, the old van switches lanes to follow me into a winding road crawling into green-grass covered hills of nothingness.

Triple shit.

I couldn't have given them a better place to shoot me. All I've got left is to push my fucking forehead into their barrel at this point.

The van manages to bump into my rear and my vehicle coughs forward. I try to speed up unsuccessfully. It's done. The Tacoma has reached its limit. Another bump follows, this time harder. My ass disconnects from my seat, my body jumps upwards. Third bump, and this time Stella's thrown a few feet forward. I need to stop this chase before they roll me over and shoot me down.

So I change tactics.

I take a left turn out of nowhere, rolling into a carved hill, and reverse back so my car faces theirs, hidden by a blizzard of dust and gravel.

Let's. Play. Fucking. Chicken.

These men want to kill me, but me? I'm actually going to let them. They may not yield, but I won't, either. It's easy to gamble your life away when you've got nothing to live for.

Playtime, motherfuckers.

Revving up my engine, I push the gas pedal so hard the muscles in my foot pull, my truck galloping in their direction. All I see is red. All I feel is the taste of their blood on the tip of my tongue.

Faster.

Quicker.

Nearer.

Closer.

The driver finally swerves to the right, and the van crashes against a thick bush. Black smoke scuttles from its engine.

The van's old age caught up with it. They're done. Their vehicle's fucked.

It's time to ruin and reign.

I fling my door open and stagger out of Stella, hurrying to my trunk and pulling out a wooden broom. That's the only weapon I have. A fucking broom. But it's long and I break it in two against my knee, so now it has two sharp edges, too.

Pacing to the van, I pull out the guy who'd sat in the passenger's seat, the one with the rifle, and toss his heavy weapon behind my back, far away from his reach.

"Who sent you?" My spit peppers his face as I drag him out onto the grassy hill. He's twisting left and right, trying to break free, but he stands no chance. I'm way bigger and stronger.

Behind me, the driver unlatches his safety belt, scrambling out of his seat. Before he has a chance to bolt for the rifle, I nail the sharp point of one of the sticks straight into the first guy's palm, pinning him to the ground. The stick is firmly planted into the soil, as is the guy who'd just tried to shoot me. There's a massive hole in the center of his palm now, and he's screaming his lungs out. I proceed to nail his other hand to the ground, crucifying him to the hill like a sick, sad, corrupted Jesus.

Then I jump on the fleeing driver like a panther on its prey.

"You're not going anywhere," I slur on a scream as I yank him by his shirt. He swings his fist at me, but I dodge it. I tackle him to the ground and he resists, pulling us together into a ball of kicks and punches. We roll down the bank, tangled and throwing fists at each other. We land in a valley a few feet from our vehicles, and I'm quick to climb on top of him, straddle him with my thighs, the way I did when Pea tried to escape, and unleash twenty-seven years' worth of wrath on his face.

I'm angry, possessed and out of my fucking mind.

My knuckles land on his nose, shattering it with a chilling sound, and I follow it with another fist as I smash his mouth with a brutal blow. A tooth pops out and rolls on the grass. I hit him until all I see is blood. I hit him even though I know that he might be dead. I hit him for reasons that have nothing to do with him. I hit him because I'm an orphan, an ex-felon, a captor and a guy who's in lust with a girl he cannot have. Because I'm a sad boy, a broken man and a lonely soul. A barbaric savage, a poet with a heart of gold and a nobody who is desperate to become somebody.

And I hit him because I need him dead. Because I can't chance him finding me again.

But I don't just kill him. No. I'm butchering him with my stone-cold heart.

Because he's not a person. He's a symbol.

Representing everything I hate.

Everything I want to turn my back on.

Everything that's taking the only thing I was born with, other than this stupid beautiful face, and that still belongs to me. *My peace.*

After I'm done, I drag his body up the hill, aware of the fact that someone might spot us. What choice do I have? I can't leave him here to be found. Luckily, by the time I climb back up to Stella, it's already pitch black and the chances of being spotted behind those hills are slim to none.

I pile the dead driver into his van and stride over to his friend, who's still nailed to the ground, cursing and spitting, kicking his legs like a toddler in a tantrum. It's a good thing Mrs. H sent me to buy a new broom not too long ago, and I forgot it in my trunk.

"Who sent you?" I growl into his face, fisting one of the sticks and moving it in circles, splitting the hole in his palm wider. I need a name I can look up. A name I can hunt down. Someone who I can turn my rage against. If the Aryan Brotherhood is after me, I want to know who the shot-caller is, who went against Godfrey's direct order and decided to kill me.

"Brown bastard," he moans at me, trying to kick me with what's left of his strength.

I drop my head to my chest, letting out a bitter laugh. "One last chance? I might let you live if you decide to cooperate." I don't want to be responsible for an unnecessary death, but I'm not dumb enough to let him walk away without a payback, either.

He shakes his head and spits his words. "Do whatever you need to do, Nathaniel Vela. You're already a dead man. We just haven't killed you yet."

I kneel on one knee, cradling his face in my palms. He has a blonde moustache, a shiny bald head and an *Aryan Warrior* tattoo on his cheek. He grins as I snap his neck in one sharp movement, breaking his spine.

His head is weirdly positioned on the grass, the stupid smile and wide eyes now staring back at me instead of the sky.

Dumping him in the van along with the rifle doesn't take long. My engine is already revved up before I throw the match I lit into the open gas tank door through Stella's window. My crime scene bursts into flames behind me, creating a rancid cloud of burnt flesh and gasoline as I speed away. My eyes prickle and my throat stings, but it's not due to the whiff of fire making its way into my lungs. No. What strikes me the most on my ride home is the fact that I am officially contaminated by sin. I'm not a killer, I'm a murderer. Self-defense or not, I've taken three lives, and I'm barely twenty-seven.

I've killed three people, two of them deliberately, not just to stop them, but to *end* them. I didn't hesitate. I didn't bat an eyelash. Goddamn, I didn't even flinch. I ventured straight into fucking serial killer territory, with neighbors like Ted Bundy and Jeffery Dahmer to accompany my new title.

Some people collect stamps. Some coins. Taxidermy. Fucking cards. I collect regrets. They don't take up much space, not physically, anyway. But inside. . .they occupy. They eat away. They ruin.

Because that's the thing about regrets. They're mistakes that left scars. Vicious, sensitive, searing wounds.

I don't feel remorse for killing those three bastards, but I feel bad about *her.*

Maybe that's why I kick the basement's door open the minute I get home.

"Vegetarian chipotle." The foil-wrapped burrito knocks on her shoulder as I toss it against her body. She's lying on the floor, her face against the tiles. I should be pissed at her for not talking to me yesterday. Correction: *I am* pissed at her for not talking to me yesterday.

I'm mad.

At her.

At me.

At everything.

Especially at everything. Yet again, life threw a knockout punch right in my face. Does Godfrey know about the AB seeking me out? And what fucking good is he to me if he can't even keep the bad guys at bay?

Pea doesn't move. Maybe she's asleep. Doubt it. She's too smart and alert, and she lives for her fifteen minutes of bathroom and food break. Glancing at the wall, I notice she hasn't chalked a white stripe today.

Not counting the days anymore? Why?

I take two steps in her direction, my pulse thick and erratic in my throat, and nudge her leg with my leather boot. She doesn't respond, her face and stomach against her blanket. I use my foot to roll her over on her back, and the stress ball she was holding rolls onto the floor. Her eyes are open, and she's staring back at my mask.

The emptiness in her expression is more unsettling than watching a man's last inhale as I snap his spine in two.

"Eat," I command.

She doesn't budge, her muscles slack. Squatting down, I drag her up to a sitting position, her back against the wall, trying to swallow my next question. It storms out of my mouth anyway.

"Has Ink fucked you?"

Irv better not have touched her. Godfrey would kill us both if he has. But that's not why my chest is burning with uncontained fury.

Something I don't recognize bubbles up inside me. It's not hate, not anger, and I hope to God it's not jealousy.

What the fuck am I doing? What the hell am I thinking? What's happening to me?

Pea doesn't answer.

"Pea!" I slam my fist against the wall behind her, expecting her to jump in fear. The wall shakes, but she just stares at a point behind my head. Apathy leaks from every pore in her face.

Fuck it all to hell.

I thought I had issues with the spunky, blabbering girl I took from Godfrey. I was wrong. *That* girl was semi-entertaining. *This* girl? She's a goddamned graveyard.

"Tell me now, before I start breaking shit. What's Ink done to you?" I take a sharp gulp of air, my body dangerously close to hers. When her mouth opens slightly, mine follows suit.

"He hasn't done anything. It's not about him. I'm not going to eat, because there's no point in me eating. They're going to kill me anyway. It'd just be a waste of everything: food, water and both of our time." She shakes her head. Her voice is so hollow, it almost echoes. "If I'm going to die, I don't want it to be at their hands." Her eyes harden. "No. I'll die here. Alone. Deprive them the opportunity of getting off on seeing me gasping for my last breath."

The mention of her death mauls at me combined with the crimes I committed a few hours ago. I resist the urge to say something comforting. I ain't a liar, and Pea's right. They'll kill her. Godfrey will make it a gory death, and no matter where the crime scene ends up being, a splash of her blood will forever stain my conscience.

But one of us has to die, and right now, my integrity is paralyzed by my survival instincts.

"Beat," she croaks. Fuck, her lips. Those pinks I'd like to touch—now more than ever—are trembling with fear. "Please kill me. I know you can't set me free, I get it. I do. But you can make my death look like an accident. Please, spare me the Archers' wrath."

She wants to become my third death for tonight, and my fourth in total. Do I look like the fucking reaper? I clutch my hair with both fists as I bite into my lip. It's a sad turn of events when you realize you don't only want to fuck the girl you're supposed to hand over to death row, but you also want to save her.

"Hey," I drop my hand to the floor to pick up the burrito, placing it in her hand. "Shut your trap about death. I'll go get my food. We'll eat together tonight."

That's the only thing I can think of that'd cheer her up. I don't want her suffering. She hasn't done anything bad to me. My dick, on the other hand, resents her round ass and suckable lips. She's been taunting it for days. If cock teasing were an art, this girl would be Picasso.

"Beat," she says weakly when I start ascending the stairs. I stop, my back still to her. "Bring your favorite book along. I'd like to read something good."

My head falls in a small nod.

She's aiming straight for my fucking heart, this chick. Shot after shot in the dark.

And sooner or later, I know, even in the pitch black, she's going to hit her target.

66

PRESCOTT

He took the bait. More like swallowed the whole fishing rod.

I don't want to hurt Nate, but I need him to set me free. And if that means compromising the truth of my mental state, then so be it.

It's not that I manipulated him. I *am* depressed. I *am* scared. Just not enough to give up on life. I'd never give up on life. That's the only thing I've got left after what they did to me.

And Nate? He gave up on his. I see how he lives. The long hours he works. Bending over backward for Godfrey. Constantly jogging to the door every time the bell rings, worrying it'll be his parole officer, that I'm going to be found. He is a trapped animal, a caged soul and a terrible liar. I know his kind.

We eat together in the darkened basement. Nate blindfolded me because he can't eat with his mask on. I don't need to see him to know that he's here.

"Thank you for the food, Beat." I munch on my rice and bean burrito. He grunts in response. Back to being a caveman.

"Why did you get thrown in prison?" I ask, sucking sour cream from my finger with a moan. I miss good food so bad.

"You want the long or short version?"

"Does it look like I'm in a hurry?"

He lets out a chuckle. His voice is great. Baritone, gruff and throaty. Not that it matters, I remind myself. *He's business.*

"Manslaughter. I smashed a vase into my dad's head. Fractured his skull."

By the way his leg nudges mine playfully, I'm guessing that he's sitting with his knees drawn up just like mine.

"That's your *long* version? Gee, how many words do you use for the short one?" I snort.

"One. *Destroy.* I'm pretty good at ruining things."

"That's harsh. And false. For one thing, you can football-tackle a girl like a pro," I joke as Nate passes me a bottle of water. I take a sip and give it back to him. "You didn't want to take me hostage. You cared when Ink hit me. . ." I trail off. "Maybe you're good."

I feel him chuckling against me.

"You hate your roommate," I say.

"I hate everything," he deadpans.

"That's not true, you just don't care."

"Maybe that's how I started this morning. Indifferent. But, today I did things I cannot undo. What's more—I don't want to undo them. Maybe I'm a monster."

"I know monsters, Beat. I know them real close. You have a long way to go until you get to that point."

I toy with the foil between my fingers. Nate is done eating by the sound of it. He is opening up to me. Something made him fragile and attentive today. Not really sure what, but I need to make another move before he slams the door to this opportunity in my face.

So I go bold.

I press my head against his huge, hard shoulder.

There's silence, the questioning kind, and I swallow every feminine fear I have of being rejected.

He shakes his shoulder lightly, brushing me away. "What the fuck, Pea?"

"I need human contact," I whisper. This time, it's not another half-lie I spew on autopilot to draw him closer to me. "You can use a cuddle, too."

I place my head on his shoulder again, and this time, Nate doesn't move. His hair tickles my ear. It's glorious. Shiny, straight and jet black. I've seen it plenty of times falling across his Guy Fawkes mask. Short and buzzed on the sides, long at the top.

He sounds beautiful. His walk's beautiful. His body's beautiful. And I'm positive that behind the mask and the blindfold awaits a man that's about to crush every single promise I've made myself about men.

To stay the hell away from them.

"You know what you need to do, right?" I snuggle into his shoulder. "Run away."

He doesn't answer, because he knows that I'm right. I don't know how he got tangled up in all the mess that he's in, though I have a feeling his little red diary will soon spill the beans. One thing is for sure, this place is killing him slowly from the inside. Godfrey, Seb, Ink, this job he hates. . .his happiness is compromised by his circumstances. But I can set him free.

I clear my throat, hoping he'll take me seriously. "You know I've got money on the outside, right? Enough to run away and fix you up with whatever you need to start a new life. I have drug routes in Oakland, Richmond and Stockton."

Nate shifts to face me, raising his palm and flattening it over my neck, wrapping his fingers around it gently. My throat constricts.

For the first time in years, I feel something that's so strange and scary, I almost tip over and collapse on the floor. *Aroused.*

"Yet you're here in my basement, and Godfrey's out and about." His voice is low and dark. "Funny how life works, huh, Silver Spoon?"

"That can, and will, change soon." My daring statement sounds thicker under the pressure he applies on my throat.

It's hot, confusing and completely unwarranted. Since I normally don't do sex, why is it that I want him to squeeze hard and fuck me even harder? I don't even care what his face looks like. It's a torturous foreplay, the wickedest kind. The one that isn't meant to be fulfilled.

"If Godfrey was stupid enough to throw together two people who have the exact same shit list, it's his problem." I pinch my lips together between my teeth, gaining strength for what's about to come out of my mouth. "You don't have to tell me who screwed you over and chained you to this situation, Beat. I already know. We can be a team. We can take our freedom back."

"Yeah? You think my parole officer will be down with that shit?"

"I think you sticking around here with manslaughter on your record and Godfrey barking insane orders at you, sinking you into deeper trouble, is just as restricting as San Dimas. What do you think is going to happen if your parole officer pays you a visit while I'm down here? You know I'm going to yell my lungs out. You can gag and tie me, but I'd still use my body to draw attention. Where would it leave you? The only reason you're still here is because you can't afford not to be. Get out of the States, Beat. Start fresh."

"Sounds like you got a plan mapped out for me."

He squeezes my throat harder, but not hard enough to cut off my air supply. I hiss a moan, rolling my head against the wall. I don't have a plan mapped out for him. All I can think about is how we walk out of here together and assassinate my enemies.

"We leave. First stop—my apartment. Get my credit cards, cash and a replacement phone. Second stop—we're getting a car with an out-of-state license plate. Third stop—Los Angeles. I know a guy who can issue us legit IDs under different names. Two passports, fresh and new, my treat. Fourth stop—we go back to NorCal, kill Godfrey, Sebastian and Camden. Fifth stop—SFO airport. You go your way, I go mine. We shake on it. Wave goodbye. I'll even buy you a cup of coffee for your trouble. This will take us three weeks, max. Camden should be here by the beginning of September. Three weeks, Beat, in exchange for a new life. You pick a place, Canada,

Mexico, South America, and I'll pay you 50k for the hassle and for helping me out with the boys. Now how does that sound?"

His palm leaves my neck and a sense of loss grips me, the kind I hadn't felt since the last time I'd been hugged. *Really* hugged. It was by Preston, who told me to take care of myself before he'd disappeared.

Nate mulls over my offer wordlessly. I can almost hear the wheels in his brain rolling as he processes my words. But even I know it's farfetched for him to put his trust and life in the uncalloused hands of a blonde girl of pedigree and designer mini dresses. Pussy is always a disadvantage in the street business. And rich pussy? That's practically a weakness in Stockton.

"You're a wild card," he says.

"Does that scare you?" I breathe.

"Not if I'm about to burn down the whole motherfucking table."

More silence.

"Godfrey will try and kill us," he booms, his warm breath crawling up my face. Am I imagining it, or are his lips hovering over mine? My fingertips tingle and I wet my lips again. I've been doing it a lot since he threw me in his basement.

"That's okay, I'm not planning on keeping him alive, either."

"Mmmm." His voice is closer, his nose brushing against mine. Hotness caresses my body. "Are you planning a bloodbath, little Pea?"

He's mocking me, and a shiver of rage jolts down my spine, making me tighten my fists.

"I'm going to kill them."

"You think you're going to kill them," he says dryly. "But when it's show time, when you're in front of your victim, no matter how much you hate them, no matter what they did to you, most people chicken out. That's what separates the monsters from the throng. Monsters switch the human button off."

"Are you a switcher?" The air's stuck in my throat, tangling into a suffocating ball of thrill.

"I'm a switcher," he confirms with a small nod that makes our lips connect.

I need him. I need a switcher. Someone to help me out with Godfrey, Sebastian and Camden. He is perfect.

"I'm taking down these men, Beat. With or without you. Now, are you in or are you out?" My brazen question skulks into his lips. That's how close we are. He laughs hard, a bad laugh, a villain's laugh, a laugh that doesn't belong in his mouth, and pulls away. Then I hear him standing up on his feet, stretching.

"Out." He tucks the book he brought for me under my arm and pulls my blindfold off in one go. I can still feel the burn of his fingers wrapped around my neck and want them to make me gasp for oxygen again. No one's ever done that to me before, but it wasn't unpleasant. Nate's face is covered by his black shirt, his abs sticking out under the dense black and blue ink. A faint trail of short, dark hair leads into his pants and I want to yank his jeans down and find out where it ends.

Never happened to me before. Not even with Camden.

"Sleep tight, little Pea."

I feel tight, all right. With nerves, fears…between my legs.

I look down to the book he brought for me. *The Perfume* by Patrick Suskind. About a serial killer who murdered women for their scents.

Time.

If Nate gives me three weeks of his time, I'll be able to kill the bastards and get my life back. Now I just need to make sure he's just business.

That'll be easy. . .right?

NATE

"What did the scumbag do?" I ask, my hands tucked under my head as I lie in bed. I shouldn't wanna know what Pea's deal is, shouldn't favor listening to her story over diving into a book. But I do. Godfrey had said that she's from Blackhawk. That she's the daughter of a loaded politician. How did she end up as a low-class drug dealer who managed to piss off some of the most dangerous men in the United States?

I shouldn't listen to her ramblings, and I *definitely* shouldn't have let her rest her head against my shoulder. Toss into this list a few more *shouldn't haves*: I shouldn't have almost kissed those pinks when my cock ached so bad to dig into that tight dress, and I shouldn't have almost choked her with my lust for her. But I did all of those things, because she's the center of my social life. Whatever fucked up relationship I'm forming with my hostage, she's the closest person to me right now. Pathetic? Sure. But it's the truth nonetheless.

"I dropped out of UCLA and moved to London to live with Camden." I hear her voice seeping from my cracked floor. The fact that Irv's always at work when we talk is a god-fucking-send. "I thought I loved him. And as you may know, in love, logic is almost always the first casualty. My parents weren't happy about me dropping out, but they didn't try to stop me either. My dad was too wrapped up in his campaign, too smitten with the idea of the Archers and Burlington-Smyths strengthening their ties. And my mother. . ." She drifts off with a bitter chuckle. "Who knows where she was at the time. She battled depression and a herd of demons that seemed to have followed her into every rehab facility she checked in to. I remember the first time I realized my mom wasn't coming back. It was on my sixteenth birthday. All I got from her was a letter. Not even a phone call. I think she lives in North Carolina now. She sometimes sends Christmas cards, and I hate it. It makes me remember her. Christmas is my least favorite time of the year."

Mine too, and for the same reason.

It reminds us we lost our mamás.

I press my palm to my cold sheets and close my eyes, thinking about how she looks like right now. Her legs sprawled on her blanket—golden, smooth and soft. My cock swells inside my low-hanging sweatpants. The only reason I ain't fondling my meat to the sound of her raspy voice is because she's confiding in me and that's a little fucked up. Okay, a lot fucked up.

"One month absorbed the next. I didn't make friends. I didn't re-enroll in school. All I did was sit around and wait for him to arrive from work every day. I was sickly in love, Beat. It was the worst form of love. The kind of love that doesn't give, but consumes. The kind of love that quickly turns into hate. Everything else—family, hobbies, friends, the outside world— was just a distraction I resented, pulling Camden away from me. Fast forward eighteen months, and guess what?"

"Spill it."

"I came back home from a Chelsea shopping spree one day to find him nailing a glamour model from Page Six on our kitchen island."

I smirk to myself, eyes still shut. I don't know much about this girl, but it's safe to say she set his balls on fire, just a starter to the main course of torture she had in mind for him. Pea's bold. She'd walk through fucking fire in kitten heels with a smile on her face and wouldn't even break a sweat. I saw it in the way she handled Godfrey and Seb.

"I closed the door quietly, stepped back and descended the stairs. Waited at a coffee shop across the street until I saw the skank leaving my apartment. I didn't want him to know that I knew."

"Because?"

The room hushes before I hear the smirk on her lips. "Because where's the fun in that?"

For the next half hour, Pea tells me about the digging work she's done, looking up Camden's bank statements, hiring a PI and doing pretty much everything a crazy bitch can to plow out dirt about her lover.

"He had seven side-pieces in total. Didn't use a rubber with any of them. I wanted to plan the perfect revenge. Something epic. The man who claimed to love me, who wanted to marry me, missed my nineteenth birthday so he could shack up with an exotic dancer in Shoreditch. He was late to our anniversary dinner because he had an orgy with two Polish tourists. Meanwhile, he was spreading promises, spewing lies, holding me captive with his charm. . .no, I couldn't just let this end with a slap and a hate letter."

She giggles, her voice rising from my floor, and to my horror, this time it makes a brief stop in my chest before migrating down to my groin for a cock-twitch.

"Do that again," I order.

"Do what?"

"That giggle."

She giggles again, no questions asked. *Fuck.*

"I take it back. *Don't* do that again," I grunt. The need to charge downstairs and fuck her is overwhelming.

"Over the next few months, I played the dutiful girlfriend. Went the extra mile and then some. Gave the best head. . ."

I adjust my junk in my sweats. I don't even know Camden Archer, but if she won't pull the trigger, I'd be happy to kill him myself.

"My boyfriend finally cracked. It took time, but he did. Camden asked me to marry him. I said yes, but that I needed to do something with my time. And what better way to spend it than doing something for him? He agreed to let me help him out with his business and signed a few power of attorneys granting me access to some of his bank accounts. He didn't get me anywhere near the shady business. Didn't trust me, no doubt, as I find it hard to believe this man would protect me from anything or anyone. Nonetheless, I became privy to his businesses. Now, I had access, a motive and the due diligence. It was time for the grand finale."

I swallow, knowing exactly where it's heading. She tried to hit him and took a blow. The ricochet was too much, and she crumbled.

"Did you know that the last time I saw my mom, I was fifteen, and the last time I spoke to her was before I was of drinking age? Camden was my first honest attempt at a genuine human relationship with someone who wasn't Preston...and it boomeranged straight into my face, breaking every single bone in the process."

"Tell me you didn't cut off his balls," I grunt. Not that it'd deter me from asking her to suck on mine, but that's pretty much the only reason I can see for Godfrey and Sebastian hate her so much. Pea giggles. Again.

My heart stutters. . .again.

My cock twitches to that adorable sound. . .*again.*

"One day Camden came back home to find it completely empty. I had moved out and gotten on the first flight back to the US. I also donated all of his furniture, clothes and belongings to the Octavia Foundation, because I'm a sweetheart like that. The bank accounts I had access to were emptied, the money thrown into an offshore British Virgin Islands account in my name. By the time he found out he was a lot less rich and very much single, I was sipping a virgin Bloody Mary in first class. I was smart enough not to go back home, though.

"I went to live in New York. The apple was big and I bit into it with gusto. London opened my big-city chakras and I was more than happy to disappear into the throng and melt into being another faceless, pea-coat wearing student. I picked up a few college courses and lived off Camden's fortune that I stole, keeping in touch with my brother and father by phone.

"Until one day, Dad called and said there was an emergency. Preston had disappeared. No one knew where he was.

"I hurried back home, taking the first flight to San Francisco and crying my eyes out all the way there. I'd felt guilty enough about leaving Preston in the first place when I'd moved to London, but this was too much.

"I walked into my family home for the first time in over two years, and Preston wasn't there. But you know who was? Godfrey, Sebastian and Camden."

I suck in a breath, eyes burning until my lids give in and flutter.

"I marched straight into an ambush, perfectly orchestrated by my own dad. He kept crying and banging his head against the wall, chanting that he was sorry, which only infuriated me even more. Dad said they told him they'd kill him if he didn't rat me out. Better me than him, right?"

I don't answer, because I have zero control over what's about to leave my mouth.

"The men sat me down and explained that despite everything, Camden still loved me, forgave me, even. Can you believe that?" A bitter laugh escapes those pinks. "Forgave, but didn't forget. Which was why things were going to be a little different from that point forward. He was going to keep me as his 'stateside piece.' What he did to me then—" She chokes on a sob. My chest fucking hurts. *Why you, Country Club?*

"He broke me. They all did. Him, Godfrey, Seb. . .they locked me in an apartment, not too far from Godfrey's office, and I became entertainment. Pure, cheap, entertainment. A pet. No cell phone, no friends, no family. Just me and my two thuggish guards. And they came for me. They came every week.

"Sometimes it was Camden, who paid a visit and played with my body.

"Sometimes it was Godfrey who wanted to have fun.

"I was a whore. A nothing, a no one. The only one who didn't touch me was Sebastian. No. Sebastian liked watching. Hetero sex was not his thing, he didn't get off on watching them fuck me. He got off on watching them *hurt* me. My pain brought him pleasure, and when I screamed, he came. Until, after a while, I stopped screaming. Just to spite them."

Kicking off my covers and springing to my feet, I punch a wall before stalking to the bathroom to run for cover. Her voice chases me.

"Godfrey said that time was of importance, so we had a timeframe. Every time he walked into the bedroom to strip me of my clothes and humanity, he turned over a three-legged, thirty-minute hourglass on a nearby dresser. He said that it'd all be over in thirty minutes or less, because he didn't want to waste too much time on a whore like me. I had to look at that hourglass every day and every night and hate it silently. Every time I broke an hourglass, he brought two along the next day. By the time I broke free, the room was littered with dozens of them, staring at me, taunting me, reminding me that life was happening and that time was moving on without me. The funny thing was that Camden didn't know his dad was raping me. He thought I was exclusively his. When I tried telling him about his dad, he didn't believe me. Said that not all fathers were bastards like mine. Then Godfrey would punish me for ratting him out."

I punch the mirror above the sink. A web of blood cracks my reflection, disturbing my false looks with the truth of my ugliness. If Pea's telling the truth, I'm the biggest asshole to walk this earth, and Godfrey Archer's a dead man.

"I never stood a chance, Beat, until I did. One night, I took a risk. I did something they couldn't foresee or expect.

"I fought back.

"I didn't even have a butter knife at the apartment, but I did have plastic cups. I stole a lighter from one of my guards and prepared a weapon in the bathroom. Burned the plastic of the cup, molded it into a spear. . ."

Storming out of the bathroom, I slide into my boots with every intention of getting out of here.

"Camden arrived and forced himself on me. Only this time, I was prepared. When he closed his eyes and moaned my name, I took the spear out of the linen and shoved it into his chest. He rolled off of me, and it was only when I watched him bleeding on the floor, that I realized I stabbed his right side and not the left. I wanted the left, Beat. I wanted the left," she says, crying loudly.

Don't go down.

Don't care.

Don't. Fucking. Care.

"I plucked the gun he always kept in his holster when he came to see me and threatened the guards behind the door with it when I broke free. They let me run away. Somehow, I was out of that place. Somehow, I was free.

"I hid under a bridge for two days. No money. No food. No friends. I couldn't contact my dad for obvious reasons. On day three, I arrived at Preston's preppy school during his lunch break and told him I needed help. He was in Blackhawk all along. Dad sold him out so I'd come and see him. Preston agreed to help. The same afternoon he came back with five grand in cash. It was more than enough to see me through the next month. I told Preston he could never talk to me again, at least until I sorted this out. I hid at Motel 6. The minute I walked in the room and turned on the TV, I saw what was left of my life hitting the five o'clock news. A story about how my dad was suspected of drug trafficking and was forced to step out of his position as mayor of Manor Hill. By then, he'd already filed for bankruptcy after Godfrey forced him to hand over all the money I stole from Camden. Dad paid my debt."

I breathe quietly, standing in my boots in the middle of the murky hallway, not making a move. Such a fighter. Such a goddamned fighter.

"Why didn't you go to the police?"

"We both know the police are on Godfrey's payroll," she huffs. "I was going to take them down myself. I'd spent that month planning. I knew when Camden was going to be in California, because I'd listened to them talking about their plans when they were at the apartment they locked me in. While I was sitting in the bedroom, flipping channels, they were in the living room, planning their next drug-trafficking escapade. With a little help from a local motorcycle club called Cutthroat Bandits, who had beef with Godfrey and his wiseguys, I not only had the when, but also the where. A warehouse in Stockton. The Cutthroat Bandits wanted nothing more than to kill the three villains in my life, get them out of the way. And me? I paid them every single penny I managed to put my claws back on from that British Virgin Islands' account to help me."

Fuck my life. *She really was planning a bloodbath.*

"Camden, Sebastian and Godfrey came to the warehouse where they were selling drugs to a local Latino gang. I showed up with the Cutthroat Bandits. We waited behind bushes and trees until the Latinos left, and the minute the loud rumble of their Harleys drove out of earshot, we climbed out of the bushes with semi-automatic weapons pointing at them. We walked in a straight line, cornering them back in the warehouse. You should've seen the look on their faces when they saw me pointing a barrel straight at Godfrey's balls.

"The Bandits did the talking. They said that the streets of NorCal don't belong to some British dude. They belonged to them. But all that time. . .all three men stared at me. Fire broke between the two gangs—Godfrey's soldiers and the Bandits—but when I saw the three cowards running up to the roof to hide from the bullets, I charged after them.

"I got to Godfrey first. He was the slowest of the three. Caught him pacing back like a cornered animal. I had a loaded gun in my hand, and that's how I found out, Beat, that I'm a switcher. I inched closer. My smile was manic. 'Time,' I repeated his own words. 'Moves differently according to circumstances.' I took a few more steps in his direction, and he couldn't do a thing. He was weaponless. Weak.

"'But sometimes, all the time in the world can end with just...a little...push.' I pushed him from the rooftop, and he landed inside a trash container. Next in line was Seb, who charged up to the roof to try and save his boss. I pushed Seb down and he landed on Godfrey. I didn't hear a sound from Godfrey, so I presumed him dead, but just in case, I shot in their general direction. I had shit aim, and it was dark." She hisses a breath.

"And then?" My fists clutch. I'm itching to kill these bastards more than she is.

"I called the police and ran away. The place was full of drugs, but empty of Camden, who managed to escape. I grabbed a few bags of God-knows-what, knowing that I had no money at this point and that I had to make a quick buck after the deal I struck with the MC. The police arrived and saw everything. Godfrey and Seb were still alive, and they were at a crime scene with enough drugs to last the whole fucking 60's. That's how Godfrey and Seb ended up in prison, and that's why they'll never rest until I'm dead."

There's no point asking why they didn't rat her out. *They wanted her for themselves.*

I know what I need to do. What my conscience begs me to do. This day has been full of good and bad. I killed bad people, and now I have the chance to redeem myself by saving a good one. But it's not that simple. My neck is on the line here, too.

And the fact that I want to fuck the shit out of her? Another complication that can backfire in my face. Do I want to help her or do I simply *want* her?

"Go to bed, Pea," I order dryly, walking back to my room, shoulders slumped.

Things just got a whole lot more complex.

Thanks a fucking lot, Country Club.

A platinum-blonde secretary in fancy clothes and with enough makeup to layer a fucking cake greets me behind a massive reception desk made out of deep oak. The title *Royal Realty* is splashed in golden letters over the fancy wood.

There is nothing royal about the asshole I'm about to confront.

"Good afternoon, Sir. How can I hel—" I don't even spare the woman a second glance. I simply charge through the double doors straight into God's office. I tell myself that it's not about Prescott. He's been jerking me around for far too long. I need answers.

The woman shoots up behind me, slowed by her heels and fears. Yeah, I wouldn't mess with me either.

"Sir! You can't go in there. Mr. Archer's in a meeting!"

I can see that for myself. I'm standing on the threshold, watching Godfrey behind his desk, two suited men sitting in front of him, in the middle of a heated discussion, which I just broke. The men twist their heads in my direction, and God stares me down like I'm a dog he's about to smack with a rolled newspaper.

He's lucky he has guests. If he were alone, I would've made a nice rug out of his dead body by now for what he did.

"Welcome, Nathaniel. I don't recall you making an appointment to see me today." He sounds composed and tranquil. But his hands are dancing. Pupils darting everywhere.

"A word," I grit, my eyes bleeding anger. Every second I stand here instead of killing him is a fucking testament of my strength. The secretary's still behind me, and I watch her in the edge of my periphery making hysterical signals to Godfrey with her hands and mouth, telling him she tried to stop me. Godfrey nods curtly, then turns to the men.

"Gentleman, I apologize, but there seems to be some kind of an emergency. During my unfortunate time at. . ." He scowls, before he continues, "San Dimas prison, I used my time and authority to try and help the young inmates. Nathaniel was one of them, and I trust he has a very good reason to turn to me so suddenly and spiritedly. Please excuse us. Melanie will show you out and reschedule our meeting."

They all shake hands, while mine is aching to sucker punch him. After a round of pleasantries, the door shuts behind us and Godfrey's agreeable mask falls, his true colors dripping from every wrinkle of his face.

"I'd slit your throat right here if the very carpet you stand upon wasn't worth more than your whole, miserable existence, you sad piece of shite."

I throw my head back and laugh. I'm not Irvin or another brainless muscle guy. I ain't scared. Pissed? You bet, but not scared. "Godfrey, cut the crap. I ain't one of your San Dimas groupies."

"You're a no one, that's who you are." He rolls his plush executive chair back and swivels, giving me his back. He pins a vinyl record into a gramophone. *Four Seasons* by Vivaldi fills the air. The only reason I know this shit is because he used to listen to this when we were working together in San Dimas.

"Why are you here?" he barks.

"When was the last time you checked on the AB?" I pace deeper into the room and he turns around to face me again. His brows furrow. His back falls to his chair as he exhales.

Underlying question: Did you send them or are you just a useless prick?

"Do I look like I work for you, lad?" he finally asks, his pupils assessing my reaction closely.

"No, I'd never hire someone like you." My ass hits the chair in front of him as I sprawl back and make myself comfortable. "I'm the one who clearly works for you, under the assumption that I'm in your debt. That's because you claim to protect me from the Aryan Brotherhood. However. . ." I trail off, leaning forward and smashing my palm against his desk when I catch his eyes drifting downwards trying to text message. The little bitch wants security to throw me out. He jumps in response, staring at me with heated eyes. "That can change. Maybe you're not as powerful as I thought you were. Maybe you can't keep me safe."

"You know, Nathaniel, everybody loves the second concerto of Vivaldi's *Four Seasons* best. It's that part they keep using in car commercials. The summer part. Everybody loves the summer. But the thing about art is"—Godfrey tosses his phone across the table and gets up—"it's quite subjective. For instance, I hate the summer, and I hate car commercials. My favorite part? The winter. Winter people are dangerous. They're not afraid of the rain, the snow or even little blonde storms. The minute you stray from my plans, Nathaniel, the minute you walk away from our arrangement, after everything I've done for you. . ." He looks around, like there's a crowd watching, and drops his voice an octave. "Caution is advised." He winks.

I stand up and wipe everything off his desk. Folders, a full coffee mug, a laptop and a pile of documents all thrown, and crashing to the floor. "You never did anything to protect me from them." My face twists with rage.

Godfrey sits back and knots his fingers together, looking smug. "Know your place, pawn."

I know my place, all right. Now I know everything about where I stand, and it's nowhere near where he wants me.

Fifty thousand dollars. Fake new passport. I know this rich kid has the money. And I've already seen a fake passport in her duffel bag. Prescott's legit. What's more? She's fucking relatable.

As if reading my mind, he asks, "How's our girl?" sounding creepily cheerful. "Camden can't wait to come here. Shame, really, about this whole wedding. Such a hassle, but it's got to be done."

"She's alive," I grit, remaining vague.

"Tried any funny business? Run away? Seduce you? Convince you to team up with her?" He cocks one brow and strokes his chin thoughtfully. All of the above. And why wouldn't she? I'm about to hand her over to this motherfucking nutjob.

Or am I? Godfrey doesn't seem to do much for me these days.

"You know, Nathaniel, I could've kept her in a million different places and waited until Camden's arrival. I chose you lot because it's a test. You've always been a loose cannon. I reckoned it'd be wise to test the water before I threw you into the deep end, into the more important fields of my business. Are you going to fail me, *inmate*?" His chin drops down, inspecting me. I smooth my hand on my chest, smirking.

"Don't test me, Archer. I'm not your fucking student."

I turn around, about to leave, when his voice freezes me in place.

"I hope she didn't mention her child," Godfrey grunts. "Poor little Prescott can say just about anything to get her off the hook."

Her child? I want to ask him what the fuck but know him better than to think he'd give me straight answers. She'll be spitting the information tonight, all right. I turn around and veer back to my reason for being here.

"So you don't protect me from the AB but still expect me to be your guard dog?" I summarize.

"I do protect you from the AB, to an extent. They are business." He taps his fingers against his lips. *Drugs.* "You can't expect me to jeopardize my business for you, Nathaniel. I keep an eye on them for you. But you are right about one thing—you're still mine, still work for me, and the minute that changes, you're dead."

A cell phone starts ringing from the pile on the carpet and he sends a fragile arm, bending down to answer it. I'd pick it up for anyone else, but not for him. I stand, tall, young, proud, and watch him flailing his arms while leaning one hip downwards miserably, struggling to pick it up.

"Now, now," he says, waving his cane in the direction of the entrance, finally gluing the phone to his ear. "I have some wedding arrangements to discuss. Off you go. Oh, and Nathaniel? Don't switch teams. Ours is awfully powerful." He winks before I shut the door behind me.

Bastard.

I spend my time reading his diary, holding the red notebook at an angle that allows a ray of sun to trickle through a crack in the boarded windows. Yellow light sheds over the pages. I'm getting to know Nate. Getting to *like* Nate. It's horrible, to feel positively about your captor. But I do. Can't help not to. He is broken, just like me. Life has fed him heartbreak, just like it fed me.

DECEMBER 25TH, 2010

"THE HEART WAS MEANT TO BE BROKEN" – OSCAR WILDE

Christmas Day.
Frank heard the news about my mom's death through the grapevine. He visits me in my cell. Brings in candy bars and Top Ramen. Pedro's eyeing the sweets like they are fucking Megan Fox. He's been trying to land himself a spot in ad-seg to get a shot of the good stuff. Again.
"Crack already, boy," the old man grunts, punching me in the shoulder.
"Yell. Curse. Break shit. Your mother just died. She was a good woman."
I agree. She was the best. Right after I killed my dad, she threw herself at the police officers' feet, begging for them to take her and not me.
"Need a shoulder to cry on?"
I sniff an arrogant "No."
He leaves, but not before he shoves a few stamps into my orange uniform. "Get yourself something nice, Nathan—I mean, Nate."
I throw the Ramen noodles against the wall and watch the slimy strings crawl downwards like worms. My throat constricts with emotions, and not the good kind. Never the good kind.
"You're a weird kid." I hear Pedro rolling over on his bunk bed. "Let me know if you get the shits again. I really need those meds."

JANUARY 3ʀᴅ, 2010

"FRIENDS ARE THE SIBLINGS GOD NEVER GAVE US" (MENCIUS)

I arrive back at the exercise yard after being MIA since news broke about Mamá.

Godfrey and his crew sit at a picnic table, eyeing me like a moving target. Seb grins and pats the bench in a silent invitation. I ignore him and go straight to Frank.

The old man's there with Stockton's old schoolers. They're standing in the corner, rolling up cigarettes and swearing at no one in particular. Frank flashes his false teeth with a rusty "Hello."

"Yeah," I say, snatching the cigarette from his hand, even though I'm not a smoker. He tilts his chin down. "Yeah?"

"Yeah, I need a shoulder to cry on."

And that night, I bawl my fucking eyes out for hours on a shoulder I used to think belonged to a veteran pirate.

FEBRUARY 3ʀᴅ, 2010

"AGE IS A CASE OF MIND OVER MATTER. IF YOU DON'T MIND, IT DON'T MATTER" (SATCHEL PAIGE)

I'm in the cafeteria when Frank shows up, slapping backs as he strides along the lengthy benches. Good mood is playing on his face. When he sits next to me, I find out why. Frank got me a gift for my twenty-second birthday. A paperback of On The Road *by Jack Kerouac. The irony tickles my lips with unfamiliar laughter. I haven't laughed in a long time, but getting a prisoner a book about freedom is pretty dope.*

The book is bent and you can see it's been rolled up for hours when it was smuggled in.

No one's given me a birthday gift since I was eight.

I cry a little on the inside, but on the outside, I let out a yawn.

He hooks my neck in a headlock and my cheek crushes against his saggy chest as he ruffles my messy dark hair.

"Fucking brat. I know you wanted this more than wet pussy."

"How?" My fingers dig hard into the book. It feels like home in my palm. Like it belongs there. His friend Sergio gives me an odd look, his eyebrows pop in surprise.

"He a fag?" he enquires, jerking his thumb in my direction. Frank shakes his head and pats my back. "He'll grow up to break bones and hearts in equal measure. Hey, Nathan—Nate," he says with a cluck of his tongue and gives me his peach. I love peaches, so I take it. "The correctional officer? Officer Bouscher? Beth?"

I stare at him blankly. I know Beth.

"She wants to fuck your brains out. Know how you talk to her about poetry and shit?"

84

"It's not poetry, it's fiction." My wry voice is clipped. Which only sends Frank into a fit of even crazier hoots.

"Poetry, fiction, the goddamned weather. Don't matter, pretty boy. She doesn't give a damn. When you talk, when she watches your lips move, all she thinks about is how they'd feel on her lips. And I ain't talking about the ones on her face."

This makes the old schoolers cackle like hyenas.

I'm not a virgin. I had plenty of sex before coming here, with so many girls I can't even try to count. Everywhere I go, women ogle me, slip their numbers into my pocket and send their giggling friends to stutter some bullshit about how they never do this. Which is why I've never been overly occupied with women in the first place. One never appreciates what he has in spades.

"She told me about that book." Frank's face grows serious. "We made it work."

Later that night, I get my first prison tattoo by a guy called Irvin. He ties an empty pen barrel to a motor from a tape player before the needle kisses my skin. I chose a Kerouac quote. Left shoulder blade.

"My fault, my failure, is not in the passions I have, but in my lack of control of them."

Since I have no passions, I pray that one day, this'll make sense to me.

So far, passion failed me. The only thing I ever did fervently was killing the man who broke my Mama's arms in a drunken fit to prevent him from hurting her again.

For now, though, I'll make do with this quote. I like the jagged pain that escorts being marked. I like the white noise of the machine, and decide that by the time I get out of here, I'll hide most of myself with bad ink.

Well, half of me, anyway. The other half I'll keep clean and pure. Who knows? Maybe parts of me are still redeemable.

I wait impatiently for the night, knowing that I've made real progress with Nate.

But when the crickets start to chirp, my heart sinks.

Tonight is different than any other night.

I hear a commotion upstairs, followed by strange noises. Feet that are not Nate's army boots nor Irvin's Crocs. (I figured Ink is Irvin—who else could it be?)

I hear cheap heels clicking like the safety of a gun, and sneakers and boots dancing together. I hear music cranking up to full-blast. Chatter.

Voices clashing like swords in my ears. Laughter. I hear women shrieking and giggling and *awwi*ng and *ahh*ing. Men swearing, spitting and drinking. There's a party upstairs, while I'm stuck here, rotting on my own stupid plans to break free. I'm terrifyingly upset with Nate, even though we're not friends. Even though I'm nothing but his victim and, if things go according to my plan, he'll soon be nothing of mine.

I confided in him, told him everything I've been through, and this is what he does?

A jolt of hatred slices through my gut. I despise every single woman who is partying up there, and I don't even know them. The idea of Nate nuzzling, kissing, straddling—even choking—someone else makes me want to scream. I'm petrified and possessive of him at the same time. Why?

Jesus, what's happening to me? I should be shouting from the top of my lungs, hoping someone would notice. But I can't bring myself to do it. The illogical part of me tells me to wait. Maybe he'll come for me. Maybe I can still make my way out of this place with him in tow.

Nate.

He hasn't come down to check on me tonight. Haven't had my meal yet. My shower time. *My Nate time.* One party and he forgets all about me?

Men. They should never be trusted.

I munch on stale chips, lying on my blanket as anger brews inside me. Tonight was not supposed to go down this way. He was supposed to come over, have dinner with me and crack completely.

I throw the bag of chips on the floor and scream into the darkness, the music swallowing the noise.

Iggy Pop is begging "I Wanna Be Your Dog" upstairs. Downstairs, I feel like a caged up pet. I knew there was going to be a downside to hearing everything through these paper walls, down to the persistent humming of their old fridge.

The music is so loud, I don't even notice when in the midst of the wild party, the door cracks open. I jump to my feet when I see the light pouring from the inside the house into the basement. Maybe the person who opened the door is a stranger looking for a case of beer and I can ambush them. Alas, I'm greeted with the Guy Fawkes mask, and Nate is standing there, a white and dirty muscle shirt clinging to his body like a slutty fangirl. His black, ripped jeans ride low, offering a glimpse of his stupid *V*, his full sleeve of monsters spitting fire crawling up his muscled arm. He is holding an open bottle of beer and a plastic plate with junk food piled high. Pizza, coleslaw and greasy fries. I turn around and toss my hair.

"Oh. You."

"Yeah, me." He sounds playful, jovial and *tanked*. He's been drinking. And by the slur I've already picked up, a lot more than one should have. "Who were you expecting? Donald Trump?"

"Honestly? I was wishing for a fucking cop." I still don't look at him, for a reason beyond my grasp. It's not a good time to be sulking. He's mumbling incoherently, drunk to oblivion and in all probability, breaking some pretty tough parole rules. The party, the alcohol and the stinking weed that's on his clothes. This is when I should be making him break even more rules. Work harder to dig my way into his heart, not push him away until he's on the other side of the planet.

Seduce. Take. Destroy. Treat men how they treat you, Prescott.

"Brought you food and booze," he offers, his muscular arm dangles the beer bottle. I don't budge from my place at the corner of the room, still moping like a two-year-old who just found out that the world doesn't spin around her.

"Leave it there." I nod my head to the table. "Now, don't let me stand in the way of your fun. Go back to your party."

Okay, who is this girl speaking from my mouth and what has she done to the ballbusting Prescott? This jealous girlfriend nonsense is not me. Ever since Camden, I've been very careful about not getting attached. Other than a handful of disastrous one-night stands I engaged in, just to prove myself that I could still do it, I haven't really paid any attention to the male population for the past few years.

Nate takes a step into the room. A sliver of a chill breaks down my skull, moving down my spine and tickling my toes.

"Turn around. I'm blindfolding you."

"What have I done now?" I throw out my arms in despair, huffing a blonde lock away from my eyes.

"Sassed around way too much for my liking," he answers with a teasing bite, clarifying. "I wanna hang out with you, Country Club. That means I'm taking off this mask. You can't see my face. I wish you fucking could, but God has a plan for me, and I don't want it to be cutting my dick off and giving it to Seb as a souvenir," he snickers. I've never seen Nate so buzzed. So intoxicated. So agreeable.

He hovers closer, grabs my hand and jerks me to his body. Then he spins me around and wraps the black cloth around my eyes tightly. I smell the beer and salty BBQ snacks as he exhales a charged breath on my skin, his lips brushing the nape of my back fleetingly. I roll my head backward as the sound of the plastic mask hitting the floor fills my ears.

"Better?" I purr, losing myself.

He leans into my body, his skin sticking to mine. "Much. I like you blindfolded."

"You like me regardless." I bite my lip, not sure if I'm trying to convince him or myself. I need him to crack if I want to be out of here soon. The good news is that whatever temptations Nate has upstairs, his focus is solely on the girl underground. "Help me take a sip?"

He grabs me by the waist and turns me around so that I face him. Nate leads us both to the corner of the room, where we sit down. The party is still alive, but I've learned a thing or two about Nate, and he doesn't need people around him. He needs silence, and maybe a good story to listen to. Parties were meant for people who run away from their minds, not soak in them until drowned by their thoughts.

"Ink's party, huh?" I elbow him, and the beer he placed in my hand sloshes over the rim of the bottle. A dash of cold liquid spills on my bare thighs, and I can't see it, but I can *feel* his eyes drop to my wet skin, heating my flesh with desire.

"How'd you figure it out?"

"Beware of those who seek constant crowds, they're nothing alone," I quote Bukowski, and hear his breaths pick up speed. He gets hot on poetry. A freak who takes comfort in other people's words. Just like me. "You don't need cheap entertainment."

"I told him he's stupid as fuck. You could be pounding this door down screaming bloody murder," he says, testing me. I run my tongue over my front teeth.

"Well, I didn't. Because, Beat, I know that I'm walking out of here before Camden and Godfrey get to me. Remember my offer yesterday?" My heart pounds faster. I'm still embarrassed about being victimized. I don't want him to see me as weak. I want us to be equal.

"Are you a mother?" he slurs. I frown.

"What?"

"Are. You. A. Fucking. Mother?"

It feels like a punch straight to my chest, a painful memory that he's slapped me with, and I'm glad he can't see my eyes through the black fabric of my blindfold.

"I'm not. Why do you ask?"

"No reason." Hiccup. "So you don't have a kid?"

"No." I grit, trying not to fume. "Already told you, Beat. It's just me in this world."

"What they did to you. . .Jesus, Prescott. That's so fucked up."

Nate is drunk. Oh-so drunk. A huge blessing, wrapped in a red sateen bow. I take a sip of my beer, the liquid washing over my throat and offering the kind of comfort only booze can, and lick my lips, knowing his predatory eyes are on me.

"That's the ugly truth," I nod.

"Then tell me something beautiful," he croaks. "I have enough uglies for a lifetime."

"There is nothing to fear except the power you give to your own demons. Sally Gardner said that."

"Good quote." His voice smiles. I smile back at it.

"Can I feel your face?"

He snorts another laugh from the shit-drunk variety. "No."

"Pretty please with a cherry on top?"

"Nope."

"I'll scream."

"I'll gag you with the extra pieces of bondage and shove the rest of the cloth down every single hole in your body. Don't tempt me, 'cause Ima enjoy it." His tone is flat, sincere, and not at all pissed off. *Peaceful.* Why is this a turn-on for me? I never had it too rough. But with Nate? I actually *want* him to hurt me. In the best, worst, most possible way.

"You'd never hurt me," I retort.

"Never ever, Country Club," he promises softly. "Unless it's fun for you, then all bets are off."

"And we've already established that you like me."

"No. You said that."

"Show me yours and I'll show you mine. Let me touch your face, and I'll let you touch me. *Everywhere.*"

"I'm not like them." His voice turns to steel. "I'm not the taking kind."

"You're not taking. I'm giving. Gladly."

Silence.

Contemplation.

I part my lips and lick them.

Persuasion.

Nate sighs in return.

He's in.

"Make it fast." He pulls both my wrists into his huge palm, placing my hands on his warm cheeks before muttering, "Silver Spoon, you little perv."

The first thing I notice are his cheekbones. They're so high, they're level with his ears. Cut, prominent and glorious. He has a Tragus piercing poking out of his left ear, which I almost yank out, because instead of an earring, he has a safety pin.

"That's rad." I grin blindly, and by the stretch of his skin, I know there's a smirk playing on that perfect face too.

"Of course you'd think so, CC."

"CC?"

"Country Club."

My hands move down to his square chin, brushing over his lips. Dear God, his lips. So pouty and soft, they feel like two pillows. My hands hurry to his nose. Just as I suspect, it's straight and narrow. My index finger runs over the smooth bone, and much to my embarrassment, I suck in a ragged breath.

"You're spectacular, aren't you, you little bastard?" My voice shakes.

He grins and softly bites one of my fingers. *Straight teeth.* "You ain't too bad yourself."

Heart stuttering in my chest, I knot my legs together, feeling warmth tickling between them. That's the first time he's said something nice about my appearance. I bite down a moan as my hands continue roaming his face, drinking in every piece of flesh, thirsty for much more than what he's offering.

"Kiss me," I hear myself plead. I'm not sure how much of it is me recruiting Nate to my team, and how much is me lusting after this boy-man.

I feel his throat bobbing with a gulp. "Fuck, Pea. You're going to get me into so much trouble, and I'm already in deep."

"Then we'll climb out of trouble together. Let's kick trouble in the ass, Beat. Crawl out of the gutter, point the gun at Godfrey, Sebastian and Camden and kill all of our problems at once. Let's claim our lives back."

His pulse drums beneath my fingers, wild and hungry and tempted, and I lean closer to his face.

"Kiss me, Beat."

"You're insane," he croaks. He's not wrong.

My body is sore, aching with want for a man I haven't seen. Never in my life have I felt like this. Sex with Camden before we broke up was. . .nice. Everything else—painfully numbing. But this. . .it doesn't even have a name.

"We'll make a pact to kill those bastards for what they did to us. Instead of shaking on it, we'll kiss on it. It'll be our little blood oath, Beat."

"Pea."

"Beat. . ."

Beat. . .

Beat. . .

Boom.

He slings me against the wall and his lips crash on mine in a hard, closemouthed, drugging kiss as he pulls me flush against his steel body. I gasp for air, parting my lips, but before I manage to draw in oxygen, he bites my lower lip and drags it into his mouth until the flesh cracks, the healing injury Seb had caused breaking open as he sucks on my blood. Horror twirls with a heady thrill inside me, and I drag my fingers through the hair of my faceless captor, pulling at his perfect locks. He takes my chin in his hand, my lip still in his mouth, sucking hard, drinking away my pain.

Excitement helixes through me, the adrenaline pumping in my veins making my whole body buzz with unfamiliar electricity I'd never felt under a person's touch. Maybe I'm going insane.

Maybe it's a place worth going.

"Blood oath," he growls into my mouth with a charged breath, dragging me up from the floor like the caveman that he is so that we're both standing up. He pins me to the wall. This gorgeous, raw, broken, sensitive monster of a boy-man hates it when men slap me, but make no mistakes—he loves to hurt me. "Make me bleed, Prescott."

And I do. I make him bleed. I bite the tip of his tongue, pulling slowly, taking his rough tongue in my mouth and sucking it with a long, husky moan that tickles my chest, tingles my stomach and ends up blowing up between my legs. The intensity of his touch is so intoxicating, it's almost like he licked me up and down. We've already sprinted over so many barriers, and I have one more to tip him over the edge.

Sex.

He needs to take from me, like the rest of them. It'd be the ultimate betrayal against Godfrey.

"Blood oath," I repeat with abandon, our lips ghosting one another, never leaving, never saying goodbye. Greedy. Ravenous. *Desperate.* "We're in this together, Beat, baby. Fuck me."

Yes. Fuck me. Against orders. Against logic. Against the fucking wall.

His tongue circles around mine frantically, his mouth drops to my neck, dragging downwards. He licks the sensitive spot behind my ear and moves down to bite my breast through the fabric of my dress, leaving goosebumps so powerful I'm quivering like a brittle leaf. He leaves a trail of that sticky blood he drew from my lips with every brush of his tongue. I feel my wetness dripping down my right inner thigh, crawling to my knee, my body begging for some action.

"Aren't you fucked up after what they did to you?" he growls. "Aren't you scared of sex?"

I grab one of his wrists and guide his hand to my inner thigh, moving it up and down my soaked flesh. "Can I fake this, Beat? Can you fake lust?"

"Why you?" A groan that sounds a lot like a beg makes his chest tremble while he pins me to the wall, lifting me so my legs are wrapped around his waist, his swollen, angry erection trapping me between his huge arms. Now he's the one grinding against me, and his willpower to resist me is running on fumes. Every little thrust of his hips hammers another pin on his self-control casket.

"I can have any pussy in the world. . .and the only one that I want is as toxic as poison ivy."

"Beat." I place my mouth on his salty skin. I have no idea what I'm licking with the blindfold on. It's even more of a turn-on. "You can have me. We could have it all. I've got the money. We can fuck and run away, start over and leave this mess."

I guess Nate is too drunk to even comprehend what I just suggested, because he snarls and tugs at the fabric of my gray dress, wanting to strip me naked but too drunk to know how.

"He'll kill me if I fuck you." He grabs me by the ass and lifts me upwards, nuzzling his perfect, straight nose into my throat and sucking. Sex is a powerful drive, and for a young man recently out of prison? It just might throw him off a cliff. "But maybe I deserve death. And maybe. . ." His teeth find my earlobe, tugging. "Maybe I don't even care anymore."

"Fuck me," I whisper into his mouth again, both of us shuddering with looming release.

His hands leave my body and disappointment slams into me, but only for a second, because then I hear him patting his back pocket and producing what might be his wallet. I hear him yanking out a condom and ripping the wrapper open.

"No foreplay," he grunts.

"No problem." I lick his skin again. He could probably drill a missile into me and I'd be fine with it. Yes, he is business, but oh, how I enjoy working my charm on him.

"It's been a while since I've been with someone." I hear the sticky rubber as he rolls the condom on and butterflies take over my chest. Am I happy because I'm close to securing my freedom, because I'm about to have sex with an obviously out-of-this-world mysterious ex-felon with a banging body or because I've played this scene in my head more times than I'd like to admit ever since I fell into his captivity?

You guessed it. All three.

"Are you telling me this because you're going to come fast?"

His hands find my waist again and spin me, throwing my body hard against the concrete with a thud. He yanks my underwear down to my knees, pulls my dress over my ass and smacks it lightly. "That too. But mostly, because it's going to be brutal."

He takes my ass cheeks in his hands, pulls me up so that my behind is against his erection and plows into me in one go.

Shit. He is huge. And I don't mean good-huge, either. No. He is this-should-come-with-a-warning-label huge. I cry out in pain, my nails digging into the wall for comfort, but nothing can dull the agony of having him inside me. Nate's so thick, my thighs spread open automatically even in this position. And he's so long, he hits my G-spot without even trying, which is good, because he *isn't* trying to please me.

And I'm pretty certain having sex with him is the equivalent of experiencing natural birth.

"Jesus," I moan, not exactly sure if it's from pleasure or pain. Instead of pumping into me, his fingers dig into the flesh of my ass, moving me in the rhythm of his frantic trance. Brutally. Repeatedly. Urgently.

"Shut the fuck up, Pea." He disregards me as his cock hits my G-spot hard again, making my mouth water with an impending orgasm. It's not pretty. It's not even sultry. His moves are rusty, feral, manic. He is fucking me like he is trying to kill me, each thrust like a knife that sends my forehead banging against the wall. His desperate growls release something that's been buried deep inside him. It's angry sex, but it's not me he's angry at. No. I'm just a hole he spills the rage he's collected over the years into.

He fucks me because he wants to ruin what belongs to Godfrey Archer and his son, and I let him, for the exact same reason.

His hand slams my ass, and I arch my back in response, my head thrown to the wall with a bang. It's like he poured hot water all over me. He doesn't rub or kiss it better, and after the first shot of pain. . .bliss. Pure bliss.

"Do it again."

"Don't fucking tell me what to do."

But he spanks me again, and I wail his name.

"Beat," I say with a shudder, chanting like a prayer to the sex god behind me, knowing that I should keep my mouth shut, but also that I can't stop. He slams so deep into me, my voice box produces groans and sobs unintentionally.

"Yes. . .oh. . .oh. . .*Nate*."

No. No. No.

His body stiffens behind me and goosebumps bloom on his skin down to his fingertips. He's still inside me, his breathing ragged.

I'm not sure what scares me more, the fact that he hasn't spoken in a few seconds, the fact that he's still inside me, expanding my body like someone shoved a chair into me, or the fact that my pussy swells around him, hot and even more turned on by my fear. I gulp.

"Ink?" he asks dryly. I nod, partly telling the truth.

"God fucking dammit," he hisses, still hard as stone. "How long have you known?"

I squeeze my swollen eyelids together.

"A while."

"Prescott," he warns.

"A week."

Body frozen with fear, I feel his hand as he brushes my hair away and kisses the nape of my neck, his other hand still holding my ass up in the air so that I'm on my tiptoes. He releases a long pained breath. I swallow hard as his silence fills every inch of the room.

"Are you going to kill me or fuck me?" My lips tremble.

He fists my hair, bringing my ear to his hot mouth. "First, the latter," he whispers sinisterly. *He's killed before.* "And then, I'll decide who deserves to be killed for this."

He's at it again. Grabbing my ass in a way that'd surely leave a nasty mark, he slams his hips into my flesh back and forth. I keep my mouth shut by biting into my lower lip hard, but even that doesn't stop the moans from escaping.

I'm working up a solid orgasm, my legs shaking all over, but Nate doesn't even warn me. He drives into me one last time and empties inside me, groaning against my sweaty back for what seems to be a full minute. I feel his condom expanding with hot cum. It feels like he broke my body and sliced my legs open with a cleaver.

And I love it.

He releases my hips and I slide down the wall until my feet hit the floor. I shimmy my dress down, my wetness sticking my thighs together. What the hell just happened? Technically, it was sex. But physically and mentally, it felt like butchery. Nate takes a step back. He went against Godfrey's order and fucked me with everything he's got and then some. His empty balls are in my cute little palm now.

Everyone knows Godfrey has a lie detector in his office. One sit-down with Nate and the needle will be dancing like a hippie at Woodstock. I'm sure we're thinking the same thing—everything's changed now that he stuck his dick in me.

"Shit," he mutters behind me as the new reality settles over the room. "Fuck, fuck, fuck!"

Even though my back is still to him, I can feel him pacing the room. I'm trying not to dwell on it, because my plans are so much bigger than being semi-rejected by a weird man-boy with a cock the size of a rocket ship. Still, it stings.

But I know his name.

And he fucked something that belongs to Godfrey.

He is screwed.

"Listen, Nate. . ." Before I get the chance to turn around and launch at him with another pep talk, the door slams shut, the walls around me rattling with the impact. I wait a few seconds before taking off my blindfold and looking around.

He left.

I kick the food and beer he brought for me, picking up the Guy Fawkes mask he forgot to take with him before he stormed away and stare at it, willing it to come alive and fight with me.

I can't believe him. I can't believe *me*. I shouldn't care that he ran off. Just be thrilled that he's played into my plan, and that I can now manipulate him even more.

Nate Vela will be back. I know he will. A whole party couldn't distract him. He came for me. He came *in* me. He has no interest in whatever the outside world has to offer. From the moment he gets to his house every day, his life revolves around me.

The way he fucked me today? It proved one thing: this man needs me just as I need him.

Bad.

NATE

I need to step out of this mess before she assassinates me in a way a whole army of crazy Nazis tried and hadn't succeeded. She's going to ruin me. . .and I'm going to let her.

No. This stops here.

I don't know this girl. I sure as fuck don't need this girl. This girl, other than being the proud owner of a magic, sleek pussy I tend to respond to like it belongs to Aphrodite herself, is nothing to me. *Nothing.* She'll pull the trigger on me without even batting an eye. She'll fuck her way to freedom even if it were under the bodies of other men. Like Irv, or Stan Hathaway, or even fucking Camden Archer himself. She'll stop at nothing to get her life back, and I can't blame her.

But I can end this.

It's her problem, not mine. Her tragedy, not mine. I've got my own fucking sad story to torture the ears of the average folk with. And that shit about a kid? I may be tanked, but I saw her face twitching when she answered.

Where are you hiding your spawn, little Pea, and who the fuck takes care of them?

Stumbling out of the basement, still thoroughly drunk, I take a wide step over a naked girl on the floor who is masturbating using an empty beer bottle in front of a cheering crowd. Jesus fuck, what kind of people does Irv hang out with these days?

I trudge straight to the stereo that's whining "Hey" by The Pixies and pull the plug out of the outlet, holding the cord in my hand like a lasso, and point it at Irv, who is sprawled out on our sofa, getting a blow job from a woman in a mini-skirt, who looks to be pushing fifty and has a pink hair curler stuck to her skull.

"Everybody get the fuck out. Party's over."

Irv bolts up to his feet, flicking his lit joint onto the hole-filled carpet and staring me down like people expect him to. This shuts up everybody in the room instantly, which is unfortunate, because I have an angry, strong woman in my basement, who just got screwed six ways from Sunday and could very well be screaming her little lungs out.

"Calm your hot ass down, dawg. Who the fuck are you to decide?" he spits. I'm so mad at him for spilling my name in her ears, I'm about to cut his ugly ass face in front of all these people.

"I'm your motherfucking roommate, and when needed, I'll also be your goddamn boss." I take a step in his direction towering over him by at least six inches. "I never agreed to have people over. Fold this shit down before I strangle you alive. I already got a rope." I squeeze the cord in my fist for emphasis and raise it to his eye level. "Now, dummy."

Ten minutes later, the house is empty. It's just me, him and Prescott downstairs. I walked out on her before even zipping up. Hell, my boxers are still damp with the cum I didn't have time to wipe off. Trying to swallow my embarrassment down—I shouldn't care what she thinks of me, she was begging to be fucked and I gave her what she wanted—I throw my pillow over my face and squeeze it, half-wishing I'd suffocate myself to death.

Pea.

Thinking about her gets me so hard I feel my pulse pounding in my dick. I'm tenting like a thirteen-year-old Boy Scout just reeling her name in my head. Sex has fucking broken her, but tonight, there was no mistaking she felt whole, even if for a second.

What is it about this girl that's so different?

She's "street" without being a hooker.

Smart without being pretentious.

Knows her fucking literature, but also how to recognize bad-blended coke from miles away, all at the same time.

No. That's not it. She's got fight, and she *wants* to live. She's actively chasing life, while I let mine slip between my fingers.

She's life, and I'm death.

Prescott Burlington-Smyth is everything I want to be. A storm moving out of a shit situation at the speed of light, not looking back to spare a glance at the casualties of her actions.

How did her pussy feel? Good. Like I remember other pussies I've driven into feeling. Tight and warm like a fuzzy blanket, a shot of heroin to a shivering junkie. But nothing special. It doesn't glitter. It doesn't spew one hundred dollar bills and it won't bring world peace. It doesn't feel any different than the last nameless chick I fucked, all those years ago. And still, she's the only woman to make me hard. The only fucking one.

I hate her.

I want her.

I need to forget her.

That stupid Pixies song keeps playing in my head, so long after I turned it off, on repeat as I roll in bed.

We're chained. We're chained. We're chained.

The following day, I arrive at Mrs. H's Blackhawk mansion. I dread that she's going to be there, but still comply with her craziness. The minute I walk into her house, I disappear into the bathroom and change into a pair of Speedos. Her favorite pair. She'd bought them for me as an Easter gift. Tends to leave a larger tip when I wear them.

I've been thinking all night, and finally came up with a plan.

I'm going to make a fast buck, let Silver Spoon go and take off myself, all while keeping my distance from her.

I'll save her life, but I'll keep her out of mine.

I need to get the hell out of here. If that means compromising my dignity, so be it. It's not like it was worth a damn, anyway. The Aryan Brotherhood is after me. Godfrey has either let them loose or wasn't powerful enough to keep them off my back. And even if he is capable of keeping my ass afloat, once he hears I screwed Prescott with enough ferocity to move a goddamn mountain, I'm going to sleep with the fishes. And Prescott. . .she'd tell him in a heartbeat. If she goes down, she'll make damn sure I'm going with her. I have no illusions why she fucked me. She wanted leverage to get me to help her. Guess what? I fucked my way straight into her plan.

"Oh, Nate!" Mrs. Hathaway rushes from the second floor down to the foyer, her pale blue babydoll loosely wrapped around her figure. "Tahoe was amazing! I couldn't stop thinking about how much you would've loved it. Wow. Speedos. What's the occasion? Have you missed me too?"

Hardly.

Literally. I've been occupied with trying to get rid of a persistent little blonde that keeps popping into my mind again and again, making me hard as fuck. In my head, she dangles her ass from side to side with that taunting smile. Pea wanted me to tap that ass and I did. What can I say? It's common courtesy to give your guests what they want. Only now she consumes half my brain, filling it with filthy thoughts.

The other half is trying to figure out how to fix this mess.

"What would you like me to do today, Mrs. H?" My jaw grinds so hard, my teeth almost turn into sand.

"Me," she jokes on a wink, before nudging her shoulder into my chest and moving forward to her couch, her thin fingers hugging a coffee mug. "For Christ's sake, Nate, loosen up. You can start with watering the plants and mulching the flowerbeds. Eddie's on vacation. *Again.* I swear that man goes on vacations more than I do," she says about her landscaper. I'm only too happy to get out of the house. It's a beautiful day. I can plug my ear buds in and let the lyrics of Morrissey and Robert Smith dissolve into my soul like morphine.

I turn and leave, trying not to hate her for degrading the shit out of me. Out of Eddie. Out of everyone. I bet she was a broke ass waitress before she married Stan. She seems hell bent on taunting people with her money, she's bound to revenge some fucked-up trauma from her past.

"Nate, darling!" Her tenor chases me down the wide hall. "Make sure you bend down real low when you clean the graveled path between the flowerbeds. Your ass is lovely when you squat!"

I water the plants with the hose, glancing sideways to the neighboring houses. I wonder which one of them belongs to Prescott's parents. Why? Why do I give a flying fuck which of these houses is the Burlington-Smyth's? So what? So I could crawl into her window and look through the shit in her baby pink room? Sniff her underwear when no one's watching? Rub one out and spill my baby juice on her Hello Kitty sheets? Or maybe so I could punch her stupid dad in the face five hundred times for handing his daughter over to Godfrey and his crew.

I still haven't recovered from that story.

Thinking about it and drowning a small plot of purple flowers in the process, I ignore Mrs. Hathaway, who ambushes me from behind. Shit, I don't want to deal with her crap right now.

"What's gotten into you, Nate? You're acting all weird. I think the coneflowers have enough water for the whole summer. Why don't you move on to the next flowerbed?"

I drop my gaze to the hose and aim it like a gun at another defenseless flowerbed. "Just wondering who can afford those big-ass houses. Stan's the owner of an accounting firm, but what do your other neighbors do for a living?"

What did you ask that for, you stupid fuck? Now she'll think I'm trying to milk her for data so I can break into their houses, when in reality, the only crime I'd like to commit is to feast on the pussy that belongs to the son of an English kingpin. But Mrs. H is always in the mood for humoring me. Her hand finds my back. She rubs it in circular movements as we both stare ahead at the sea of lavish mansions from her front porch.

"Well, let's see. Those are the Simpsons. We play tennis with them every weekend. They're old money," she snorts. "Texan oil. Then the Cruz family, right over there." Her index finger travels in the direction of another manor. "Lawyers. Best in the country. They can get you out of anything, if you can afford it. Easy-T over there is a rapper. The Greenspans own publishing houses in San Francisco, and the Browns are in real estate. And those," she says and points to a Spanish colonial villa, boasting a lush tropical garden and iron gates, "are the Burlington-Smyths. Surprised the electricity is still running. The house belongs to Godfrey Archer now. An English lord or duke or. . . Ah, I have no idea who that man is, other than the fact that he's my husband's client. Shady business, either way."

I give a small, indifferent nod. So that's how Godfrey got me this job. Everything's connected, calculated and intentional. "Howard Burlington-Smyth was the mayor of Manor Hill. But not anymore."

My stomach knots just from hearing his name. My silence prompts her to continue.

"I don't know the whole story—you know how it is, the more gated the community is, the deeper the secrets are buried—but word in Blackhawk Plaza is that the mother of the family is suffering from schizophrenia and has been MIA for the past decade. I always thought that Howard was a widower. Raising his two kids alone earned him some serious points when he ran for mayor. But this was before. . ." She trails off, her hand sliding lower, massaging the two ridges of my back.

"Before what?" I almost snap. She gives me a onceover before continuing slowly.

"Before the scandal. He was involved in a shady, under-the-desk deal gone wrong, and he had to sell his house to the English guy."

Normally she could tell me that she was attacked by four grizzly bears on her way back from the tennis court and I'd shrug it off and not even offer her a Band-Aid. I look like I have a dog in this fight. Mrs. Hathaway's gaze scrutinizes me, trying to peel away my layers of aloofness. After a stretched silence, she finally says, "Why are you interested in the Burlington-Smyths, Nate?"

"I ain't. Just making small talk. Isn't that what you rich people do?"

That seems to pacify her, and she sucks in a breath.

"So now the Burlington-Smyths live in a house that doesn't belong to them, and Howard throws favors around to keep that expensive roof over his head. I think that's what got him kicked out of his position in the first place. They say"—she drops her voice down to a whisper, despite the fact that we're all alone in her colossal property—"he was involved in drug trafficking. Knows people at the border checkpoint. I personally don't believe it. He seems like a decent man, then again," she says with a shake of her head. "His daughter ran out of the state a few years ago and his son, Preston...no one's seen him in years. So there's no telling what goes on in that family."

I rub the back of my neck, trying to peel away my reaction to her story. We barely know each other, but I guess I figured that Prescott lived the kind of charmed life I couldn't even dream about, because I didn't fully fathom life's potential. Sheltered. Wealthy. Whole. I catch glimpses of this kind of life here and there. When I mow Mrs. H's lawn and watch stick-thin women in sundresses walking their poodles, pushing flashy strollers. Cooing and drinking iced coffees and talking on the phone about their fucking family vacations. Life's a casual thing for them. They don't even realize that one day, they'll be dead. They *know*, but they don't *realize* it. There's a difference. Rich people think money can buy their way out of the darkness. They're wrong. We come from darkness and go back to it when we're done. Nobody lives forever, and everybody's grave is equally as dark.

I know that, and surprisingly, Prescott knows that too.

All this time, Pea was like me. The shattered pieces of her broken family are hiding in piles upon fucking piles of secrets and hearsay that have her whole neighborhood just dying to dig up the shards.

"Sucks to be a Burlington-Smyth," I grunt. What the fuck? I'm one step away from growing a fucking vagina. So what if Prescott had a shitty life? I bet it's still a lot less shitty than mine. Besides, I've already decided that I'm going to spare her life. No need to buy her fucking flowers to make up for the awful men she had to deal with.

Mrs. H creeps closer, brushing my arm as her eyes drop down to my package, squeezed into rubber Speedos. My balls are sweating like they're in a sauna. They've been tingling for Pea's attention for days now. I wonder what it'd take to get her to suck on them.

"I can tell you a lot about this neighborhood if you're interested, Nate," she says. I guess she's talking to me, but she's still staring at my junk. "The Browns have a bastard child and the Simpsons are divorcing. You can stick around when you're done. I'll open a bottle of chardonnay."

"Thanks for the offer, but I got plans." I turn my back to her and point the hose at a mound of flowers.

I do have plans. And they're starting to look crazier and crazier with every tick of the clock.

Tick, tock.

Am I switching teams?

Tick, tock.

Playing right into Prescott's scheme.

That night, I send Irv to give Pea her food and fifteen minutes of bathroom time. But not before warning him for twenty minutes about the importance of not being a total cunt. I also kindly ask him not to volunteer anymore crucial information about me, such as my last name, license plate, social security number or favorite porn star.

Though deep down, I know it's too late. She's on to me. She knows my name and would be able to piece together a pretty accurate picture to the cops.

An ex-inmate from San Dimas named Nate, tattoos covering only the left side of his body.

Yeah, not many of those walking around in the world.

Then again, for the sake of my conscience, I can't, correction—*won't*—hand her back to Godfrey after everything that he's done. And if she's a mother on top of everything, I ain't gonna be responsible for her kid becoming an orphan.

I'm going to let her walk away and make it on my own, without her fifty grand. I have a feeling doing this together would only throw us into a deeper pool of shit. Besides, she's small and blonde and on fucking heeled boots. She'd only slow me down.

There's no way I'm going down there again. She's been manipulating this whole house, reigning it with her sweet pussy and philosophical quotes. I have some thinking to do, and going down there means I'll be handing my dick the key to this out of control train wreck.

Even though I send Irv to take care of her, while trying to read *American Scream* in bed, I still strain my ears to hear them. I hear every curse that leaves his lips as he talks to her and every sarcastic comeback she throws back at him. I keep telling myself I'm eavesdropping because I want to make sure he doesn't hit her again, but it's not the truth. Not the whole truth, anyway. The whole truth is that I'd like to hear if she asks about me. She doesn't.

When her time runs out, she goes back to the basement and doesn't try striking up a conversation. It's been thirteen days since she got here. Not too many more to go before they'll come and take her. She knows it. But she has no idea that I've made up my mind.

They're not touching this girl again. I won't let that happen.

If Prescott Burlington-Smyth dies—it won't be on my watch.

FEBRUARY 27ᴴ, 2010

"DEATH IS THE CURE FOR ALL DISEASES" (THOMAS BROWNE)

Time. Is. Death.

That's why there's an overhead clock in ad-seg, its needle always stuck on 12:00. Midnight or noon? Day or night? You don't know, and after a while, you stop caring. If you want to kill a person from the inside, forget about knives and guns.

Use a fucking watch.

Coming out after a week in the hole, the light of day feels unnatural and almost unwelcome.

I ain't proud of the reason why I got thrown in the hole, but I'd do it all over again if I had to.

It was yard time, and I was sparring with an inmate while the old schoolers and Frank were watching.

I don't remember when exactly Marco disappeared from my eyesight and Hefner entered my vision. But when it happened, fear trickled into my gut, for the very first time in my life.

Something bad was going to happen, I knew it, but not to me.

Hefner took two steps toward me and curled his fingers around my neck. "Yo, Bitch." His Aryan friends grouped behind him, armed with glowing smirks and not much wisdom to accompany their glee. "If you wanna stay alive, you gotta join your brothers."

I peeled his fingers off and muscled my way away, stoic. "You're not my brothers."

"You're white." A guy behind him with a tattoo on his forehead took a step forward, holding me in place. "That means you're a brother."

"Hispanic," I corrected. "And an only fucking child. Now get the fuck outta my face."

"You don't look Hispanic." Since when did this bunch turn into a movement of genetic experts?

"Leave the boy," Frank said, shuffling to my side. He was half my height and delicate in build. He was old and weak, and they were immoral and cruel.

"Says who? You?" Hefner shoved the old man. Frank collapsed on the dirty ground. Hefner's friends picked him up, clutching his arms tight. I yanked Hefner by the collar and threw him against the fence. "Touch him again and you're dead."

"You let the old man ride you, handsome fuck?" Laughter bubbled out of him. "It's not him I'm after, idiot. It's you."

This made me feel better. I can deal with the Aryan Brotherhood myself. But I didn't want to drag Frank into this mess. I threw a punch straight to Hefner's smug face, knowing that I was about to get beaten up by at least fifteen men, but what happened next surprised me.

They turned to Frank.

The guy with the brow tattoo dragged him by the arm across the yard, his frail body grinding against the sizzling concrete. His friends followed, kicking and punching the old man.

I had showed weakness. It was Frank. So they kicked me where it hurt.

Him.

I launched at them, peeling body after body from him, before two Aryan Brothers held me in place and glued me to the wall as Hefner strangled Frank with his bare hands. He sat on my old neighbor's chest in the middle of the yard and squeezed his throat so hard, the veins on Frank's forehead popped out like purple snakes. I screamed until my throat felt raw, until my lungs bled and my yells became labored breaths, kicking and shoving, trying to break free.

He was killing Frank.

He was killing Frank, and I was standing on the sideline, letting it happen.

He was killing Frank and slaying what was left of my small, meaningless world in the process.

Hefner didn't care. He was a lifer, anyway. What could they do? Sentence his rotting body to another life without parole?

When I finally broke free, Frank looked dead. The guards were roaming the yard, approaching us with murderous faces.

"You need to get in the hole, or they'll kill you," someone whispered in my direction, and I recognized the accent. I turned around, puzzled. "Punch me, boy. Make a mess."

"What?" I spat blood. I didn't even realize I was injured. Godfrey was the most infamous, dangerous inmate aside from the death row crowd. . .and he wanted me to punch him?

"If you punch me, they'll throw you in the hole. Your life will be considered in danger," he explained calmly, even though the guards were seconds from getting to us. "Make it bloody, lad. I'll take care of the Aryan bastards before you get out of ad-seg."

I wasn't thinking. I just did as I was told. I swung my fist and hit him so hard, he rolled back and collapsed to the ground with a thud.

Godfrey was right.

I got thrown into the hole, and by the time I came out, he had cleaned up the mess with the Aryan Brotherhood. I know that I'm out of the woods because they keep their distance from me in the yard. The cafeteria. When I'm at work. They don't talk or approach me. And I know that I've opened a debt that will be collected at some point. My freedom's price is far more expensive than what money can buy.

But I don't care.

He can't ruin what's already tarnished.

MARCH 3RD, 2010

"WHERE GRIEF IS FRESH, ANY ATTEMPT TO DIVERT IT ONLY IRRITATES"
(SAMUEL JOHNSON)

Beth takes me to an isolated corner at lunchtime. You can see us behind the glass door, the way she puts her hands on my shoulders, like it's okay. Like we're friends. She tells me Frank's not dead, and I release the breath I've been holding since they threw me in the hole. He had, however, lost his voice box and Hefner broke his spinal cord and cervical spine. The bastard hit the important nerves. C something and C something. Frank won't be able to talk anymore. Or walk.

He will spend the rest of his life in bed.

Assisted by life support.

Because of me.

She looks like she wants to kiss me, the fabric of her green uniform rubs against my orange clothes, and I turn around and leave before I do something I'll regret.

Like cry.

Or fuck her.

Or cry and fuck her.

The old schoolers don't want me around anymore, and I can't blame them. I'm responsible for what happened to Frank. Godfrey signals for me to come sit with his crowd, but I don't.

One week, two weeks, three months. . .loneliness is a terrible thing. A close cousin to death. Sometimes, you need company, even if it's from the devil.

After a month of courting from Godfrey, I cave in and join them. Irvin, the tattooist, is there too. Seb, who's in his early forties, nudges my shoulder and offers me his peach. I take a juicy bite off it, my eyes still trained on Sergio and the rest of Frank's friends.

The peach doesn't taste good in my mouth. Kinda sour. Kinda rotten. Maybe it's not the peach.

Maybe it's me.

107

MARCH 13TH, 2010

~~I grind through my sentence in~~

APRIL 16TH, 2011

~~Got bored so got a few more tattoos and~~

OCTOBER 3RD, 2012

"ALL THINGS CAN CORRUPT WHEN MINDS ARE PRONE TO EVIL" (OVID)

Godfrey arrives at my cell and gives me a parental hug. Over the last couple of years, that's what he's been to me. A fatherly figure. In my world, that means he's someone who lives under the same roof and who I'd like to kill at some point.

If the yard is a circus, Godfrey's the ringmaster. He orders fights—bloody fights— for his entertainment only.

He manages his business on the outside from the confines of these tall walls like it's his goddamned office.

I'm beginning to see why the DA threw every resource they had at locking him in here for forty years on drug trafficking offenses when he stood trial.

He's a dangerous man. His place is among other dangerous, soulless people.

"Happy birthday, lad," he congratulates. He clasps me, hissing in my ear. "Got a proper gift for you this year. Much better than a book. Wanna off Hefner? I have a nice opening for you to walk through."

I shake my head. I killed a man, but I'm not a murderer. All the same, I understand the underlying order in his invitation. Saying no is not an option.

"I'll just mess with him a little." I won't break his spine, but a few ribs—sure. Why not?

I find Hefner scrubbing pans after dinner. Godfrey's soldiers are behind me, and they signal the kitchen workers to fuck off with a nod.

Everyone leaves Hefner and me alone.

I stalk in his direction, much bigger in size and presence than the useless prick. I've spent my years here working out and bulking up, while he spent his years stirring shit and causing trouble. Hefner wipes his forehead with the back of his arm, wheezing.

"Looky here. There's our pretty boy." He still sounds cheerful, but underneath the make-believe smile lies fear. I can smell it. The acidic sweat, the labored breaths. Un-fucking-canny. I want to bottle it up and smell it every time I think about Frank.

I brush my fingertips against a row of pots and pans hung neatly beside the stovetops as I stride toward him wordlessly, my eyes dead.

"Don't do anything you'll regret." He sniffs, still scrubbing the sink clean. "I got brothers inside and out."

108

My hand that's traveling through the pans stops and yanks out a heavy metal tray.
"You killed Frank."

"He ain't dead," he spits. Swallows. Stops what he's doing.

Scared, scared, scared.

"He's as good as dead," I correct, "and so are you."

I smack him in the face with the tray. He stumbles backward, his back hitting the wall. I shove the tray against his middle, creating a gap between two of his ribs. They snap and break like twigs, the sound sending chills down my back.

Hefner collapses on the floor, tipping over a full bucket of lard.

I kick him in the middle twice, letting him roll over the greasy ground as my Converse sneaker targets his sensitive spots. Spots that bleed easily. Mouth. Nose. The less meaty parts of the legs, ankles and arms. After I'm done assaulting him, when he's red and purple and swollen, I bend down, baring my teeth next to his ear. "Next time, it'll be your dick I snap in two. Just to give you a heads-up. Now, get back to cleaning, little bitch."

Hefner offers a bloodied smile, looking like the Joker. He didn't yell or scream once I'd beaten him up. Never tried to fight back either.

"He set you up," he mumbles through broken teeth, collapsed against a wall, his head rolling from side to side. "God told me to kill Frank. Frank worked for him on the outside. There was a contract on Frank's head before you even arrived in here, you stupid little shit," He throws his head against the wall and laughs manically. "He was always dead meat. Oh, man, you're so fucked."

Crashing the tray against his head, I speed out of the kitchen, leaving Hefner injured, yet very much alive. I skip over the pool of blood under him, anger and fury rattling my chest. Rage detonates in my gut, nausea washing through me.

I'm sick.

I'm seething.

I'm fucked.

The next morning, I find out that Hefner was beaten to death. Not by me, but killed nonetheless.

Lockdown.

Big mess.

And back to ad-seg until further notice.

People don't get offed too often in prison, let alone at one that's as high-security as San Dimas, and especially when there are no traces of a murder weapon in sight. Fortunately, I figured shit like this might happen and ran straight into the arms of correction officer Beth Bouscher after the Hefner incident. I have an airtight alibi, but that doesn't stop people from suspecting.

The death of the Aryan brother sparks a prison riot. Word is I sought retaliation after Frank.

I have a motive. I was seen by the security cameras, walking into the dark corner of the kitchen. Snitches get stitches, so no one's going to say a word even if Hefner's killer was seen doing the deed.

109

Words are weapons, and the ammo on me is being spread by the correction officers who are on Godfrey's payroll. In cells, hallways, canteens and on the outside, where the real life I hold grudges against is awaiting my return. Jabbers with mouths working overtime, and the good-souls of San Dimas are all too happy to let the rumor loose.

A rumor that Godfrey himself put in everyone's mouth.

Godfrey knows that now, I need his help more than ever.

Hefner was a dick, but he was also right. My so-called "fatherly figure" set me up.

And now? All I'm left to do is wait and see what plans God has for me next.

NOVEMBER 8ᵀᴴ, 2014

"THE QUICKEST WAY OF ENDING A WAR IS TO LOSE IT" (GEORGE ORWELL)

My release day is in two weeks. Godfrey's sentence was cut. He's been pardoned, let go with nothing but a slap on the wrist. Will be out in a month. The governor, no less, pulled some strings to make it happen. Godfrey told me Irv's already waiting for me on the outside and that I can crash at his until I figure shit out.

The outside world is bad, but Godfrey is worse. He harvests on oppressing people, a powerhouse of corruption. To tell you that I hate him would be an understatement. He put me in a debt that would chain me to his good graces forever. There's nothing I'd like more than to see him and his right-hand man, Sebastian, losing their lives in an unfortunate accident involving a hazardous waste truck, gasoline, fire and a fucking missile for good measure.

Whatever wicked plans he has, I'm sure my spilled blood will be a part of them. I'm a pawn, a soldier, a slave at his mercy. If I don't comply, he'll unleash the Aryan Brotherhood and let them feast on me alive.

For now, I obey, bow down and submit to living under the same roof as Irvin the tattooist. As I wait for my fate to be sealed, I know one thing for sure—whatever mess I landed myself in, in prison, it's about to get a whole lot messier in the real world.

Nate hasn't come down in three days, and fear's most loyal companion, panic, oozes into me. Getting into Irv's good graces is a task that's as equally impossible as sneezing with eyes wide open. Scientifically, it's bound to fail. He is about as compassionate as a brick wall and holds the exact same amount of brain cells.

Godfrey was right. Time is precious. Yet, I spend my days doing nothing. I've already read *Dreams from Bunker Hill* a thousand times. My stress ball is all torn, most of it scattered on the floor like sad snowflakes. I have no fingernails left, they've all snapped out of my skin during my attempts to try and peel off the wood on the boarded windows.

My future depends on Nate's goodwill, and even if under the rough interior and cheap ink hides a compassionate soul, he is a man first. A man who proved to be just like the others. He took, then he left.

If Nate won't come to his senses, I will lose mine. What will happen then? I'll attack Irvin with my bare hands and try to make a run for it.

I could get killed.

But at least it won't be *them* who kill me.

"Come on, Nate. Come back to me," I murmur as I hug my knees to my chest.

No, he is not like those men who took. Because he also gives.

Nate gave me the one thing I almost forgot how to feel.

He gave me hope.

NATE

Turn around and walk away.

That's what I've been telling myself for the past ten minutes. I'm standing in the middle of Draeger's, a preppy, uppity, expensive-as-fuck supermarket in Blackhawk Plaza. I've been here twice before. Mrs. Hathaway sent me to buy her groceries while she was hiding at home after a neck-lifting surgery, and both times, I wanted to crawl out of my body and run for my life, leaving a crust of epidermis on the floor, like a snake who molted its own skin.

I stand out here like a good idea in congress.

I'm surprised I haven't been arrested merely for walking in here yet.

Towering at least ten inches above everyone else, my full sleeve of black, morbid ink sticks out of my black tank top just as much as my unconventional haircut and muddy leather boots. Everybody around me is wearing pastel cardigans and sharp suits. There's even an elderly man with suspenders and a bowtie.

But I don't need to make friends with these assholes. I just need to use the ATM here, withdraw some money, go back home, give Prescott a ride and take off.

No. I can withdraw money somewhere else. Doesn't have to be here, where I'm looked at like a circus freak.

I turn around and walk toward the automatic doors, my legs trying to buckle under the strain of working under the sun all day in Mrs. H's garden.

My foot already touching the sidewalk, I hear the old man with the suspenders behind me, saying, "Why, look who it is! Howard Burlington-Smyth. Haven't seen you here in a while."

I spin back on instinct. I see the asshole approaching Bowtie gingerly, a small green basket tucked under his arm, looking sheepishly in all directions.

Hate. It froths within me, consuming every cell in my body. I hate him so much, it takes me long seconds to register what he looks like through the mist of disgust.

Howard Burlington-Smyth looks nothing like his daughter. She has blonde hair, pouty lips and a curvy body that was designed to be played with. Her father, on the other hand, is tall, fat and has dark brown hair, speckled with patches of silver.

I look down to his basket and see a simple loaf of bread, butter and some canned food. Then I remember what Mrs. Hathaway told me about him. *Broke.* Pea's family is considered virtually penniless in these parts.

"How've you been?" Bowtie asks my captive's father. But Howard continues wiping his sweaty forehead, looking left and right. His shapeless figure is clad in a cheap suite. He looks like a waiter at Olive Garden who just pissed into someone's dish and is afraid to get caught. What the fuck is he so scared about? Maybe he senses the presence of someone who'd gladly nail his head to one of the decorative spikes in his iron gate.

"It's going great." Howard clears his throat. "My wife and I are looking into buying somewhere in the Hamptons. Get away from all the hustle and bustle around here."

Liar. Prescott's mom's gone.

"Is that right? But aren't your kids living around here?"

I watch Howard, maybe too intently. He waves his hand, his face plastered with an insincere grin.

"Preston is studying in Boston. . ."

Preston is fucking missing.

"And Prescott. . .well, God knows where that wild-child is these days. She never picks up the phone, you know. Kids."

This much is true. God *does* know where she is. But in about an hour and a half, he'll have no fucking clue.

A shot of fury runs from my throat down my arm, making my fist choke the wallet in my hand.

"She has always been a bit of a free spirit. Shame about her," Bowtie tsks. *Fuck you, old man.*

"It is indeed, but we did what we could." Yeah, like setting her up.

Loser dads are a touchy subject for me.

I killed mine for less than disowning me—oh, mine owned me, all right. So much so that he beat me up every time I said the wrong word or acted the wrong way.

I march straight to Burlington-Smyth and the man's eyes widen in terror with every step I take. I love the way his face drains of blood as my shoulder brushes against his, and I feel his body tensing against mine. I continue moving slowly without looking back. This was a threat. I wanted him to shut up, and he did.

Nobody cares about Prescott Burlington-Smyth.

But that's about to change.

The minute I get back home, I jump out of the car and head to the basement without even taking a shower, pulling on the Guy Fawkes mask Irv retrieved from the basement and adjusting it on my face as I descend the stairs.

I've never had a girlfriend. Before prison, I had sex. Booty calls. One-night stands in cars and bathroom stalls and national fucking parks on crisp nights. But I don't know how to grovel. Never needed to before, and the only reason I need to now is because I want to switch teams.

I'm a switcher, after all.

I find Pea trying to tear the wood on the windows down, her movements listless and desperate at the same time. Blood runs down her arms, no doubt from her busted, nail-less fingers. Her head turns around at the sound of the squeaky door and that's when I notice her eyes are nothing but swollen slits. Doubt she can see through them at all.

"Stop it, Country Club. You'll never succeed."

She physically winces at my words.

This girl's walking out of here alive and well, out of an open door. She'll give me money to run away, and I'll give her a life to run back to.

Pea looks at me like I've just murdered her whole family, biting her lips to contain whatever it is she really wants to say to me.

"Why are you here?"

"Because it's probably where I belong."

"Is it?" Her voice is hoarse.

"You're crazy, uncalculated and lethal for me." I take a step in her direction. "So yeah. Being by your side is exactly where I should be."

Checkmate, Godfrey. Your clock starts ticking now.

It should alarm me that I'm more excited about the prospect of killing Godfrey and Seb than I am with getting my own life back. But the truth is, life has become such a chore to maintain over the last few years, it'll take me a long time to find my lust for it again.

He is standing in front of me, wearing his mask and to my dismay, my toes curl against the damp floor.

Even through the mask, his chin is strong and high. There's something incredibly proud about this broken man. Nate's fingers brush the wall as he paces like a predator in my direction.

"I fucked up. You confided in me, told me what they did to you, then I went and did the very same thing on the grounds of being drunk, horny and a prick," he admits, his tone calm. "But I want you to know one thing. I'm a killer, I'm a murderer, *I am* a prick, but I'm *fair*. The minute you told me your story, you were already free. These walls," he knocks on the concrete, "they mean nothing. Up until this afternoon, I thought I was going to let you walk away then go do my own thing. But then something dawned on me," he says and inches closer causing my jaw to go slack in anticipation. "I'm *not* fucking done with you, Pea, and if it's up to me? I'm not done fucking *you*, either."

I hug my body, trying to protect myself from something that's already embedded deep inside me, to shake away the looming calamity that's moving my way. He rattles something within me that's not ready to be moved. Not right now, and certainly not by him. "Nate." His name on my lips sounds like a warning. On some level, it is. He stops, his mask still offering this wild, up-to-no-good smile. "I don't want us to part ways yet. I want us to flip hourglasses. To stir up chaos. To start a blood bath."

He stops next to me. His hand drops to his hip and he lifts the hem of his shirt, rubbing his six pack.

"Prescott?"

"Yes?"

"I'm switching teams."

My knees turn to jelly as my body starts quivering with released tension.

He is switching teams.

He is setting me free.

God, he's going to help me glue the pieces of my broken soul together.

All the tears I kept from him come spilling down, my face damp and happy and my heart so, extremely full. I'm a crier. I cry when I get a paper-cut, when it's that time of the month and when Bambi's mother dies. The only reason I haven't cried in front of Nate yet is because I don't let my enemies see me break.

But he is not an enemy. Not anymore.

"You won't regret it," I say, shaking my head, trying to gain control over my emotions. He needs to see me strong. "Together, we'll overthrow his empire."

Nate doesn't answer, but his eyes are hungry behind the mask. It dawns on me that I'm about to see his face, and something unsettling stirs in me. It's not that I don't want to see him. I do. I'm dying to lay my eyes on the man I had sex with, who's about to give me life back, who's been the center of my world for the past few weeks.

But I'm not ready.

He's become a fantasy; a bubble I don't want to pop. A feather of hope that's tickling but not quite touching me the way I crave. The minute he takes off the mask, the mystery is solved, and reality will kick in. A reality I'm not entirely prepared for, despite the fact I pushed for it for so long.

A reality that consists of people getting killed, of us running away, of trying to get by, of peeking over our shoulders, every second of every day.

Life starts here.

He erases the space between us with a long step, his abs bumping into my chest. My breath hitches and my spine tingles. This is bad. No, bad is forgetting to turn off the oven when you leave the house. This is disastrous.

"Where will you go after this is all over, Pea?" His mask touches my lips.

"Iowa," I answer. "I want to go somewhere peaceful."

"Cabo for me," he replies, his thumb stabing his chest. "I wanna go somewhere wild."

"Send me a postcard." I muster a weak grin, but it feels wrong on my lips.

We don't actually know if we'll get out of this alive, and even if we do, I'll dump him and move on with my life as soon as we kill the bastards.

We're polar opposites. He's peace looking for color, and I'm a storm looking for serenity. And somewhere between my chaos and his peace, we found each other. Even crazier—we want to save one another.

"Pea." He rubs my chin with his thumb, staring at my lips with burning eyes. "I'll fight your war while I'm winning mine, but you have to be honest with me. When I took you like an animal the night of the party. . .did it remind you of them?" "It was different," I answer. "Intense, yes. Wild. But it reminded me that I could still enjoy how another body feels against mine. I didn't think I could anymore."

His jaw tenses and he looks down at his palms as he speaks.

"I'd like to be the person who reminds you of that again," he says, his usually cutting tone sounds softer now. Maybe it's just what I want to hear. "I'll be whatever you want me to be. Wild, gentle, good, bad, rough, delicate. Your pick."

I swallow and look down to his chest, blinking away my embarrassment. "I'd like that too."

"Would you like that now by any chance?" he growls, his forehead dropping onto mine. "Ink's out of town. Some family shit. I need inside you."

You're already inside me, I think. *You crawled in the minute you showed me mercy, the minute you decided to switch teams.* But I know what he wants. He wants what all men want.

He wants sex. My flesh, my warmth and what's between my thighs. Because after all, before he became a killer, a captor, an avid reader and even my savior, he was the one thing I hate—a man.

The only difference between Nate and the others is. . .well, I want his body, too.

"Are you going to take off your mask?" I ask, staring at his army boots.

"Do you want me to?"

"Yes."

No.

My eyes are still trained on his feet as his mask floats to the floor, landing next to his shoes. This is it. The mystery man who has been occupying my thoughts all this time is standing in front of me, exposed and open, offering me everything I've ever asked him for.

I drag my eyes up, lingering on his groin, his hips, moving on to his flat stomach, memorizing his triangular upper-body, tan, inked throat, and once I get to his face. . .

I lose it. Completely lose it.

Cruelly beautiful, that's what he is. A beauty so violent it demands to be appreciated despite my best efforts to ignore it. I can actually *hear* his face, and it's loud. Screaming at me to drown in his perfect features.

Every bone in my body melts and my skin spikes with the need to touch him.

His cheekbones are high, prominent like blades, and sharpen his face into something that's ruthlessly male. Which is good, because everything inside this frame is sickly pretty. Roman strong nose, bee-stung lips with a cupid's bow, upturned, hooded eyes of a predator. Hard, dark, expressive, *perfect.*

I look away before it burns, like staring directly into the sun. I shift my gaze, feeling something funny crawling from my neck up to my face. Something I haven't felt in a long time, maybe even ever.

Something I promised myself I'd never feel.

I'm about to get out of here and instead of being filled with joy and ecstasy, I refuse to look directly into my new partner in crime's face.

I open my mouth, not sure what might come out of it, but before I get the chance to say anything, he braces a hand on the wall above my head. His eyes fall to my lips, then return to my eyes.

"Let me do filthy things to you, Prescott." His husky tone breathes fire into my body. "Let me dirty you up with who I am."

I close my eyes. I can do it. I can master my emotions. I've done it so many times before. Years of not letting anyone in made me resilient to whatever men throw at me.

But how do you let someone inside you without letting him into you?

My eyes travel to his, and I dare look at him again. So perfect. So, disgustingly, unwarrantedly perfect.

"You think you can rub your filth on me?" A lopsided grin pulls from the right side of my mouth. "I'd like to see you try."

That's all the invitation he needs. He picks me up, fireman style in one arm, and rushes up the stairs, tackling two at a time.

My nails are already digging into the flesh of his lower back, squeezing out the scent of his manhood and sweat—sweet and sour and animalistic.

"We'll fuck, then we run away?" I pant.

"We're not *running*. Running is for pussies. We do this shit in a stride."

He marches the short distance from the narrow corridor to his small room, which I've never seen before, and bangs the door shut, me still on his shoulder. Before I know what's happening, he throws me onto his bed like a ragdoll and looks down at me, still standing.

He's huge.

Tall.

Tatted.

And completely stunning. This is not the first time I've gotten into bed willingly with a man since I ran away from the Archers, but it's the first time I'm scared about how I'm going to leave it once it's over.

Before Nate, I had sex to prove to myself that I could still feel.

But with him? I'm going to have sex and convince myself that I don't.

"You're beautiful," I say breathlessly.

"You're *safe*," he answers reassuringly. Exactly what I needed to hear.

"Make peace to me, Beat." I call him by his nickname purposely, my smile sly and cunning.

"Make fucking storm to me, Pea," he says, doing the same.

He dives onto the bed on top of me, grinding his huge, scary hardness against my body. My legs spread on cue. Know that old cliché you read in romance books, *Our bodies were made for one another?* Well, that's not the case with Nate and me. My body was made for an average-sized man, while his would be more fitting for a 6'2" Viking girl, or a full-grown elephant. He's so much bigger than me, but it works. For us, it's perfect.

His puffy, swollen lips find mine. Warm, fierce and comforting. I should probably close my eyes like he does, but I can't, still crippled by his good looks. I watch him wide-eyed as our kiss deepens and his tongue attacks mine, his body grinding against my own. I gaze at him, mesmerized, as I feel his needy erection poking between my thighs, barely contained by his jeans and boxers. The bastard doesn't have any bad angles. At all. He must've spent all his years in jail walking with his back pressed against the wall.

His fingers spread my thighs open roughly, and my dress rides up past my chest. His mouth sucks on my right nipple long and hard, teasing it with lazy circles he creates with the tip of his tongue. Then he pulls my panties down with one tug and slides his index finger inside me. Nate is so huge, his finger is probably the size of a typical cock. Simple math: Two fingers = Two cocks.

His finger pulls out of my folds and drags my wetness along with it. We both watch in awe, eyes half-closed under the mist of lust.

I never get wet anymore. Only for him, I do.

He uses my wetness and rubs the same finger around my clit, my head falls to his cheap, flat pillow.

"No hourglass in here, Pea. With me, we take our time."

"Yes," I groan.

"Yes," he repeats with conviction as he starts rubbing my clit up and down, his tongue striking mine like it's trying to punish me. "Fuck." Kiss. "You." Bite. "Godfrey."

I smile into his mouth and reach for his cock, the sound of his zipper rolling down is the only thing audible other than our moans in the murky room. "Fuck." I grab his junk in my hand. "You." I move my palm up, rubbing the tip, then slide the pre-cum along his shaft. "Camden."

"Fuck them," he concludes, reaching back and yanking his shirt up over his head and throwing it to the floor. His tongue finds my neck, swirling downwards in swift movements.

"Fuck them," I agree, letting him slide my dress up as he undresses me, toss it on the floor next to his jeans, and watch his head travel south.

He French kisses my inner-thighs, his warm tongue dancing in passionate circles around my hypersensitive flesh, only hovering over my folds, but never touching. Circling, applying pressure, then biting softly. He's giving every valley and curve in the area special attention, and I begin to spasm, rocking myself against his face, completely possessed. Nate's tongue hasn't even touched my sex yet, it's still licking my thighs, biting my flesh. . .but I'm already well on my way to a furious orgasm. I'm quaking all over, thrusting myself into his face, begging him to put me out of my misery. When he does, when his beautiful, hot mouth closes on my clit, his rough palms nail me to his bed and he doesn't let me move.

"Fuck Sebastian." He pulls my clit between his perfectly straight teeth and I actually throw my fists on his shoulders because the orgasm is too much. I'm losing control over my body, my muscles, my skin, even my bones. My hips move erratically to the rhythm of his mouth. Every time he speaks, his charged breath tickles me from the inside, making every inch of me tingle with pleasure. "And fuck the Aryan Brotherhood and fuck San Dimas and fuck this world. We're getting outta here."

I explode in pleasure and jerk back and forth on a scream. He finds out just how hard I come by pushing his tongue deep into my channel, meeting the warmth trickling out of me in a wave of satisfaction. He swirls his tongue inside me, licking up every drop of my want for him.

Just when I think I can't take it anymore, he starts fucking me with his tongue, completely disregarding my current physical state as a human pond of hormones.

I'm a goner. I'm on fire. I'm done. No, wait. I want more. So much more.

"Hand me my wallet," he says, signaling in the general direction of his jeans next to the bed. I lean down, fumbling with the back pockets, until I find it. I hand it to him and he flicks it open with one hand and pulls out a condom.

"How many condoms do you have in your wallet at any given moment?" Jealousy leaks into my tone.

"One. Which I never use." He leans down for a demanding kiss, pulling up on his knees above my opened legs and sliding the condom over his cock. I forgot to ask him if they even make them for his size. What is he? XXL?

"Women bore me," he croaks.

"I'm pretty sure that I'm a woman," I reply.

"You're not a woman." He guides his cock to my entrance, sinking his teeth into his lower lip. "You're a storm."

He thrusts into me and I arch my back in pleasure. It's not as painful as it was the first time, probably because I knew what to expect this time. He's riding me like the devil's inside him. I'm holding on to him like he is a hurricane I have to survive, and the bed creaks so loud, I'm afraid its frame is going to break. When he comes, sprawled out on top of me, our foreheads sticking together, both dripping wet in the tiny, windowless room, I actually let out a laugh, my lips searching for his again.

"Can I ask you for a favor?" I murmur.

"Ask away."

"When I finally get my hands on Camden, I want you to fuck me in front of him with his eyes propped open by toothpicks, like in *Clockwork Orange*. It'd drive him crazy. Think you can do that for me?"

He chuckles, a laugh that fizzes out from the pit of his stomach and makes his abs shake against my stomach.

"It's on."

We fuck.

On his bed.

On his floor.

Against every surface in this grimy, horrid house.

In the tiny bathroom where we stole so many small, hauntingly painful and blissful moments.

Against the tiles.

Under the rusty showerhead.

My sex is burning with the relentless friction and my insides feel numb. The majority of my muscles—abs, quads, even glutes—shake under the strain of working his body so hard. But we keep at it.

On the kitchen counter, the shelves behind us shaking, their contents spilling onto the floor.

We're an earthquake, and we destroy everything we bump into.

The last time we do it, we're back in his bed. My whole body throbbing and my muscles shaking like I spent the last couple of years working the fields under the sun. But Nate? He has all of his early twenties to make up for, sex-wise. It takes him exactly twenty minutes to get back up again and the minute Nate Junior is ready, so am I.

Because injured or not—it is still Nate Vela.

I'm not supposed to know his last name. . .but I wonder if he trusts me just a little now?

"What's your last name?" I pant above him. I'm riding him reverse cowgirl-style, his hands on my hips, bouncing me up and down. Reverse, because I can't chance him having access to my throbbing nipples anymore. He just spent twenty minutes sucking and biting on them until they turned from pink to red, the flesh around them bruised and cracked. At one point, he dragged them so slowly and painfully through his teeth, they pulled like an elastic rubber for about five seconds too long before he let them free.

He halts only for a second before grunting, "No offense, Baby-Cakes, but I don't trust you with a fucking plastic spoon. No way in hell am I telling you my last name."

"No," I pant. "No." My voice matches the rhythm he thrusts into me with. "If we're going to do this, we need to trust each other."

A reluctant grumble leaves his mouth.

"Vela. Nate Vela."

"I'm Prescott Burlington-Smyth." I snake my palm behind me for a handshake and peek at him. He cocks one thick eyebrow, shaking my hand while still using the other one to hold my waist and drive my body onto his cock.

"Nice to fuck you, Nate Vela."

"My pleasure."

He is just about to show me exactly how much pleasure he is in—I can feel him expanding inside me—when we hear the front door open, then bang shut.

Irvin.

He was supposed to be on a family visit for the next two days. What happened?

I stop moving on top of Nate and swivel my head. Our eyes lock. Wordlessly, Nate jerks his hips forward in one go and squeezes my waist, his fingers digging into my flesh, and comes inside me. He opens his mouth in a mute moan, rolls me over so that my back hits the wall by his bed and stands, pulling on his briefs and black, ripped jeans. I lie on his bed, watching his every move. For all I know, he could throw me back into the basement any minute now. Just because we fucked for the past three hours doesn't mean he really is on my team.

But this time, I'm not going into the basement, even if it means shedding blood. No matter whose.

We hear his roommate moving around the house. His Crocs squeaking in the hallway while he mumbles to himself. He's taking a leak with the bathroom door open, then moves to the kitchen, raiding the fridge.

"What are we going to do?" I mouth, my head propped on my hand. Nate throws me a calm look.

"Stay here. Don't move."

Don't count on it, buddy.

I watch his shirtless figure walking out of the room, shutting the door behind him. As soon as he does, I jump out of the bed and yank open the drawer to his bedside table.

Perfect. Thank you, Nate. Lying there and waiting for me to embrace it is an old-school dagger. I slip into my underwear, pick up the weapon and slide it into my waistband. I pull my dress on to hide my new best friend. After I'm done, I press my ear to the door. I hear their muffled voices and my heart picks up speed.

Please don't betray me like everyone else.

I hear furniture creaking and the sound of Irvin getting pissed off.

"You want me to take care of the bitch? That ain't fair! I wasn't even supposed to be here. Not my fault my fucking mom came down with the flu."

My pulse thickens against my throat. *Take care of me? What?*

"Do it," Nate prompts.

"No." I hear Irvin's voice approaching Nate's room, the thuds of two sets of feet on the carpet. Shit. They're both going to come for me. I can maybe take one of them, though even that's farfetched, but both? With just the dagger? That'd be damn near impossible.

I stumble back until my knees hit the edge of Nate's bed.

"You better do it," I hear Nate's baritone. This is a nightmare. I let the guy into me—*again*—and now he's going to have his roommate throw me into the basement?

I pull out the dagger and wait in a southpaw stance in front of the door. I hear their footfalls going back and forth, some more shuffling, and after a while—who knows how much time's passed—the door swings open, and I run straight to the body in front of me and stab the dagger into his flesh.

Nate.

"Fuck!" he growls, stumbling away, his back hitting the wall. I rush out, about to stab him a few more times as he nurses his bleeding bicep by squeezing the wound. "What the hell are you doing?"

"I heard you." I point the bloody dagger at his face, seething. "You sent Irvin to deal with me."

"I sent him to the fucking *basement* so I can lock him in there. What in the actual fuck? You talk about trust, but you give me none."

"Of course I don't trust you," I shriek, hysteria closing in on my throat. Which part of our encounter together so far would have made me trust him? The part where he took me in as a hostage, or the part where he fucked me and then disappeared for a few days until showing back up to the gates of my own, personal hell? It's been a long time since I trusted a man, and just because he said he switched teams, doesn't mean that I fully believe him.

"Well, that'll have to change." He makes a tsking sound, looking down to his right bicep and slowly peeling his hand away to assess the damage. I managed to cut deep. Well, at least I have that going for me in case I find myself engaged in a knife fight.

Only now I feel bad about doing this to him. Not overly bad, he deserves some kind of punishment for my captivity. But it was probably not the best idea to injure the guy who is about to help me run away and take down three of the most dangerous men I've ever come across.

"Fine. I'm willing to admit that there may have been a bit of an overreaction on my end." I fold my arms around my midsection.

"Ya' think? Wow, it takes a big woman to admit that." He bites every word, pushing his healthy hand through his hair.

"Hey, Pea, are you going to stand in the hallway with the knife pointing at me for much longer or are you ready to hit the fucking road?" he nearly barks. "Go get the first aid kit. It's in Irv's room." Nate nods his chin to the door right in front of his. "On his desk."

I quickly grab the kit and sit my sexy partner-in-crime on the kitchen counter while I take care of his wound, bandaging it up tight. The orange of the iodine leaks around the white fabric and his arm looks like crap, but I think he's stopped bleeding. I'm standing between his thighs as I tend to his wound, grateful for every second that I touch him but knowing that this is exactly why I should get rid of him as soon as possible.

"Are we all set? Should we run over our plan one more time?" I ask quietly as I roll another clean white cloth over his muscular arm. I can hear Irvin banging on the basement door, screaming and shouting and swearing like a madman.

"We pack our shit, get the money and fake IDs and disappear to different places and time zones." He shrugs, his husky voice tickling my hairline. "Simple plan."

"We need to kill them first." I'm hoarse, yet determined. "They'll follow us anywhere, down to the pits of hell."

His eyes meet mine, and for a brief moment, I want us to be something else. Something normal. A boy and a girl who live in neighboring cities and met somewhere neutral, somewhere safe, a club or a park or a flipping Starbucks. Our options are unlimited. I'm not broken by previous, awful men. He's not broken by a previous, awful life. It's just us, and the scent of opportunity, of first dates and picnics and rolling on lush summer grass, laughing into each other's mouths.

For one brief moment, I imagine that he walked into my world without tearing it apart, bloodily and messily, and that I stormed into his without making him face the dilemma of his life.

I shake my head when I realize where I let my mind drift off to.

"It's either us or them." My pulse quickens with urgency.

"You know, Prescott, if you wanna mend your soul, killing people is not the way to do it."

"Of course it is." I kiss his wrapped arm without breaking eye contact. "Because each of these men still hold a part of my soul. I need to take it back, don't I?"

A hint of a smirk finds Nate's face, but it disappears just as quickly as it came.

Our heads snap in unison at the deafening sound of shattered wood, and it takes us less than a second to realize that Irvin has managed to kick the door down. Nate shoots up from the table, sidestepping and shielding me behind his back, charging out of the small kitchen and toward the hallway. The gesture doesn't escape me, but I don't allow myself dwell on it.

You're safe, he said before we had sex tonight. Maybe I am.

I follow his steps as he stalks to the hallway, where Irvin already scrambled for his cell phone, which Nate must have tossed across the room before he threw him in the basement. He's clutching the phone and the discarded Guy Fawkes mask Nate had left on the floor, a dirty Crocs footprint flattened the plastic and disfigured the smiling face. This is the first time I've see Irvin without his ski mask, and he's got the face of an albino eel.

"I'm calling Godfrey." He averts his eyes from my face and back to Nate's, his jaw quivering wildly. I've never seen someone so manic in my life. "You guys are done, you hear me? Fucking done!"

Forget the packing. We have to run away now.

"Nate," I say, touching the massive back that shields me from his roommate. "It's time."

Nate is still staring at Irv and I wish he'd stop. We haven't got time to dwell on betrayal.

I slide into my boots, yank the keys from the fruit bowl and grab Nate by the hand.

"Come on. He's deadweight. Godfrey will never keep him alive after our escape," I bite, happy to see Irv's face behind Nate's shoulder twisting in surprised horror. It's the truth, and he knows that.

Nate grabs his mask from Irv's hand and we storm out. He shuts the driver's door to his Tacoma and punches the wheel three times, honking loudly in the process. I watch him wordlessly, knowing that it's not only Irvin he is mad at, but also himself. He's running away from his only chance at normalcy. From a parole officer. From the real world, and from his real identity. He can never undo what he's doing right now. Me? I haven't been a part of the real world in such a long time, I barely miss it anymore. It doesn't miss me, either. Case in point: I was locked in a basement for two weeks, and other than a few crackheads who are probably wondering why I haven't shown up with their supply, nobody gave a damn.

Other than him.

"Do you want me to drive?" I try not to sound too panicked.

His face is buried between his arms against the steering wheel, and I see him shaking his head.

"Where to?"

127

"West. We need to stop by my place, get a credit card, go to the ATM and drive to Concord to get a new ride. Your license plate will be easy to detect."

He starts the car and throws it into drive, heading for the Stop sign at the end of the street and passing through it unblinking, speeding forward as the highway and darkness swallows the truck. I buckle up, treating myself to a glance at his profile. Magnificent in his beauty and peaceful in expression. Whatever got into him—he overrode it.

He is a switcher, I think. *I bet that's exactly how he looked when he killed his father all those years ago.*

"You sure heading home is a good idea? One of Godfrey's wise guys might be waiting with a fucking Magnum for us." He leans down, opens the glove compartment and retrieves a pack of gum. He throws a peachy-flavored one into his mouth and chews, offering me the pack with a silent gesture. I put it back in its place without taking one.

"He has no clue where I live. Trust me, if he did, he wouldn't have targeted me in the middle of Oakland. He would have done it quietly and professionally, plucking me out of my apartment in the middle of the night. My lease is under someone else's name. I paid her well for it. I don't leave footprints."

Nate gives a sharp nod.

"Fake Passports Guy needs to know that we're on our way," he reminds me.

"I'll call him when I get to the apartment. I saved his contact on each and every one of my SIM cards. He owes me big time." I sit back, trying to let some of the tension roll off my shoulders. I'm out in the open. On a highway. With a beautiful, larger than life man who wants to stick around until we're both out of the woods. Silk black sky above me, golden sandy hills engulfing the road, I suck a deep breath.

Freedom.

I keep throwing glances over my shoulder, making sure no one is after us. The road is empty. The only witnesses to our deed are the stars, glaring at us like pairs of shimmering eyes, waiting to see how we'll get out of this mess. Otherwise, it's just me and him. I like it. What's scarier is that I could actually get used to this, to being around him.

"Should've done it when I first got out," Nate ponders aloud, sinking his teeth into his lip like I so desperately want to do right now. We've spent the last few hours touching and licking and sucking and biting every single piece of flesh on each other's bodies, and it's still not enough.

"Everything happened for a reason. You'll help me finish the Archers and Seb, and I'll give you money and everything else you need to start fresh. This life has nothing to offer you. You need to start fresh. Under a new name. Under the pretense of someone innocent. You *are* innocent,"

I stretch. "Go to Mexico. Live the life. Get a house by the beach. Start every morning with a margarita. Get a nice tan."

He offers me one of his gorgeous smirks, looking at me briefly before turning his attention back to the dusky road.

"I'm going to live somewhere the sun's always shining," he announces in a voice that's almost child-like. This is new. And so flipping adorable. "Just like Cali, but less fucking expensive."

"You deserve it," I reassure, squeezing his hand that's resting on the console.

"Hey, Prescott?" he says, after a minute. "Tell me something beautiful." He squeezes my hand back. "I like your words. You got some solid brain between those slightly big ears."

I chuckle. My ears *are* a little bigger than the rest of my head. That's why my hair is so long.

"'You wanna fly? You got to give up the shit that weighs you down.' Toni Morrison, *Song of Solomon*."

"Good stuff, Pea."

"I try."

"No, you don't. That's what I fucking like about you."

I like him too. Not just because he gave me freedom. But because he treats my body more roughly than any of the men who raped me did, yet makes me feel incredibly cherished.

We get to my apartment when it's still pitch black. It's weird to be here, in a neighborhood I never thought I'd see again. It looks so normal and oblivious to everything I've been through over the past couple of weeks. Nate grabs my hand and rests my knuckles against his lips, willing me to look back at him. I do, and his honey-yellow-greenish-freakish eyes tell me that we're on the same page.

About everything.

"This is going to be one hell of a ride."

"That's okay, we'll get a faster car." I smile, then proceed to explain myself. "I can't let them get away with what they did to me. For me, it's personal. I'll go down with them if I have to. If it ever comes to it, if I need to go with them, kill me if it means they're dead too. Promise me, Nate."

He shakes his head, but doesn't answer.

"Move your hot ass, Baby-Cakes. We've got some baddies chasing after us."

NATE

Don't judge a book by its cover. Remember *The Catcher in The Rye* cover? Ugly as the darkest sin committed on earth, but once you jump inside, something beautiful and raw awaits.

Prescott.

On the outside, she's a generic, attractive shell. Busty and blonde, not unlike that chick from *Legally Blonde*. Flippant and wrapped up in an expensive dress. Then you dig deep, and you discover a scarred, scared, bold, frightened warrior. A survivor who will not let her enemies get away with what they did to her. A caring sister, a loving woman who's been betrayed. Angry but still cute, like a fucking Pink song. She's so much. *She's too much.* But I understand why she wants them dead.

Godfrey.

Sebastian.

Camden.

I'd happily assist with the first two, because I have beef with them that runs just as deep. Camden, on the other hand, is not my problem. I'll help however I can, but that one's on her.

I follow Prescott up the stairs to her apartment, watching her calves swelling as she climbs. We didn't take the elevator to make sure the stairway is clear. She reaches a black wooden door, one of a few in the clean, casually lit hallway, and takes out my dagger from the waist of her underwear. She fucking kept the dagger she stabbed me with. And she's about to use it to break into her own apartment. I watch in awe and ignore my twitching dick. This girl has managed to get me hard the way no one else could for a reason.

Prescott is a storm, and she's sweeping up my ass faster than a tornado, ripping apart shit in her wake without even giving me the opportunity to take a step back and examine the mess she leaves behind.

I'm not going to give a name to what I feel toward her, but there's one narrative that's always hanging above my head like a guillotine when she's around.

Crashing.

Not falling. Falling takes time. I'm thrown into whatever this is, crashing fast, hitting every goddamn branch of the Feelings Tree on my way down before hitting rock bottom with a chilling sound. Landing so hard, I leave a fucking dent in the shape of my heart.

She pops the door by crushing the dagger against the handle at a perfect angle, pushing it open and signaling me with a head tilt to follow her.

Shorty got moves.

Pea ambles into her bedroom and opens her drawers as I take in her apartment. It's a simple one bedroom, beige carpets, black couch, flat screen TV, zero pictures, zero furniture, zero personality. She didn't get comfortable here—she got by. Pea zips open a backpack on her naked mattress and throws a thick batch of credit cards tied together with a rubber band into it. Then she proceeds to throw in some underwear, a bra, approximately five hundred stress balls, cash she'd apparently been hiding under her bed and a fossil tin covered with pictures of Paris and London.

"What's in the box?" I enquire behind her back, feeling like a tool. I'm just standing here doing nothing, helpful as a fucking doormat.

"Heroine, crack, rat poison," she answers flatly, still packing. "We might need to get creative when we strike them. It's nice to have a few tricks up our sleeves. I'm going into the shower." Her drawer snaps shut with a bang. I want to come with her. Hell, I want to come *in* her. But rationally, I know that in order for her to trust me, I need to keep my dick in my pants until she's ready for more. She's been sexually abused, and I'm not going to pretend like it never happened. We're chasing down the motherfuckers who did this to her and won't rest until our fingers are smeared with their blood. Besides, this journey is not about pussy. It's about wonderful, twisted, dark paths, all of them leading to one destination: *Freedom.*

On a more practical note, somebody needs to watch out in case Godfrey and his lap dogs show up downstairs with enough ammo to wipe out North America.

"Make it count. I'll watch." I finger a slit in her black Venetian blinds and peek through it.

She hesitates for a moment before touching her cheek, like she's just been offered a compliment. Which makes me feel like even more of a douchebag. She's touched because I don't force myself into both her bathroom and her pussy.

"Thanks. I'll be right back."

Prescott likes me, but she still doesn't trust me. She locks her bathroom door twice and I know my dagger is still tucked inside her delicious underwear. She asked me for my full name but probably lied to me about having a kid when I asked her about it. I need to remember that she's keeping some secrets from me. She's not to be trusted, in any way or form.

When Pea comes out, looking fresh and prettier than I've ever seen her before, the scent of heaven drifting from her body, she joins me near the window. I haven't left it since we walked in. I'm staring down her sleepy Danville street, counting cars, joggers and dogs on fancy leashes. This place, it doesn't suit her. She was born for something less restrained. More. . .*chaotic.*

She puts on a blood red dress, which looks like a huge shirt but somehow hugs her body like it's a fucking condom, and a tailored leather jacket.

"Are we good to go?" I ask. She nods and throws her backpack over her shoulder. "Yeah, I texted Hussein. He's waiting for us."

I nod to the door.

"Let's wrap this shit up."

"Don't you want to have a quick shower first?" She's still rooted in place. I walk straight for the door and mumble a definite "No" before I stop dead in my tracks.

"Why, do I need one?"

"Well," she says with a shrug. "You reek of sex."

"And that's a bad thing?" I test, cocking a brow.

"It's a distracting thing." There's a private grin on her lips. I haven't seen it before and immediately decide that it belongs to me. Glancing at the door and back to her, I'm trying to figure out if she's buying time before getting down to the dirty stuff. To say I ain't happy about leaving her to watch for Godfrey and Seb on her own is an understatement, but if I smell like a stale fart, I wanna get it out of the way. Especially seeing as I'm waiting for her to make the next move, and it'd be in my favor if I didn't smell like a five-day-old rotten fish.

"Watch the street and holler at me if something's wrong. I'll be quick."

"You always are." She wiggles her brows, resting one shoulder against the wall by her window.

"Fuck you." I smack her ass hard enough for it to be considered a warning before I disappear through her bathroom door, throwing my clothes off on my way to my point of destination.

"Been there, done that," she shouts from the living room. "Five times tonight, actually."

My cock twitches, but I keep my cool. I can mess around, smack her here and there. She loves that shit, but full-blown sex? That's for her to decide the ifs and whens.

I shower with her fancy coconut-vanilla products, and by the time I saunter into the living room, I smell so good I have to check if I still got my balls intact. Pea is squeezing on a stress ball, her hazels never leaving the window.

"You ready? Hussein is probably wondering where we are. We need to make a move."

"Yeah." I yank the backpack from her hand and swing it over my shoulder. "Where to?" I ask, already out the door. Prescott stops, her hand on the doorknob as she inspects her darkened apartment one last time. Sorrow pings through me. I didn't look back when I left Irv, because I never cared for that house, or for the little shit I lived with.

But this was the place where she learned it was okay to be broken.

Grief is thick in the air, making it harder to draw a deep breath, and I find myself wrapping a hand over her shoulder, planting a cautious kiss on top of her head. "They're just walls."

"That's what I'm afraid of," her voice is hollow. "So many walls to break, so little time."

Our first stop is the ATM across the street. I wait in the car. Prescott borrows my black hoodie and pulls it all the way down her face. Jogging to the machine, I watch as the deep black sky swallows her figure whole. The white light pouring from the ATM screen highlights the arcs of her face. I see the outline of the dagger—*my* fucking dagger—under her dress. She doesn't trust me.

And the worst part? I don't trust her, either.

As she punches the screen, looking left and right, fiddling with an old cell phone she jammed a SIM card into and texting an unknown number, it dawns on me that I really don't know what her next move is, and whether it involves compromising me.

In other words, I put my trust, life and what's left of my soul in a girl I don't trust enough to pour me a glass of water without suspecting she poisoned it.

She jumps back into the car with a pile of one hundred dollar bills in her fist, counting the money by licking her thumb and flipping through it.

"I can only withdraw one thousand at a time, but it'll get us through today and tomorrow." She punches an address into my GPS app and places it in its stand. "What? You're looking at me funny."

I didn't even realize I was staring. But I am.

I shake my head, and my weird mood, then throw Stella into drive.

"Just make sure my fifty grand is ready by next week. I'm planning around it." My tone lashes against her face.

We spend our journey to Hussein, her Iranian car dealer, in unwinding silence. It gives me time to think about what I've done. The parole officer will be knocking on my door sooner or later, and Irv is going to tell him the truth. That I ran away. By then, I'll need to be at least out of the state, if not the country.

But no one promises me that I will be.

I break the silence. "How long will it take your guy to produce the passports?" Prescott's face twitches, her eyes still trained on the road.

"I'm hoping we'll have them by tomorrow morning. It depends on when we get to Los Angeles today. We still need to take passport pictures and give them to him. Why? Jumping ship already?"

She's trying to disguise her anxiety with a chuckle. She's nervous, as she should be. It's going to be hard to take down three grown, pissed-off, powerful men by herself. Prescott tried once, and we all know where that brought her.

"I have a week tops to fuck around before the authorities hunt my ass down. Camden's not in the states yet. And frankly?" I shoot her a look, partly to gauge a reaction from her, but mostly to linger on those lips. "He's not my fucking problem. I'm not gonna wait around for him. But we'll take Godfrey and Seb together before I leave. That, I guarantee."

Okay, asshole, now let's try and figure out what made you say that.

Maybe I wanted to prove to myself that I'm not so pussy-whipped that I'll kill someone I haven't even met just for a girl.

We all have vices, and I'm starting to believe Pea's mine.

Prescott (I still can't believe I caved in and called her that. I also find it difficult to stomach the fact that this stupid name's growing on me.) narrows her eyes into slits and takes out a stress ball, clasping it like it killed her puppy.

"Don't worry. I want Camden all to myself. You were never a part of the plan."

Touché.

I kill the engine in front of a one-story bungalow in Concord, and a tan guy in a blue robe holding a cup of coffee saunters casually through the door.

Now that the sun is almost up, the clean morning air sweeps through my nostrils and the reality of what we're doing sinks in. I drink Hussein in. He's got a week's worth of stubble on his face and a head full of black hair. When he opens his mouth, a thick accent accompanies his words.

"Prescott, you little troublemaker, how've you been?"

Pea unbuckles and jumps out of the truck, slamming the door in my face. On purpose, of course. She walks to his spot on the yellow grass and shoves her hands into her leather jacket.

Man, she's got a great ass.

Focus, idiot.

"Trust me, you don't want to know," she says a little louder than necessary, making sure I'm within earshot. "Hey, Huss, I need a favor."

"You mean, *another* favor," he enunciates, taking a slow sip from his coffee. "I'm listening."

"I need to trade this Tacoma for another car. Preferably something with an out-of-state license plate. Something fast, but not flashy."

I jump out of Stella and shut the door behind me, walking toward her. She doesn't even turn around to acknowledge my presence, let alone introduce me to the guy.

"Why don't we change the license plate? We don't need to replace the whole fucking vehicle." I rage. "I can't part ways with Stella yet."

She spins slowly, her face still blank.

"Stella?" she repeats, tilting her chin down as she inspects me. "Think again. Your truck looks more like a Gladys. Stella is a hot girl's name."

I stare her down through a hooded gaze, but this time, she doesn't budge. "And to answer your question—do you really want to run away from the baddies with your signature tinted-windowed, red Tacoma? I mean, it's a good idea, but you might want to just walk straight into Godfrey's office, unzip, place your balls on his desk and give him the hammer to smash them with."

I offer her a long, middle finger, but she's got a point. Hussein behind her chuckles into his mug.

"You guys are cute."

"Shut up," we both say in unison, still staring each other down. I really want to kill her, and really, really want to hit that shit. I'm not going to lie, though, part of her charm is the fact that she's fearless, no matter my size and track record, even though she's been burned by men before.

Tough cookie, but delicious all the same.

"This truck's in good condition," I grit. "Whatever's left from the trade ends up in my pocket."

"Fine," she shrugs, turning her attention back to Hussein, who is grinning from ear to ear, still planted on his front lawn. His unkempt grass is the opposite of Mrs. Hathaway's lush, green one. It reminds me that on a normal day, I would've hit the road by now on my way to her house to avoid traffic. It's not like me to not show up. I've never taken a sick day in my life. But I won't risk my neck in the name of etiquette. After all— Godfrey hooked me up with the job. I've no idea how tight he is with Stan Hathaway and how far his accountant is willing to go for him.

Prescott and Hussein exchange words while I continue staring at the back of her head, wondering how the hell I got here and why I am placing my future in the manicured hands of a twenty-five-year-old blonde from suburbia. We're going to trade Stella for a beat-down, black Corvette. Tinted windows. Nevada license plate. Rough state. When Hussein leaves for the back of his lot and rolls around the corner with it, I snort out a laugh. I'm not sure what year the car is, but suffice to say we're about the same age.

Hussein slaps cash into Pea's hand and she gives me the difference without counting the bills, before awarding the middle-aged man with a hug and a tap on the shoulder.

"Take care of yourself, Prescott," he says, eyeing me suspiciously. I nod a goodbye at him and climb into the driver's seat. I can barely fit into this low, small car with my height and width. My knees touch the steering wheel and I need to bend my neck if I don't want my head to hit the roof. Shit, my nose is almost touching the windshield.

"Good choice, Prescott. Next time, why don't you fix us up with a fucking unicycle? That'd be fun."

"Hey!" She throws her bag to the backseat. "It's not my fault you're the size of a Costco warehouse. This is a great car. Looks like the Batmobile."

"It's beat-down and old," I retort.

"Beatmobile," she concludes. "We shall call it the Beatmobile."

"I liked you better when you were blindfolded and locked in my basement," I murmur, starting the car, the rumble of its engine roaring to life.

"And I liked you better when you were locked in a cell in San Dimas, watching your youth waste away."

Yeah. I fucked up bad by telling her I would ditch her after this week. The worst part about it? I didn't even mean it.

Shit, I didn't even *think* it.

Planning ahead requires attention, and right now, the only thing I'm focusing on is staying alive and killing Godfrey and Sebastian before they kill us.

Where am I going after this murder crusade? Canada? Mexico? What am I going to do in Mexico? My Spanish isn't good enough to live there. Unless I plan on sticking to ordering food and swearing at soccer teams for the rest of my life. Then, I'm good.

No. I'll move to Canada, which will give me the language advantage. But fuck, the weather. It can get real cold. Although, I'd be one state away from Iowa. Prescott could visit me all the time. . . Wait, what the fuck am I thinking? Visiting me in. . .whoa. Slow down there, stud. She's just a brat who's using you to get ahead in the game. You should be doing the same. Get your head out of your ass, Nate.

Thankfully, Miss Fucking-off-to-Iowa smacks me out of my reverie. She throws the stress ball at my forehead and it bounces back into her hand.

"Earth to Nate. This is the direction we're heading. And it's jammed as hell." She points at the GPS with the hand that clasps the ball. "We won't get to Los Angeles for another six to seven hours, if we're lucky."

"We're good. We'll just have to stop at the first L.A. mall we get to, take photos for our fake IDs and get some more money. We'll hit downtown L.A. before dinnertime, give your guy everything he needs, check into a motel and wait it out." I signal the blinkers and swerve onto the highway, rolling down the windows and letting the hot, dense summer air breeze into our car. The noise of the outside swallows Prescott's delicate voice, but I can still hear her yelling through the wind.

"You're a shithead for not sticking around for Camden, Nate."

Is that right? The girl's still keeping a fucking dagger in her panties. My dagger, by the way, and she's pissed off about me not throwing myself under the bus for her?

"Let me ask you something," I start. My nostrils flare, and I slide the shades I retrieved from Stella up the bridge of my nose to cover my eyes, because I can't chance her seeing what's behind them. "If your sensitive soul is so crushed about me not sticking around, why don't you come with me to Canada when we're done? Didn't we say something about a blood oath?"

"You might want to rethink that incident, because, if I remember correctly, that's around the same time you fucked me and bailed on me for oh, four days or so?"

"I came to my senses." I crush my teeth together. I wanted to fight it. Us. Whatever this fucked-up thing was, I didn't want to be a part of it.

The Beatmobile slows down to a stop, and we're stuck in traffic, moving south from Concord to Los Angeles. I check on Prescott through my darkened sunglasses and know that she's just as uneasy about this as I am.

Standing still is not an option in our situation. There's a police car five vehicles away, and if they decide to stop us, my life is over.

"I'm not coming with you to Canada, or Cabo, or wherever the hell you're going after this is all over," Pea whispers hotly, licking her lips. "I'm going to Iowa, just like I said. You held me hostage, for crying out loud."

"Give me my dagger," I fire at her.

"No. You still haven't convinced me you're trustworthy enough not to stab me in the middle of the night."

I wrench my eyes back to the road, shaking my head. We spend the next four hours in silence. I use the time to mull over the whole Mexico versus Canada debate. I'm leaning toward Mexico. Closer and less chance of me being handed back into the open arms of the US authorities.

When the afternoon rolls around and I hear Prescott's stomach complaining loudly, I pull in at a gas station. I need to stretch my limbs. This car is fucking killing me.

"Would you like to hear our specials for today? We've got Twix for a starter and glazed-BBQ Lays for an entrée," I stick my head into her window. The blonde spitfire bounces the soft stress ball off my nose a couple of times as she speaks.

"Two Red Bulls and a sandwich. And chips. Oh, and something sweet. Chocolate. I'd like a Diet Pepsi, too."

I come back with approximately sixty percent of the convenient mart's goods and switch on the ignition. Prescott pumped gas while I was inside. I groan when my knees hit the steering wheel again. I shouldn't have let her shake hands on this car. By the time we're done, I'll shrink to half my size in this thing.

"I miss Stella. The Beatmobile sucks ass," I say, pulling back onto the main road. Prescott throws her hands up in despair.

"Would you stop moping? I hate to break it to you, but there's probably another guy deep inside Stella right now, riding her like there's no tomorrow."

"Bitch," I drone, creamy clouds move away to make room for the blues and pinks of the sun. This day is turning out to be fucking stunning. Maybe it's the weather.

And maybe it's the girl.

"I'm joking, Nate. Would it help if I gave you head?"

My neck heats and my eyes water with the possibility. *Okay, it's definitely the girl.*

"A little. Let me lick your crack when we get to the motel. That'd put a smile back on my face."

She rolls her eyes on a smirk. "Fine. In the meantime, I'm unzipping you."

I don't dare move my gaze from the road. My blood is pumping so hard in my veins, I'm surprised I'm not bursting like an overcooked wrapped meal in a microwave. I'm not even sure I'd like her to give me head. I'm liable to throw us right into the ocean with those lips on my junk. After all, we're passing beach towns. It's damn likely I would.

"Here?" I ask coolly.

"Why not?" She pushes her hair up off of her face, angling closer. "Tinted windows, and I've been meaning to see how much of you I can take. I have a suspicion it'll be just the tip."

I suck in my cheeks so that my mouth won't break into a shit-eating grin of the douchebag variety. My left hand is still on the wheel, while I use my right one to grab the back of her head roughly and pull it into my lap. She unzips me and I help her by lifting my ass from the seat to give her better access. My dick is swollen, stiff and ready to get to know those pinks up-close. She reaches for my boxers and strokes my cock in her hand. It jerks its appreciation in response. I'm still not sure why she's doing this. We weren't on good terms when we left Hussein's house, and I was under the impression she'd let me sweat before letting me into her pussy or mouth again.

Prescott leans farther down, her hot breath on my cock. I roll my head back and fight to keep my eyes open. Crashing into a traffic light would slow us down, but it would be fucking worth it with her mouth on my dick.

Generally speaking, I'm not a fan of blow jobs. Girls usually suck (no pun intended) at knowing the pace and rhythm that works for me. And Pea's right, most chicks can't even get half my cock down their throats, anyway. But this is fucking Prescott Burlington-Smyth. I'd take anything she offered me. Herpes included.

I feel her tongue swirling around my tip, painful desire tensing every muscle in my body. Her mouth is sweltering and her silky locks pale, but dirty like her soul, are all over my lap like a sheet of gold. She hasn't even sucked me yet, but my balls are already tightening, ready to burst.

"Oh, fuck, Baby-Cakes." I fist her hair and drag her mouth deeper into my groin, lurching myself up from the seat as far as this fucking car allows me, begging for more contact. My head lolls against the headrest and I'm struggling to draw a steady breath. What is it about this girl that makes me forget how to breathe?

She opens her mouth and takes some of me in a leisured suck, then comes up for air. Then she does it again. And again.

After a few minutes of her licking and nibbling through my length, even I have to admit—she gives terrible head. The California highway is potholed, scarred with the impact of earthquakes and the blistering sun, and the car hits bump after bump. Every time it does and my dick meets the back of her throat, she gags with a ghastly sound. She sometimes moves her jaw from one side to the other. *I can feel her teeth*. It's like a getting a BJ from a shark. But even though she's exceptionally untalented at sucking cock, I don't want her to stop. Her mouth's on me and that's enough to make me want to say crazy things to her. Things I'm sure I'm incapable of feeling, anyway.

Ten minutes into the blowjob, Prescott throws in the towel and straightens her posture, eyebrows pinched together. Rage lights up her face.

"You're not going to come, are you?" Her lips are puffy and bright pink. Just thinking about the fact that they're swollen because they were wrapped around my cock puts a dark, sinister smile on my face.

"Nope."

"I thought you said you're always hot for me."

"I am." Is it a good time to tell her she shouldn't quit her day job as a drug dealer because she sucks like a garbage disposal? "I'm saving my spunk for marriage," I joke. But she doesn't laugh. She stares at me seriously, tears pulling at the edge of her eyes. I move my gaze quickly from the road to her face, back to the road. We can't stop. It's too dangerous. . .

Fuck it.

I swing onto the shoulder of the freeway, inches from the concrete divider, and lift the handbrake quickly.

"Yo, Pea, what's up?"

I know she cries. A lot. Over the past few weeks, I saw her pink eyes, the puffy skin beneath her lashes. She cries, but never in front of men. Always alone and in the dark. So why now?

"This is stupid." She shakes her head, wiping away a tear using the sleeve of my hoodie. Even now, she looks sad, but not helpless. "We need to move. We still have to take pictures for the new IDs."

"Why are you crying?" I insist. Fuck the fucking pictures.

"It's stupid, just start the car. We're running out of time."

"Tell me what's wrong."

She looks out her window, tapping it with her fingertips, obviously embarrassed.

"I'mscadyo mighsto likee me," she mumbles.

"What?" I move closer, which rewards me with another hit from her stress ball, right into my groin this time.

"I'm worried you might not like me anymore!" She yells, throwing her arms in the air. "What if you decide to ditch me before we get to Godfrey and Seb, or the minute you get your new passport?"

I take her face in my hands without thinking much of it. The need to touch this girl is overwhelming in a way that fucks up every single working cell in my brain. Carefully, I bring my nose to hers, my lips hovering over her pinks, staring right back at her.

"If you think I'd ever bail on you, you're out of your beautiful, twisted mind. And if you think just because I didn't come, I don't find you attractive anymore, you're a psycho. Because there's nowhere I'd rather be than between your legs. *And* if you think that you're damaged goods because of what those lowlifes did to you, then you're an idiot. It's just the opposite, Pea. They built a woman who's untouchable. So many people have tried, me included. But you're stronger than anything, which is why we're sitting in this stupid car right now, chasing freedom. You think I don't like you?" I breathe into her mouth.

I'm fucking crazy about you.

It's a depressing realization, not one that I'm willing to admit out loud. But the thing about the truth is, sometimes you don't need to look for it. Sometimes it finds *you*.

I wouldn't have killed Godfrey and Sebastian. But she asked for it, and, well, what she asks for, she'll get. At least from me.

"I do like you," I finish quietly, not stupid enough to entertain myself with the possibility of giving her the whole truth. "I like you, all right."

"I like you too." Her nose brushes back and forth against mine in an Eskimo kiss.

Breathe, assclown. Fucking breathe.

I pull away and look back at the highway while I rev up the engine.

"But I didn't say I was damaged goods."

"You think it. Which is even worse. Now, repeat after me: I'm not a victim, I'm a goddamned survivor."

"I'm not a victim, I'm a goddamn survivor." She rolls her eyes. I hit the accelerator and speed south, determined to get to our destination before night falls.

"Lift your head up, Baby-Cakes. Don't let your crown fall. And just for the record, I didn't come because you were using your teeth like my dick was dental floss. Trust me, I'm so hard for you, the thought of checking into a motel tonight makes my mind work overtime."

"Who said we're sharing a room?" she asks with a sly smile.

That's my Prescott.

"We're sharing a room. And I'm licking your crack. You owe me one for the Beatmobile and the loss of Stella."

"Nate Vela, you're a vile man."

"And I'm going to violate every hole in your body tonight."

PRESCOTT

Great. I cried in front of him.

I'm a crybaby. During my captivity, I made sure I cried when no one saw, because I remember what Camden told me all those years ago. *Never let your enemies see you break. Your indifference disables their victory.* So by the time Beat came for me, my eyes were always dry.

Nate is wrong. I'm not untouchable. I've been touched too many times. Each handprint left a scar. It would take years to scrub off the marks and dig out my true self again.

I fall asleep curled into myself, next to him, while he eats up the rest of the journey to Los Angeles at an absurd speed. The minute we hit La La Land, we walk into the first mall we hit, take the passport pictures and get out with our fingers laced together. I'm not sure who makes the first move, it kind of feels like our hands just magnetically connected. The silence between us is comfortable and accepting, and most of all—content. But I'm keeping secrets from him, at least two that'd make him walk away from this arrangement, and I hope to God he doesn't find out before we split.

Nate has his hoodie over his head to hide the tattoos—although it's hard to go unnoticed when you're a six-foot-five pile of muscles and hotness—and I wear my best innocent expression.

It's time to get down to business.

BRYAN

Is actually a hot shot in the Department of State. Fortyish years old. Neat hairstyle. A real life Walter White, only less relatable. You'd never guess what this suited, respectable man does to make an extra buck. But the extra cash is needed in order to pay for his dark little cocaine addiction.

No one knows.

Not even his wife and three picture-perfect kids.

But me? I sold him two pounds of cocaine when he was on a business trip to San Francisco and cut his price by sixty percent under the condition that he would owe me. Big time. It's time to cash in on his debt.

It's time for everyone to cash in on their debts.

We meet Bryan behind a kosher bakery on Fairfax Avenue. I'm wolfing down a chocolate babka, taking long sips from my Americano and watching Bryan and Nate through my big dark shades. I hand Bryan our pictures with chocolate-covered fingertips and he tells us that by tomorrow at noon, we will both have passports under different names.

Nate Vela will die, and from the ashes of his cursed name, a phoenix named Christopher Delaware will rise.

As for Prescott Burlington-Smyth—If you thought my parents burdened me with an unfortunate last name, you'd be surprised, because the only name Bryan managed to snag that fits my physical profile is Tanaka Cockburn. And while Tanaka is a beautiful name. . .

Cockburn.

Nate sprays his coffee all over Bryan's white dress shirt when he hears my new name, then proceeds to turn away, walk to the corner of the alleyway, and rest his hands on his knees as his massive back shakes with wild, unrestrained laughter.

"I shouldn't have to pay for a name like that," I mutter into my foam cup.

But what Nate doesn't know is that I'm barely paying for this service. I'm only footing the bill for the actual production of the passports, which sums up to a few hundred bucks.

He doesn't need to find out that I'm flat broke and won't be able to help him in any way to cross the border. Fifty grand? I don't even have five thousand. Hey, don't judge me. You'd do the same in order to save your life too. *Lying to your captor included.* And his question about me being a mother? Well, that's none of his business, either.

Seeing as we have 24 hours to burn in Los Angeles, Nate suggests that we check into a motel and use the time to plan our next move on Godfrey and Sebastian.

I still want him to lust after me, even though I shouldn't. Seducing him should no longer be part of the plan—I'm already free. But the truth is, I crave him.

Trying to remind myself that he's a criminal, a killer and a guy who— up until a few hours ago—had every intention of handing me back to my ruthless enemy to be skinned alive and fed to his twisted son, I disconnect our hands and keep to myself until we arrive at our next stop.

We check into a rundown motel in a rough neighborhood downtown. The one-story complex is unevenly painted in baby blue, with pink lettering announcing *Palm Spring Apartments*. A Mexican pop station greets us when we walk in, its tunes swallowed by a loud portable fan directed at a heavy lady wearing taffy lipstick at the reception desk. Her curly hair has been violently straightened, a flowery dress barely covers her huge cleavage and a coat of sweat mists 100% of her flesh.

"No AC," I cough into my fist when Nate and I walk in.

"Hey, Dorothy, I don't think we're in Blackhawk anymore. Unless you want to waste your money on the fucking Chateau Marmont. Your call."

I grimace. At this point, he probably has more in his bank account than I do.

The woman ignores us, despite me punching the bell on her counter several times. When she finally looks up from an erotic paperback, it's because she sees Nate approaching from behind me. When he rests his elbows on her reception desk, she puffs a cloud of cigarette smoke into his face. Her blue mascara is so clumpy, blinking must be an exercise for her.

She lets out a primal growl. "Well, you're a treat, aren't you, gorgeous?"

Am I see-through? Nate and I are clearly together. I'm not sure why I care. He is not my boyfriend and it's not like he's going to run away with this middle-aged woman. Besides, the bastard is probably used to it. I haven't seen him interacting with the outside world yet. I know the man in the darkened basement, the captor who will hurt me if I disobey, but something tells me this isn't the first time a woman has blurted out something embarrassing in real-life Nate's direction.

He looks like the reason women buy Pocket Rockets. This probably happens to him all the time.

Nate leans his waist on the counter and flips through a wrinkled travel magazine, chewing his peachy gum, the signature flavor of his mouth. Completely unfazed by the attention he's drawing.

"We need a room," he says, ignoring her compliment. "One night. One bed. Paying in cash."

"No problem, sweetie. Name?" Her pen floats over a page listing the rooms. Almost none of them are highlighted in yellow as occupied. Jesus. This place doesn't even use computers. I hope there'll be a lock on the door.

"Baby-Cakes"—he drapes his arm over my shoulder, his mouth invading my cheek with a charged groan—"should we put it under your name? What do you say? Yeah, let's just put it under your name." He angles forward and pronounces slowly, "Tanaka C-o-c-k-b-u-r-n. That's her last name. Cockburn."

"Shut up." I swat his arm, barely biting down my laughter.

"Do you need me to spell that for you again?" Nate points at the form the receptionist fills out, and she licks her lips when her gaze moves up to his tattooed fingers. Stone-faced and perfectly composed, he continues, "Cockburn. Like a cock that burns. You know, like an STD side effect."

He is so not going to get backdoor access tonight if he continues this.

Who am I kidding? Him being funny just kills every attempt to dislike him even more.

Five minutes later, Nate is dangling a small key with a pink hoop and we both stroll to room number 13. The receptionist directed us (well, directed Nate, he was the only person she was looking at throughout our short encounter with her) to a bar down the road that serves all-you-can-drink beer beginning at five p.m.

Even poor people need one happy hour.

As it happens, I desperately need a drink. This could be a good way to clear my mind and think about our next step. If everything goes to plan, we should be back in Northern California by tomorrow evening.

Are we starting with Seb?

Are we starting with Godfrey?

The possibility of hurting those two sends a hot rush down my back.

"Let's go have drinks down the road," I suggest as Nate pushes the squeaking door to our room open. We walk into a small, stuffy space, the scent of stale smoke rubbed into every sheet and piece of furniture. Cigarette holes in the comforter and yellow, indiscernible stains sprayed on the walls. I say a little prayer before walking into the bathroom, only to find a peeling tub. The vent is hanging out of the ceiling and the toilet is filthy with other people's waste. Swiveling my head to Nate, I see him giving me a casual headshake.

"Can't risk it. We gotta lay low. Godfrey's got people everywhere, Cockburn. You know that as well as I do."

"Stop calling me Cockburn." I kick my ankle boots and collect my wild, wavy hair into a high ponytail. "I need a drink."

"I'll go get you something from the K-Mart downtown." He walks to the window overlooking the street, peeking outside and searching for something Godfrey-related. Should I be as alarmed as he is? Somehow, I find it difficult to believe Godfrey is already on to us. He has no idea we're in Los Angeles. Technically, there's nothing for us to do here. Also, Archer had spent years and years in prison not too far away from me and none of his men ever got to me. Not even once.

But I know better than to think that it's because he couldn't have. He just wanted to keep me alive so he could kill me himself.

146

Maybe Nate is not only worried about Godfrey, but also about the Aryan Brotherhood. This guy is practically a dead man walking in the state of California. He has many reasons to watch his back.

All the same, I'm not going to sit and rot in this room until our IDs are ready. Going down the road for a few drinks is not going to kill me. The chances of being spotted and recognized are non-existant. It's just an old, poor neighborhood in the middle of Los Angeles, where Godfrey has never set foot. Besides, Nate has had the outside world for a while now. I've spent over two weeks stuck in his basement, trying to dig my way out with nothing but broken nails.

"I'm going."

He turns around and jerks me into his body by the arm, his face murderous. "Like hell you are. I'm gonna have a shower now. When I come out, you better still be here, and have pulled out a number for a good place that delivers greasy food."

I open my mouth, about to sass, but he's already shut the bathroom door behind him.

The faucet running on behind the door. I clutch my stress ball in a death grip. He thinks I need his permission to go to the bar? Well, he's in for an unpleasant surprise.

I throw my backpack over my shoulder and charge out, storming past the reception area. I don't stop until I reach a corner bar called Three Bullets, the one the receptionist recommended.

I push the door wide as I walk through and slide onto one of the barstools, adorned with clouds of foam growing from its torn black leather. Tapping the bar twice with my knuckles, I ask the bartender for whatever it is that's on their all-you-can-drink menu.

Three Bullets.

Godfrey.

Camden.

Sebastian.

Nate would appreciate the irony. I need to stop thinking about what Nate likes and dislikes. Scanning the room while the old, bald barman hands me my glass of lukewarm beer, I decide that I like this place. It's got this old-school, Barfly vibe. Either the blue-collar, bearded old men in here haven't heard of the no-smoking law enforced in California, or they simply disobey it. A bunch of retired men are playing poker at a round table behind me while a few greased-up younger men just back from their manual labor jobs are seated at the bar, peering into their drinks in hopes of finding the answers to how they ended up here.

Cheap, broken décor. Everything is peeling, everything stinks and everything is dirty. *Just like my soul.*

I gulp my first drink in one go, studying my surroundings, and tap the rim of my glass, asking for more. A few of the men notice me. They look at me. *They stare.* And even though it makes me feel slightly uncomfortable, I'm not scared.

I'm way past scared. Everything I've been through sharpened me into someone who's not easy to intimidate. A guy around my age, maybe slightly older, swivels the stool next to me, his ass landing on it. I focus on my drink, knowing that I'll have to brush him off.

"Passing through?" he cuts straight to the chase. I offer him half a shrug and take a sip of beer. People are watching us intently. I'm the only woman in the bar, and I bet that other than an occasional visit from the receptionist at my motel, this place hasn't seen a woman within its four walls for a lifetime.

"I would have remembered if I saw you before. You're pretty."

I turn to face him, smiling sweetly. I want to drink and think about my plans. Not have a quickie in the filthy bathroom.

"Can I just enjoy my drink, please? It's been a long day."

"I can make it a long night, too, if you want." The guy scans me over. He is not ugly, but not attractive either. I wrinkle my nose.

"Doubt it."

He doesn't take the hint and instead moves closer, his chest almost bumping into mine. I'm ready with the dagger. Ready to show yet another man that I'm not to be messed with, but I'm hoping not to have to go there. Drawing more attention is the last thing that I need.

All eyes are on me now, and the thought that Godfrey may have moles here after all creeps into my mind. Oh, shit. What if Nate was right? What if I screwed our whole plan in the name of cheap beer?

"Do you have a boyfriend?" Jesus. The guy is still here?

"Yeah, she's got a boyfriend." I hear the nonchalant, curt tone that makes my heart quake and overflow behind me. *Nate.* "He's a real fucking asshole, too. You're better off trying to shove your dick into a food processor than hitting that ass. Come on, Cockburn." I feel his huge hand scoop me into his midsection, his fingers digging into my skin angrily— telling me I fucked up—as he pulls me into him, planting a possessive kiss on my temple. "Let's get back to our room. Wednesday is anal night."

I giggle as Nate slaps a twenty-dollar bill on the bar and yanks me back to meet even more of his body, guiding me back out into the humid, scorching night.

I know I need to break free from his touch.

But I don't.

In fact, as he blankets me with his frame, my back brushing his flexed chest as we awkwardly wobble across the road back to the motel, my guard is down.

So down there's nothing separating me from my raw emotions toward him.

"What did I tell you about going to the bar?" he whispers into my skull, making my skin crawl in a delicious way.

"You're not my boss," I reply, trying to sound indifferent. We enter the crumbling motel, walk past the receptionist and I shake him away, picking up speed. "And now you're not my captor, either. So I can do whatever I want without giving a damn what you think."

"Oh, Cockburn," he says, throwing that stupid nickname in my face again. "When are you going to get over the little fact that I held you hostage in my basement? Stop holding grudges. It's bad karma."

When we get into the room, he locks the door behind us and shoves the key in his back pocket. I stand with my knees against the edge of the bed and lift my head.

"I was doing some thinking at the bar. Who are we going to take out first, Godfrey or Sebastian?"

"Sebastian," he shoots back, unblinking. Now that we're alone, he doesn't touch me. Doesn't seek the warmth of my skin. Is it bad that I constantly crave his? Of course it's bad. He told me he is ditching me in a week. I need to shake off this stupid crush and realize he won't be here by next Thursday.

"Explain." I open my backpack, sifting through my stuff and making sure it's all there. I haven't left it once since we started this journey, but doing inventory when I feel stressed or cornered soothes me. Stupid, I know, but I have to keep my hands busy.

"Makes more sense." Nate arches one eyebrow. "He goes to a gay club in San Francisco every Friday. Irvin's ex-cell mate sees him there regularly. Perfect opportunity to find out where he lives." Nate walks back to the window and peeks out. "We'll be able to follow him back to his place and do it quietly. Also, if we off Godfrey first, Seb would get word and run away. He's got no ties to NorCal. Godfrey, on the other hand, can't simply fuck off and hide. He's got business here. No. He'll stay, and even wait for us."

Clearly, he's thought this out.

"We don't have a weapon." I chew on my lower lip, dragging papery skin through my teeth as I mull this over. I used to have a Glock, but Godfrey took it. It's not going to be easy to get my hands on another one so soon. Archer supervises and knows of each and every unregistered gun that's on the market in NorCal, and I don't know anyone who sells here in L.A.

"We've got plenty. We don't have a gun. But guns are for pussies, anyway."

When he sees the doubt pouring from my face, he snarls with conviction. "I've got your back, Baby-Cakes. I can kill him with one arm tied to my back, on fucking roller-skates. Clear?"

I swallow hard, looking away, my eyes burning with impending tears of emotions I don't fully understand. Him being around me is both the best and worst thing that's ever happened to me. I'm losing focus. I'm losing control. *I'm losing it.*

"Revenge is better served cold, and personal, Prescott. Hands. Marks. Fingerprints. Mess. Sharp objects. Pounding hearts. Guns are for those you show mercy to. And what do we lack, my dear prodigy?"

His shoves his face into mine, his devilish eyebrows knotted together.

"Mercy," I answer. He brushes his thumb on my cheek, diving down to my mouth, dragging the soft coat of dead skin from my lips and pulling it leisurely. It hurts, and I love it.

"That, we do. They didn't show us any mercy, and we're not bigger people."

Good God, this man is ruthless, yet so soft when he handles me. I can't even begin to read him.

I clear my throat. "Go get us something to eat." I bark out the order to disguise the storm that's swirling inside me, but I'm sure he can see through me. My cheeks are cherry red, my pulse is so fast you can see it pounding in my neck and I constantly lick my lips. He nods curtly and leaves without even asking me what I want, locking me inside.

But he doesn't need to ask, he knows what I want.

I want him.

I wake up to faint red flickers of the clock on the nightstand. It's 3:30 a.m.

Time.

It's my only fortune nowadays. Other people, people who took and used and abused me, are running out of it.

Stretching my arms and spreading my legs over the cool sheets, I notice I'm alone. My throat bobs and I blink away the sleep.

Where is he?

Looking around, I take in the empty room through glassy eyes. I remember falling asleep minutes after he'd left to get us food, but he never woke me up.

Christ. I should have never trusted this man.

Scrambling up to my feet, I throw the bathroom door wide. Empty. I'm consumed by the darkened room, all by myself, and instead of launching for my backpack, making sure he hadn't stolen anything, I fight the tears that are quietly flowing down my cheeks. The thought that he left me makes me want to throw myself off a building.

He wouldn't leave without getting his passport and 50k first—would he?

Maybe one of Godfrey's guys got to him. Shit, maybe I'm next.

After checking my backpack and making sure that everything I brought along is still with me, I pace the room back and forth. We're only using one burner phone, and it's on me, so I can't call him. I check the window overlooking the street. Nothing. Slipping into a pair of flip flops I'm not even sure belong to me, I get out of the room with my backpack in tow, cursing him for taking the key because I can't lock the door behind me.

I'm sweating buckets as I get close to the lobby, fearing I'll come face to face with my English enemies. With every step, my prayers become louder. At first they're just in my head. Then, they come out as whispered chants. Launching into the empty reception area, scanning, searching, hyperventilating, I pass by the small pool the place offers and a blue shadow dances in my periphery. I twist my head in surprise and stop with a screech.

Nate.

He's swimming to and fro, slowly, gracefully. *Taking his time.* I stare at him, allow my pulse to slow down and wipe the cold sweat from my brow before I snap out of my stupor and walk to the pool, not making a sound. The motel is practically deserted, the only noises that can be heard include the surprised swooshes of a pool that's probably never been used before, and the whimpering of a faraway coyote.

I'm still wearing my red number and a small leather jacket when I walk over to him. He has his back to me but when a twig snaps under my flip-flops, he turns around sharply. His expression relaxes from tight back to peaceful when our eyes lock.

"What in the actual hell, Nate?" I disguise the panic that swirled within me moments ago by burying my hands in my jacket's pockets, even though it's hot outside. I always dress up in cute clothes. It reminds me of my previous life as a Blackhawk princess. But I always wear something on top to hide my body. That, however, is all thanks to the second part of my life, the one after the Archers bulldozed into it. "I thought you said you were bringing food!" It's supposed to be a question, but it comes out as an accusation.

"And I did. You were snoring. What was I supposed to do?" his eyes narrow into dangerous slits. I can see it from here. Even in the blackness of the night. He's only wearing his boxers, and looks delicious bare-chested.

151

"You were supposed to not get out and swim in the open, where everybody can frigging see you. Should I remind you that you're violating your parole, and that we're running away from kingpins with blood on their hands?"

Hysteria consumes me. I'd be shaking if it wasn't for the fact it's 300 degrees outside and I'm wearing a goddamned leather jacket. Nate shrugs inside the pool, disregarding me completely. I shake my head, exhaling.

"You're so stupid, Nate. You act like it's the first time you've even been to a pool," I turn on my heel, about to walk away.

"It is," he says. I freeze, spinning slowly. His eyes follow the hand he uses to splash the water around.

"Huh?" I ask, dropping my backpack on the floor. My face pinks but the night blankets my skin, keeping this our secret.

"Yeah," he repeats louder. "I've never been inside a pool, even though I clean one regularly where I work in Blackhawk. Grew up in California, twenty-seven years old, and this is my first time." He barks out a laugh, but it's not bitter. He doesn't give a damn about what people think, me included. Nate seems like he's always been keenly aware of his circumstances. "Anyway, thought I'd check it out. See what all the fuss is about. Just in case. . ."

Just in case they kill us. I nod, offering him a small, knowing smile.

"Why is it that you only tattooed one side of your body?" I stand at the edge of the pool. I want to change the subject, but am also genuinely interested in the answer.

"The bare side represents my virtue. My ambitions. My good intentions. And the other side. . .that's the dirty side of me. Violent and primal. It's the side that kills without blinking."

"You're good," I whisper.

"And bad," he argues. "I'm the guy who took you as a prisoner, to be murdered by sacks of shit, remember?"

"But also the guy who ushered me out, and promised to help me seek revenge," I maintain.

"And that, gorgeous, is why I have a clean part. Even on my skin."

Even in your heart.

I shake my head. He may enjoy my words. . .but I'm mad about his.

Bending down, my knees touching the damp floor, our eyes level silently. His lashes are dark wet curtains and his mouth is even more perfect dripping with water, bathed in the moonlight. He breathes heavily. I don't dare breathe at all. Complete opposites, with so much to give to each other. A storm and calm waters, we can create a natural disaster, but it would be beautiful and broken and ours.

Kiss me, my heart sings as my stare falls to his lips. *Please, want me.*

"I got scared when I saw you weren't in the room," I admit. He rests his head against mine, our bodies inches from one another. *Pull me in.*

"You ain't listening when I talk, are you, Baby-Cakes? I told you to trust me."

"I can't trust a guy who wants to sleep with me. But I can trust a guy even less when he *doesn't*," I half-joke. But I'm scared. So scared. Because the odds are against us. Hell, everything and everyone is against us.

His lips laugh into mine, and the rumble of his wet chest dampens my dress. My underwear too, despite the fact he's nowhere near them.

"You know, Pea, even though it's been years since you and Camden broke up, I know that on some level, I'm still the goddamn rebound. This is the first time you've allowed yourself to get sucked into something that even vaguely resembles companionship. I need to tread carefully, figure out what you're willing to give me on this short journey of ours. You wanna know the truth? I don't know how. No one's ever been careful about *my* feelings, about *my* trust. You've been sexually abused. I can go and spit some 'I understand' bullshit, but you're too smart and I'm too honest. I *don't* understand. So I'm letting you make the first move. If I touch you, I need permission, but make no mistake," he says then catches my lower lip between his teeth and pulls, at first softly, and then hard enough to suck me into the pool with him. I willingly let my body drop forward but he catches me at the last minute. "I want you. I want your words and your body and your brain and your little stress ball bouncing against my face, even though it's annoying as fuck. I want more than you could ever give me, so don't worry about that part, Cockburn."

Our chests are so close now, I feel his heartbeat in my own ribcage. And his words. I feel them, too. Everywhere. I've gone and done it again. Only this time, it's ten times worse.

I fell in love.

I fell in lust.

I fell in stupid.

I nod, my forehead bobbing against his, feeling pleasantly yet sickly light-headed. "Thank you." My voice croaks. "For asking for what they demanded. For what they took. But it's unnecessary with you."

Silently, I plead for his touch by beginning to peel off my clothing. He takes a step back in the blue pool, watching me through eyes heavy with desire. The jacket falls to the ground first, my armor against men. My red dress and flip-flops follow and are discarded near a stripy yellow and white lounge chair. I slide into the pool, clad only in my bra and panties, and straight into Nate's arms.

The water is cold, but all I feel is his heat.

He takes my mouth with his and kisses me desperately, my legs wrapped around his waist. I feel his want for me, and again, am surprised by my reaction. It doesn't feel sleazy or scary. It doesn't hold a promise of something devastating.

I drag my tongue along his neck, sucking his pulse and his life into me, my back still pressed to the edge of the pool as his erection moves up and down my stomach. A muffled groan disappears into my hair every time our groins touch. He tastes salty and male and like my own, personal heaven.

"Cockburn. . ." He bites my earlobe, his shaft digging between my legs. Our lips find each other and our tongues move together erotically. I don't even care if people can see us from the dozens of windows overlooking the pool. Let them look and eat their hearts out. Life's too short to care about what other people think.

Time.

I want to use it wisely as long as he's around.

"Delaware," I tease back into his mouth, panting with what's beginning to feel like an orgasm building between my legs like a hot Saharan sandstorm.

"Tell me something beautiful, Cockburn," he whispers behind my ear, stroking my lower back, igniting something sinful. "Tell me something pretty like you."

I sift through my thoughts, even though it's damn hard with his hands roaming all over me.

"'A poem begins as a lump in the throat, a sense of wrong, a homesickness, a lovesickness.' Robert Frost."

Hot lips land on my collarbone.

"How rough do you want me tonight, Little Poem?"

"Rough," I pant.

"Turn."

I spin around and he lifts my upper body so that I'm lying flat on the concrete next to the pool, my cheek resting against the surface. I feel his fingers peeling down my underwear, my ass facing him. I grin into the cold tiles under the hot night.

"What are you doing, Delaware?"

"I don't have a condom here," he says, dodging my question, spreading my ass cheeks with his firm fingers. Embarrassment tickles at the pit of my stomach. I've never done this before. Not willingly, anyway. Godfrey sodomized me, but I wasn't there when it happened. I blanked out. Now, I'm here completely, ready to feel it.

I get over my doubts and worries by reminding myself that it's Nate Vela. Or Christopher Delaware. I'd let both versions of him do anything they wanted to me. Hell, I'd even let Beat tap it any time of the day.

"That could be a problem." I feign innocence, my teeth crushing gritty, salty sand from the floor. Nate digs one finger into my pussy, borrowing my wetness and rubbing it against my anal rim in circles.

154

"I'm clean," he continues. "Checked myself when I got out of prison, and haven't been with anyone on the outside."

That's a surprise, unless you really know Nate. Women don't interest him.

Storms do.

"And on the inside?"

He smacks my ass hard, a slap that lands on my left ass cheek and makes my face crash against the floor. The boom of his palm on my skin ricochets between the palm trees, and a red sting follows.

"Watch it, Cockburn."

I chuckle, knowing that this guy is way too intelligent to be a homophobe. I love when he hurts me. Pain feels different under his touch.

With him, we're sharing, not distributing.

With him, pain is just another way to feel.

He spreads my ass again and places his hot tongue on the flesh between my ass and sex, giving me a thorough, warm lick. I shiver, feeling my erect nipples grinding against the concrete, and lift my ass to his face, asking for more.

Sinking his head into the pool, he comes up with his mouth to my pussy and starts fucking me with his tongue. Thrusting his hotness between my folds hard and fast from behind, his nose buried in my ass. I whine in need, my hips bucking, rocking, circling, *searching*. His square jaw scratches my thighs, the stubble burning my skin in a way that's almost too painful if it weren't for the cold water splashing over them with every move of his head. After a few minutes, his mouth moves north to my ass crack. His tongue swirls around my hole, and I'm quaking all over, jerking into his face every time he presses his tongue hard against my skin, applying pressure on my sensitive spot.

I'm soaked. So soaked.

"I'm clean too," I cry into the ground. Before Nate, I hadn't had sex in a long time, and had visited a clinic since. I feel his hands ghosting my waist as he drags me back down into the water, his mouth on my shoulder.

"You're a delicate flower I'd like to smash to pieces, Pea. But only with permission." He pushes his boxers down and off. I see them floating beside us.

"Smash me," I groan.

And he does.

He smashes me.

The first thing I notice is not that he slams into my ass—not starting with the tip—going all the way in, but the fact that my face hits the edge of the pool and my lip splits open. The exact same place Seb left me bleeding. But the experience is anything but similar. I suck on my own blood and shriek in a mix of pain and pleasure as he guides my face up, his palm on my neck, so my head is flush against his chest.

"Sorry. I didn't mean to hurt you. Not in this way."

Slam.

"Fuck, Prescott, fuck."

Slam.

"You're killing me."

Slam.

"And I'm loving it."

Slam.

Words so beautiful, spoken in such an ugly place, under the same stars that are watching the people who want us dead. He drives into me like he's trying to mold us into one, and with every thrust, I'm beginning to believe that it can actually happen. My heart cracks open a little more with every push.

I'm falling in love with this guy.

I'm going to kill two people with this guy.

Soon, this guy will hate me when he figures out that I have no way to pay him and fulfill my commitment to him. That I lied to him about the money, and kept the truth from him when he asked me about other things, too.

Slam.

Slam.

Slam.

We need to hurry up and go our separate ways before it backfires on us both. Nate Vela is not an easy guy to read, but our ending is still written in the sky. It reads *heartbreak* and *death.*

Slam.

"I'm coming," he says, and I arch my back in response. I would have probably come too, had I not been so occupied with my stupid feelings for him.

"Are you close?" he produces a guttural hiss through his teeth. I shake my head, no.

"Come inside me, Nate."

He slams into me a few more times before stilling, and I feel his warm release pouring into me. We stay like this for a few moments—him standing on the pool's floor, holding my ass against his groin, his favorite position, before he spins me to face him and nails my back to the wall. My ass is sore and I'm pretty sure I won't be able to sit down for at least a couple of months.

"Did I hurt you, Cockburn?" His full eyes cut to my split lip, and I'm filled with horror, because I can actually feel the tears stinging the backs of my eyeballs again.

I'm taking this partnership way too far.

"No. Well, yeah, it hurt, but I still enjoyed it."

"Then why are you crying?" He pushes his hair back, furrowing his brows. "Tell me."

I shake my head no. It's starting to get a little chilly in the pool, but I don't budge.

"Hey, Nate, can I ask you something? And don't get offended."

"Okay."

"I'm serious."

"Me too. What am I not getting offended about?"

"When exactly are we parting ways? I need to have a real date in my head, so we can. . .you know, plan everything and make sure we're ahead of the game."

Nate moves his hand over his beautiful wet hair, drops of water decorating his thick eyebrows, eyelashes and strong jaw. God, his face. It's only been twenty-four hours and I'm already addicted. How will I live without seeing it every day?

"How about next Wednesday I take off to Mexico? It leaves us plenty of time to take out those two clowns. Camden will have to come to the States once he hears his father dropped dead, so maybe I can even help you out with him. A whole week is enough. Trust me."

I nod silently. There I have it. A date. A deadline. A defined, obvious end to whatever it is I've built with this guy.

"Thanks."

"You're shivering," he says, rubbing my arms up and down, splashing water around us. "Let's get back to the presidential suite. Order some room service," he jokes. I laugh a little on the outside and die a lot on the inside.

Hell, I'm in love with three men.

Beat, the felon.

Nate, the poet.

And Christopher Delaware, who I don't even know yet.

NATE

We've got them. The motherfucking passports.

It's bittersweet to see my ticket to freedom clasped in Pea's small hand. I've never had a passport, so I'm no expert, but this one looks legit. It has my face on it, and the identity of Christopher Delaware is real. Meaning, the poor motherfucker does exist. Only now, I've regressed back to being twenty-five and apparently I was born in Nebraska.

Nebraska shares a border with Iowa, the bane of my existence and Pea's next stop.

Did I mention I fucking hate Iowa?

Prescott has her new ID. I'm glad she does, because it's a great way to cover her ass. And what an ass that is. Speaking of, she's been walking funny all day today, so I'm glad we spent most of it in the Beatmobile, heading north back to Stockton. I know she's sore from yesterday, and I should feel guilty, but honestly? Couldn't be more thrilled. She let me into her ass. That's like code for *Ask me on a date* or something.

I was just about to. For a second there, when we were in the pool, I was about to throw all the fucks I give about my safety out the window and just go for it. I wanted to ask her if she'd like to go to dinner when this is all over. Not here in California. But maybe somewhere else. Maybe even in fucking Iowa, for all I care. After all, by then, I'll be Christopher Delaware.

Then she threw the deadline in my face, and reminded me that we're just a business arrangement with a little pleasure tossed in.

A lot of pleasure tossed in.

Still, it's work. She wanted to know when I'd leave, and I gave her an exact date because she put me on the spot. It's not like I'm counting the days and hours I have left with her, but I'm not gonna lie, it stings like a bee-tch.

I fling a look in her direction from the driver's seat, watching her squeezing her stress ball, eyes trained on the road.

"We need to crash somewhere outside of Stockton. The deeper we get into their territory, the better their chances of finding us," I say.

"I know a place in Lodi, so far away even the owner isn't sure where it is exactly. I'll pull the address." She turns her body to the back seat and fiddles with her backpack. I peer down to check the time on the dashboard and see that time is on our side. It must be a sign from God.

"I'm pulling over to take a piss and pump some gas."

"Cool." She awards me with the same treatment as her word. She's never been so cold to me before.

Fuck it, she doesn't have to like me, and it's probably even better if she doesn't. It'll only make things easier when she pisses off to Iowa.

I shut off the engine and stride into the bathroom while Prescott pumps gas. It's becoming harder to leave her to do things on her own without the nagging fear of them taking her again. This time, I may not be there to release her. I take the fastest leak in the history of piss, and when I get back, I spot her standing just outside of the gas station, next to a payphone, one finger stuffed into an ear and the other ear covered by her cell phone. She's talking to someone animatedly.

Who the fuck is she talking to and how is it more important than guarding our stupid, impractical car?

I stride in her direction, knowing that I'm intruding and not giving a damn. Our destinies are chained for the time being. This is not about acting like a jealous boyfriend.

Because I'm not her boyfriend.

And I ain't jealous.

Right.

"Okay," she says and nods into the phone. "Yes, of course. Whatever you want. Whatever you need. Thanks again for reaching out, I really appreciate it."

Pea, polite and well behaved? That's new and unbecoming. When she hangs up and slants an eyebrow in question, I fold my arms on flexed pecs. I'm tense, and not just because of this phone call. Something feels off. It's in the air. It's in her eyes. It's fucking everywhere. Life taught me how to recognize when things are about to explode, and right now, I need a bulletproof vest.

"Who was it?"

"None of your business," she chirps with a sugary smile. I grab the hem of her jacket and pull her to my body, invading her personal space.

"Spill it, Cockburn, or I'm riding your ass dry tonight."

"I swear to God, Nate, call me Cockburn one more time and I—"

The payphone behind her starts ringing. We don't pay attention. At first, it doesn't even register at all. All I hear is snippets of our conversation. Some are things I tell her, some are things she tells me.

160

". . .maybe if you didn't act like a cold-hearted bitch. . ."

". . .I've never met someone so self-centered. . ."

"Next Wednesday can't come soon enough. . ."

Finally, when the payphone doesn't stop ringing for a full minute, and the sound somehow becomes ear deafening, it dawns on me that:

A) Our car was left unattended and we're in a fucking rundown gas station.

B) Payphones don't usually ring, let alone for so long.

C) We better pull our shit together if we want to get out of this alive.

"Shut up, Prescott, I mean it, just shut the hell up." I'm tired of her hot and cold behavior, and I'm really pissed with her for not letting me in on who she was talking to. It's making me edgy and suspicious of the girl I like.

The girl I like. Great. So I did grow a bushy vagina after all.

I trudge toward the payphone, pick it up and press it to my ear. I don't even have to say *hello.* The second the receiver hits my skin, a cockney accent seeps from the other end.

"Hello, Nathaniel. You know, I thought you were a lot smarter than this. Granted, not a bloody genius, but clever enough to know my game is too dangerous for you. You're lucky you're in the middle of a highway."

I look around me, trying to spot him or one of his wise guys. Where could they be? Cars flash by from each side of the highway, golden mountains fill every corner of our landscape. There are two other cars and one truck driver lazing around the gas station, so I bet wherever they are, the only reason we're alive is because they can't aim straight at our heads without missing. I'm trying not to panic, but one look at Prescott, and I'm seeing red. Her eyes widen in shock when she realizes who I'm talking to. Well, technically, I haven't spoken yet, but that's about to change.

"Now, now, Nate. You know I'm a saint, so I'm willing to let this one go. Just this time. Go back to the car. Act as if nothing's happened. Hand the girl back to us. I'll be waiting in my office. I want her delivered straight to my door. Do it, and I'll spare your miserable, meaningless life. Got it?"

The hair on the nape of my back stands up in warning, but I take comfort in one thing. God's in Blackhawk. Otherwise he wouldn't have directed me to his office. That means someone else is watching us. And I bet it's his little toy soldier, Sebastian.

"Am I clear?" he repeats, this time louder. His urgency doesn't escape me.

"Yeah," I answer indifferently, propping a lazy foot on a step under the payphone, holding the receiver between my ear and shoulder. Purposely looking like I couldn't give two shits. "But there's one little problem."

"And what would that be?"

"She's not going to be any good for you."

"How so?" He seems intrigued.

"Well. . ." I glance fleetingly in her direction. She's looking at me like I'm the Messiah, shifting her weight between her feet nervously, choking the stress ball in her fist. "Because soon, you'll be dead. And dead people? They don't really need a companion, Godfrey my friend."

He barks out a laugh that bounces off my ribcage, not quite reaching my heart, but having enough impact to make me shiver.

"If you're going to shoot the king, you better make sure that he's dead. I'm so much stronger than you, *Nathaniel*."

"And I'm so much angrier, *Godfrey*," I warn quietly. "You better start running, because we ain't stopping until we play fucking football with your head. No hourglass in the world is going to stop us this time."

Pea's eyes are so big right now, I can see my whole reflection dancing against her irises. I'm trying to read her face, and if I ain't wrong, I see admiration, surprise, panic, anger and confusion. It's a lot, but it's all there in those hazels.

"Goodbye, Godfrey." I smirk then slam the phone with a loud bang. Prescott rubs my arm, eyes bright and wide. She looks startled, but there's also something soft behind those brown-greens.

"I don't know how to. . ." she mutters, looking away. Heartbreaking expressions of surprise, terror and gratitude paint her face. She can trust me, and she knows it. No more fucking around with my dagger in her panties. "Thank you."

"Who were you speaking to?" My tone may be dry, but my heart is doing cartwheels. I guide her to the car by throwing an arm over her shoulder, mainly to shield her whole body from behind. I'm not sure why I'm protecting her life with mine.

Actually, I am. But saying it aloud, or even thinking about it makes me want to punch my own face. We practically run to the car, working our way so that we're always close to the other customers at the gas station.

"Someone named Dorian. He says he's Preston's counselor." She's breathless, trying to keep up with my pace. "Dorian said Preston is in rehab in Vallejo. Got into a bit of trouble with booze, but he's getting better now. That's really good. That means that he's alive, Nate."

"Why wouldn't he be alive?" My brows furrow. She lifts her shoulders. "He was always haunted by a lot of things. Our family, his sexuality, life in general. But this. . .this is a breakthrough. I need to go there, Nate. I need to see my brother."

Alarm bells. Loud and deafening, fill every space between my ears. She can't hear them, clouded by the euphoria of finding her only loveable family member. But it seems really fucking convenient that Preston shows up right along with Godfrey and Sebastian. In a rehab facility in Vallejo, a place we don't know, a place with miles and miles of dead zones where they can corner us, catch us and end us.

Still, I gotta tread around this subject carefully.

"When were you planning to do that, Baby-Cakes?"

"Tomorrow," she says. I open the door for her and shove her in, slamming it in her face. "Come on, Nate." Her head pops out through the open window. Goddamn, does she want them to shoot her between the eyes? "It'd be quick. If we get suspicious, we'll make a U-turn. What do you say?"

Hell to the no with a side of absolutely no chance.

"Get your head in the car, Cockburn." I push her forehead into the vehicle. "And slide the fuck down before I kill you myself."

With that, I jog to my side of the car. We gotta get this freak show back on the road, before one of Godfrey's spies slays us.

Jumping into the Beatmobile, knowing full well that we're being followed, I zigzag into small towns, populated residential areas and busy highways. There's a RAM that's about as low profile as a circus clown shadowing our every turn. I bite down on my tongue to stop myself from barking at her. She's fucking insane for wanting to go after Preston when we're being hunted like easy prey in an open field.

"I can see the bastards," she swallows uneasily, her eyes narrowing into slits. Her gaze clicks with the young black man in the RAM, who drives behind us, through our rearview mirror. There's a fat white guy next to him, grinning like a crocodile. If I get my hands on him, he's going to look like he's been mauled by one.

Pea's knees are shaking. Probably seconds away from fainting. I'm just glad we're in a place so populated, they can't pull out a fucking rifle like the AB.

"Check for traffic jams," I motion toward her cell phone with my chin. "I want to get into a standstill from hell where we can lose them."

Prescott looks for the most congested roads, the ones marked in red on her GPS app, and that's where our car heads. They can't do shit with busy traffic surrounding us.

Two hours later, when we're sure that we've lost the intruders, we're back on the main road, heading north. Both Prescott and I are watching all of our mirrors, making sure we're spy-free, for long minutes before she opens her mouth again.

"I know what you think," she starts. "But the number connects straight to a rehab center. I called again and hung up when I got the receptionist. It's legit, Nate."

It's no big deal to dial from a number that doesn't belong to you. There are a lot of ways to hack through it, and I'm sure Prescott knows that full well. She doesn't want to think about it right now, and I ain't going to taunt her with the truth.

"Look," she exhales. "This is not a part of our plan, and not a part of our arrangement. You don't have to come with me."

"I want to." My words cut the tension in the air. Do I? No. I know it's a trap. But I also know that if she's walking into the open arms of Godfrey and Seb, I'm walking in with her. She's not doing it alone. Correction— she's not doing it at all. "But you need to do your boy a solid, Cockburn. Give me a day. One day's all I ask. We're going for Seb tonight. Let's get him out of the way then visit your brother. Cool?"

Time.

I'm trying to buy as much of it as I can, but right now, it's goddamn expensive. After Sebastian, I'll ask for one more day. Then we'll kill Godfrey. Then we can go wherever they want us to go, because none of it will matter anymore. They won't be able to hurt her. *Us.*

Prescott considers it before nodding once. "Okay, but promise me that we will?"

"Baby-Cakes," I warn. "You know I only promise things I can deliver. By the time tomorrow rolls around, I'm not sure you're still going to want to do it."

Knowing that Godfrey is going to be stalking every single motel near Stockton, we decide to blindside him and check into a Marriott in Santa Clara, some long miles away from Godfrey's wise guys and snitches. The Marriott has top-notch security, and when we check in, we specifically ask for our room to be located in the middle of a hallway. The receptionist looks at us like we're complete freaks but doesn't ask any questions.

Prescott's one-thousand-dollar piggy bank is running thin, and when I carry her backpack to the room, I tell her it's time to go downtown and get some more dough. She fidgets with the hem of her tattered red dress, looking down, *looking guilty*, before her gaze glides back up to meet mine. The deflated smile on her face tells me everything I don't want to hear. I just saved her ass, telling Godfrey I'll kill him before he gets his hands on her, and all this time, she's been keeping something from me.

"Nate." She sniffs and stops walking, avoiding my face. "Please don't be mad."

But it's too late, I already am. We stop by the door to our hotel room. It's hard to stay calm under the stress of our current existence.

"What now?" I grunt.

"There's something you should know before we. . .before we go to the bank."

Fuck, no. More complications? This chick is like a fucking infection. She spreads inside you, fast, then before you know it. . .boom, you're dead.

"Spill it."

Her eyes are hard on the floor. We don't have time for this shit.

"Prescott."

She just sniffs. *Fuck!*

"Prescott, are you broke?"

She doesn't answer, just shakes her head, fat tears dropping from her lower eyelashes.

Fuck me.

"Prescott!" My voice notches up. An impending storm passes through her eyes. My peace is collapsing. How can this girl ruin yet make everything better at the very same time? I knew the little witch was a fraud, but my dick dragged me into her mess.

And now an entirely different organ is keeping me from smashing my fist into her face.

She conned me. Fucking set me up. She can't pay me, can't help me, and I'm about to run away penniless, with not a dime to my name. I have about five hundred bucks in my bank account, and I need to withdraw them before my parole officer realizes I favored a crusade against drug lords to sitting pretty in my crumbling house, playing nice.

"How much money have you got?" I pin her to the wall by the neck. Not erotically. Not longingly. But not too painfully either. My eyes play her a horror film that'll become her reality if she doesn't comply, and she quickly settles back into her role as a captive and a victim, pinching her lips together. I squeeze harder. "How much? In all of your bank accounts. Altogether. What's your funds situation? You better not fucking lie to me."

"About two grand," she whimpers, looking scared beyond belief. And I hate it. And I hate *her*. My skin is burning with anger. "Probably, like, two grand."

I pick up her backpack from the floor with one hand and clasp her arm with the other, leading her back to the elevators in a bruising grip.

"We're withdrawing everything we have right now."

"Why?" she questions. "I can take it out whenever I want. The police aren't after *me*."

"*Yet*," I snap. "We don't know what Godfrey has in store for us."

Ten minutes later, we cancelled our room reservation, got a full refund and are walking into Bank of America. We take out her money, almost $2,500. I do the same. I end up having $780.

With the money in my pocket—Prescott doesn't argue or asks any questions as she hands over every penny she has—we drive north, looking for a hideaway. We can't stay where we withdrew money. It's too risky.

We wander into a small motel in Martinez an hour later, and the reason it appeals to us is because no one speaks English here and there's no way we'll get ratted out. It looks a lot like our Los Angeles hotel, only not under the haze and charm of doing this together, Bonnie and Clyde style. I haven't spoken to her since I found out she's almost as poor as I am.

Locking the door to another dingy shithole behind us, I give her a warning: "Stay here. Don't move. Don't fucking breathe. I'm getting in the shower. Watch the window and holler if you see anything fishy."

The minute the cold water hits my skin, I hear a screech. *Ignore it.* She probably sat on the crumbling bed. Better yet, she probably opened the door and took off again. This time I won't be chasing her. It's her funeral if she wants to keep wandering alone when kingpins put a bounty on her head.

Another screech.

I'm suddenly aware that Prescott may have company outside. Company she hasn't invited.

Pulling my jeans over my wet thighs in a hurry, I jump out and kick the door open. A horror scene plays before my eyes.

There's the guy who drove the RAM earlier today sitting on top of Pea. She's pinned under him against the dirty mattress, and he's throwing punches at her. She dodges some of them, clawing into his eyes with her nail-less fingers, screaming and kicking. She's hurting him. He's yelling, twisting his head violently, trying to escape her fingers. My storm is blinding him with her strength. A ruthless bitch. *My* ruthless bitch.

Then I notice a huge, pink and fresh bruise on her left cheek, and a little blood trickling from her nose.

My nostrils flare and my jaw tightens. I blink my eyes open, and it's like I'm watching everything through a first-person shooter video game and I'm about to die. The edges of my vision are splattered with red and everything darkens. In a few seconds, I won't be able to see anything at all.

He hurt Pea, and he's going to pay.

I jump onto his back and peel him off of her, dragging him by his neck and throwing him against the wall. He's not going to die. He's going to live.

Too bad for him.

Pinning him until his body molds with the exposed bricks, I signal her with my index finger to come closer behind my back. Her figure appears next to me in no time. My fingers sink into the flesh of his neck, cutting off his air.

"What's your name?" I ask the young guy. He looks to be in his early twenties, fat, thuggish and ugly. There's a red handprint of her small palm across his cheek.

"I ain't telling you nothing," he hisses out, along with whatever oxygen's still left in him, and then spits blood. Prescott hands me my dagger, and I shove it deep into his thigh, until I hear the tear of his pants as the edge pokes through the other side of his leg.

"All right, let's go through your options"—I shrug, sporting a polite smile—"Tell me what your name is, and you'll live, plus, I'll let you go. I got a little message to send Godfrey, anyway. However, if you do not cooperate, I will kill you, find out who you are, then go and butcher your family. Seeing as you know who I am, I trust you'll go with the sane, user-friendly option number one. Now, I'll ask again—what's your name?"

"T-T-T-Tony," he sobs, snot running down into his mouth. What a fucking wimp. It makes what Prescott went through with her chin up so much more admirable.

"Listen to me carefully, T-T-T-Tony," I repeat mockingly, yanking his cell out of his pocket. "Call your backup downstairs and tell them you need help dragging our bodies down. When he gets up here, we're going to sit down and discuss your next move. Am I clear?"

He nods frantically and follows my instructions. Three minutes later, another guy walks in. He's black and tall, and looks like he's seen a ghost when he enters the room. Prescott points with her stress ball to the corner where T-T-T-Tony sits.

"Please, sit down. Would you like anything to drink?" Her upper-class manners kick in, and our new guest's mouth hangs open.

I drag the dagger out of the first guy's thigh, slowly as I possibly can so that it'll hurt more than necessary, and bring the dagger to the black man's throat, the blade stroking the pulse in his neck.

"You know you've been playing for the losing team, right?" I poke at his skin, producing a pea-sized dot of blood, before withdrawing it and admiring the blood at the tip of the blade from all angles. "The good news is, you can still atone for your mistake."

The dagger flies down the guy's T-shirt, and I tear it almost completely, letting the blood on it stain the cloth. I squat down to his legs and slash his pants. Then I go back up and punch him in the face, so that it'll look like he's been in a fight. All while Tony is still slumped against the wall, staring at his thigh wound in horror while holding his leg like it's about to run away and leave him behind at any moment.

"Here, that looks better. Now, as the lady said, please sit down." I throw him head first to collapse next to his injured friend and then bend down.

"Gentlemen, driver's licenses." I open my palm and wait for them to slap their IDs into it. I'm starting to think that this is the best thing that's ever happened to us, being discovered by two of Godfrey's wise guys. Prescott writes down their names and addresses on the back of her hand with a pen we stole from the motel. As if she'd ever use 'em.

"Caleb," I go through the black guy's wallet, walking back and forth in the tiny room that's now crowded, with three grown men and my girl inside it. "I see you're a baby-daddy. She's cute. I'd hate to fuck her up, ya' know?

Look at that smile." I pass his wallet to Prescott. There's a toddler, around two years old, in a photo behind the dirty plastic of his wallet. A big, innocent smile adorns her sweet face, pink flowers in her braids. Pea tsks and shakes her head, playing along with my game. "We can make a good buck selling her across the border. Too cute," she agrees, straight-faced. I almost snicker. I'd rather slit my wrists than hurt a kid, but *he* doesn't know that. He thinks like a scumbag. And sadly, a part of me, the fresh-out-of-San-Dimas part, thinks like one, too.

"What about this guy?" Prescott nods her chin to Tony. "Who has he got to lose?"

"Please," Tony gulps. "No."

"Yeah," I reply, throwing Caleb's wallet into Pea's hands and flipping through Tony's paperwork. "We know everything about you. But you only need to know one thing about us—to Godfrey and Seb, we're dead. Go there. Tell them you killed us. Take our clothes with you. Take some of Prescott's hair. Tell them you dragged our bodies out at night, to avoid drawing attention. Make them think they're not in danger. Disobey, and I will slay each and every one of your relatives."

Tony lives in Stockton, and judging from the screensaver on his phone, he's got a girlfriend. One he wouldn't like to see in a coffin.

"How can we be sure they won't rat us out, anyway?" I hear Pea enquire from behind me. That's a fine question, with a very fine answer.

"They'll have us on speaker phone the whole time. From the moment their asses hit the seats in their car, to their point of destination in Godfrey's office. Try and signal to him, scribble something down or warn the old man—and I'll know. I'll go straight to your families. I've got the addresses."

"Godfrey's order was to bring you in alive," Caleb jeers, rubbing his swollen cheek.

"We put up a good fight. It was a life or death situation. He'd rather us be dead than still on the run." Bullshit. Godfrey will kill them, they're deadweight, collateral damage, the minute they come back empty-handed.

But they don't need to know that.

"You sure?" Tony's shiny, crooked eyes glance over to Prescott, who stands behind me. She nods.

"Positive."

We escort Tony and Caleb back to the RAM and press the call button. We hear everything, sitting on the bed and listening to their every move. They drive silently, grunting and whimpering the whole journey. We hear the noisy road and the bell of the elevator to Godfrey's office building, which I recognize, and we hear them delivering the news we put in their mouths.

Nothing to worry about.

Nate and Prescott are dead.

The bodies will be retrieved soon after dark falls.

"Why should I believe you?" Godfrey's voice is dripping doubt. There's shuffling over the line, presumably the sound of the men producing the chunk of Prescott's hair which we plucked out of her skull—from the root, we simply had to—smeared in their own blood. And I know they must be showing him one of her stress balls and a slice of my black jeans. "We'll go back up to Martinez and get the rest at night. We couldn't do it in broad daylight."

"My people will handle it," God growls. "You better not be lying."

More whimpers. "Godfrey, we'd never."

"I know, because then you'd be dead."

No, motherfucker. By the time you figure out we're alive, they'll have already packed up their shit and their loved ones and have run away from your claws, I think to myself.

The phone conversation doesn't end until they crawl back to the hole where they came from, but I'm not worried about them coming back to warn Godfrey. He may be powerful, but not as powerful as their love for their families. We disconnect the phone call that had us sitting in thick silence for hours, our only form of communication was our eyes. The minute I click the line dead, Prescott turns to me, pink on her cheeks.

"I was going to tell you sooner," she mumbles, staring at her hands resting on her thighs. "About being broke. What was I supposed to do? Let you hand me over to Godfrey?"

I shake my head. It's not an answer, but it's the only thing she'll get right now.

I'm about to head into the bathroom to try and finish that shower I started a few hours ago. Prescott flings up to her feet, standing in front of me. I scan her, my lower lip pulling my upper one in frustration.

"You're in my way." I warn.

"Baby. . ." It's the first time she's called me that, and her hazels are two pools of misery. They beg me for something. I'm not sure what, but know that it's already hers. "When this is all over, I'll give you everything I've got left. I'll walk out of this with nothing but my bag. I promise you, Nate. Just please forgive me. I can't bear the thought of you hating me."

That's another problem I'll have to deal with. I can't let her walk away penniless. She's a lone, beautiful girl in this dark world, and she's as poor as my fucking social skills. She'll have to pay her way through her next meal somehow.

I know exactly how.

And I'd never let it happen.

"Where the fuck did all your money go, huh?" I push her away, angry heat rolling from my body. "You sure as hell were able to afford a glitzy-ass apartment in Danville, and last time I checked, the crack business ain't exactly in recession." She looks away, embarrassed. Her eyes catch a glimpse of the outside through the filthy window, following the graceful movements of a tiny bird.

"Private investigators." She swallows. "I wanted to find out what happened to my brother."

"Goddamn," I groan, rubbing my face with my palms.

"They all came back with the same conclusion, either he left the states or he's dead."

Whimper. Sniff. Less storm. More heartbreak.

I have to tell her.

"Look, I didn't bring it up until now because I didn't think it meant shit, but when I was working in Blackhawk, I bumped into your old man at a grocery store. He's been telling people your brother went to college on the east coast."

Her brows knit together. "My brother dropped out of high school," she tells me, and I nod. That's what Mrs. Hathaway said as well. There's a second in which her eyes flicker with understanding, and she realizes what this means.

"He's covering up something." Her jaw clenches. I drop my forehead to meet her blonde little head. She knows the drill. Plot threads connect. Pieces fall together. He's probably not alive, and if he is—he's not well.

"Whatever happened to him, my father knows."

I tug at her blonde locks softly, planting a kiss on her head. "What else did he say?"

I'm not going to tell her what he said about *her*. The way I hurt her. . .it's different. I don't want to break her, I don't want to cut deep. I just want her body to feel what I feel when I see her come alive in my hands. No. Inflicting real pain on her, the kind that stays under your skin, is something I'm incapable of doing.

"Nothing," I lie. "Overheard him making small talk with some dude in a bowtie."

"Mr. Simpson," she gasps. "How did he look? My dad?"

"Like a sack of shit who created something beautiful and doesn't know how to take care of it." Raw truth leaves my mouth. "Forget about him, Cockburn. He's a nobody. But what else are you hiding, Pea? Godfrey said something about you having a kid."

Her eyes narrow and she takes a step back. "I don't." She shakes her head, fighting more tears. "I don't have a kid."

"Another lie?" I tilt my head down, inspecting her. She's hiding something.

"I swear, I'm not a mother," she finishes quietly, looking away.

I make a move, resuming my quest for the shower, but her hand ghosts over my abs, stopping me. Then she goes and does something completely unreasonable. *She hugs me.* Straight up embraces me with both her arms. I don't think I've been hugged in, well, ever? So I just stand, rooted to the ground, not sure what to do, my arms flailing at the side of my body. She squeezes harder, burying her face in my chest, the scent of her coconut shampoo drifting into my nose.

"I'm sorry. And I'd completely understand if you abandon ship. You have a fake passport, you have the Beatmobile. I'll give you my money. All yours. Just please. . .forgive me. That was *before*."

Before we found out we were more than just fugitives with the same hit list.

I peel her away from my body, keeping her a step away from me by holding her shoulders.

"You fucked up," I grunt.

"I know," she murmurs, but her chin is up, liquid fire in her eyes. *Still my fucking fighter, ready to break some bones.*

"But here's the thing, Pea," I rub her split lower lip, the one that keeps healing and breaking again and again, before I plant a kiss on the dry scab. "You're a shit person. You're a liar, a con and a witch. You're a storm, and you want to hurt those who hurt you. You're bad. And when you're mad? You're even worse. Capable of lying. Of deceiving. Even, I suspect, of killing. And I love you. I'm wholeheartedly, desperately, unapologetically in love with your sorry ass."

Her mouth falls open, probably because I just made an already complex situation even more explosive, but I continue, undeterred. "You know why? Because you pulled laughter out of me like no one else has. You made me smile more in three weeks than I've smiled in my entire twenty-seven years. That's enough payment, in my opinion."

"You love me?" she whispers, pointing to herself, disbelief coloring every corner of her face. I nod once.

"I do. I love you." *I love her.*

"Say it again."

"I love you," I say louder, understanding her need to hear it.

No mom. No dad. God knows where her brother is. She needs it. She's getting it. I'm going to give her everything she wants before we say our goodbyes.

I erase the space I created between us—I hated it anyway. "I love a chick named Cockburn," I admit, "and even more embarrassing, I love a girl named Prescott. I love you, Pea. I love you, Miss Burlington-Smyth. Who else?"

Her arms circle around my neck, our bodies sticking together. There's that smile. That beautiful, confident smirk that even Sebastian couldn't wipe off with his fists and pointy shoes. "I'm sure you can think of a few other things to call me. Words are your trade."

"I love you, Hot Ass." I grab her butt and crush it, until she flinches in pain, and release slowly, knowing that she clenches from the inside every time I hurt her. "I love everything about you. The sun-kissed freckles on your shoulders and your taste in books and music and the way you laugh, that angelic blonde hair, and the way you let me lick your crack when you know I've had a long, stressful day."

She laughs, but her face coils in agony. We're either not getting out of this shit alive, or if we do, we're going our separate ways. I can't stay in the states and she has nothing to do in Mexico. Besides, I know her by now. She'll try and find her brother, dig until the truth hits her in her pretty face with a fucking shovel.

Her hands roam my chest and when she looks back up, her eyes are menacing.

"I miss the feeling of your cock filling every space in my body," she admits.

"It misses you too," I breathe, pulling her to the bed and yanking her into my lap. She sits on top of me like I'm Santa and she's a shy kid, but my plans for her are the kind of shit children under eighteen aren't supposed to see.

"Maybe it's time him and I get together again. Release some of that tension. Tonight is a big night." She wiggles her brows. I pat my junk.

"Show me what you've got."

"Prepare to be amazed, Mr. Delaware." Her husky voice trails downwards, kissing its way from my throat to my chest. She stops with her lips on my neck and pushes me back, until I'm lying down, then continues her journey south.

"Just don't suck Delaware Jr. You're terrible at giving head," I warn when she unbuttons my jeans. Who am I shitting? I'm dying for those pinks to meet my dick again.

My jeans are tossed aside and she peppers my groin with wet, starving kisses, her eyes are closed, and she looks *pained*. Not the kind of pain I want her to be in; not the kind I can control.

I play with her hair, admiring the view under my chest. She doesn't stop kissing the swollen flesh of my cock, dragging her tongue and treating it like a lollipop. This is actually pretty good.

"I love your monster cock," she sighs and I groan, letting my head fall back to the flat pillow. Her hand snakes under me, and she caresses my asshole with one finger while massaging my balls with her thumb. *Fuck.*

"Actually, I love this whole area."

"It thinks of you highly, too," I reassure. Her mouth finds my balls. I'm so turned on I might blind her with a shot of cum. She spends a minute or so sucking on them, licking them slowly, tickling, creating tension that's begging for release, before I yank her up and throw her aggressively, her back slamming into the mattress.

"I love it when you're rough with me," she continues, but I shut her up with a kiss. "It reminds me of Beat. That's who I'd like to have sex with tonight."

I throw my head back and laugh. I'll humor her if she wants Beat. Hell, I kind of miss him too. He liberated me from a face that's been a distraction and objectified me like I'm a fucking Playboy Bunny for years. I prop myself up on one elbow and send my arm to her backpack on the nightstand, pulling the mask out.

"You sure about that? Nate was in the mood for slow, fun sex. Beat's an angry motherfucker."

She nods. "He has good reasons to be. You don't let him loose too often. Tell him I want him to destroy me."

"Message received."

I hear the snap of the rubber against my skull as I put the mask on and arrange it so my eyes meet hers through the tiny holes. She curls into herself, looking scared in the best possible way.

I roll on a condom with one hand and pull her hair to yank her up with the other. My voice, which is always dry and low but is somewhat forgiving when directed at Pea, looms into something beastly.

"You scared?"

"Yes," she says breathlessly.

"Good. At least your instincts are still in check."

I drag her by her hair until she falls on the floor, her knees hitting the wood with a loud thump. I stand above her, my erection in her face. She whimpers in pain, rubbing her injured legs and looking up at me for further instruction.

"Take off your dress. *Without* standing up."

She worms out of it quickly, her eyes still trained on the floor, too scared to look up.

"Now crawl to the window and sit your naked ass on the sill. Facing *me*."

She starts crawling seductively, rolling her hips, a glitter of wetness sparkling at me from between her thighs. Her pussy's already peppered with some hair that's grown back. I kick her ass with a growl. "Faster, Country Club. We got business to attend to."

By the time she waits for me with her legs wide open, sitting on the windowsill, her naked body pressed against the glass, with everyone in the fucking neighborhood watching her milky white ass, I'm just about ready to burst. The pink of her pussy peeks at me demurely between her dark blonde patch. I stride, completely naked except for my mask, in her direction. Every step I take, she shrinks into a smaller version of herself. Petrified. I love that. I crack my neck and my fingers like I'm getting ready for a fight. When I'm inches from her, I stop.

"You really did a number on me, didn't you, Silver Spoon?"

Her gaze travels up and her chin sticks out. "Please hurt me."

I allow her a small moment of silence and anticipation—and then I do.

I slam my sheathed cock between her thighs, finally feeling home again, and slap her ass with a whip that sounds like a scream.

Time.

I wish it'd freeze right now so I could have her this way forever. Nothing in the world will ever live up to this moment. I fuck her against the window and peek through the curtain of her soft hair as she moans Beat's name again and again and again, digging my dirty fingers into her ass. There's a small crowd forming under our window, a few Mexican men back from their day of work and two black teenagers. One of them sticks his hand inside his pants when he catches a glimpse of my girl rolling her head sideways, exposing those full pink lips and long lashes behind her long pale hair. With every thrust she bangs against the window, her silky flesh pressing against it for all to see and admire.

"Beat," she wails, touching the mask, and I feel my cum making its way to the tip of my dick. I swat her hands away and use the base of my palm to bang her head against the window as a warning. "No touching."

"But, Beat," she sighs again, a little frustrated, her pussy clenching around me in a death grip. She's about to explode on my cock. Pea thrashes and bucks, rolling her hips frantically, her inner thighs soaking and dripping with her want for whatever form of me she's calling to. Neither of us answer.

"Bring me Nate again," she pleads and bites into my skin, trying to claw the mask away from my face, but I don't let her. Every attempt to peel the mask off is rewarded with a loud spank. She comes hard, tightening with a force that almost traps my cock in her pussy. "I need to tell Nate something important." Her mouth almost drips with ecstasy.

I wait for our releases to subside, throw another look to our audience and yank her off the windowsill. She trips into my chest and finally peels my mask away, almost tearing the rubber in the process.

"Nate?" her uncertainty almost makes me laugh.

I'm drenched in sweat and bliss, but I know I need to get my ass into this shower and bolt out of this room before the police end up nailing us for indecent exposure. Wouldn't that be ironic?

"Yeah?"

Her face battles surprise, her eyebrows knitting together.

"I love you. All of you. Your perfect face. Your beautiful soul. Your ugly deeds."

"Say it," I demand, collecting her hair into a ponytail I let loose over her left shoulder. "Again."

No mom. No dad. No siblings. I need it. I'm getting it. I'm going to take everything she's willing to give me before we say our goodbyes.

"I love you, Nate Vela. And it scares the living hell out of me. Why'd you have to go and steal my heart like this?"

I don't answer her with words. They won't do justice to what I have to say. I kiss her sweet lips that are just starting to heal from splitting open again yesterday. A deep kiss that's not at all sexual. I wouldn't call it romantic or soft, either. But it's intimate. Lazy. Content. Happy. And it's got our names on it.

I pull her into the bathroom with me, and after a quick shower together, we're out of the room and back on the road. We still have a few hours to burn until show time, but we won't spend them like sitting ducks in the apartment where Godfrey's people found us and a bunch of horny bastards watched us having sex. I stop outside a Walgreens and Pea jogs in to buy some stuff for our operation tonight. The automatic doors swallow her but I can still see that bright red mini dress as she walks up and down the aisles.

While staring at her through darkened windows, I come up with a plan. Something that will help us out of the quicksand we're drowning in. It's going to be even harder to face myself after I do it, but I have to do whatever I can to make sure that we've got the best chance of getting out of this shit alive. When Pea is done getting the syringes and nail polish remover, she walks straight out of the Walgreens and inside a neighboring Dollar Store. I punch the steering wheel and curse her silently for making a stop she didn't inform me about.

They think we're dead. Nobody knows what we're up to, I keep reminding myself. But I don't know that for a fact. Wanting to chew my nerves away, I grab the backpack she left here to look for my peach-flavored gum. I find it buried at the bottom of her bag, along with something else I didn't even know still existed. Something I forgot I even had.

I pluck out my red notebook and stare at it, moving it in my hands like it's some sort of magic fucking wand. My prison diary. My words. She always says they're so pretty, but these are my ugly words, the ones she shouldn't be exposed to.

Has she read it? Of course she's read it. Goddammit. She knows my story through and through. The horrid bits and the painful parts. My jaw clenches so hard it almost snaps and pops out of my mouth. I don't even notice when she gets back into the car, falling into her seat in a fit of wild, youthful laughter. The giggles die down quickly the second she sees the diary in my hand.

"Shit," she gulps, swiveling her whole body to face mine. I don't look at her. I'm still staring at my old diary. Violated is not the right word for what I feel. Disgraced comes close, but it's still not quite there.

Her hand grips the door handle, ready to run away, but I dig my fingers into her thigh.

"Five seconds to explain. It better be good."

"I'm sorry I took it without your permission. I tucked it into my dress when you carried me from the basement before we. . ."

Before we fucked like animals. She knew everything about me. And she still wanted to do it.

I love her.

"It didn't feel right to leave a part of you back in that awful place. Your words deserve freedom, not that dingy basement. Besides—" She hesitates.

"Besides?"

"That red diary made me fall in love with you," she finishes.

A few seconds pass before I hand her the notebook and motion with my chin to the nylon bags she's holding.

"Got everything?"

She nods. "Can I take your diary with me when we're done? You were going to leave it behind anyway, and I want to carry your words with me everywhere I go," she says quietly, not meeting my eyes.

"Take whatever you want." I rub my face in frustration before looking away. I mean it too. If she wanted my balls, I'd hand them over in a heartbeat. But man, it's hard to talk about the day after we part ways. "Just keep it safe."

"It's yours. Of course I'll keep it safe," she says. I believe her.

In a lot of ways, she's already saved me.

PRESCOTT

When night falls, our guards go up.

It didn't surprise us that Seb arrived at the club clad in a dapper, checkered gray and red suit, accompanied by two bodyguards.

Sebastian may believe we're dead, but he knows there's still a chance we're after him. And him? He's after young boys. Sex is a drive just as powerful as revenge. Tonight, he is going to find that out.

We sit low inside a white Tacoma Nate broke into earlier tonight. He said Seb might recognize the Beatmobile and besides, he missed Stella. We made a stop in West Oakland, where he strode into an alley, yanked an antenna from one of the parked cars, wedged a space in the door and effortlessly hit the unlock button.

"Looks like you're an expert when it comes to breaking into cars," I said in hushed disdain when he slid into the driver's seat.

"Yeah, well, you didn't look out of your element yourself when you broke into your apartment." Touché.

We watch Sebastian breeze through the doors of Think Pink, a gay nightclub just on the curve of Mission Street, without even coming face to face with the bouncer. I recognize the two muscle men who plucked me out of that Oakland alley the night he found me and handed me to Nate.

I don't feel too bad about hurting his soldiers—they didn't shed a tear when they handed me over to death row—but I hope Seb doesn't come out of here with an innocent, unsuspecting one-night stand. That would be a complication we don't need right now.

Beside me, Nate is flicking a Zippo lighter absentmindedly, moving his jaw from side to side while chewing on his peachy gum. The fire engulfed by his huge palms is dancing on his irises, revealing the complete peace behind them.

He doesn't look like boyfriend-material right now, despite his good looks.

He doesn't even look like Beat, the scary masked man who takes violently but with consent.

He looks. . .like a killer.

And Godfrey told him about my child. He knows.

"How come you're not nervous?" I ask, shifting with discomfort that has nothing to do with the small space we're sharing and eyeing the entrance to the club religiously. We can't afford to lose Seb. With little means and barely any intel, tonight is our only clear shot.

Nate shrugs, rolling his gum with his tongue. So serene. So sickeningly serene.

"He rapes young men. He took a piece of my girl's soul. He's a bad guy and he deserves to die."

"Are we good people?" I swallow visibly, ignoring his remark about me being his girl. I can't allow myself to drown in fantasies right now.

"We're better than good," he flashes a smile that doesn't reach his eyes. "We're fair."

Three hours after he walked in, Sebastian leaves the nightclub with his two bodyguards in tow, sans an innocent male companion. My palms are sweaty. I've been constantly wiping them over my bare thighs. Who the hell shows up in a dress to kill someone, anyway? I bet there's a sensible dress code for these kinds of occasions. Well, at least it's red, so I got the bloodstains part covered.

Seb and his men disappear into a flashy silver Cadillac and head out of the city and into the playground where everything, both bad and good, happens. The East Bay.

We follow them silently, careful to have at least two cars between us at all times. Nate is wearing his hoodie and I'm wearing a Raiders cap. Luckily, it's Saturday night and the roads are pretty busy, despite the late hour.

The Cadillac stops outside a glitzy apartment building in Dublin, not too different from the one I was living in just a few weeks ago. Seb steps out of the car, and it's almost too good to be true—I'm literally rubbing my eyes in astonishment—when I see him saluting a curt goodbye to his bodyguards before disappearing through the reception doors.

Jesus Christ, they're not even guarding his apartment from inside. He's just leaving them there, on the street, sitting in their car, in the unlikely case we show up. The driver folds his arms over his chest and closes his eyes, while the guy in the passenger seat takes out an iPhone, playing a game, the glowing screen highlighting his broken nose and a jaw the shape of a rock.

My gaze meets Nate's, and he's already grinning from ear to ear. A lucky break that fell from the sky and right into our laps.

We wait for a few more minutes, looking up, watching the light on the second floor of the building as it switches on. Nate slides the car past the crosswalk, making sure there's an easy getaway route in case we need to make a move quickly, and once the engine is off, he turns to me, grabbing my shoulders so that I'm facing him.

"Sure you wanna do this? I won't hold it against you if you pussy out. No shame in changing your mind, Baby-Cakes."

I snort, shaking my head. These men are going down. I appreciate him giving me an opening to back away, but I wanted to kill them before he, and his golden dick, marched into my life.

"I'm good," I say.

He angles forward, grabbing me by the back of my neck and placing a kiss on top of my head. "You're not good, you're the fucking best."

Taking out the syringes from the Walgreens bag and the tin with the drugs, I mix a deadly cocktail of cocaine and nail polish remover, shaking it together into something that'll leave his bodyguards begging for their deaths. I know this powdered crack, and it's full of the worst ingredients the market has to offer. If the ammonia and rat poison straight to the veins don't kill them—the nail polish remover will finish the job.

All I need to do is make sure I hit the right spot. But years of dealing with junkies who resorted to sticking needles in their feet and genitals made me somewhat of an expert on human anatomy when it comes to where to stick a needle—even in battlefield situations.

Sliding out of the car first, Nate—clad in his mask and hoodie—walks in the direction of their car, hands shoved in his pockets. When he stops in front of the driver's window, he taps it with his gloved knuckles. I watch from the Tacoma as the window rolls down and a meaty hand darts in his direction, trying to stab him in the stomach with a sharp object. He dodges the knife elegantly and twists the guy's arm out of the window, breaking it against the door with a popping sound that makes me swallow back a lump of puke. The arm dangles limply. Nate's mask lifts and his eyes zero in on me. It's my cue. I open my door and run in his direction, clutching the syringes in a death grip. He nods toward the broken armed man, and I jam a needle into a nice, blue vein in his neck. Nate is already dealing with the Candy Crush guy, who had time to round the car with a gun at his waist, a gun he is clutching on to but doesn't pull out. Shooting someone on Main Street is not a stellar idea. Even he knows it.

"Put the gun down." I hear Nate's low growl dripping authority and immediately come to the depressing realization that I needed someone like him all this time. If he were by my side when I first tried to take my enemies down, they'd be long gone by now. "The chick behind me has two Magnums, and she won't hesitate to make Swiss cheese out of your saggy ass if you point that shit at me. Pull your sleeve up and gimme your arm."

"And why the hell would I do that?" The muscle man panics, waving the gun in the air but not at anyone in particular. "Whaddaya' need my arm for?"

"Baby-Cakes," Nate signals for me to come closer. The broken armed guy foams out of his mouth, gagging as my lethal cocktail fills his blood stream with pure venom, but Candy Crush can't see it, since his friend's upper body is spilling out of the window in the opposite direction. I eat up the space to Nate and the armed muscle guy. "Tell the man why you need his arm."

"So I can poison you," I smirk. The guy turns around and tries to bolt for the apartment building, but Nate hooks his fingers into the back of his collar and swings him effortlessly into a back alley behind a local restaurant. Muscle Man is slammed against a trash dumpster and crashes to the ground. Nate picks up his gun and unloads the revolver, throwing the weapon into the trash.

We could have used that gun.

I know he says guns are for pussies, but what the hell does he think I have between my legs, an In-N-Out Burger?

"Give me the keys to his apartment," Nate barks at Seb's bodyguard, his voice uncharacteristically loud.

"I don't have them."

Kick to the stomach. Muscle Guy rolls into the fetal position, wincing and hugging his middle. Nate picks him up, opens the heavy lid to the dumpster and shoves his face into it. The guy's limbs are flailing. He can't breathe. Lifting the lid, Nate yanks him up by his hair, and the guy gasps, gulping oxygen.

"Keys, asshole. Don't make me fondle you."

"I don't have keys to his place!"

Another kick, this time straight to the face. Blood. Blood and dust everywhere. The scent of his life seeping away makes me gag and shiver, but on the outside, I'm leaning a shoulder against the wall, crossing my arms and snickering.

This guy didn't flinch when Seb kidnapped me from that Oakland Street.

"Do you want to know what it feels like when your organs explode from the inside? It's about to happen."

"I told you! I. Don't. Have. . ."

Another kick, this one to his back, but he doesn't scream and writhe this time, which makes me put a hand on Nate's lower back. Peace can be violent. I've learned that from my short time with him.

"Baby, time is wasting. He's not worth killing. Let's go."

My lover squats down and looks through the guy's jeans to see if he has the key. He doesn't. I think the man is either out or dead, but we don't bother checking as we make our way back to the main street.

We wait patiently behind a giant plant decorating the entrance of the building, and once a drunken man in a suit uses the touch-screen keypad and pushes the front door open, we muscle our way in, shoving him deeper inside. We bustle into a lobby that's probably wired with countless cameras. Doesn't matter, as our faces are covered down to our necks. My Frankenstein mask is anything but sexy, but it does the job.

"What the. . .?" The young, suited man stumbles his way past the plush sofas and toward the elevators, and we follow him, Nate holding the middle of his dress shirt like he's a dog on a leash, jabbing the elevator button with his gloved finger.

"Good evening, Sir." Nate's voice is as cheery as his Guy Fawkes mask. "Had a good time tonight?"

The guy stares at him with eyes like two, shiny moons and nods his head slowly, not paying me any attention. Despite my scary mask, you can still see that I'm small, curvy and a woman.

The silver doors slide open and the three of us walk into the elevator, Nate still holding the poor guy by his shirt.

"Floor?" he asks politely.

"Two." The guy's throat bobs, and our masks turn toward one another in a silent celebration.

"That's exactly where we're heading. What apartment does Sebastian Goddard live in?"

The guy's lips are pursed. He's looking at Beat's mask with fear, watered down by suspicion. "Look," he starts. "I don't want any trouble. . ."

The elevator pings again, and Nate thrusts him into the hallway of the second floor in a firm shove. "I believe you. Which is why you should start singing right about now. Apartment number?"

"But. . ."

"Number, kiddo."

"I don't know," the guy exhales. He's lying. It's that little twitch in his lips that gives him away. The building complex is small, and there are no more than ten apartments on every floor.

"Let's try again." Nate throws the guy's back into the wall, hard enough to break a bone or two. "This time, we'll use a little thing called honesty, okay? Keep in mind that it's late, and my companion has a curfew. She should be in my bed in approximately forty minutes, and every minute I'm here, talking to *you* instead of fucking *her*, is a terrible inconvenience for us both."

I flush red and my thighs clutch together.

"Show me to Sebastian Goddard's door. Now."

This time Nate speckles his request with a fist to the guy's nose, and his head finds a glassed painting behind him. The frame shatters, raining glass on the guy's face. Nate has to yank him back out by pulling on his short, damp hair.

"Okay. Okay. Fine! It's apartment 34. Now please, just please, let me go."

"Happily. We'll even escort you to your place."

The guy looks between me and Nate like this is some kind of a terrible conspiracy. Nevertheless, Nate herds him to the far corner of the hallway, hurrying past apartment 34. When I notice the number, my heart thumps so hard against my chest, it a hurts my ribs. The guy looks between us and his door, sighs, and takes out his keys, pushing his door ajar. Nate walks into his apartment, and I follow suit.

What's he doing?

Where is he taking this?

We already have Seb's apartment number, why is he still harassing the poor guy?

Nate walks around the living room, his fist still clutching the fabric of this guy's collar. "Nice place." He pushes the guy to sit on the floor under his kitchen sink and jams his wrists against one of the cabinet handles. Next thing he does is take the black cloth he used to cuff me with out of his back pocket and wrap the guy's arms tightly against the doors. So tight, in fact, that the guy grimaces and jerks his head from side to side, fighting tears.

"Oh, shit, oh, no," the guy curses, and Nate shakes his head and throws me a glance from behind his shoulder.

"Just for the record, it was so much more fun to handcuff you, Baby-Cakes."

I flip Nate the bird and he laughs. I love this guy so much, the need to be around him overwhelms me. So perfect. So flawed. Ironically, in very similar ways.

Nate squats down, shoves his hand into the guy's pocket and takes out his cell phone, tossing it aside. It lands on the floor on the opposite side of the living room in a bang.

"Sorry, bud. It ain't personal. You look like an all right kid, but see, we can't chance you calling the cops on us. Thank you for your cooperation and have a wonderful weekend. And let me just spare you the guilt trip—we would've found him with or without your help. So don't spend a minute thinking you were responsible for Mr. Goddard's death." He slaps Suit's cheek endearingly. "Sleep tight."

Nate stands up, hooks his arm around my shoulder and guides me out of the apartment. We close the door silently and pour back into the hallway. When we get to Sebastian's door, holding hands, our bodies draw deep breaths in perfect harmony.

It's happening. I'm getting that piece of my soul back.

"He's mine," I whisper, more to myself than to him.

"He's yours," Nate whispers back. "So am I. So is everything in this fucking world, as long as I'm by your side. I love you, Storm."

"I love you, Peace." My heart collapses with excitement, flowing in dangerous waves. It's like feeling an emotional orgasm, and I blink away my tears. By the time I open my eyes, Nate releases his hold on my hand, takes a step back, gaining momentum, and kicks the door down with a loud bang that fills the hallway with noise and my gut with fear.

"Surprise, motherfucker," Beat's mask announces into the thin, cold air of Sebastian Goddard's apartment. "Guess what? We're alive, well, and fucking pissed."

It's show time.

Sebastian's living room looks like a psychiatric ward. The walls are heavily padded, due to his inability to stand the sound of life. Furniture, couch, paintings, and even the TV is white. Everything is hollow, empty and bleached. Arranged neatly and obsessively in straight lines. Nothing is misplaced and everything has a purpose.

Nate moves smoothly toward the bedroom at the end of the hallway. Again, I find myself following, kicking myself mentally for thinking I could have done this on my own.

Nate kicks Seb's bedroom door open to find him already up on his feet, reaching for his gun and loading it with bullets. His quivering fingers fail him. He's wearing boxer briefs and a plain white dress shirt. He was going to sleep good tonight, thinking he's safe. It makes me hate him even more.

I haven't slept well in years. Not since what they did to me.

Beat rushes to his side and sends an uppercut right to his jaw, stunning him with the impact of his strength. Sebastian stumbles back and lands with his back against the bedframe, his ass hitting the carpeted floor. The gun drops to his feet and I hurry to pick it up and fill the revolver with kisses I'd like to plant on his skin, just like the one he left on my forehead before we said our goodbyes the last time we saw each other.

"How did you—" he starts, not quite sure what's going on.

"Seek, and you shall find," Nate explains. "We found, motherfucker."

"You're supposed to be dead," he whispers.

"Yeah, well," I say with a shrug, "killing you sounded better."

My idea of fun is killing everyone.

"Remember what we said, Baby-Cakes. Guns are for pussies. Only Seb, Godfrey and the likes of them use 'em," Nate reminds me, casually picking Seb up in a chokehold. Sebastian roars in pain, in the same way I held myself back from doing when he hurt me less than a month ago. The man I love leads him out of his bedroom with his grip.

"Yell, and I'm cutting off your balls and letting you bleed out while you're gagged. Shut up, and I let my girl decide how she wants to finish you," Nate singsongs.

"*Your girl*," Seb spits. "Oh, *Diabla*. Always fucking your way to more drama."

"And you love watching," I say, still holding his gun close to my thigh. We all stumble to the padded living room, where noise is swallowed from the inside and out.

"Ah, men and their love for dangerous pussy," Seb huffs. "No wonder I prefer dick. Less hassle."

Beat thrusts Sebastian's face into the nearest framed picture, and the blow is so intense, Seb almost crashes back against the opposite wall. His face is now full of little shards of glass poking out of his skin.

"Oops. At least you didn't yell like a bitch this time. Good dog."

Nate throws Sebastian on the sofa and kneels down, so that he is at eye-level with him behind his mask.

"You know, Seb? Out of all the things you did in prison, out of all the boys you raped, the people you conned, the murders you plotted, there's one thing that sticks out for me." His voice is so calm. So *light*. He's my peace, and having him around right now ensures that I won't get dragged into a tempest of fear and pain. "You watched my girl being raped," Nate finished. "And you got off on it."

Seb's small, gleaming eyes travel up to meet mine. When our gazes lock, he uses whatever strength he has left to pull a satisfied smirk. "It was bloody fantastic. Watching them tossing her around like a football. Father and son. Pass after pass after pass. Kick after kick after kick."

My stomach turns and rolls. I sway lightly, feeling woozy with humiliation. "There's nothing more erotic than watching a little soul break." His dreamy grin conceals his physical state. "You know? Sometimes I'm not even sure if I'm a homosexual. Maybe I'm not. If they're not young and unwilling, I lose interest. But she. . ." His eyes roam over me in a way that makes me want to hug myself. "She was a weak girl when she got to us, and look at her now. A monster. *Diabla*. I'm proud."

Nate's fist lands on Seb's face, nailing him to the back of the sofa with a thud. The shards dig deeper into his flesh.

"Asshole!"

Seb's face swings back with a bloody smile. "I think the best part was when she bled. Out of her pussy. Out of her arse. Out of her mouth. God, it was beautiful to watch. The rich and entitled became poor and broken."

Another blow follows, and this time I hear Seb's nose crack. He yells, then groans, then swings back up, looking dizzy and disorientated, yet eerily happy. He looks up to me, his head tilting sideways, seemingly unfazed by the thick pool of blood spreading on his white carpet. I can't stop the tears from falling. I'd give up anything to make him shut up.

"Does he know you fell pregnant?" Seb asks, and my vision clouds with thick black mist. "What we had to do to terminate your pregnancy so that we wouldn't have any more whores to look after?"

My knees turn to sand and I feel Nate's gaze slowly revolving in my direction. I lift the hand that holds Seb's gun to his face, but I'm shaking. Shaking so badly, I'm afraid it'll be Nate I end up shooting.

"Pea?" I hear his voice, and for the first time, it's not so peaceful. It's scary. Edgy. It's a nightmare. I shake my head, taking comfort in the fact that the tears are invisible under my Frankenstein mask.

"Move away," I order. He does as he's told, still looking at me. I know he said guns are for pussies, but maybe I am a pussy. Seb took it too far. No. I didn't tell Nate that I fell pregnant when one of these assholes—hell knows if it was Godfrey or his son—knocked me up. Because the way they aborted the baby. . .I shoved it so deep into the back of my head, sometimes I'm not even sure it happened at all.

The gun is swaying in my trembling hand, a dance of fire and hate.

"You didn't know." Seb licks his swollen lips on a smile. His whole face is disfigured and purple from Nate's beatings. "Gutted like a fish, thrown in the shower like a whore. She actually wanted to keep that baby," he says with a cackle. "The stupid little cunt."

I shoot Sebastian James Goddard three times.

Three bullets.

One in the chest, one in the face and one ends up eating a hole in his sleek ex-white vinyl couch. I stand there for long seconds after, letting it sink in.

I killed a man.

I killed a man who abused me.

I killed a man who killed my baby.

I killed a man who doesn't look human anymore.

Still rooted to the floor, my feet immobile, I can't stop staring at Sebastian's face. Or what's left of it. There's a hole where his nose used to be, and dark red blood, slimy clots and other inner waste is pouring from it. It kind of looks like the inside of a minced meat lasagna after you tripped and it spilled all over the floor. What have I done? What has *he* done?

My baby.

Sebastian's blood against the contrasting white of everything else in the room is beautiful. Almost picturesque. A calm smile starts making its way to my mouth. But I'm not happy. I'm in shock. Nate's hand finds mine. He's dragging me out the door, taking the stairs, and when he realizes how out of it I really am, he yanks me up and tucks me under his armpit, like I'm an envelope he needs to deliver, and paces down hurriedly. When we get to the truck, he buckles me up but stays outside.

"We need to run," I mouth urgently.

"Padded walls," Nate grunts. "No one heard. Be back in a second."

Then he disappears between the building's doors once again.

I hate that he is not next to me, paranoid by the prospect of being taken by Godfrey's men again, snatched in the middle of the night, nothing more than a daily newspaper your neighbor can grab from your front porch. My fears, however, don't materialize. A few minutes later, Nate jumps into the driver's seat and speeds away from the crime scene after tossing something into the trunk. The gun is still clutched in my hand. I release it slowly, without even realizing that it drops to the floor of the car, still deep in trauma.

He drives to an office block I don't recognize, but the minute I see the name Royal Realty glittering in gold over a big sign next to the names of the other corporations, I throw up on my knees. The Archers' company. Why's he doing this?

"Shit," Nate mutters, and I hurry to clean my mess with paper towels I grab from my backpack. "You okay, Baby-Cakes?"

I nod, but it's only so I won't have to utter a lie. I'm not okay. I killed a man, and I'm not Nate. I'm angrier and more vocal about my hatred—I'm madness driven by revenge—but I'm not like him. He's a dark, quiet killer. A peace. His abnormally beautiful face was given to him, and not by accident. It's to disguise all the ugly things he is capable of doing without batting a pretty eyelash.

He's not a bad man, but he is fair. Even when justice means doing something terrible. He turns to look at me, and my heart swells before shattering in my chest. I'm not going to survive parting ways with this guy, but do I really have a choice? Can he accept and love something so broken?

"I don't think you should see what happens next. But if you do, wear your mask. This place is wired like the fucking Pentagon."

He kisses the corner of my lips softly before slapping on his Guy Fawkes mask and jumping out, opening the trunk and taking something dark and round with him. I sit and watch him disappear into the underground parking lot of the building, jogging down the wide concrete road and sliding under the automatic barrier.

I think back to the first time I saw Beat's Guy Fawkes mask. He said he chose it because it was the easiest mask to find, but I know the truth. Guy Fawkes represents chaos, anarchy, and dark deeds that are done behind closed doors.

He represents the part of our relationship I didn't even know I craved before, but awakened a part of me that I didn't know existed.

I can be a ruthless. I can kill. I can take from those who deserve to be punished.

The strength in knowing that, in some ways, he's already fixed my soul is what makes me slide my mask on and push my door open. I walk into the parking lot. My small feet make very little sound, but this is Nate. He's aware of my presence.

There's something cinematic about the vision of his huge, muscular back as his fist clutches Sebastian's short hair. I don't know when he had time to decapitate my archenemy, but his pasty skin transformed from white to bluish in the short time he's been dead. Blood drips from what's left of his throat, but it's more of an annoying trickle, like a broken faucet that *drip, drip, drips*.

The sound of Nate's steps in his army boots echo off the walls of the empty parking lot. When he gets to a parking space that's painted with Royal Realty's title, he drops the head, letting it fall to the ground. Going down on one knee, he produces something small from his back pocket and arranges it neatly next to Seb's head. I take a few breathless steps forward to see what he's done.

It's a small hourglass. Something he must've bought when we were in Los Angeles, while he was getting us some food.

Time.

Godfrey Archer is running out of it.

I open my mouth for the first time since I killed Sebastian.

"I'm sorry I used the gun. I know guns are for pussies."

Not sparing me a glance, his back still to me, he shakes his head.

"You're brave. Too brave. You did what you had to do, and I respect the shit out of you. Got it?"

The need for him to tell me that he still loves me is devastating and sucks the oxygen right out of me. Sebastian's death is the least of my worries right now. It's what's been revealed in this visit that makes tears chase each other down my cheeks.

I had a violent abortion at the hands of Sebastian and Godfrey when they found out about *the thing*.

"My world ended that day." My voice is small and sad.

"I know. But you're building a better one. A stronger one. You've got this, Baby-Cakes."

Nate marshals me into another dingy motel room—all of them are starting to mold into one another in my head—while I stumble to keep up with him.

The thing about trauma is, you don't really know the extent of it when you're looking from the inside. On the outside, though, Nate must see something incredibly alarming, because he pulls me into his arms and hugs me so hard my bones scream in pain.

"I loved it," I say quietly into Nate's chest. His heart beats against my ear in a slow, steady rhythm. He's got the heartbeat of an athlete. Just one more thing that makes him my peace. He exhales hot, peachy air into my hair.

"Promise me you won't break. You did so well today. So well."

"I've got no more strength." I'm quivering so violently, I bump into parts of his body without even noticing. "I don't have any more fight in me."

He cups my face in his hands, so that I can't escape his penetrating gaze. "Then I'll give you some of mine."

Shaking my head, I suddenly feel hot. So hot. Too hot. I hate this place. This room. This life. I worm out of his touch.

"They're monsters, but they're going to pay for what they did to you, all of them. One day when this is all over, one day, sometime in the future, you'll have it all. I promise. A big swollen belly from the man you love."

You, I want to shout. *You're the man I love.* Only we promised each other we'd say goodbye. Knowing I'm way too screwed up right now to face rejection, I still put myself in the most fragile situation I've ever been in. Rejection might kill me, but I have no choice.

I lift my eyes to meet his and my lips flatten.

"I want to come with you. Forget Iowa. Forget my stupid dreams. Can I come with you, Christopher Delaware?"

His gorgeous face pulls into a badass smirk and my heart stutters in my chest.

"Why, Miss Cockburn, I thought you'd never ask."

I'm too exhausted, shocked and irritated to smile. But he picks me up honeymoon style and carries me to the dirty bed. We're holding each other's stares like neither of us believes we're good enough for the other person to stick around. Somewhere underneath the painful reminder of my pregnancy. . .I'm at *peace*. I have a home now, and that's with Nate.

We fall asleep like two dead people sometime after the sun breaks over the skyline. I don't think I've ever been so sad in my entire life. But also happy, and confused. Hopeful and hopeless. I'm a mess. I'm his mess. And that's *something*.

That's *a lot*.

And as I drift off to sleep I wonder. . .could it possibly be *everything*?

NATE

Blindsided by the whole pregnancy ordeal, I find myself staring at her as she snores softly, exhausted by life. Jesus fuck. This girl has been through and seen so much in her twenty-five years of life. Her baggage must weigh about five hundred tons. But I'll happily shoulder whatever shit she carries in her heart if that means spending time with her.

She wants us to stick together. I want that too. Even though I know that, it doesn't change the fact I need to piss out of the state, out of the country, before the end of the week. Today's Sunday—one day after she killed Sebastian—and she doesn't look ready to get out of bed. Actually, that's a bit of a fucking understatement. The truth is, her face is buried in the pillow, crying, crying, crying. Amazingly, she doesn't run out of tears.

"We need to get up."

"I want to see my brother."

"We're killing Godfrey first."

"No. I want to go to Vallejo, now."

"No fucking way, Cockburn. Erase the idea from your head. We ain't getting near that place until we finish Godfrey. It might be a set-up." *It is a set-up.* She's too distracted by grief to see it. "Pack up."

"No. I need Preston."

Goddammit.

I'm starting to suspect that she's on the verge of depression. I can't let it happen. She needs a dose of adrenalin, and since I can't try to fuck my way into improving her mood, I have a better idea. An idea that can do us both a lot of good, even though it's a very bad deed.

"Get the fuck up. We're leaving." I throw her backpack on the bed she's buried in. She doesn't respond, so I order her again. Still, nothing. I can understand her state of mind, even what she's feeling. I lost my mother, after all, and couldn't even attend her funeral. But we don't have time for her sulking. She can sulk all she wants when we're done. I grab her by the arm and yank her up, pulling her flush to my chest.

"You're getting over it, hear me?" I growl in her face. She doesn't look at me, just slumps her shoulders and lets me guide her to the door and into another car we stole to cover our footprints. This time I chose a Camaro. For our next act, we'll need something fast.

We drive toward Danville, going east. At some point, she stops her sulking and turns to me. I can see how devastated she is by the way her cheekbones are sunken and her eyes are shut off. Prescott's eyes used to glitter in the dark for me when I came down to the basement every night.

"Where to?"

"Blackhawk." I twist to the backseat, still driving, and pull out the two masks from the Walgreens bag. At this point, the damn bag can write a fucking memoir about us. "Put it on after we go through the gates."

Blackhawk is a gated community, but Prescott breezes right in. She's a resident. Actually, I'd be able to walk right in too, considering I'm still technically employed there. But we'll have to be quick when we run away, because rich people are pretty sensitive about getting their shit stolen.

And I'm about to steal some expensive fucking shit.

She rubs her face, looking up and sighing.

"What are you up to?"

"No good, just as usual."

I've been sexually harassed for months. Not with the kind of brutality Prescott has been handed, but still enough to feel a tad less guilty about it.

We drive through the gates with no problem, and I leave the engine running as I park about a hundred yards from Mrs. Hathaway's house. I learned her schedule during my time as her help and I know that today, she and Stan are playing tennis at the Simpsons'. It's unfortunate that I have to do it on a sunny Sunday, the streets are relatively busy (though less so in the sleepy neighborhoods of Blackhawk) and it's going to be a bitch to get away if things go south. I motion for Pea to sit her ass behind the wheel.

"We'll need to move fast. Do you drive like a chick?" I throw a jab at her, curious to see if she's still got those killer instincts.

"Nope, but you sure fuck like one," she bites. I turn in her direction and grab my junk, already making my way across the road to Mrs. Hathaway's mansion.

"You're addicted to this." I slap my mask over my face, even though it's futile. If Mrs. H is home, she'll recognize me from miles away. She's spent the last few months memorizing every ridge of my muscles and every drop of ink in my tattoos. I'm not bothered by it. She'll know that it's me, but if my plan goes accordingly, by tomorrow we'll be gone.

"You caught me." She hugs the steering wheel, a devious smirk on her beautiful pinks. *That's my girl.* Seb called her Diabla, like it's a bad thing. She *is* a little devil, but I like her brand of evil.

"I'm riding that dick tonight if you come back with some money," she mouths.

"You're riding it even if I end up in jail. You know you'd try to sneak in for me."

With that, I turn my back to her and stride ahead to Mrs. Hathaway's house like I own the place. The Hathaways have a high, wrought-iron gate with golden spikes along the top, but I climb through it easily. I saunter right into the house, the front door might be locked but they always leave their balcony doors wide open. Mrs. Hathaway likes it when the landing is airy. My strides are confident and long as I walk past the little fountains and statues scattered across her massive marble floors, climb up the spiral stairway, straight to her bedroom and into the walk-in closet. Here, right here, was the first time she tried to seduce me. I was three days into my new job, scared shitless of the outside world and even more worried about the possibility of pissing off my new boss. I've learned that the female population is divided into two sections: the women who are weary of felons like me, who believe I'd rape them if I got the chance, and the women who get hot on my stained past. The last thing I wanted was to be in a room alone with her only to find out she falls into the first category.

I stand in the middle of her giant walk-in closet, taking in the cherry wood of the walls and the rows and rows of shoes, suits and dresses. Taking three steps forward, I swing a painting of a woman lifting her hair into a bun and the big iron safe stares right back at me.

Hello, you.

Three strikes, that's all I have. I remember Mrs. Hathaway telling me this as she leaned into the safe, pulling out a whip and some leather cuffs and dangling them in her hands.

"This is where I keep my toys." She smiled seductively, but my eyes travelled to the huge stacks of cash piled behind her in the safe, just like in the movies. Why did they have so much cash? Fuck knows, and I certainly wasn't stupid enough to ask. But she saw the awe on my face. Her gaze trekked to the loaded safe, and when it landed back on me, a sly smile accompanied her words.

"But beware, Mr. Vela. If you're going to try and steal something, make sure you get the password right. After three times, both Stan and I get an automatic phone-call and the local neighborhood officer gets paged. That's how we know someone who is not supposed to have access to the safe is up to no good. Are you up to no good?"

Three strikes. There's a four-digit combination, and I just know these two old idiots picked something obvious like a wedding date or a birthday or some shit.

My gloved finger drags through button number four, because I remember Mrs. Hathaway's birthday is in April, when I hear the front door shutting downstairs.

Well, fuck.

I strain to listen and hear a set of feet, but it's tennis shoes, so I don't know if they belong to a man or a woman.

If it's Stan, I can take him down without even blinking.

But if it's Mrs. Hathaway. . .

I hear a feminine voice humming along with the whoosh, whoosh of her stupid pool, and know for a fact that it's her. She's fucking around downstairs doing hell knows what, but she'll be up here soon. An idea so sick, twisted and perfect rises in my head, and I do the craziest shit I've ever come up with. Taking my clothes off, down to everything but my briefs, I jump into her bed and wait.

And wait.

And wait.

After ten minutes, she walks in and lets out a scream, followed by a giggle, followed by slapping her cheeks like an idiot. Giddiness dancing all over her uncontrolled facial muscles. She's now eyeing my dick like it's some sort of a holy grail.

"Oh my gosh! Nate! Where the hell have you been?"

My head is propped on one hand, and I give her what I hope to shit is a sultry look, because I'm not a good faker. But I do know how to get women wet. Even years in prison couldn't take that away from me.

"Get naked and come here," I order sharply.

She swivels her head to the open door and turns back to me, her cheeks flushed. Maybe it's because she played tennis for hours this morning, but more than likely, it's because she sees me willingly shirtless, lying on her bed.

"Stan is having drinks at the Simpsons'. He'll be back in about forty minutes." Another giggle escapes her lips. I hope Mr. Simpson and his bowtie choke on their stupid girly cocktails.

"That's nine orgasms." My voice is flat and cool. "By the fourth, you'll be begging for me to stop. Now show me those beautiful tits I've been dreaming about."

I pat the plush mattress. She gingerly steps forward, but stops, her brows creasing. Astonishingly, her forehead doesn't wrinkle an inch. Jesus fuck. She's got enough Botox up there to sculpt an actual size baby.

"Where have you been this week, Nate? I've been trying to call."

"I wanted to fight this." I get up from the bed, walking toward her, hoping my movements don't give away my impatience. I don't have time for this crap. I lift my hand and brush a strand of hair behind her ear. The cheesiest thing a man can possibly do. I have no idea why people do it. Is there anything sexier than watching Prescott's dirty blonde locks getting all messy and tangled, knowing a part of the reason it's a hot mess is because I fucked her senseless?

"I was reaching my fucking limit, Mrs. H. How long can a straight guy work for you, deal with your advances, without breaking? I wanted you so bad, keeping away from you was the only thing I could do to fight this. Until I realized," I say and take another step toward her, my eyes turning to slits as my palm cups one of her cheeks. She leans into it. *Such a fucking goner. Like taking candy from a baby.* "I realized that I'm done fighting. I want this just as much as you do. Now tell me, Mrs. H, How. Hard. Do. You. Want. To. Be. Fucked?"

Her face is beetroot-red and she falls to her knees, her thumbs hooking each side of my boxers. An uncomfortable shiver breaks down my spine. Hell no. This man belongs to one chick, one who's sitting in a stupid-ass car right now, waiting for him to come back with shitload of cash.

"Baby." I fist her hair and jerk her face away from my junk. My dick is so soft and uninterested. How can she not notice? "We've waited so long. I want the whole fucking deal. Get me the whip and the handcuffs. I'll show you a good time."

With skepticism playing on her face, she rises to her feet slowly, her eyes searching mine. All she sees is a devious grin, and my heart skips as I pray she doesn't see the Guy Fawkes mask I threw under my clothes. After long, agonizing seconds, she spins toward the closet and the painting. I follow her footsteps, knowing how hypersensitive she is to my movements.

"Why are you following me?" Her tone is quivering with excitement. Her suspicion grows beyond her want for me. This needs to be rectified. I keep a good distance between me and the safe, so I can't pounce on her when she opens it.

"I want to cuff you to the old man's tie rack and fuck you against his suits while you scream my name. Problem?"

She smiles over her shoulder. "You're sick, you know that?"

"You're about to find out just how much, sweetheart."

She punches in the code to the safe, and my eyes follow her fingers religiously. 4.5.2.9.

4.5.2.9.

4.5.2.9.

4.5.2.9.

I chant the combination in my head like a fucking choir boy, slapping it with a catchy jingle, and watch as she produces the handcuffs from the safe and gives them to me.

"Hands up, against the rack." I push her to the left side of the closet and she does as she's told. Her wrists to the rack, I handcuff her tightly enough so she can barely dangle from side to side, her body long and erect, her feet barely touching the floor. I scowl, leaving her personal space at once and shaking my head.

She's helpless, caged and locked onto the tie rack. I turn around and walk back to the safe.

"Jesus Christ, Nate! What the hell?" Her voice is low but panicked.

"Sorry." I knock half her closet down and throw shit on the floor, looking for something I can use to stuff all the dough into. "I never planned on taking a penny I didn't earn from you. It wasn't my intention. Alas, shit happens. And when it does. . ." I punch in the numbers with steady fingers: 4.5.2.9. The door to the silver safe slides open, and all the cash smiles back at me, like it's happy to see me too. I walk back to the master bedroom, get dressed and return to collect the cash, shoving it in one of her big purses, my boxers and my pockets, anywhere I can fit one hundred bills. "Let's just say, I appreciate the help."

"Help! What help?! Nate! Come back here right now! You can't do this! Stan will kill me if he sees me like this. How could I explain it to him?"

I pause, and look back at her like I'm actually contemplating the question. She's trying to wriggle free. "That's a very good question. And not my fucking problem."

"You low-life!" She swings from side to side. "You're nothing but a stupid servant with swim trunks," she spits.

"Yeah, well," I grab a ludicrous amount of cash and shove it into the back of my pants, "the fact that you're tied up to a fucking tie rack less than four minutes after you walked in on me in your bedroom doesn't put you up for the smartest person in the world award, either. Have fun explaining this to your husband, Mrs. H."

I jog back across the street with my mask on, my body heavy with all the cash I have tucked into shit knows where. Do I have dollar bills between my ass cheeks? Damn right I do. The stolen car is waiting for me, engine revved up and Pea sitting behind the wheel with her shades sitting on the tip of her nose. She's glaring at what used to be her house, but snaps her attention back to me when I slide into the passenger seat and order, "Get the fuck out of here, fast."

We bolt through the neighborhood, every mile we put between the car and the Hathaway house relieving a bit more of my panic. When we cross the gates, she zigzags out of the rich area of Danville, out of the town, out of the region, moving north toward Sacramento. Good call. We need to fly low until this evening.

"Your zipper," she states, glancing briefly to my jeans as she maneuvers the vehicle. Gotta hand it to her—she's a class act behind the wheel. Drives like *Diabla* and looks much more comfortable in the tiny, confined space of a sports car than I am. "You're unzipped. Please enlighten me as to why your cock came out to say hello at Mrs. Hathaway's house."

I keep a straight face and casually roll my zipper up, before I start plucking out stacks and stacks of the one hundred dollars bills I need to count.

Where I expect her to be ecstatic, she remains silent. "Did you do anything with her?" Her voice shakes.

I place all the bills on my thighs and start counting. "This dick only salutes to you, Baby-Cakes. Didn't even touch her. Actually, that'd be a lie. I did tie her up to a tie rack."

She sniffs, making a U-turn in the middle of a town I don't know. We're just cruising along, getting farther away from our crime scene. I ease back into my seat and count silently, my eyes bulging out as I keep adding more digits to the number.

Six thousand. . .eight thousand. . .no wonder it felt so fucking heavy on my body. *How much money does Stan Hathaway keep in his safe?*

"Has she touched you?" I hear Prescott ask from the seat next to me. I still mumble the numbers as I answer, "I don't think so."

"You don't think so or you know so?" she presses. My head shoots up.

"Problem, Cockburn?"

She chews on her inner cheek, tapping on the steering wheel fast with her fingers.

"I hate not knowing what happened in there." She hitches one shoulder up, looking fucking adorable doing so. I have a few more stacks of bills to count, but I'm already at fourteen thousand dollars.

"I got to the safe, she walked in on me, so I had to act fast. I stripped down to my boxers and waited for her. Pretended to seduce her. Didn't touch her. I tied her up to a rack, grabbed the money and went back to the girl of my dreams, who was waiting in the car, feeding herself useless fears. Got it?"

She finally relaxes, taking a deep breath. She's acting like a cute, jealous girlfriend. An unsolicited desire for her to be all those things stabs at my gut.

I want to treat her like a girlfriend. Wish I could take her to a restaurant nearby, or even a drive-thru, but it's too risky to get out of the car or even make a brief stop at a junk food chain. Especially now, when not only is Godfrey on our heels, but also, more than likely, the police. By now, they've probably figured out I broke my parole, stole from my previous employer and might have even tied me to the Sebastian Goddard murder case. It's all about the timing, and a lot of shit's gone down since I went MIA.

As if on cue, we pass by a digital billboard, and when I see my face looking back at me from the panel, I choke on the very air I breathe.

WANTED BY THE FBI

FOR DRUG CONSPIRACY

REWARD UP TO $25,000

I lose my balance and blink in amazement. Drugs? What drugs? What fucking drugs are they talking about? Your homeboy doesn't even toke up.

Godfrey.

I'm wanted by the fucking FBI, with my face plastered on billboards, probably all over this side of the state, because of Godfrey.

Life closes in on me.

"Stop the car," I order Prescott, whose face is paler than chalk. She saw it too.

Pea turns her head from side to side, trying to make sure that it's safe to slide onto the shoulder of the road. I slam my fist against the console.

"Pull the fuck over, Prescott."

When she does, I open the passenger door, stumble out of the car, and try to take as much air into my lungs as I can. Everyone's after me. After *us*. Me? I know what I'm facing. Life in prison or death. But Pea, she doesn't deserve this kind of crappy life. We need to get out of this place as soon as possible.

Bending down, my hands over my knees, I draw in deep breaths and feel her hand circling my sweaty back with her comforting touch.

"I love you," is all she says. I take a few moments before turning around to face her.

If we're being fair, how come this whole world is so unfair to us?

"This is going to shit," I grit.

"But it's still going there with *you*. Nice journey, if you ask me." Her smile makes me want to breathe regularly again, so I try. This girl is dealing with a missing brother, loser father, MIA mother and a violent abortion. And she still smiles. *For me.*

I straighten up and hook my arm over her shoulder, pulling her into my chest.

"Cockburn—" I start.

"I know," she says, cutting me off. "We can't afford to stay here. We're taking Godfrey down tonight, then driving to Vallejo to see Preston and then getting on the first flight to London to deal with Camden. We have enough for tickets, right?"

Preston is not in Vallejo, a guttural scream tickles my throat, ready to jump out, but I just nod. "Plenty."

"Good. Nate?"

"Yeah?"

"We're getting out of this."

"You bet your fucking ass we are."
"Promise me."
"I promise."
"I love you."
"I fucking love you too, Baby Cockburn."

PRESCOTT

Nighttime falls on California by the time I see the blues and reds bouncing on and off my rearview mirror. I'm trying to remain calm, tapping on the steering wheel to the tune of "Hotel California" on the radio, but inside, I'm a mess.

The police are asking us to pull over, and there's no way we can get around that.

Nate is sitting next to me, his face blank, the money neatly rolled and stuffed under his seat, well hidden.

Is this how we're going to end? After everything we've been through? A police car stopping us in the middle of the road?

I slide to the shoulder, resting both hands firmly on the steering wheel after combing my blonde hair and sitting straight like a good schoolgirl. Nate's jaw is clenched and he is looking ahead, on the road.

He can't break.

I won't let him.

Not now, after everything we've achieved.

A chubby officer in a dark blue uniform with a flashlight saunters from his SUV straight up to my door. He flashes the light in my face, before arranging his belt on his round stomach.

"License and registration," he commands, his flashlight traveling to Nate's face. My heart is beating so fast I'm on the verge of breaking down in tears. Instead, I take out my wallet from my backpack and pluck my real California license, under my legitimate name. Nate might be wanted, but I'm still just a groomed kid from Blackhawk to the unsuspecting world.

Although I know that if the cop recognizes Nate, it's all over for me. I'm going down with him. Nate knows that, too, because his eyes almost roll out of their sockets in amazement when I hand the officer my driver's license. His hand twitches next to his thigh, and I hope he's not going to do anything stupid to try and spare me.

I don't want to be spared, I want to be his.

"Prescott Burlington-Smyth," the officer repeats my name, looking at my paperwork. I nod curtly. "I need your companion's ID, too."

"Sure. Chris?" I smile sweetly to Christopher Delaware. Reluctantly, he pulls out his passport, and I pass it along. The officer's brows pinch together.

"No driver's license?"

"Lost my wallet," Nate fires. "Waiting for a new one to arrive."

"Funny." The officer flips through his passport. "I see no stamps on this thing. Brand new. Planning to go somewhere?"

"Mexico," Nate answers calmly. "Family vacation."

"Huh."

This is going bad, I know, but what can we do? Run away? We will only draw even more unwanted attention. Tapping the steering wheel with my fingers and swallowing loudly, I look exactly like I feel—a fireball of nerves, on the verge of exploding.

"Ma'am, is everything all right?" The officer sticks his head into my window, and I open my mouth, about to say everything is great, when he takes a step back and yanks his belt over his big belly.

"Step out of the vehicle, please."

My fingers are shaking as I punch the unlock button and my head swivels in Nate's direction. He looks taut, severe; his forehead wrinkled into an expression I've never seen on him before. It's the first time he looks less than the most delicious and confident man on earth.

"Forgive me," he whispers.

"For what?" Tears tickle the back of my eyeballs, and I feel my lungs shutting down. I'm drowning, unable to come up for air. I need to breathe, but an impending catastrophe is threatening me.

Please don't try and save me, I beg him with my eyes. *I've only known you for a short time, but I already can't live without you.*

"I want you alive and protected. This ends here."

"Ma'am, I said step out of the vehicle." The cop's screechy voice is louder now, grating on each one of my nerves.

"Nate, no!" I call, punching the dashboard as he yanks out the gun we got from Seb and squeezes it to my temple. I'm shaking all over. The officer steps back and lowers himself to get a better look at what is unfolding before him. His mouth hangs open and his eyes grow wide.

"Tell the bitch to step out of the car. I kidnapped her for the money and now I don't need her anymore. I want the car and the cash, but most of all, I want her fucking gone. Do it," Nate says coldly.

Jesus Christ, no!

He's throwing himself under the bus for me. *Again.*

"Get out of the car," he repeats, his voice like steel. "Out. Before I put a bullet in your fucking skull."

"Ma'am, I ask you to step out of the vehicle immediately," the officer says.

Nate knows exactly what he's doing. If I step out of this mess right now, they're going to either arrest him, if he doesn't run away—or kill him, if he tries. As for me, I could walk away unscathed. But that's not what I want. Not what I signed up for. We're in this together, and I don't care if he's wanted by the police, Godfrey, the Aryan Brotherhood *and* the FBI.

"Beat," I warn. It makes no difference whether the officer recognized Nate or not, because every version of him is breaking approximately five thousand rules in a row right now.

"Get out," he says, this time almost pleadingly. The look on his face tears me to shreds from inside. "It was a cool ride, but we're done here. Save your ass, Pea." Then, on a whisper only I can hear. "*Please.*"

In the background, the officer is calling for backup while begging me to step away from the car. There's a lot of commotion, more blue and red lights approach us, and the gun is still glued to my temple. Nate's eyes are beseeching. He really does want me to get up and leave, even though it was my idea to send the world up in flames. He was getting by just fine until I barged into his life.

And now he wants to take my heat? To burn in hell for my sins?

This guy is delusional. I'm not leaving him. Ever.

"Screw you," I mutter, revving up the engine and throwing the car into drive. I almost run over the officer's feet as I pump the gas several times to gain more speed. The acrid scent of burnt rubber seeps into my nose and I open my mouth, gulping air. Say what you want to say about this car, but it is *fast*. Faster than Stella, God bless her heart. Or engine, in this case.

"What the fuck!" Nate yells while the car shimmies under the strain of its new speed. "What. The. Fuck?! Do you realize what you've just done? Why? Why, Cockburn? Why are you fucking your life up to try and save an asswipe with no future?" He is yelling and punching his seat, the door, everything around him but me. Though I suspect I'm the only thing he wants to punch right now. "I'm done, but you can still go and live in fucking Iowa, which, by the way, was the home of the person who invented sliced bread. Did you know that? I do. You know why? Because I googled the shit out of the place you want to live in. Because I love you. Because I fucking need you alive and safe! Pull over right now and go with Officer Incompetent before it's too late. Do it fucking now."

"No!" I pump the gas again, sliding off the highway and onto a side road. The officer didn't even have a chance to get into his cruiser yet, but I know that soon enough, the police are going to be on our tail.

I hope it doesn't end up on television. I always wonder who those idiots are who actually run away from the police. Well, now *they're us*.

"I'm not leaving you," I tell him. "And I already told you, Iowa is out of the picture."

"I'll shoot you." He jams the gun in my ribs. Numbing pain spreads across the area. I don't flinch.

"You won't." I say calmly. "You love me."

"Fuck!" he kicks the dashboard with his long leg, unable to contain his boiling frustration. "Cockburn, I don't want you to be locked up for life. Please, please," he begs, gluing his palms together, the gun clasped between them. "Pull over and let them take you. They'll take care of Godfrey. I'll tell them I killed Seb myself. Please, Prescott."

"No."

He grows quiet for a moment, rolling his lower lip in his fingers as he always does when he thinks.

"I'll kill myself." He suddenly aims the gun at the base of his throat, just under his Adam's apple, which is decorated with dancing flames and laughing demons. "Do it, Cockburn. I won't ask again."

"Guns are for pussies," I hiss his words back at him, not even sparing him a glance, my focus solely on the road ahead. "You'll never kill yourself. Let alone with a gun."

We're riding deeper into the dense woods. What woods? Who the hell knows? I have no idea where we are, only that we're heading north. Shit. If I accidentally wandered into Yosemite Park, I'd never know how to get out of there. Finally, Beat pulls the gun away from his neck and shakes his head.

"What are you doing, Baby-Cakes?"

"I have no idea." My tears make another frustrating cameo. "But I'd like to find out with you by my side."

Rubbing his knuckles against his cheek, he exhales loudly. I silently pray for him to come up with a plan, any plan, that can get us out of the woods.

"Break back south. We'll look for somewhere residential. Gotta ditch this car and find another."

Veering out of the woods, we get back on a highway, its lanes divided by a long set of tall trees. We're heading south, flashing by a row of police cars making their way north, presumably to try and find us. Soon, we stumble upon a real gem. It's a small town, deserted, or at the very least not fully occupied. Darkness engulfs us, unlit by city lights, and it takes us exactly three minutes to dump the Camaro in a swamp and break into a white Kia Soul. Talk about keeping a low profile. There's an unwritten rule somewhere that you can't purchase a Kia Soul unless you're between the ages of forty and eighty or have at least three whiny kids in the backseat.

Nate sighs in relief when he slides into the driver's seat and rests his forehead against the steering wheel, relishing the feeling of space between his legs and the pedals. I bet it's a lot nicer for him than the Corvette or the Camaro.

"I'm going to ask once again. Do you still want to go through with Godfrey, or do you want us to drive straight to SFO and board the first plane out of this goddamned country? Forget about Vallejo. We can always come back when shit cools down."

I fall back against my seat and fold my hands over my lap. I know what he wants to hear. He wants to hear that we're getting out of here as long as we can. *If* we still can. The more time we waste, the greater our chances of getting caught.

But I can't have Godfrey walking around free and happy, and I definitely can't leave without knowing what happened to my brother. Life wouldn't be worth living that way.

"He still has a piece of my soul," I say, not daring to lift my eyes to see what's in his. "And my brother is the only reason I didn't give up on life."

There's a brief silence before he nods.

"Then let's get them."

NATE

Archer got Sebastian's head, the hourglass and most importantly—the message.

Godfrey's smarter, or at the very least, more aware of our abilities, than Seb was. I know that because his Danville mansion is crowned by guards. And not just any guards. Pigs with pink, alcohol-swollen faces and tattoos inked on their foreheads.

The Aryan Brotherhood.

Ten, maybe twelve, brothers lean against their bikes and vans, arms crossed, watching the plush neighborhood through narrow eyes. They're waiting for us, no doubt. Godfrey figured it'd be nice to kill two birds with one stone.

They're the stone—we're the birds.

Archer lives in a European-looking mansion, rising from loose gravel. It looks like it was freshly planted by evil, watered by fear and grown into something dark and dangerous, standing out like a sore thumb against the California landscape. The light in his front terrace is on. He's home. I know where he lives because I've had to visit him a few times since we got out, mainly to deliver him drug-related shit. I never dabbled in drugs, but on occasion, when his contact people in Stockton weren't able to make it, I'd do him a solid and move stuff from point A to point B.

Prescott's swiveling toward the backseat, her shoulder pressing against mine as she recovers the backpack and our masks.

"We have to get rid of them," she says, referring to the AB. "You can be the bait."

I snap my head around to face her. Either I didn't hear her right or she's drunk. The latter is less than likely since we haven't left each other's side in fuck knows how long.

"Say that again, louder now, so I'll have a good reason to bend you in half against that tree over there and spank your ass until your skin sheds."

"I'm serious." She licks her lips, turning to face me. "Get rid of all of them, and I'll take Godfrey myself. I have the gun and the dagger. I can do this."

"He's got more weapons than you can dream of in his house, and even if, hypothetically, I was able to get all those sons of bitches out of the way, there's no telling who's waiting for you inside. And in case you've forgotten"—I yank her by my hoodie, our noses crushing together—"you're carrying around the heart of the girl I'm fucking in love with. Be more careful with her life."

I shake my head. "This is out of the question. You're not going in by yourself."

"Nate," she starts, her voice spikes with an edge, and I grind my lips against hers. I've fucking missed them. We've been too busy dodging the police over the past few hours to fool around.

"Pea," I breathe into her mouth. "Screw this. Let's turn around before they see us. We have our whole lives to live. Who cares about these fuckers?"

"I do," my girl says, eyes traveling to meet mine. "I'm sorry, Nate, but I do."

She swings the passenger door open and runs out of it before I get the chance to blink.

Without the gun.

Without the dagger.

But with my fucking heart.

She runs straight to the gated entrance of Godfrey's mansion and the air is trapped in my lungs as I fumble to get my own door open before my hand freezes. If I walk out of this car, I'm dead. They'll shoot hundreds of holes in me without even flinching, like in *Gran Torino*. I won't be much help to Prescott if I'm dead. I tuck my head low and watch as Pea crosses the road, running straight into the arms of the Aryan Brotherhood, and I know, I just fucking know that my nerves are not going to survive the next few minutes.

The moment she rounds the corner, the tall oak trees that cover our car hide her from my vision, and I'm in the dark.

Pulling on my hair until patches of black are left in my fists, I fume. Crazy bitch.

I'm staying in.

I'm coming out.

Fuck.

Whatever I'm doing, suffice to say—I'm going mad.

PRESCOTT

He exhales into my ear, his white moustache tickling the curve of my neck as he brushes a strand of blonde hair off of it. It's something Camden used to do a lot and I hated it. It's corny as hell.

"This is going to be our little secret, isn't it, my darling girl?"

"I always thought you were asexual." My gaze is lingering on the weather report dancing across the flat screen TV. It's going to be a glorious week, but of course, I won't get to experience it. I know what's to come, but I have to keep it together. I won't let him see me break. "I thought Camden was a fluke. That maybe you tried pussy one time and it resulted in a kid. You don't have a wife and you're not divorced. Who's Camden's mother, anyway?"

I don't actually care. I just want to taunt him. In all the time I've been with Camden, he'd always kept silent on the identity of his mother. Said he never wanted to talk about her, that she was off-limits. I know that he and Godfrey are very close, but if his mom is alive and well, there is no way that they're in touch.

"None of your bloody business, sweetheart. None at all." Godfrey's cold, cracked lips trace my collarbone as his palm moves under my shirt, cupping one breast, rolling my nipple between his fingers. "If you ever tell Camden that I've touched you, I'm slicing you up and feeding you to the hounds. You're good meat."

I don't answer. I just remind myself of all the good times to pull through this one bad moment.

Pistachio ice cream.

The scent of the ocean as it breaks against my sandy toes.

Playing Monopoly in my PJs with Preston and Dad, stuffed to the max after Christmas dinner.

Jumping on my waterbed when the nanny wasn't looking.

The movie *Amélie*.

Feeling the tears tingling your nose when you read an angsty book.

"Lie down," he says, and I do, because I know that he can kill me. Kill me and tell Camden that I tried to escape and one of the guards had to stop me. I don't want to die. Not until I figure out if there's a way out of this hell.

"Don't worry, beautiful. It'll be over before you know it. True, it'll feel like forever when I break into you. Time. It moves differently according to our circumstances. It's very slow when you're being tortured. But what are your choices?" He turns over an hourglass on the dresser near the bed. "Resist—and your time is up."

Godfrey is taking from me.

Taking my happiness and my soul and my sexuality. Taking things I have no intention of giving. He reaches for a Vaseline tube that's next to the bed and slides his fingers into it. Over the past few weeks, Camden had been the only one to take. Sometimes he let Sebastian watch, as a punishment for what I did to him. But this is the first time Godfrey is having a taste.

Camden would've never agreed to such a thing. He's possessive and jealous, a bratty prince who considers himself more worthy than the mad king.

I start crying, my body shaking against the sheets. He's not even naked yet and I'm already trembling like a wrinkled newspaper trying to survive a hurricane.

"Christ," Godfrey moans in annoyance. "I can't shag you properly. Not like this."

For a second, I mistake his annoyance with my tears for kindness, and sniff as I prop myself on my elbows, but then he says. "Turn around."

My stomach pressed against the cold sheet, I hear him sliding the lube up and down his bare dick with a slurping sound before he guides himself into my tight hole. I've never been touched there before. Camden asked me to do it when we were still together, but I said no. He respected that. Even after we'd broken up.

But his father doesn't know, and more than likely, doesn't care.

It hurts, more than just physically. I have no doubt that I'm bleeding. But I take it and barely grunt, my lips pressing hard against the pillow, closing my eyes. I will not break.

"You know, Miss Burlington-Smyth. Fucking you over is almost as fun as doing it to your dad. It must be quite disappointing, being deserted by your parents because of money and greed."

Blue skies after the rain.

Playing peek-a-boo with the neighbor's sweet toddler, Charlie.

A cup of fresh brewed coffee at the airport after a long flight.

First dates.

First kisses.

First everythings.

Not breaking. Not breaking. Not breaking.

Godfrey comes inside me, groans in pleasure and rolls away from my body.

The next day, he rapes me again, this time driving into my pussy.

Three weeks later, I find out that I'm pregnant. Godfrey never used a condom.

Neither did Camden.

The baby is an Archer.

It doesn't make me hate it. In my mind, it's US against THEM. I need to save it from the Archers no less than I need to save myself.

Only I fail my baby.

And it's the moment when I'm bleeding out a clot the size of a pea, watching it sailing on the sea of red in the toilet, that I truly break. It's that moment that changes everything, that lets me know that it's okay to want to kill them.

I failed my baby.

But I won't fail me.

I stride to Godfrey's timber gates, surrounded by Aryan brothers. Eyes zeroing in on the door, I feel more confident with every step I take.

They let me walk by freely, because they're shocked.

Because they know who I am.

And because they can't kill me—Godfrey wants to do it himself.

When I reach the edge of the cobbled path leading to his entrance, a fat man in dirty Levi's and a white wife beater pushes me away.

"Now what the heck do you think you're doing?"

"He wants me alive," I say calmly, bouncing a stress ball up and down in my palm. "Ask him yourself. Tell him Prescott is here. *Alone*, and ready to talk."

I hope Nate is keeping a good distance away from this scene, but know that he's livid with the way I handled things. I didn't even ask him before I charged to Godfrey's house, and now I'm standing in front of six burly, Nazi-looking men. They all have shaved heads and blue, faded tattoos all over their bodies. Their faces are mapped with fury. Life failed them, and they failed life. It's a catch 22, but I have zero sympathy for them. We all have demons. True fighters chain them to the pit of their dark souls.

"Stupid bitch," one of them spits, his phlegm landing right next to my boot. "Thinks she can boss us around. Your rich ass will be raped if you don't shut your pipe."

"Ask Godfrey." My chin is up, my cool façade on full display. "I'm here to collect. He thinks it's the other way around, and he's been chasing me for years now. Better not keep him waiting much longer, or your head will be on his dinner plate tonight."

That makes them cackle. They're so dumb, they mistake my small size for weakness. I don't care. I don't dare turn around to check on Nate. If I even flinch in his direction, they will try to see who I'm looking for. More than likely, they already know Nate and I should be together. That's why they've agreed to watch over Godfrey in the first place.

Finally, one of them, a tall man with a thick, blonde beard puts his phone to his ear.

"She's here." His tone is clipped. "Alone. I'm sending four guys to look around and try and find him."

My stomach twists in pain.

Run away, Nate. It's not your war.

Though what hurts me the most is my stupid pride. I've gotten myself into this situation because I cared more about ruining Godfrey than giving Nate and I a fresh start. As the bearded guy guides me into the depths of Godfrey's front yard, I have an epiphany. If we make it out alive, there's so much I want to show and do with him. I want to recreate all those happy moments that kept me from breaking. With him.

Watch a heart-wrenching play at the theater with him.

Have pistachio ice cream under the sun.

The ocean breaking over our sandy toes.

First dates.

Wet kisses.

Reliving everything that gave me hope. With. Him.

Not running away, his voice echoes in my head as the double doors to Godfrey's mansion swing open. *But chasing freedom.*

"Before she sets foot inside the house, check her for weapons." Godfrey's voice carries from the second floor as we reach the threshold, along with the faint sounds of Beethoven's "Ninth Symphony." Godfrey and Camden are big on classical music. I look around his foyer. It's everything I expected it to be. Big and built to intimidate, with marble floors, antique furniture and the empty echo of a house that never truly made it to becoming a home.

We all hide behind walls we're desperate to break.

The only personalized thing in here is a creepy portrait of him and his son, something the size of the wall, in the middle of the living room. Godfrey is standing above a sitting Camden, clasping his shoulder with pride. They're both looking straight at the person who painted them. Both wearing navy blue suits.

Their gazes. The choral playing in the background. An uncomfortable shudder rips through me.

"You heard the man. Arms out to the sides."

I do as the Aryan Brother tells me, though my mind is elsewhere. Less than a month ago, it was Nate who searched me. But even back then, three minutes into our relationship, I knew there was something different about him.

There's nothing different about the Aryan Brother. He is a barbaric savage, just like all the men in my life. *Except for one.*

His rough hands stroke the curves of my tits to the sound of the dramatic music, lingering, pressing, moving down to my stomach and fumbling with my sex and ass. He is chuckling to himself as he spends long seconds sliding his hand up and down my behind. I remain stoic, knowing it's not as fun for him when the woman isn't distressed. When his hand moves from the length of my arm to my fisted palm, he pries it open.

"What's this?"

"A stress ball."

"Give it to me."

"No. It's made of foam. It's not a weapon. Don't be ridiculous."

"Godfrey?" He raises his voice, his eyes hard on mine.

"Let her keep her stupid toy."

After a bit more touching and fumbling, he finally lets me go, thrusting me in the direction of the staircase.

"Godfrey." It's my turn to yell, gripping the golden rails of the fancy stairway with one hand and my stress ball with the other. I release the rails with a gasp when I realize what I've done.

Fingerprints, stupid.

"I'd expect you to cater to your guests and play some flipping Wagner. They'd probably be all over the anti-Semitic bastard. Hope you're not pussy enough to have your wise guys upstairs. It'll be just the two of us, right?"

The booming sound of violins and cellos is unnerving before he finally speaks.

"Don't worry, sweetheart. We'll be completely alone. I want that just as much as you do." A chortle.

Looking down at the first stair like it's a challenge to put my foot forward and climb it, I close my eyes and inhale. I can do this.

I climb up, stair after stair after stair. As I do, the music gets louder, swallowing my thoughts. When I reach the wide, lengthy hallway of his second floor, I'm barely shaking anymore. The place is empty, occupied only by the intense symphony of notes and chords.

The minute I'm in his hallway, his voice sings.

"Second room to your left."

Cameras everywhere, I note. If I get out of here alive, I need to flee the country ASAP. Making a stop in Vallejo is a death wish. It's risky as it is, with the officer who stopped us and the police chase.

I push the door open and stand in front of him.

He's still weak.

Still clutching a cane.

Still in his stupid, big, orthopedic shoes.

Closing the door behind me, I notice he is indeed alone. His bedroom is simple, humble, even, with a queen-sized bed, no TV and sad, bare walls.

"It saddens me, what you did to Sebastian," he says, getting up from his bed by pushing onto his cane. I erase the remaining distance between us. Pulling the sleeve of my leather jacket over my fingers, I reach for an hourglass sitting on a tabletop by his bed and turn it.

"He got what he deserved. Now it's your turn to part ways with *time.*"

The stereo is humming in the background, changing movements.

"Let's not get ahead of ourselves," he says with a smile. "I have a flight to London tonight and I am going to catch it. I wouldn't miss my son's wedding for the world."

Squeezing my stress ball hard and releasing it slowly, I shrug.

"If you say so."

Godfrey takes out a Glock from the back of his Bermuda shorts and points it at me. *Guns are for pussies*, I remind myself when my pulse grows erratic and I become light-headed. When I look into the barrel of his Glock, I realize that it's not only a gun, but it is *my* gun. Bastard's got a nice touch. He wants to end me with my own weapon.

"Thank you for making it so easy for me. Catching your boyfriend will be anything but a challenge. And you. . ." He shakes his head, grinning. "I wanted to give you to Camden, wanted to kill you from the inside before I slaughtered you in flesh, but I have underestimated you, Prescott. You can give real trouble. Now I simply want you dead."

"Flattered," I say, moving leisurely toward the bed and sitting on its edge, crossing my legs in complete nonchalance. My gun follows my every move, and Godfrey's eyes widen in disbelief. I confuse him, and it's making him stall. He's wondering what I've got up my sleeve, when in reality, I've got nothing at all.

Confused people don't act intelligently, they act stupidly. That's what I'm counting on.

I've been on death's door so many times recently, but never took that first step past the threshold. One more time is not going to kill me. Or maybe it will, but it's a chance I'm willing to take.

Godfrey's throat bobs, his gaze shifting from the night outside the window, to the door that's still shut and then back to my stone-cold face.

"Why do you hate us so much? Me. My dad. My brother. . ." I choke, but my expression is icy. "You don't normally ruin the upper-classes. You stick to the unfortunate souls, the ones who can't fight back. Why us?"

This question has been bugging me for years, and it finally slipped between my lips. Today, I have a feeling, I will get an answer. No matter what happens in this room tonight, I know, only one of us walks out of here alive. It may not be me, but it doesn't matter anymore. Any secret spilled inside these walls is not going to make it past the threshold.

"Her name was Marcia. She was American. Lived right here in San Francisco." Godfrey's fist chokes the gun tighter. I blink.

Camden's mother.

"Was?" My stress ball keeps bouncing from side to side, dancing in my hands. "She's dead?"

"She is." He nods once. "Your father killed her."

My blood runs cold, making my whole body numb. My dad? He's incapable of deliberately hurting people. He's too much of a wuss. Proved it time and time again. The way he treated Preston. The way he compromised me. The way he played into Godfrey's game. . .

"My dad would never—" I start.

"It was an accident," Godfrey interrupts. His tone is indifferent, detached. *Off.* "You weren't even born yet. Camden was a wee baby. We'd just moved from England to San Francisco to be close to Marcia's family. Marcia went across the road in the middle of the night to buy Camden formula at the Seven Eleven. Camden had been crying so badly, she was in a hurry and didn't take the crosswalk. She always used the crosswalk, but not this time. Your dad wasn't drunk. He didn't lose control of the car. He didn't go over the speed limit. . ." Godfrey's eyes narrow on me. "But he was careless. Your mother took it hard, what happened to Marcia. She was the first to get out of the car and see what was left of her. Your mother lost it. That's what ultimately led to her mental breakdown and the reason she checked into her very first rehab facility."

My heart freezes in my chest but I never stop bouncing the ball, because it's important.

Keep playing with the ball, Cockburn, Nate's voice teases me in my head. *Keep it moving.*

My parents never told us. But surely, dad knew when he got into business with him. . .

"I took Camden and moved back to London. We had nothing to stay for in the States after her death. He was raised by nannies while I tried to move on. Your father was let go, and there was nothing I could do about it. Believe it or not, back then, I wasn't after him. It was the phone call that made it all change."

I'm looking away. Blinking the pressure out of my eyes. Still bouncing the ball.

"The phone call?"

I take a deep breath, gritting my teeth. This can't be right. All of this happened. . .because of my dad?

"Remember what I said about only forgiving once? One chance, no more. The plan was to ruin your father. Not you or your brother. But when our business ties grew tighter and you'd met Camden, I couldn't stop you two from falling in love. I told him to stay away from you. Told him the Burlington-Smyths were not our allies, but our enemies. He didn't listen. He knew who you were, and that made him bitter."

Is that why Camden cheated? To get back at me for his mother? To avenge something that had nothing to do with me? I'm shaking, tossing the stress ball faster from one hand to the other, squeezing the death out of it every time it switches hands.

213

Don't stop moving. His gun is still pointed at you, but he is getting used to your hands flying around.

"So when you emptied his bank account and ran away with the money, I had no choice, I had to take care of you too."

"And Preston?" I grit. "Did you do anything to him? Is that why he ran away?"

"Ran away?" Godfrey takes a strained step toward me, my gun now just inches from my face. "If you ever get to Camden, which you won't, I'm sure he'll be able to let you in on what happened to little Preston. Your brother came to us willingly."

"When? Why? Where is he?"

I'm not even sure I want to know.

The symphony gets louder, the violins shriek in horror.

"Don't let me ruin all the fun. That's our grand finale. You'll know if you get out of here. But. . .that's not going to happen, is it?"

Tears stream down my cheeks. I'm breaking in front of him, because it won't make any difference. He'll be dead soon. The trumpets roar.

"It's a terrible thing, taking a life. You should know. You took Seb's. But sometimes," Godfrey says, leaning forward, pressing the gun to my lips and digging them open until it looks like I'm sucking on the barrel. Our eyes are holding each other's stare. *So close.* "We've got no choice."

Do it now, I hear Nate's voice in my head.

I shove the stress ball straight into Godfrey's left eye with full force. He stumbles back and falls to the floor with a bang, surprised more than hurt, and a bullet fires from the gun, slicing the mattress open. I jump to my feet and rip the gun from his fingers. It's not difficult to do, seeing as he's weak and lying on the floor, unable to lift himself up without his cane. So weak. So troubled. So dead.

Guns are for pussies.

I tuck the gun into the waistband of my underwear and roll my dress back down. Walking behind him, I grab the collar of his Hawaiian shirt and twist it around his neck from behind, knotting it against his throat.

Horns. Flutes. Chaos. War. A symphony of life and death in the background.

Now *that's* more personal. The noise Godfrey is making is unbearable. Gagging and gurgling, gasping for air, he tries to free himself of the shirt that's choking him to death. I remember what Nate wrote in his diary about Frank. How they suffocated him on Godfrey's order.

Turning red.

I glance at the hourglass. The sand is running out, and I squeeze his jaw with my free hand, willing him to look at the hourglass I hate so much.

Time.

It represents all the evil in this world.

"This is for Nate," I growl, pulling the shirt tighter, using all the strength in me, dripping sweat all over. The fabric slices his pink and wrinkled skin, creating a growing necklace of blood around his throat. The music screams in pain, absorbing Godfrey's cries for help.

Turning purple.

"It's for Marcia too. I bet she would have hated to see how you and your son turned out."

Turning blue, and not fighting as vigorously as he did before.

"But you know what, Godfrey? More than anything, this is for me. When I walked into this place today, outnumbered and out of my mind, I thought to myself that there was no way I would be leaving here in one piece. But the need to kill you was too strong. Now I see that God—the real God, not you, Godfrey—is on my side. Not because I'm good, but because I'm fair. That's why I'm going to England, on that plane you planned to take tonight, and I'm going to kill Camden. I'm going to take from everyone who took from me and save my brother. Time is too precious for second chances, remember? Your words."

At the mention of his son's name, Godfrey lets out a pained final choke before his body goes limp. Driven by paranoia and fear, I keep choking him for a few more minutes for good measure. Then, I put two fingers to his throat, checking for a pulse. Nothing. It's time to figure out how I am getting out of here with the Aryan Brothers swarming outside. I didn't bring my phone. It's still with Nate.

Aware of the presence of a dead body in the room, I peek outside the window. I'm not sure how many of them are standing behind the door of this room, but there are at least four walking back and forth at the entrance of the house. I look down, calculating the height. If I jump down, I'll break a leg. Maybe a hand. Probably both. I won't be able to run away fast enough to get away from them. And I have no idea how far I should run. Maybe for miles. No promises Nate stuck around.

Though I know he has. I know my lover. My man. *My peace.*

Trembling fingers covered in my jacket's worn leather grasp the doorknob, intending to swing it open, when I hear a shot. Then another one.

They didn't come from my gun.

What the hell?

NATE

Ten minutes later, homeboy officially loses his shit.

Fuck it. I'm going in and if I die, at least the pain of knowing she didn't make it will go away. Dead people don't feel. Ghosts can't be haunted.

I don't know how I managed to hold off for more than a second knowing she could be in danger. What was probably only ten minutes seemed like a fucking century.

Yeah, *guns are for pussies*, but when it comes to Cockburn's life, I'm not brave. *I am a pussy.* I can take a gamble with my own life. Take the gun we stole from Sebastian and figure shit out for myself. But Prescott? I'll use every dirty trick in the book and out of it to make sure she's safe.

I count the bullets in the gun before I go in. Six rounds.

Six. That means I'll still have to handle at least some of them with my fists. The first two to go down are the Aryan Brothers standing at the front door. I've never used a gun but my aim is good. I have steady hands and a knack for doing all things violent.

In all probability, people from neighboring houses heard the shots. There are only two houses on Godfrey's cul-de-sac, and judging by the fact that they let a bunch of criminals hang out here for hours without calling the cops, there's a chance I might have a bit more time to pull my shit together. Maybe they're not home this time of year, those rich bastards. Here's fucking hoping.

I storm into the house and two more assholes run toward me with fists and knives.

Boom. Boom. Gone.

"Pea?" I call out, looking around the open-space foyer. I can see most of the kitchen from this angle, and it's empty. I hop up the stairs, taking two at a time, my quads burning.

"Prescott!" I boom, kicking the first door in the hallway open. Nothing.

"Baby-Cakes?" My voice breaks. Two more Aryan Brothers appear from the far corner of the hallway and I shoot them down immediately.

I'm out of bullets, but I don't give a fuck.

"Try and kick something, make some noise," I prompt her.

If she's dead, I'm burning down this whole house, with me inside. But she's not. She's tougher than Godfrey, and he doesn't even know it.

Maybe he found out.

I'm just about to kick the second room's door when it swings open, and I take a step back on instinct, only to find the face of the love of my life staring back at me. Wide-eyed, shocked and trembling. . .but healthy and still standing.

Thank God.

"Jesus fucking Christ, Cockburn. Why didn't you answer me?"

"I ran and hid in his closet when I heard gunshots," she murmurs and throws herself into my arms. I pull her into a suffocating hug, one that'd hopefully glue her back together. When we break away, I run my fingers over her face, her nose and her mouth, then touch her hair. Doing inventory, making sure they're all still there. "Where's Godfrey?" I ask. She takes a step sideways and I see him on the floor, his Hawaiian shirt torn around his neck. She killed him with her hands.

"Guns are for pussies." She grins, pressing her hot, sweet mouth into mine, and I feel like fucking her right here on the floor, but that'll have to wait.

"Come on," I grab her hand. "We need to rethink this law on guns. If you see someone coming, shoot them. We don't have time and I don't have bullets." I gesture toward the gun she's clutching.

Descending the stairs, she halts near the first step of the staircase, takes my sleeve and wipes the railing.

"Fingerprints?" I ask. She nods. I grab one of the Nazi bastards who are lying dead at the foot of the stairs and crash his head against it. Blood splatters all over the railing. "That covers it."

We storm out of the house and into the car in record time. When I rev up the engine, my girl tells me, "We have one more stop. London, England."

"What about Vallejo?" I ask.

"Preston is with Camden." She smiles. "I can feel it. Besides, you're right, if he's in Vallejo, I can come back for him when we're no longer wanted."

I tilt an imaginary hat down.

The drive to SFO is so quick, we barely have time to catch our breaths.

My baby has just one final piece to glue together before her soul is whole again. I intend to help her in any way I can.

PRESCOTT

Fake passports or not, both Nate and I are a wreck when we show our IDs at the security check-in point. Every law enforcement official in the state is probably looking for him by now, and unfortunately, his good looks, endless tattoos and huge frame only work against us in this case. His face is ridiculously memorable.

We ask the girl behind the United Airlines counter for two tickets to London, first flight out. I shift my weight from foot to foot, chewing on the inside of my cheeks and gawking at everyone and everything like they mean me harm.

Nate is stoic, quiet and peaceful, but he's also human. There's a storm inside him too, he's just better at hiding it.

"Ma'am?" Her forehead crinkles, and I shake my head.

"My father's just died and I need to hurry make it for the funeral," I tell her from behind my big shades, even though it's nearly dawn. That's the only way I can justify the sunglasses.

"I'm sorry to hear that." The young woman puts one manicured hand over her chest and moves her attention to my companion. Her eyes glint with something, and for a second, I worry that she recognizes Nate. But no. It is not recognition that peaks her interest. It's the fact that he is a walking, talking masterpiece.

"Sir, may I have your passport please?" She offers a smile, and he hands her Christopher Delaware's passport.

"Mr. Delaware," she mumbles to herself. He nods once. She begins punching information into her touch screen monitor, her gaze scrutinizing. I want to yell at her to stop, but know that it's a less than stellar idea.

My heart pounds violently, and I feel it everywhere in my body, down to my fingertips. Behind the shades, my eyes land on a photocopy taped to the woman's workstation. It is one of several labeled as "no fly," staring up at her—Nathaniel Vela's face is included.

Shit, shit, *shit.*

I'm trying to tell myself that he looks different now. He hasn't shaved in weeks and his slicked back hair is a tousled mess of curls. Nate has changed after what we've been through. He's older, colder.

She takes my passport again and examines the picture, lifting her eyes back to me and dropping them down to the picture. Chills run down my arms and back. I *am* the person in the picture. Then why is it so difficult to breathe?

My eyes are twitching and I want to scratch my face until I peel it off completely. She could put a stop to our whole journey. I can't let that happen.

Another glance at the passport.

Another glance back at me.

Happy thoughts.

Listening to The Lovecats by The Cure on repeat.

Being kissed by a puppy, wet, smelly tongue and all.

Nate looking at me.

Nate smiling at me.

Nate inside me.

Nate, Nate, Nate.

Why didn't we cross the border to Mexico by car? How could I have been such a fool?

She picks up the phone at her station. No. Please don't do this.

She speaks into the phone, but I can't hear what she's saying. The air around me is white and thick with panic. Nate grabs my hand and squeezes it hard. This can't be happening to us.

I want to scream, to go back in time, to choose another desk, another flight. *Another plan.* I should have paid more attention to who would be serving us.

No. No. No.

Her manager arrives. He's a man. I can't see anything else about him through the blur of tears. He's asking me questions. My date of birth and other stuff I answer on autopilot. I remember Cockburn's date of birth because I did my homework.

Long minutes pass, but they let us go. When they do, I'm dripping in cold sweat. I'm so clammy, my sockless feet squeak inside my ankle boots.

When we get the passports back with the tickets tucked inside, I shriek in relief. We pass security, despite our backpack being stuffed full of cash. My boyfriend grabs me by the waist and guides me to the terminal. We jog across the airport. We don't have any bags. Just my one backpack. This could probably raise some questions, but no one seems to notice. We just need to get on that plane and everything will be okay.

Time.

I want it to move quickly and see me through to the other side of the planet.

Nate slumps into one of the plastic chairs at the gate as we wait for our flight to board and I buy us some Jamba Juice. His face is covered by the hoodie and he keeps quiet. I rest my head on his thigh and curl into a ball. We're too nervous to talk. Too nervous to even blink. We just sit there. Two mute people, wishing we were invisible for the duration of the flight.

Once we get on the plane, I release a huge breath and close my eyes. It isn't until our plane is in the air that Nate visibly looks well again. From erect and alert, he returns to his normal self. The hardness is gone, replaced with the charmer look he was born with. When we cross California's border and the little screen on the headrest shows that we're above Nevada, I let loose a little smile. His lips find my ear, and he doesn't care that a flight attendant is passing by us with her cart, offering drinks.

"The minute we land in the UK, we're checking into a hotel and fucking the shit out of each other. I still owe you a punishment for going all G.I. Jane on those Aryan Brothers' asses."

I lick my lips and turn around, my teeth grazing his chin lightly.

"You like 'em dangerous, don't you, Delaware?"

"Yes, I do. And what's more dangerous than a Cockburn?"

He falls asleep in the tiny, narrow chair, and I spend hours just staring at him. I love him so much, I can feel the weight of this love on my body. I swear it's like I'm pregnant with feelings.

In a lot of ways, he's the only thing that's kept me sane. In the past three weeks, I've been kidnapped, thrown into a basement, seduced my captor, ran away with him, fell in love with him and killed two people. And I know Nate killed at least six more at Godfrey's house.

This is not a joke. It *is* a blood bath. Godfrey said Camden holds the answer to Preston's disappearance. The burning question is—*does he actually hold Preston?* The old Prescott wouldn't take any chances. She'd go to Vallejo before boarding a plane, consequences be damned, to do whatever she could to find her brother. But I'm not the old Prescott anymore. Nathaniel Vela changed me. He changed my priorities. He changed my heart.

What's keeping me sane is the knowledge that what we're doing is right.

I killed Sebastian, Godfrey, and now I'm going to kill Camden, because they don't deserve to live. They took life from me. Not just in the spiritual sense. They literally ripped me open with a hanger, shoved it deep inside of me and plucked out the life I was growing. The life they themselves put inside me.

An eye for an eye. A life for a life.

We land at Heathrow, greeted by a slight London chill. It's enough to make me shudder in my ragged red mini dress. Nate, who woke up after eight hours of sleep, notices and pulls his hoodie—filthy from everything we've been through—over his head and offers it to me, then proceeds to wrap his arm around me.

We stand in customs for forty minutes before they let us out, but when they do—when we walk through those sliding glass doors, pass the Duty Free shops, pass the meeting point where dozens of people wait behind barriers, clutching balloons and flowers and signs with names we don't know—we laugh. Happy, joyous laughter. *We made it.* Hand in hand, our chests rattle. A symphony of bliss. We're free.

No longer on US soil.

No more Aryan Brotherhood.

No more FBI.

No more Sebastian Goddard.

No more Godfrey Archer.

My fingers dig their way into his back for another grateful hug. Amid all the chaos of the airport happening all around us, he stops, faces me, pulls my hands into his, and levels those honey browns on mine.

"My fault, my failure, is not in the passions I have, but in my lack of control over them," he says, repeating the words from his diary. The words to his first ever tattoo. The words he so badly wanted to relate to. "Thank you for helping me find my passion, Cockburn. My passion, as it turns out, is you."

NATE

Camden Archer wasn't difficult to find.

He's been all over the news, giving interviews about the death of his father. He said he died in his sleep, probably because he didn't want to tell the world the horrid, revolting truth. Camden's now officially the heir to his father's businesses, and the last thing he wants is for people to find out just what happened at his father's place the night Pea took his life.

Archer's long awaited wedding to Lady Hilary Thompson (can you believe that shit? The guy who raped my girlfriend continuously is marrying a *lady*) is off. I'd say I feel sorry for him, but the truth is, I can't wait to meet him so he can get to know my fist.

One thing's for sure—Camden Archer knows that we killed his old man, and that we're coming for him. His death won't be as easy as Sebastian's, or as lucky as Godfrey's. We'll need more. More resources, more planning, more luck. More fucking everything.

According to the news, Camden flew to California to deal with his father's funeral arrangements, and will be back next Friday. We've got a plan mapped out for him. He'll go back to his father's house in Kent, thinking we'll be waiting on him near his Marble Arch apartment in London.

But he'll be wrong. We'll be waiting in Kent. This time, with actual weapons and a detailed strategy of how to take him down.

As we wait for him to arrive back in England, we get some down time. The last four days have been nothing short of fucking heaven.

The minute we landed in London, Pea and I checked into Piccadilly Backpackers, a hostel in the center of the English capital. We've been sharing communal showers and toilets with high school graduates from all over Europe and Australia and sleeping on the same level in a bunk bed, curled into one another like sardines. We eat Kettle chips for breakfast, lunch and dinner and drink pints of Guinness at the Dublin Castle in

Camden Town. At one point, we even decide to splurge and spend a few pounds to get into the Music Room and listen to a local indie band perform.

The band is shit but we don't care. We make out on a wooden bench the whole time. My hands slide into her new Primark skirt (she made us go all the way to Tooting Broadway because she didn't want to visit the Primark in Marble Arch. It reminds her too much of Camden.) I finger her through soaked panties in front of a bunch of drunk people we don't know. Stifling her moans against my lips. Making her come against my whole fucking fist.

We go to Madame Tussauds and I take a picture of her cupping David Beckham's balls, and she takes a picture of me pretending to plow into Kylie Minogue from behind.

Subsequently, we get kicked out of Madame Tussauds, but we're laughing so hard while stumbling out, our abs hurt. It's definitely worth the slap on the wrist.

We sneak into buses and stand for two fucking hours in a London Eye capsule next to a Japanese couple who are fighting furiously and their kid, who smears snot all over the glass.

At night, I hold her so close my heart expands, filling every inch of my body. I make love to her and make hate to her, because sometimes, the best kind of sex is the angry shit you just want to screw out of your system.

But in London, Prescott doesn't ask for Beat. She asks for Nate. For the first time in my life, I dig inside myself, trying to find who he is. How he'd act in bed with the woman he loves.

Turns out I can be a gentle little shit. Not vanilla, I still like to bite and pinch and pull at her nipples and her clit until she swats my shoulder and twists away, but Prescott introduces me to something called 'relationship sex'.

"It's basically a lazy fuck," she grinds herself on top of me cowgirl style, placing her fingers on her lips, kissing them and then brushing them against mine. She moves leisurely, and I enjoy my view, a relaxed smirk on my lips. "It's how people fuck when they're not being chased by the whole goddamned world," she winks.

"Hmm," I slide my hands up and down her body, rubbing her nipples with my thumbs before moving down to flick my finger over her swollen clit. "I ain't familiar with this concept, and frankly, don't care for it. What the fuck am I supposed to do with my life if no one's after my ass?"

"Live it," she pants, relishing my touch on her skin. I pinch her clit and bite her wrist. "Enjoy it."

"I do enjoy it," I suck on her fingers. We hear the Italian girls in the next room giggling. They've been eavesdropping on us having sex for days. "Do you enjoy fucking me as much as you enjoy killing people, Cockburn?"

"Yes," she pants. "Of course."

I hook my finger into her pussy and curl it. That's when she bends down to kiss me and I whisper into her face. "Because sometimes I think you're hungrier for blood than you are for cock."

She comes on top of me, shaking and smiling, and I come inside her, groaning and laughing.

I could get used to that. Live like this forever. I'd take the fucked up Burlington-Smyth baggage she brings along with her, Preston included. But my girl wants to kill the man who ruined her, and we'll do it, one way or the other.

She's got one more piece of her soul to collect.

Dealing with Camden will burst our bubble. After we're done, we'll figure out where we want to live, what we want to do.

Today, we are going to go over our plan to corner him after his father's funeral. We sit at a small coffee shop in Chelsea, expensive as fuck but this place is dear to Pea's heart. It's where she often ran away from her cheating boyfriend to window shop. I stand up from my seat, stretch, gulp my small shot of espresso in one go and slam it against the wooden table.

"I'm going for a piss. Wait here."

"Worry not, I'll never leave your side," she says with a wink.

I kiss her lips and walk toward the restroom. While taking a leak, I whistle and watch my cock through lazy eyes. It's been buried in Prescott's pussy and ass so many times recently, it can practically call them home. I wash my hands and look at myself in the mirror, and the shit-eating grin I'm sporting these days will have people thinking that I'm happy. Shockingly, I am. I'm really fucking happy, for the first time in my life.

I've been through so much shit, killed so many people recently, and still, I've never felt more alive.

Alive because there's another heart I need to live for.

It's beating against mine every night.

Beat. Beat. Beat.

PRESCOTT

I look down at my phone, texting a guy from Brixton who offers muscle for hire. We'll need all the help we can buy when we strike Camden in Kent. Typing fast, my finger pads furiously tapping the screen, I pause when a whiff of an expensive cologne hits my nostrils. My hands stop, my brows furrow. It's familiar. . .and revolting.

I don't dare lift my eyes from the screen.

"*Diabla,*" his low voice is so chilling, he sounds like the reaper himself. "So beautiful, kissed by the Californian sun. Shame you won't be seeing it ever again."

I dart up from my seat, about to charge through the door and run for my life, but I'm too perplexed. Camden clasps me in his arms before I get the chance to slip away, engulfing me in an embrace. His arms circle my neck like we're old friends sharing a moment, and I feel a blade pressing against my carotid artery. People can't see it. His hand is curtained by my long hair. But it's there, and the insanity twirling in his sapphires tells me he's still crazy. *Crazy enough to kill me.*

He buries his face in my shoulder as he hugs me tighter, inhaling my scent like an addict snorting a line of coke.

"Show the smallest sign of distress, and I'm slitting your throat and leaving you to die on this floor, sweetheart."

I gulp, staring at the car that's waiting for him outside. A flashy Alpha Romeo. I recognize his driver through the rolled down window. Simon. He used to drive me around when Camden and I were together. My ex said we were too good for the tube.

"Follow me. Don't worry, your lover will join you soon." He grabs a napkin from under my coffee mug and jots his address down with the same object he threatened me with. One end is a pen and the other is a knife. *Clever.* And so very Camden.

I let him throw me into the backseat of his car for no reason other than the fact I'm in shock. He's not supposed to be here. Yet he very much is.

Camden slinks onto the leather seat, crossing his legs and lighting a smoke nonchalantly. He stares out the window as he speaks. "You did me a huge favor. I always wanted to inherit the family business. My old man got sloppy with age and with pride. Those are the things that usually kill you."

Should I attack him? The doors are locked and it's just us and Simon. Camden is not Nate. He's not as tall, strong and monstrous. As if reading my mind, my ex-boyfriend shrugs, turning his gaze to me. He blows smoke into my face as he speaks. "See this pen?" he fingers his weapon. "It's a custom-made blade. Sharp like a hunting knife. It could cut your skin like butter. Gorgeous, really. My fiancée bought it for me for Christmas."

"Lovely," I fold my arms over my chest, mimicking his posh accent. "I'm glad she nurtures your inner psychopath. I let it starve for years."

Camden laughs and tsks, moving closer to me. He brushes my hair away from my neck and kisses it softly, speaking into my skin in a hushed tone. "I've missed our banter, Diabla."

I suck in a breath. The scent of cigarette and expensive cologne suffocates me. "And I wouldn't go around labeling people as psychopaths with your track record. You murdered my dad."

"Your dad murdered my soul," I hiss back, scooting so close to my side of the car, my whole body is pressed against the door. "*And* my baby."

He lets out a groan, twisting my face by squeezing my jaw in his palm, forcing our gaze to meet. "Look at me now, Prescott. Has my dad really raped you?"

I nod slowly, not breaking eye contact. "I wouldn't have killed him otherwise."

His azures drown in my hazels. He's getting lost deep inside me, and me? I'm pulling him in. I can see it through his dilated pupils. The compassion. The guy who bought me a ticket to London after a first half-date underneath the stars. The guy who fell in love with a girl whose father is responsible for him becoming an orphan. It's all there, in our messy, dirty truth. His eyes drop to my lips.

"Prescott." He breathes. He moves to kiss me, and I purse my lips instinctively. "Let me go."

It's an order.

"Never."

It's a promise.

He kisses me again, this time harder, on the mouth. I gag a little, but remain composed. When his lips leave mine, he's still gawking at me, taking another silent drag of his cigarette.

"Tell me the truth, Prescott. Is the giant twat a pawn?"

I shake my head slowly. "I'm in love with him." I find the strength in me to smile. That's the last thing I say before he smashes his fist into my nose and my eyes roll back into darkness and I see stars.

Nate.

NATE

Even before I walk back to our seat by the window, I know something's wrong. I can feel it in my bones. They're cold. When I round a corner and Prescott is not seated on the sofa overlooking the busy street, cold turns to hot. When I pace over to where we sat, cutting through charged air that seems to lack oxygen, hot turns to sick. There's a small napkin on the table with an address scribbled on it. I look it up on Google Maps, unsurprised to see that it's in Marble Arch.

Fucking Camden.

I jog out and signal for a cab, but they're all busy. It's early in the afternoon. Suited men and women pour in and out of taxis. Time is wasted, and I hate that I'm running out of it. She needs me *now*.

Finally, a black cab stops in front of me and I jump into it and rap the divider frantically, giving him the address.

He got to us before we got to him. He conned us into thinking he was out of the country. We were so drunk on being happy once in our fucking lives, we lost focus.

The driver's trying to strike up a pleasant conversation from the plastic screen, but soon realizes that my current state doesn't really allow talking. Or breathing, for that matter.

We were so sure Camden would run or hide behind burly, brainless soldiers like the rest of them. We committed the very same sins that made Sebastian and Godfrey's hourglasses run out of sand. We got comfortable. And cocky.

Pea and I had gotten away with so much during those short few days. Unplanned and uncalculated, we took them down, one by one. It was almost too good to be true. It made us feel invincible. Now, I worry that I might soon find out that we are anything but.

When the cab stops in front of Archer's building, I bolt out, leaving fuck knows how much money behind me. Maybe more than a fat tip. Maybe not enough to cover the fare. I jog up the stairs to the second floor, taking them three at a time, and throw the door open without knocking. I'm met with a beefy guy in uniform—a waiter or a driver or fuck knows what. He charges from a tuxedo sofa in the living room right in my direction, waving a vaporizer pen in his hand.

High on adrenaline and fury, I let him run all the way to my spot near the door before slamming his head into the nearest wall. But then I feel it. In my stomach.

He digs the pen into my abs on a throaty roar, leaving it inside as he collapses to the floor. The scent of blood comes before the sting of the blade. Then I see it. And when I see it—it's everywhere.

All the red.

The pen is not a pen. The pen is a fucking knife. A sharp motherfucker, too.

I stagger back, staring down at the hole in my middle. Not too big, but way too deep.

The cocksucker gutted me. I need to get to Prescott before I drop dead from blood loss or fucking Peritonitis.

Maybe it hurts. I believe that it does. Bile shoots up my throat and a blood stain spreads rapidly across my white shirt. I pull the knife out in one go, sighing in relief when it doesn't come out along with my intestines, roll my attacker on his back and stab him in the throat. The knife slides all the way through until it meets the floor. His limp body comes to life, jerking one more time before he gives in and drops dead.

Pen in hand, I stumble into the corridor, the *drip, drip* of my blood sounding against the floorboard. I see a door ajar and know what awaits inside. I crack it open. I want to charge through it like a blizzard, but with every step I take, my vision becomes blurrier, my steps wobblier. Am I dying? I might be. But I don't care.

Prescott.

The bastard's back is to the door. Who does that? Who gives his rival his back? *Someone who wants to die.*

Someone who wants to be surprised.

Someone who knows I won't kill him because he's got something of mine that I want back.

I sway like a drunk, bumping into the wall and the dresser in his bedroom, until the knife is pressed against his throat. He probably thought I'd never get this far, that I'd be intercepted in the living room by his muscle man. *Surprise, scumbag.*

"Let her go."

I'm blinking furiously, trying to regain focus, and I know I'm dripping blood all over him, but when the sight in front of me registers, I have bigger problems than losing consciousness.

Camden Archer is sprawled on a plush recliner in his room, facing a window.

Underneath him, on the floor, sits Prescott, beaten to a pulp.

A gun to her temple. A hand wrapped around her neck that's bruised in purple and red. I feel my throat tighten. *Breathe. Inhale. Don't lose your shit.*

"Diabla was the only disease I couldn't seem to shake." His posh English accent sounds so far away right now. He's stroking her head. Why's he stroking her head? I want to stop him but can't. I know that if I don't kill him soon, I'll die myself. But I can't chance pressing the knife to his throat, because he might pull the trigger.

"What is it about Prescott Burlington-Smyth that brings grown men to their knees?" he wonders aloud. My body failing me, I collapse and grab the back of his seat for balance. He doesn't care that I have the knife pressed to his throat. I have a feeling he doesn't care about anything anymore.

But I do. I care so much about the girl who's forced to sit between his legs. And it's ruining me that I can't save her.

"It's okay to fall, Nathaniel. We all fall sometimes." His gun strokes the hair away from her forehead in a way that's almost endearing. "You know, I saw you a few years ago when I visited my father in San Dimas. No one came to visit you. You were burning time in the yard. You looked so invisible inside that big body of yours. You think you found something to live for, but she belongs to me. The art of letting go. . ." He snickers. "I was never good at it."

"Kill us both and walk away, Nate. I want him dead," my brave girl commands in the background, but I can't hear very well anymore. Everything becomes white. Voices are muffled. My watch stops ticking.

I'm selfish. I will never let him kill her, even if that's what she wants.

"Yes, Nathaniel. Kill us both," I hear him echo through red, searing pain that throbs between my temples. "Our time is up."

For the first time since Pea and I got together, something dawns on me. *I can't save her.* This time, she's on her own.

It takes me long seconds to realize that I'm down on the floor, my eyes wide in terror. I stare at the legs of the recliner, Pea's back between Camden's legs. I want to move. I *need* to move. To jump out of my skin and be strong for her. A river of blood, my blood, starts streaming toward her.

Struggling to keep my eyes open, I try to talk to her, even though I can barely move my lips. White becomes black, and the wild ride we had together is coming to an end. If there were one last thing I could feel before I die, I'd want it to be her stupid stress ball bouncing off my face. She looked so hopeful and lively the day we rode out of Stockton together. It made me fall for her. All that spirit. She fucking sparkled, a stick of dynamite in the pitch black of my existence. Country Club didn't give me any choice. She ripped my heart from my chest. Is it a surprise that I can only get hard for one girl, that she is only wet for me? She gives me storm, and I give her peace.

But I can't give her my peace right now.

Because I'm gone.

PRESCOTT

CAMDEN

So plain looking, he couldn't stand out in a sea of black. But he wears tailored suits, a cunning smile and the confidence of a man who never had to count his pennies. *Likes:* Drinking, screwing and using his father's power to get his way. *Loves:* Me. *Hates:* Everything and everyone who might get between him and me.

"Put the gun down." My pitch dances high and low. Shit. It could have been different, if Nate wasn't here. I would care much less about my death.

I know Camden, and if he kills me, he'll grieve for me more than he grieved for his dad. He's been peppering me with kisses, wet with tears and his stinking cigarette saliva, ever since he hit me and dragged me out of his car. He ordered Simon to stay in the living room and wait for Nate as he pulled me into his bedroom, kissing, crying, apologizing and slapping me across the face all at once.

So mad. So crazy. So, so insane.

He's rambling, something about how we could've been great parents. I don't hear a word he says. The only sound that bounces inside my skull is *Nate, Nate, Nate.*

He's hurt. I can't turn around to look because of the gun that's digging into my temple, but the blood. . .Nate's blood is making its way to my feet. I see it running over to where I sit on the floor like a wounded animal begging to be saved, the copper scent so strong it fills my mouth, even though it's nowhere near my tongue. Trying not to gag, I pop my neck back and forth and inhale deeply.

Please don't die on me. Please don't go.

It would hurt so much more than the beatings I endured from my ex-boyfriend.

"I need to take him to the hospital, Camden. You're not your dad. You can't get rid of two bodies without leaving evidence. Just tell me what you want, and I'll do it."

He wrenches me by the hair so that my ear meets his lips, the skin of my forehead stretches from the impact of his grip.

"You can't give me what I want, because you already gave it to the poor sod who is dying on the floor behind us. That'd be your heart, by the way."

My goddamn tears betray me again. I'm shaking violently. He's dying. My peace, my everything, may already be gone.

"Camden, anything. Name it. I'll give it to you. I came here for my brother, not for you," I lie. "I'm over what happened between us. I just want my family back."

And Nate *is* my family.

I'm trying to sound firm, but not desperate.

"I don't want your life, Prescott. I want what I set out for. Even after everything you've done to me. . .to my family. All I want is you. That cold thing that beats inside your chest," he hisses, grabbing onto my left boob and pinching hard. I feel urine trickling between my thighs, which prompts my eyes to leak too. "That's the thing I ache for."

"Then have me. Let me take him to the hospital, release Preston, and I'll come back. I promise."

Nate has his fake passport and some money left. He could make it, and help Preston. Complete my quest in my absence. I trust him. That's if he's still alive. I might fall behind and become a slave again. But it's a price I'm willing to pay after everything he's done for me. It's a price I *want* to pay, despite the consequences.

Camden places his lips on top of my head again, stroking it like I'm a fragile doll. It's chilling. His way of treating me like nothing more than an object.

"You miss your brother."

Careful not to react, I stare blankly at the wall. Camden wants to squeeze the shit out of my despair and agony. Breaking apart will only make him stall.

"How old is he now?" Camden muses, his fingers tickling the sensitive spot behind my ear. He used to do that when we fell asleep together. Now, he does it to taunt me.

"Shouldn't you know? Your father said he's with you," I sniff my runny nose, unable to keep this inside me anymore.

There's a dramatic pause of words and movements, before he resumes running his fingers through my hair. His tone is calm and blasé.

"Prescott, love, what are you on about? Preston is dead." I feel a shot of pain straight to my heart. He tugs my hair a little, enough to make my skull burn, still brushing my blonde waves. "He practically begged us to kill him. After you had my father and Sebastian locked up for years"—he smiles, reminiscing about the time like it was a sweet memory—"I got mad, and naturally, wanted to get even. I know you don't care for your dad very much, and that your mom is in a crazy asylum. That left me with. . ." He extends my neck, forcing me to stare at his broad smile. "Baby Brother Dearest."

I want to cry, to scream, but am too paralyzed to do any of those things. Preston is no longer alive. My brother. My only real family. Nate, by the lack of sound or labored breaths, is dead too.

Everything I care for—gone.

"In hindsight, I could've handled it better. He came to me trying to find you. Bad timing."

Shit, Preston, shit. I told him not to look for me after he gave me the money. He wanted to save me and got killed for it.

"When he realized what I'd done to you, it was too much. I gave him two options—end up as my slave or say goodbye. He didn't even blink." Camden rests his forehead on mine and our eyes level. "Preston pressed his forehead to the barrel like a trooper. He had balls, I'll give him that."

I'm peeing myself. Doing exactly the thing I wanted to bring Camden to do. Shattered into mosaic pieces of pain and agony.

"You pulled the trigger?" My teeth chatter.

"I did," Camden confirms. "I'm sorry, Diabla. I was quite mad at you back then. Well, we both were a little over the top, weren't we?" He chuckles.

My fists flex and my vision clouds. "Please. No more death. Let me take Nate to the hospital. You want me? You can have me. Just let him go."

Camden shakes his head, sighing heavily. I look at the man I thought I used to love and hate myself for letting him into my life. His face drips malice, his usual cocky glint replaced with a mad glow. It's the same insanity I saw in his father's eyes before I finished him. An electrifying intensity that will shut off like a power outage the minute he's dead. He blankets me in the scent of stale cigarettes and Royal Mayfair fragrance. His lips press into my throat.

"You'll never be mine. I saw the way you looked at him. If I keep you, you will kill me. It would only be a matter of time. You're a hurricane, Diabla. I can't risk you blowing up my life."

"No." I shake my head. "I won't, I won't. I promise. I'm done. Let me take him and I'll leave. You have my word."

He seems to be considering this. His hand is still buried in my hair as he strokes it lightly. Lovingly. Sickly. Is Camden about to do the right thing for once? He finally believes me when I say his father raped me all the time I was trapped in that apartment.

"What happened to us, Prescott? We could've been good together. Now I have to kill you, so you won't kill me."

"No you don't. I'll stay away."

"You'll be desperate and poor," he snaps. His palm twitches as he fights the urge to slap me. "And you'll get back to doing what you do best—hustling. If I let you go, I'll need to make sure you're being taken care of financially."

The conversation confuses me. My head is about to explode. Does Camden want to help me now? After killing my brother? After killing my *lover?*

"My father touched you." I hear his voice above my head. "Repeatedly."

I nod, eyes on the ground. "Seb would watch. It was the only thing that made him smile."

When I look up, a tear hangs on his fair lashes. That's when I see that behind the cheater, the abuser, the man who ruined me, my baby-brother's killer, is still the thirty-year-old guy I once fell for. His eyes flicker as mine turn off.

"Kill me," I whisper. I mean it. I've nothing to live for anymore without Nate and Preston.

He kisses my lips and I let him, because it doesn't matter anymore.

"No, Diabla. That wouldn't be fair. Know what is fair? Russian Roulette. A game of chance and dare. Now, there's only a single round in my revolver. Then again," he says and brushes the barrel softly across my cheek, whispering into the shell of my ear, "It's my lucky bullet in there. Life or death? Decisions, decisions. Where do you want me to aim the gun?"

"Temple," I swallow. I want it to be quick.

"Not very original, but whatever tickles your fancy."

I feel the gun sliding against my sweaty temple effortlessly, plowing into my flesh like a nasty migraine, and squeeze my eyes shut.

The sound of the spinning cylinder dances in my ear, so terribly close, and I hold my breath, the air trapped in my lungs. I want to die. I need to rest. I need my peace. Maybe it won't be in the form of Nate, but at least it'd be quiet. *At least I'd be safe.*

The cylinder stops spinning and everything is illuminated by the silence. *Click.*

Am I alive?

I don't know.

I feel my body quivering frantically, sweat and my own urine making me glide across the floor. But I also feel pain. I need to do something. Try and lift my hand or blink. Why is it so hard to move? My brain commands me to do something, but my body doesn't comply.

My brain. It still works. The realization sends shivers down my arms.

I'm alive. I'm going to be okay. *If Nate makes it out of this room with me.* If not, the bullet might have been the best thing that could've happened to me.

"Camden," I plead. He knows what I'm asking for. Uttering it aloud is unnecessary.

"This guy doesn't deserve you." Camden throws himself back on the recliner and pats his pants for his pack of smokes. Lighting up one, he sends a rancid cloud to the ceiling. "Besides, he's probably dead."

"It's over. Everybody got what they deserved. Let's just move on." I prompt. Other than you. You get to walk away unaffected. I killed his dad, but Camden only ever cared about the money and the power. The thought of letting him walk away from this makes sour bile tickle my throat, but I care more about Nate.

"I want you out of my life and off this island, Prescott. And I'm willing to pay. One hundred grand. In cash. If you walk out of here and promise not to retaliate. See this as my farewell gift to you. . .and as my apology about Preston."

He's going to let us go. He really does love me in his own, screwed-up way.

My voice shakes. "I promise."

"So now," he says, while his hand snakes to my jaw, his finger tucked under my chin, angling me to face him. "All I need is a souvenir."

"Anything." I feel his other fist gripping me from the base of my hair and dragging me to his crotch. For a second, I think I know what he means and am tempted to bite off his dick. It was bad enough to go through this when my heart didn't belong to anyone but myself. But with Nate lying here, I'd never be able to do it.

"Something of yours," he continues, twisting my head to face him. I collapse backward and reposition so that I'm sitting with my body facing his. He likes that. His smile suggests victory.

"What?" I keep peeking behind him, trying to catch glances of Nate.

"An arm? An ear?" he wonders aloud. "A finger." He grabs my palm and strokes it, his scowl melts into a grin. "You always had beautiful fingers. Thin, delicate. . .and mine."

White dots fill my vision. He wants one of my fingers? How the hell would he. . .I know exactly how. I get it now. Camden wants to punish me. Not for what I did to his father and Sebastian. He wants to see me tortured for giving my heart to someone else.

"This is punishment for Nate, isn't it?" I grit out.

He nods once. "Smart girl."

"You asked for someone else's hand," I argue. "The wedding might be postponed, but you're still going to take her as your wife."

"Marriage of convenience," he says simply and pats my cheek, like I'm a loveable puppy. "She's a bloody Lady. And a rich one, at that. But my heart will always belong to you."

Yeah, but your dick was everyone else's. But I don't care anymore. I just want to crawl to Nate and mourn him quietly. Screw my fingers.

"Take a finger, Camden. Just be quick."

He gets up from his chair. "I was never one to stall when it comes to violence."

The minute he strides out of the room, I slither toward Nate's prone figure. There's so much blood around him, his white shirt is soaked. I'm crying and grabbing on to his cold cheeks, begging him to say something, but he's limp. There's a faint pulse in his neck. I need to get him to the hospital as soon as possible. I don't have my phone on me; Camden tossed it out of his car when he took me, and if I yell from the window for help, my ex-boyfriend might backtrack on his offer.

Camden steps back into the room with a wrench.

"Give me your hand, pretty lady." He's still standing up, me kneeling before him, his index finger curled for me to crawl closer. I do.

"Pick a finger."

I offer him my left pinkie.

"Oh. Come on now. Give us something you'd actually miss. How about your right hand's index?"

"Fine," I bite. *Just take the whole arm and let me attend to my boyfriend*, I want to scream.

When the cool iron touches my bony finger, I wince and look away, but when I feel it twisting against my skin, I think about Nate. How it would feel to have it all with him. The life he offered me. We would have it by now had I pushed away my thirst for revenge. I don't even want Camden's life anymore. It's so hollow and meaningless, now that I know what real pain feels like.

Not the wrench. Physical pain is nothing.

Nate.

After my bones disconnect with a chilling sound, Camden produces a knife from his back pocket and cuts the skin surrounding it. The burn is agonizing. The pain is everywhere. I want him to tear my whole limb apart so that I don't feel the throb between my fingers. I shake my head back and forth, biting back my scream.

"All done," Camden says cheerily, tucking the wrench in his back pocket and fisting my ripped body part. "Remember, sweetheart, if you come after me, I will pluck the rest of your organs one by one."

I collapse on my stomach and moan.

"Please, let me make one phone call. I have to take him to the hospital," I groan in pain.

"Don't take advantage of my kindness," he taunts, laughing to himself. "Drag him down to the street. It's only two floors. Goodbye, love. I wish I were strong enough to kill us both. But the truth is, I love you too much to see you go so young. Enjoy what's left of your life, Prescott. I fully intend to enjoy mine."

With that, he strides out of the room with my finger clutched firmly in his hand. I'm confused, but I don't have time to dwell on my grave situation. Camden caught me, exposed and unprepared, armed with a muscle man and a plan, two things I didn't have with me.

Still bleeding from where my finger used to be, I grab Nate by the hem of his jeans and drag him out of the room into the corridor. He's heavy as hell, too tall for me to be able to maneuver him alone. I bang his limp body against the doorframe by accident, but he doesn't even flinch. My arms burn and my legs shake under the strain of his weight, as I pull him out to the living room area of the apartment, one inch at a time. I catch Simon lying flat on the floor, his neck cut open. I drag Nate outside the apartment, but this is an old Victorian building. There's no elevator.

The adrenaline that exploded in my veins subdues, and I feel the sharp pain in my hand and my thighs itching with my own urine. I have to hurry up before I faint.

Reluctantly, I round behind Nate's head and grab him by his shoulders, each arm hooked under an armpit, and protecting his head. I slide him down the stairs, all while trying to pull him up to me so his head won't take a hit. He looks so fragile, even with his huge size, with his eyes closed and that hole in his stomach.

The minute I get out of the building, I lose it. Every ounce of self-control evaporates as I yell for help. I grab strangers by the collar, staining them with my blood and sweat, begging them to call an ambulance, knowing that they are going to call the police too, but I'm far too gone to care. Trapped in a bubble made of insanity, I desperately want to burst. It's ironic, my need to be strong for a man who is my only weakness.

I can't lose him. Can't let go of my peace.

Fifteen minutes later, we're both at St. Mary's Hospital.

Nate is being ushered to the operating room while I fight the staff who are trying to tend to my wound, demanding to join him.

The art of letting go. Camden thought he was bad at it, but me, I'm worse.

Five hours later, my hand is wrapped up and Nate is recovering in the other room. He lost a lot of blood and had to have a transfusion, but Simon didn't manage to reach any of his inner organs. I was not allowed to stay by his side as I'm not next-to-kin, but the minute he wakes up, he asks for me. A nurse approaches my sad plastic table in the cafeteria and places her palm over my bandaged hand. "Your companion said he'd like to see Miss *Cockburn*?"

Nate is still subdued under mountains of morphine, but he squeezes my healthy hand when we meet. His lips are chapped and he has an IV drip attached to his arm.

"He's dead," I croak as soon as my ass hits the chair beside his bed. I'm too tired to cry. "Preston. Camden killed him."

"Baby-Cakes." His sucks in a shaky breath, stroking my palm in his. He doesn't need to tell me he's sorry. It's all in his facial expression, wrapped in grief.

He knew this all along, I didn't want to listen.

Our foreheads meet, and I take a whiff of my peace. Fragile and hurt, it's still there. I used to look at Nate as someone invincible who could catch a bullet in his hand. Now I know that he is mortal, like me. It makes me love him even more.

"Tell me something beautiful," his lips speak into mine. This time, I don't have to search my brain for an answer. No words written by someone else can do us justice.

"Us," I rasp. "We're beautiful and ugly and broken. . .and whole."

Four days later, the police finally come to terms with the fact that they aren't getting anything from us. "Snitches are bitches," Nate whispered to my neck when they first arrived in his hospital room. I stick to my story that a bunch of teenagers in beanies cornered us in an alleyway, stabbed Nate, cut my finger out when I didn't want to give them my bag and ran away with our money. We're just two tourists from America who want to go home and lick our wounds. It's a crazy lie no one believes, but you can't force the truth out of people. Especially people like us.

A week later, we're free. Me sans a finger, Nate with a new, fresh scar on his stomach. Simon hit a spot that's already heavily covered in ink. His "tainted" side, as Nate calls it. The scar will not be visible under the steampunk clock scribbled on his stomach.

Time.

Our whole lives are ahead of us now.

I need to live mine in memory of my loving brother, who couldn't handle hearing how much I suffered at the hands of monsters. In memory of my mother, who went crazy with grief. And with Nate in mind. For all the time he lost in prison. While being Godrey's do-boy. But he's not a memory. He's my future.

We walk into the tube station hand in hand, taking the train back to our room to get our stuff and move into a hotel that can better accommodate our new, fragile situation.

The missing finger bothers me; it feels unnatural to do the simplest things, from flipping pages in a book to browsing the touch screen of my phone or even making coffee.

I pluck a free copy of the Metro from a stack of newspapers before getting into the subway, my mind begging for a distraction. We walk the length of the platform silently before I freeze. Camden's face is smiling back at me from the first page, hugging a beautiful young woman who looks like some kind of a ginger princess. "The Wedding is On!" The headline celebrates. My knees buckle and nausea slams into me once again.

Nate's nostrils flare and he grabs the paper, balling it in his fist and throwing it behind his shoulder without looking back.

Our train arrives, and he finds himself dragging me inside. This was a bitter reminder of my defeat. This man raped me, killed my brother and ruined my life, and he walked away free of punishment. What's more, he bribed me with money, and I took it. Because I'm a coward. Because I'm a loser. Because I'm the very lowlife he treated me as. A part of me wants to chase after him, screw the money, and kill him. But a bigger part knows I value my second chance with Nate too much to fuck it up again.

"Camden is still alive. We lost," I tell Nate, resting my head against the blue seat of the subway and moving my palm across my face

"No, Baby-Cakes." He pulls my head to his shoulder. "We survived."

EPILOGUE
TANAKA

Even the hookers don't look so down and depressed around here.

Not a surprise, considering they live in a place called Nice. It is nice. More than nice, actually. Sprawled over the French Riviera, this city offers yummy ice cream, a beach with little pebbles—the kind that heat under the warmth of the sun and massage your feet when you walk on them—and yachts. Beautiful, gorgeous yachts you can stare at for hours at the promenade. Across the street, prostitutes stand and wait to be called for by tourists.

Stinking wealth against unbearable poverty.

Flashy against degrading.

They all live here, under the same sun and stars. Strong and weak. Takers and givers. Just like in the US. Just like everywhere else.

But here, I'm not a giver. I'm not a weak one. I'm a fresh, clean face.

I like the little tram that passes through this beautiful city, the street dancers who come out every night, making a show in front of dozens of tourists, and the main street restaurants.

Nice is not nice. Nice is perfect.

There was a lot of debate about where we wanted to live after we got out of the hospital.

We received the suitcase stuffed with cash a few hours after we left the hospital—Camden sent one of his dirty workers to hand it over—and checked into the Ritz. Nate and I called room service, asking for someone to get us a map of Europe and tipped the bellboy fifty quid for his trouble. We spread the map flat over the giant bed, eating greasy pizza and slurping cold beer as we debated the question of where we should live.

In the end, we have shortlisted two places: Spain and France.

I wanted to go to Barcelona. Nate to Cannes.

We drifted off to sleep, still bickering about things like climate and healthcare. Neither of us really gave too much of a damn at this point, we were so high on being with each other, alive and well, and so low on not killing Camden, that nothing else mattered.

At around five a.m. one early morning, Nate woke me up the good old-fashioned way, by licking the length of me underneath the sheets. His huge body bulged out of the covers above me, making it look like I was suffering from the biggest morning wood in history. Sucking hard on my clit, making warm waves wash under my navel, he groaned into me.

"I bought us two tickets to Nice, France. Nice has your name on it."

"It does?" I moaned, spreading my legs wide to grant him more access. His teeth rubbed against my pussy, creating delicious friction that made my nipples hard and sensitive.

"I did some reading about France while you were waking the dead with your snoring." His voice was muffled as he spoke into my pussy. The fact that I was moaning loudly didn't help, either.

"Let's hear it."

"Did you know, Cockburn, that the Bay of Nice was named after a miracle that happened in the third century? There was a young Christian woman who was arrested for her faith in Palestine, just across the Mediterranean. Her torturers did everything they could to convert her faith, but she stood her ground."

"Tough lady." I felt my thighs quivering against his head uncontrollably, my limbs turning into jelly. Oh, God. So close.

"She reminds me of a little storm I know. When her torturers realized that she wouldn't cave, they beheaded her. As was the custom after such an execution, her body was put on a raft and sent across the sea."

"Assholes." I threw the covers off of his body, my fingers twisting in his hair. I rode his face with my eyes shut, feeling my mouth watering with pleasure.

"They, too, remind me of some people we know. Logic dictates that her body should've been desecrated by seagulls. Logic dictates that her beautiful head wouldn't have made it past Greece before it would have rotted under the sun. But logic doesn't live where there's love. The myth is, angels took over her raft and guided it across the Mediterranean all the way to the Bay of Nice. Her body arrived pristine and untouched. A miracle, stronger than the circumstances and the sea."

I came hard against his lips. My angel wanted to take me to the French Riviera. I wasn't going to argue. I'd follow him to the stairs of heaven or the pits of hell. *Doesn't matter where we go, I'll always enjoy the ride.*

"The young woman became a martyr, Saint Reparata, the patron of saint of the Cathedral in old Nice," he said as his face rose up from below to meet mine, his lips glistening with my passion for him. I placed a soft kiss against the hot flesh of his neck.

"What happened to the angels?" My voice was hoarse with sleep.

"They named the bay after them," he whispered. "But the angels aren't the point. They didn't give two shits about the glory. All they ever wanted was to see the girl through her journey and give her peace."

"I love you so much." I clasped his face, noting that the space where my missing finger once was, was starting to heal. I survived the world's greatest torture under the arms of powerful men, but it was this broke guy from Stockton who managed to snatch my heart and soul, and I know that he is the only person who can ever break me.

I also know that he never would.

"My martyr, my storm, my passion. . ." He kissed every inch of my face. "My Cockburn," he finished on a rumbling laugh.

I hugged him, his cheek against mine as I inhaled his unique scent.

"No, seriously. My cock fucking burns. I need to shoot a load. Spread your legs, Country Club."

I smile at my neighbor from across the hallway. We live in an antique building on Rue Segurane, close enough to everything we care about. The gardens, shops, restaurants and promenade. Chris and I take long walks every evening and drink our coffee every morning on our balcony overlooking the jade Mediterranean Sea.

"Bonjour, Mademoiselle Cockburn." Auralie, my old, friendly neighbor doesn't even bother locking her door after she closes it silently, so as not to wake up the young students who party all night down the hall. I smile back and nod, bending down to pet her old Yorkshire terrier. Despite her friendliness, Auralie, like the rest of my neighbors, refuses to communicate in English. Not because she doesn't speak it. She's knows it fluently, I suspect. It's a matter of principle.

"Ça va?" her sweet voice enquires. She always speaks extra slowly for Chris and me. We're still learning, and if I may add—we're terrible students so far.

"Jamais mieux." My lips smack. Never better. *Never.*

I skip down the stairs like a giddy four-year-old on Christmas morning, sticking my earbuds in, *La Valse D'Amelie* providing a soundtrack to this beautiful summer day.

All my favorites. Recreated, with *him.*

My gift waits for me one block from where we live, and I can't wait to unwrap whatever it is that he's wearing. Holding my long, yellow summer dress just above my ankles so I won't trip over it, I charge to one of the places I call home nowadays.

Throwing the door to the coffee shop open, I thunder into our place. We called it *Le Journal Rouge*. The Red Diary. We bought it because it looked like crap, but inside, was a soul in the form of a library with hundreds and hundreds of books. In English, French and Spanish. In Hebrew, Mandarin and Arabic. Tourists come here and tuck their favorite books into our shelves like it's the Western Wall, their wish is to immortalize their love for their favorite novels. Here, we share beautiful words and heartbreaking art.

Customers love sitting here between 2 p.m. and 4 p.m. when everything else is closed for the afternoon rest. They drink our terrible coffee and read our wonderful books.

My boyfriend lifts his eyes from the coffee machine and bangs the filter holder into the trash. He wipes the steam wand clean with a dishcloth then throws it over his shoulder. Leaning forward, his elbows resting on the counter, he takes my hands in his. People look at him weirdly here in Nice. He stands out even more, with his size and sinister tattoos. He doesn't care. He never did.

"What can I get you?" My palms disappear inside his and he brings them to his lips, planting kisses all over my knuckles, halting a few more seconds on the one without a finger.

"Do I look too demure in this dress to say something crude like 'your eleven inch dick'?" I giggle into the yellow strap of my dress.

"Yes, you do," he confirms, looking around like he is searching for someone. It's early in the morning, hence why the shop is busy as hell. There are a lot of people sitting around on the sofas and barstools, sipping coffee and eating pastries. "Meet me in the restroom in two minutes."

I don't ask questions. I don't even want to know how he is planning to neglect his station as the barista. What I do know is that the quickie we had this morning is not going to cut it. I need more of him, now.

"Now less talking, more showing me that fine ass as it walks its way to the restroom. Move it, Cockburn."

NATE

So many names crammed into so little time.

Beat.

Nate.

Christopher Delaware.

Prescott.

Pea.

Country Club.

Silver Spoon.

Tanaka Cockburn.

And it all boils down to one thing at the end—*us*.

It took Prescott a while to get over Preston's death, but I suspect that she always knew deep down that he hadn't made it. Her family was torn apart, after tearing apart the Archers. She had no choice but to build something new, and I hope that someday, she'll do it with me.

My argument for the past couple of months was simple and valid—I can't be with a girl whose last name's Cockburn. It's embarrassing. For me, for her, for everyone involved. Tanaka said that Cockburn is a perfectly legitimate last name, and even pulled out some bullshit facts from the Internet, including a Wikipedia page for actress Olivia Wilde. Apparently, her original last name is Cockburn (can't argue with that. She's legit fuckable).

Since my girlfriend refused to take the hint, I've decided to lay it out pretty fucking simple and straightforward, Stockton style. No hearts and pink pony crap. When she arrived at the coffee shop we own together in her yellow dress, the one that reminds me that we still live under the same sun that makes the freckles on her shoulders pop out, I directed her to the restroom. She looks like gold in this dress. Pure. Cherished. Precious.

Daniel, our eighteen-year-old neighbor, who has been eyeing her in a way that makes me want to cut his tongue out and shove it down his throat, jogged from the corner of the street and I watched from the wide window as he entered Le Journal Rouge, just as she disappeared behind the wooden door to the restroom.

Now that he's here, it's show time. We're always ready for show time, Tanaka and I.

"It won't take long," I growl as I slide under the counter and charge for the restroom.

She's waiting for me the same way she did the first time we had sex. Her hands against the wall, her legs wide open. I love watching her fingerless hand. The wound has healed and now her outside matches her inside. Imperfect, broken and hurt, but so very beautiful. I flick her long dress up and unzip.

"No foreplay," Beat whispers into her ear.

"No problem," she says, just like she did then. I know this woman well. She's always wet for me. Him. Us. *Always*.

I ride her from behind, just like I did the first time. Only this time, I'm not angry. A little anxious, yeah, but after the shit I've been through for her, she better say yes. I hold her waist with one hand and slip the other into my back pocket, producing the engagement ring I got for her last week. We have money, thanks to the late Camden Archer, but it's nothing fancy. Just a silver hoop with a small yellow diamond that shines like her blonde hair. Linking my fingers with hers while fucking her, I slide the ring onto her engagement finger.

No words necessary.

No love declarations.

No *You're mine*.

Everything is said in the way we move together.

"Oh my God, Nate." My old name slips between her pinks. I can't see her face but I can feel her pussy clutching my cock tight, like she's about to see stars. "Are you. . .?"

"I am," I confirm. "And I will. Forever. Fucking. Take care of you. That is, if you'll let me. Will you?"

"Yes," she says breathlessly.

We come together hard, and I spin her to face me. Her hair is stuck to her temples, sweaty and beautiful. She's every ambition I've ever had.

I love her like a slave, I kneel in front of her like a subject, I crawl back to her at night like a drunk and I worship her like a believer.

She's my truth, my lie, my storm and my peace.

Prescott Burlington-Smyth turned Tanaka Cockburn soon-to-be Tanaka Delaware has created a dystopian chaos only she rules, but I'm happy to be her soldier.

Godfrey.

Sebastian.

The Aryan Brothers.

And Camden, who tragically died in a lethal car accident on the outskirts of London, on his way to a vacation in York three weeks after we left the UK.

I didn't quail. Godfrey was right—I'm not a killer, I'm a murderer. But with her, I don't have any hard limits. And I will take my own fucking life to put a smile on those pinks. We're going to be all right. We're going to stick around in a place where no one knows us and no one cares. We're going to make French babies together.

Wherever we're going, we're going there together.

"I love you," she tells me, tears in her eyes. I kiss them away. She's such a big fucking softie.

The dust has settled over the blood we've shed. Our previous lives are behind us.

The future is bright.

And clean.

And most importantly—it is ours.

PRESCOTT

Time.

A wise, vile *dead* man once told me that it moves differently according to circumstances. Sometimes it's slow. But sometimes. . .it moves exactly as it should.

I don't want to pause, and definitely not to rewind. If anything, a part of me wants to press fast forward.

To life without stress balls.

To domestic bliss.

To babies.

To growing old next to this man who occupies every inch of my soul.

All you need to know about life is that it's just like an hourglass. Sometimes you're down, and sometimes, up.

And right now, I'm up, baby. So. Flipping. High.

THE END

ACKNOWLEDGEMENTS

Hello, acknowledgements. We meet again.

For those of you who aren't aware, this is the part where I forget all the cool people then beat myself about it for the rest of my life. So here's a massive shout out to the people who keep me (relatively) sane. Bear in mind that I probably forgot a few of you. Sowwie with a side of oh-you-know-how-bad-I-am-at-these-things:

Special thanks to Mr. Shen and Baby Shen, who always put up with my crazy mood swings, weird schedule, sugary cravings and overall awful behavior (remember, you cannot leave me. I'm the only one who knows where we hide the Oreos in the house.)

A huge thank you to Vanessa, my amazing editor, who has taught me so much (including the fact that 'alright' is not an actual word. That was earth-shattering news right there.) I'm your number one fan, and working with you is always a pleasure.

To my street team – you're THE SHIT. It's pointless to try and explain how grateful I am. Amanda Farmer, Paro Madhur, Ilor Tsabar, Paige Jennifer and Lin Tahel Cohen – you girls are my anchor. You keep everything together. Thank you, thank you, thank you.

Also, thanks to Erika, Alexandra, Avivit, Sabrina, Hen, Liran, Lisa, Tanaka, Denise, Erika, Donna, Cristina and Kerissa (see? I know I'm forgetting a bunch of people.)

To my beta readers – Author RB Hilliard, Amy Halter, Sunny Borek, Julie Kitzmiller and Sabrina Shalalashvili. Thank you for being patient and reading the earlier drafts of my work. For the helpful suggestions and ruthless advice. You rock.

To MY MAIN GIRL, my PA, rock star, soulmate and sister-from-another-mister, Amy Halter. Baby, you make me feel like I can climb Mount Everest when you're around (don't get any ideas, though. And this is DEFINITELY not turning into a bet). Thank you for everything. I couldn't have done it without you. To my PR manager/Mama Bear Neda Amini. Love, love, love you. Thank you for taking the not-so-fun-stuff out of the way and leaving me to do what I enjoy, writing and mingling with my readers.

Thank you Sunny Borek, Lin Tahel Cohen and Bree Shalalashvili for the moral support. I have no idea why you put up with my nagging questions and insecurities. But you do. And I'm so grateful. To the Beat Museum in San Francisco for the muse and to the cool guys there for humoring the little weirdo girl with the muscle tees.

To Letitia of R.B.A Designs for this beautiful cover and for being so attentive and supportive, even when I clearly had no idea what I was doing or what I was saying.

Thank you, awesome bloggers who signed up for my release, reviewed, talked and shared my book. Where would I have been without you? Probably exactly where I am right now, sitting on my couch sipping light beer, only, you know, without nurturing a career from the comfort of my living room. You took a chance on me even though you didn't have to. I'm forever in your debt.

One last thank you is to *you*, my readers. My main fear when releasing a book is that no one will read it. *Ever.* When that doesn't happen, I get giddy and thrilled and all kinds of weird. I said it in Sparrow and I will say it again – you make my dream come true. You're my heroes.

Thank you!

AUTHOR'S NOTE

After I wrote Sparrow, I told everyone who'd listen that I'm taking a break to try and spend more time with my family and friends. Enjoy my sweet son, catch up on Veep, Game of Thrones, Silicon Valley and wine. But after I finished writing Sparrow, they came to me.

Nate and Prescott. Those sneaky bastards.

I wanted to fight it, but found myself binge-writing into the night. *Again.* Those hours of sleep I promised myself when I was editing Sparrow? Yeah, I never got them. I wanted to give you a totally different experience than the one you had in Sparrow, someone who is still badass, but not as cold and distant as Troy, and another strong woman – but in very different ways to Sparrow.

Again, I am asking you to put me out of my misery and leave an honest review. I want to know what you felt and thought when reading Blood to Dust, what you liked and disliked. Writing is a lonely job, and editing is the reason they invented beer. You guys are the fun part.

So be fun, okay?

As always, I invite you to engage in my reading group, where you can talk about my books freely and where I make an ass of myself on a daily basis: https://goo.gl/lKsquA

For my latest releases and to stay in the loop, feel free to sign up to my newsletter (all the cool kids did it):

https://goo.gl/T1AziV

Thanks for taking a chance on my books.

L.

xoxo

Made in the USA
Columbia, SC
31 July 2024

39714332R00159